Beckett's Art of Absence

Also by Ciaran Ross

LECTURES D'UNE OEUVRE: En Attendant Godot, Fin de Partie (*with Christine Lombez & Herve Bismuth*)

AUX FRONTIÈRES DU VIDE

SUB-VERSIONS: Trans-National Readings of Modern Irish Literature (*editor*)

Beckett's Art of Absence

Rethinking the Void

Ciaran Ross
University of Strasbourg

palgrave
macmillan

First published 2011 by
PALGRAVE MACMILLAN

Palgrave Macmillan in the UK is an imprint of Macmillan Publishers Limited, registered in England, company number 785998, of Houndmills, Basingstoke, Hampshire RG21 6XS.

Palgrave Macmillan in the US is a division of St Martin's Press LLC, 175 Fifth Avenue, New York, NY 10010.

Palgrave Macmillan is the global academic imprint of the above companies and has companies and representatives throughout the world.

ISBN 978–0–230–57518–9 hardback

This book is printed on paper suitable for recycling and made from fully managed and sustained forest sources. Logging, pulping and manufacturing processes are expected to conform to the environmental regulations of the country of origin.

A catalogue record for this book is available from the British Library.

A catalog record for this book is available from the Library of Congress.

10 9 8 7 6 5 4 3 2 1
20 19 18 17 16 15 14 13 12 11

Transferred to Digital Printing in 2012

In memory of my mother and to the future of my sons Milan and Noah

Contents

List of Abbreviations

(All French texts are publications from Editions de Minuit, Paris, unless otherwise stated.)

AST	*As the Story Was Told: Uncollected and Late Prose* (London: John Calder; New York: Riverrun Press, 1990)
ATF	*All That Fall* (London: Faber, 1957)
BT	*The Beckett Trilogy. Molloy, Malone Dies, The Unnamable* (London: Picador, 1979)
C	*Company* (London: John Calder, 1979)
CA	'Cascando' in *Collected Poems in English and French* (London: John Calder, 1977), 30
CSP	*Collected Shorter Prose 1945–1980* (London: John Calder, 1984)
CSPa	*Collected Shorter Plays of Samuel Beckett* (London: Faber and Faber, 1984)
D	*Disjecta. Miscellaneous Writings and a Dramatic Fragment* (ed.) R. Cohn (New York: Grove, 1984)
DFMW	*Dream of Fair to Middling Women* (Dublin: Black Cat Press, 1992)
EAG	*En attendant Godot* (1952)
G	*Waiting for Godot* (London: Faber, 1985)
H	*How It Is* (London: John Calder, 1977)
HH	'Henry Hayden, homme-peintre / Henry Hayden, Painter-Man' (1952), in Philippe Chabert and Christophe Zagrodzki*, Hayden* (Paris: Fragments, 2005)
INN	*L'innommable* (1953)
KTP	*Krapp's Last Tape in CSPa,* 53–63
LSB	*The Letters of Samuel Beckett, 1929–1940* (eds) M. Fehsenfeld, L. Overbeck (Cambridge University Press, 2009)
M	*Molloy* (1951)

MM	*Malone meurt* (1951)
Mu	*Murphy* (London: Picador, 1973)
NOV	*The Expelled and Other Novellas* (London: Penguin, 1980)
OH	*Ohio Impromptu,* in *CSPa*, 283–8
P	*Proust and Three Dialogues with Georges Duthuit* (London: John Calder, 1965)
PI	*Ping* in *CSP*
TT	*That Time* in *CSPa,* 225–35
W	*Watt* (London: John Calder, 1976)
WH	*Worstward Ho* (London: John Calder, 1983)

Acknowledgments

The author and publishers wish to thank the following: Faber and Faber Limited for permission to quote from *Malone Dies*, *The Unnamable* and *Waiting for Godot*; *The Journal of Beckett Studies* for permission to quote from various articles; Rodopi Publishers for permission to quote from *Samuel Beckett Today/Aujourd'hui*; Les Editions de Minuit for permission to quote from *Molloy*, copyright © 1951 by Les Editions de Minuit, *L'Innommable*, copyright © 1953 by Les Editions de Minuit and *En attendant Godot*, copyright © 1952 by Les Editions de Minuit; Cambridge University Press for permission to quote from Martha Dow Fehsenfeld, Lois More Overbeck, George Craig and Dan Gunn (eds) *The Letters of Samuel Beckett 1929–1940*, © the Estate of Samuel Beckett (2009), published by Cambridge University Press; Grove/Atlantic, for permission to quote from *Molloy*, translation copyright © 1955 by the Estate of Samuel Beckett; from *Malone Dies*, translation copyright © 1958 by the Estate of Samuel Beckett; from *The Unnamable*, translation copyright © 1958 by the Estate of Samuel Beckett; from *Waiting for Godot*, copyright © 1954 by Grove Press, Inc. (copyright © renewed 1982 by Samuel Beckett); from *All That Fall*, copyright © 1957 by Samuel Beckett; from *Eh Joe*, copyright © 1967 by Samuel Beckett; from *That Time*, copyright © 1976 by Samuel Beckett; from *Ohio Impromptu*, copyright © 1982 by Samuel Beckett; from *How It Is* by Samuel Beckett, copyright © 1964 by Grove Press, Inc.; from *Company*, copyright © 1980 by Samuel Beckett; from *Worstward Ho*, copyright © 1983 by Samuel Beckett; from *Three Dialogues*, copyright © 1949 by Samuel Beckett; from *Ping*, translation copyright © 1995 by the Estate of Samuel Beckett; from *The Capital of the Ruins*, copyright © 1946 by Samuel Beckett; from *Theatrical Notebook: Waiting for Godot*, copyright © 1993 by the Estate of Samuel Beckett; notes and editorial matter copyright © 1993 by Dougald McMillan and James Knowlson. All excerpts are used by kind permission of Grove/Atlantic, Inc.

In bringing this book to completion, I owe a great debt of gratitude to many people who have helped me in different ways. I am particularly indebted to Angela Moorjani for reading earlier parts of this work and giving me the benefit of her great scholarly ability at all times. I also wish to warmly thank Tom Cousineau for his very helpful comments and Dan Gunn for his personal encouragement.

At a very early stage in my studies in Dublin, Ross Skelton was an inspiring force by introducing me to Winnicott's *Playing and Reality*. This proved to be a decisive moment in the development of my views and I sincerely thank him here.

I am very grateful to my editors at Palgrave Macmillan: Paula Kennedy who immediately expressed her interest in the initial project, and, in particular, Ben Doyle for his continuous professional support. I also wish to thank Nicci Cloke at Faber & Faber and Dara Hyde at Grove/ Atlantic Inc., for their assistance in getting me through the long process of securing permissions to quote from Beckett's works.

As this work was started during a sabbatical leave, it is only fitting that I should record my gratitude to the University of Strasbourg. In this respect, I am grateful for the support I received from my colleagues in the English Department and equally for Ersie Leria's precious editorial assistance.

In conclusion, very special thanks go to Lore Schacht for listening to me time and again and providing support at moments when I had doubts about continuing this book. I also want to express my gratitude to my sister, Catriona, for her constant encouragement. To my wife, Kathrin, and my sons, Milan and Noah, it is with love and appreciation that I can acknowledge my deep gratitude to them but I can never repay back the debt I owe them. I sincerely thank them for their patience, forbearance and admirable endurance during these last years.

Preface

If one is prepared to accept that academic criticism presents its own elaborate fictions and might be likened to a form of intellectual storytelling, then this book is no exception. It tells a story about the significance of absence in Samuel Beckett's major writings. This may be a familiar story to many Beckett specialists. But the particular story being told here is concerned with the peculiar way the different modes, forms and discourses of issues such as negativity, death, emptiness, the void, 'serve' Beckett's aesthetic vision and cannot be restricted to just being symptoms. Beckett's art of absence is about the art of 'thinking' absence and 'playing' with the limits and at the limits of such 'thinking'. My point is that this key-theme need not be seen as something inherently tragic or negative, in the pejorative sense of the word. It may be rather seen as having a fundamental aesthetic value, a key perhaps to Beckett's concern with a negative sublime.

I begin in the first chapter by charting Beckett's Irish background, looking at personal and cultural factors that may have been decisive in his decision to emigrate and settle in France. And here I take into consideration his early environment, his need for analysis in London with Bion, his bilingualism and his war-time experience. This briefest and indeed schematic 'history' is not meant to be essential background for reading the Trilogy and *Waiting for Godot*, since these texts can be read without any prior knowledge of Beckett's Irish world. The emphasis here is on Beckett's personal experience of exile and estrangement and to show that the sense of emptiness that prevails is not simply on account of some abstract 'human condition', but rather has its 'roots' in an identifiable, even normal early experience.

The decision to centre the study on the later 1940s has to go down to my long-standing fascination with this period. I acknowledge, with hindsight, that more emphasis could have been made on the later shorter texts and these may have even provided more fruitful material. But my contention, too, is that despite the extraordinary attention the Trilogy and *Godot* have received from critics, there are still areas of bafflement and obscure zones that have been left fallow by critics.

In using psychoanalysis as my principle method of investigation, I am also mindful of the fact that 'absence' in a literary text and 'absence' in the clinical world, as theorised by Winnicott and Bion, are probably two very different irreducible orders. Concepts like 'transitional object', 'playing', 'thinking', 'attacks against linking', have simply allowed me to find, if not any 'meaning', certainly form and pattern in Beckett. Methodologically they serve to structure my reading. Hopefully from the readings provided, I will be seen as being involved more in exploration than in explanation.

Like the 'history' chapter, the 'theory' section in Chapter 2 is meant to be a partial exposition of the theoretical background to this study and the methods of analysis intended for use. Between Bion, Winnicott and even André Green there is a common ground in the way they think about absence, negativity, void. Winnicott and Bion might be seen as the Siamese twins of my critical thinking – Bion being drafted in for helping me to 'think' the destructive side of Beckett's imagination and Winnicott for the more paradoxical and playful side. The reader will be undoubtedly prompted to ask if Bion and Winnicott, why not Lacan? The short answer is that the biographical importance of Bion alone seemed engaging and relevant enough to devote a whole study, never mind leaving room for Winnicott. On a personal front I had discovered and had been reading Winnicott long before I came across Bion. It was then a question of finding space for both Bion and Winnicott in my critical thinking about Beckett's writing.

This present book was initially planned to be a translation of an earlier study I published in French, *Aux frontières du vide*. This simply proved to be unfeasible for many reasons. Hence my decision to rewrite and restructure everything anew even if the essential ideas and themes of the French are still to be found in the English.

This study recapitulates my long personal and professional involvement in Beckett's work, divided between two countries, two languages and two very different Becketts, the one taught by French Departments, and the other by English Departments. If nothing else, this study has helped me to give expression to my unnameable fascination for Samuel Beckett the man and for Beckett the writer. I owe him a lot, I suppose. It was he who created the absent Godot, that imaginary companion of mine, who has kept me company during the writing of these pages.

Introduction

Nothing doing

'Nothing is closer to the supreme commonplace of our common-place age than its preoccupation with Nothing', wrote Robert Martin Adams (Adams 1966, 3). The same could be said about the content and reception of Samuel Beckett's writing where the negative has albeit constituted a commonplace for reading and interpreting the texts of the Irish writer. 'There are many things I don't understand in my books', Beckett once confided to Patrick Bowles, in a discussion about his enigmatic writings, before immediately going on to quote, in French, Democritus: '"*rien n'est plus réel que le rien*" [Nothing is more real than nothing]. They are a positive statement of a negative thing' (qtd in Knowlson 2006, 109, Bowles' emphasis). Similarly, in a letter to Aidan Higgins (8 February 1952), Beckett, while acknowledging the primacy of the nothing for his work, realised that his writing resembled more of a journey 'in gathering thinglessness':

> I used to think all this work was an effort, necessarily feeble, to express the nothing. It seems rather to have been a journey, irreversible, in gathering thinglessness, *towards it*. (qtd in Morin 2006, 137–138, my emphasis)

More celebrated formulations of the 'negative thing' were to appear in the interview with Georges Duthuit, on the painting of Tal Coat, where Beckett memorably defined his ideal of artistic expression as 'there is nothing to express, nothing with which to express, nothing from which to express, no power to express, no desire to express, together with the obligation to express' (*P* 103).

He might have had his own work in mind for, to a large extent, 'the questions of Beckett's writings' are 'questions of negativity', to quote Leslie Hill (1990, 163). But, more than that, Beckett's very success, with critics and audience alike, has to do precisely with the questions his work raises as 'to the *shape and character of the negative*' (ibid., my emphasis). The same critic makes an even bolder claim when he points out that 'the fate of Beckett's texts hangs, quite uniquely, on the issue of how the power of the negative in his work is understood'. It follows, then, that 'the history of reception of Beckett's texts could be written in terms of the different interpretations put forward as to the force and significance of the negative (ibid.).

While this is not the place to rewrite the history of Beckett criticism, the least we can say about the early existentialist – 'human condition' – critics is that a pervading idealism and essentialism pervaded their 'search' for the 'ultimate' meaning of Beckett's 'negative' or, what was commonly called, Beckett's 'absurd' world (Esslin 1964, Elevaara 1976, Baldwin 1981). Similarly, as Peter Boxall tells us, the liberal humanist criticism that came to dominate Beckett studies from the sixties to the early nineties, saw in Beckett someone 'who represents universal truths about human reality in concrete dramatic form, who rejects cultural and political concerns as trivial and illusory, and whose artistic merit stems from an unflinching, penetrating depiction of the world as it is, seasoned with ineffable poetry and grace' (Boxall 2003, 51). Unsurprisingly, such liberal humanism was 'geared to humanising Beckett's "representation of the void"' (ibid.). With the emergence of theory in the eighties another Beckett emerges, argues Boxall, 'whose drama is a dangerous challenge to the very notion of a universal humanity, whose *negativity* is a residual and mournful form of protest, and whose poetry is generated by a restless, formless antagonism' (50, my emphasis).

This book is very much about the 'other' Beckett, alluded to by Boxall, since it seeks to give critical expression to some of the major negative issues with which Beckett's post-war writing confronts us: absence, emptiness, void, death, hatred. Where other interpreters may 'have occupied themselves with "emptiness", "the void", "nothingness" in an abstract way' (McMillan and Fehsenfeld 1988, 9), my concern will be with the affects and those emotional experiences underlying things negative *chez* Beckett. Using alternative modes of reading informed by British object relations theory, particularly by the work of Bion and Winnicott, I wish to argue that a new psychoanalytic discourse is required for the interpretation of Beckett's negativity, a discourse that is able to articulate the radical negative without absorbing it into the very bourgeois humanist ideology that Beckett's writing strenuously resists.

The single simple idea behind this book is that the negativity of Beckett's texts is not something that psychoanalytic criticism has to overcome, since it provides its 'own' logic and form, discourses and strategies which we, as readers or spectators are incited to read, think and ultimately to accept. The purpose of re-reading the first prose trilogy (*Molloy*, *Malone Dies*, *The Unnamable*) and *Waiting for Godot*, is to see how the negative operates in the writing and, in doing so, to reclaim its 'real' place in Beckett's narrative and dramatic art. Such re-reading will hopefully convince us of the need to re-think Beckett's negative status and to revise those familiar psychoanalytic images of Samuel Beckett's writing as being solely dominated by regressive and tragic forces where memory of birth or those catastrophic reactions to birth are seen as pathologically obsessional.

So, how are we to understand Beckett's renowned attraction to the negative, negation and, more widely, negativity in terms other than the earlier clichéd perception of Beckett as a tragic nihilist? Before outlining the approach favoured in this study, a brief review of the general relationship between Beckett and psychoanalysis is essential.

Beckett and psychoanalysis

The feasibility of interpretative discourse depends on a prior context. There is no naked, pristine, uninterpreted mode of literary experience. This does not just mean that this current psychoanalytic study of Beckett has already been preceded by many other ones, but that when we turn to Beckett's extraordinary relationship to psychoanalysis, it proves to be a daunting one, the context being a rich one at that.

Psychoanalysis had an obvious attraction for Beckett, ever since his personal therapy with Bion (which will be dealt with at length in Chapter 1). His therapy was also the occasion for attending with Bion a lecture by Jung at the Tavistock Clinic where he was fascinated by the case of a little girl whose archetypal dreams seemed to announce her early death, Jung's enigmatic explanation being: 'she had never been born entirely' (Jung 1968, 107; Moorjani 2004a, 175). In Beckett's subsequent fictionalisation of the Jung lecture in the radio play *All That Fall*, Maddy's comments have the quality of an unspeakable secret, the visit of a ghostly revelation, a potent mystery (*ATF* 37). Not unlike Beckett who prematurely terminated his analysis with Bion, Maddy too left the lecture before the end, but at this moment in the play, she enigmatically breaks down and weeps (ibid.). The Jungian motif has subsequently become 'an unavoidable presence in Beckettian criticism' (Thurston 2009, 128).[1]

While Beckett's work has long attracted the attention of psychoanalytic critics and their innumerable schools, no real attempt had been made to sketch out some general history of Beckett psychoanalytic criticism until Angela Moorjani's pioneering article in 2004.[2] She roughly divides the vast domain into three areas: firstly, Beckett's psychoanalytic culture and intertexts, secondly, Bion and other post-Kleinians and, thirdly, Lacanian or post-structuralist approaches. To complete this critical picture, I would add another division and situate it historically prior to the 'Bion' critics. These would be the first generation of Beckettian psychoanalytic critics who contributed greatly to the cult of the 'negative writer', 'negative' meaning here pathological, neurotic, regressive or tragic.[3] Accounts of disintegration, loss of identity, schizophrenia, sado-masochism, oedipal fixation, which largely relied on either traditional Freudian or Jungian motifs, tended to focus on reductive issues such as the mother–son relationship in the trilogy or the Molloy–Moran relationship in *Molloy*. One is reminded here of Lukac's famous indiscriminate critique of Beckett and modernism as pathological nihilism (Weller 2005, 6–11) or Alvarez's absurd claim that Beckett writes like someone who never had a childhood (Alvarez 1973, 18).

Fortunately, second-generation psychoanalytic criticism has proven to be somewhat more responsive to the complex question of Beckett's relationship to psychoanalysis and, as Moorjani shows, can be seen to provide a timely corrective to the somewhat stultified image of earlier Beckett psychoanalytic criticism. One neglected factor in this complex relationship was Beckett's own therapy.

As Steven Connor wittingly puts is, the temptation to find in the analysis a particular determinate cause for some immediate and contemporary effects in Beckett's writing is irresistible (Connor 2008, 11). This is the line taken both by Bennett Simon and Didier Anzieu, who see Beckett and Bion as 'imaginary twins', whose meeting in 1934–5 established the terms of a shared 'gestalt', defined by the concern with the possibilities of understanding and communication against the background of psychotic denials of meaning and human communication (Simon 1988):[4]

> For each of these creators the other seems to have been his secret imaginary twin [...] the complementary double who constitutes a decisive stage in the creative process. (Anzieu 1989, 168)

Simon hypothesises that the imaginary twin phantasy that Bion conceptualised only in 1950 was based on Beckett's therapy with him. More daringly, Simon claims that Jung's comments about his young mysterious patient, arguably served as a kind of shared creation, a transitional object that allowed Beckett and Bion to separate and yet remain in touch via the theme and phantasy of intra-uterine psychic life (Simon 1988, 335).

In Didier Anzieu's *Beckett et le psychanalyste* (1992) written as an autobiographically styled diary, which partly charts the author's reading experience of Beckett, the Beckett–Bion relationship plays centre stage. Anzieu takes the risk to imagine, to think and to re-write the clinical reality of their encounter, taking it in turn, as it were, to play the role of the patient – by imagining the notes that Beckett wrote – and that of the training analyst that Bion was. The thesis that emerges from Anzieu's provocative imagination is that the form of Beckett's mature post-war work is a significant response to the experience of his analysis which Anzieu categorically takes to be a traumatic failure: 'le sentiment traumatisant d'un échec' (84). Such a painful interruption is paradoxically necessary for the 'economy' of the future work, since it provides an irreducible nucleus that will never be mastered, but can at least be formally 'represented' albeit negatively: 'donner des représentations à cet irrépésentable, telle est, nouveau paradoxe, la visée créatrice' (ibid.). Beckett, consequently, pursued the interrupted analysis with Bion in the shape of a fictionalised self-analysis going from *Watt* through to *How It Is*. Steven Connor suggests that Anzieu's 'voice' may be seen to add 'to the transferential conversation established between the work of Beckett and Bion, both triangulating it, and bringing it full circle' (Connor 29). The 'voice' that Anzieu hears in Beckett's autoanalysis 'depends upon a voice which provides the one who emits it with that sonorous envelope with which it has failed to be surrounded, a voice as precious to be heard as a birth in the pharynx' (ibid.).[5]

Anzieu's conception of voice as sonorous envelope is closely related to his own original theory of the importance of the skin as an ideal, ego-forming container, a theory which he derives a great deal from the work of Bion on the relations between the container and the contained (Ross 2004, 73–6). The 'skin ego' (le moi-peau) could be loosely described and defined as a phantasmatic interface between the body self and the outer world (Anzieu 1985). For the skin ego, phantasies of protective envelopment that recall fusion with the mother in the womb or in a common skin defend against separation anxiety (Moorjani 2004a, 181; Ross 2004, 73–6).[6]

Jean-Michel Rabaté tracking a number of allusions in *Murphy* to Beckett's therapy with Bion, also contends that there is an unconscious connivance or correspondence between the former analyst and his Irish analysand (Rabaté 1984), but these need not be narrowly or magically related to Beckett's analytic experience. More broadly, Rabaté shows that the discovery of the 'nothing' as a fundamental object of unconscious desire, thematised in *Murphy,* was also one of the major discoveries of Bion in the thirties. In another article, he argues that both Beckett and Bion are both concerned with 'ghosts', with the issue of an infinitesimal (and ghostly) lessness, and with the question of the positivity of the 'void' or 'nothing' for the elaboration of a general logic of subjectivity' (Rabaté 1996, 25)

In Steven Connor's admirably detailed and comprehensive exploration of the Beckett/Bion relationship, the suggestion is that both careers may be seen to interpret each other in significant ways, the English psychoanalyst and the Irish writer sharing the same critical interface as it were (Connor 2008). For example, both Bion and Beckett's fertile period was after the war, with Beckett writing the trilogy and Bion developing, in the early fifties, his key concepts that were to lead to a theory of thinking, in particular 'Attacks on Linking' (1959) (to which I shall return). For example, not just content to show us how Bion can be used to interpret Beckett – a reading I shall be using in a later chapter – Connor daringly suggests that we can use Beckett's work to interpret Bion. A text like *The Unnamable*, for example, with its oral-excretory forms and verbal-corporeal phenomenology called for the terms of a new theory 'that Bion was not to develop until the 1960s' (Connor 25), namely the theory of the container and the contained. Or where Beckett's later texts may appear 'to move towards the depressive position' (a concept that will be explained in the next section), Bion's later experiment with fiction (*A Memoir of a Future*) resembles more 'the pluralising of consciousness and cognition achieved in *The Unnamable*' (32).

Finally, Lois Oppenheim (2001) takes issue with the notion of a profound reciprocal influence of Beckett on his analyst, refuting the idea that the clinical material of Bion's 'Attacks on linking' was based on the Irish author – 'where is the proof?' (768). Like Steven Connor, she sees more fruitful links to be made between Bion's later concepts, such as that of transformation, and what she terms Beckett's highly dissociative writing and 'profoundly visual thinking' (771).

The second critical factor that problematises any analytic approach to Beckett is the Irish author's own extraordinary psychoanalytic culture. The notebooks Beckett kept on his readings in psychology and psychoanalytic theory at the time of his treatment, were discovered only after his death. He took notes on his therapy but these, by Beckett's own confession, are apparently lost (Knowlson 1996, 171–2, 652n.51):

> I used to go back to my digs, and write notes on what had happened, on what I'd come up with. I've never found them since but maybe they still exist somewhere. (68)

For Beckett's readings in psychology, the list is impressive. It includes: Karin Stephen's *Psychoanalysis and Medicine: the Wish to Fall Ill* (1933), Robert Woodworth's *Contemporary Schools of Psychology* (1931), Otto Rank's *The Trauma of Birth* (1929) and Freud's paper 'The Anatomy of the Mental Personality', updated from his 1923 study 'The Ego and the Id'. Beckett also read Ernest Jones', *Papers on Psycho-Analysis* (1912), Adler's *The Neurotic Constitution* (1930) *and Practice & Theory of Individual Psychology* (1923).[7] It now emerges that Woodworth's compilation of schools made Beckett familiar with Behaviourism, Purposivism, Gestalt Psychology (configurationism), the Külpe School, Adler, Jung (Analytic Psychology), Purposivism or, Hormic Psychology, not to mention Köhler's works *Gestalt Psychology* (1920) and *Mentality of Apes* (1925), or Koffka's *The Growth of the Mind* (1921).[8]

Confronted by such a vast analytical culture, it is no surprise that many commentators working in the field of Beckettian psychoanalytic criticism have articulated the relationship between author and text in terms of Beckett's use of psychoanalytic intertexts. Ironically the remarkable insights of critics like Rabaté (1984, 1996), Moorjani (1982, 2004), Baker (1996) or O'Hara (1997), came long before the discovery of Beckett's notebooks.[9]

For example, Phil Baker looks at the ways Beckett's writings reflect and refract psychoanalytic ideas and notions constituting a 'mythology' of a sort (Baker 1997). The intertextual presence of psychoanalysis is proof of what Baker calls 'structural debts' (xii). Locating Beckett in 'a whole retrospective landscape of loss in mid-twentieth century culture constituted by notions such as the paradise of the womb, pre-Oedipal plenitude, maternal prohibition, oceanic regression, narcissism, and the narratives of mourning and melancholia' (xv), Baker argues for a natural structural indebtedness on Beckett's part to psychoanalysis. The affinity between the Beckettian imagination and psychoanalysis, or what Baker calls 'psychoanalytic myths and models' (xiv) is taken to be so evident and natural that Phil Baker puzzlingly takes them 'as read' (xii). Here he is loosely referring to the double Oedipal structure of *Molloy* where 'the knowingness of Molloy's Oedipal material [makes] it a form of unstably ironised citation' (xiv), not to mention its well-known Freudian quips such as: 'Obidil' (libido), or 'the fatal pleasure principle' (ibid.). It follows, then, that 'psychoanalytic myths of origin and selfhood also have a privileged place among the abandoned bases of the Trilogy's progress' (xiv).

The wide-sweeping compendium of analytic ideas and of concepts Baker finds in Beckett's texts is of course illuminating and very useful. While I agree that psychoanalysis can be intraliterary just as much as literature is intrapsychoanalytic, Beckett's reappropriation of analytic discourse is however more than just a quotational practice. I am particularly critical of the way Beckett's texts have been reduced to simply categorically representing such psychoanalytic *intertexts* as *contexts*. Irrespective of whether one is dealing with the early work or the later work, what is contextually given and what is textually made, however, are two irreducibly different orders of things. Bringing psychoanalysis to Beckett – and Beckett's writings to psychoanalysis – necessarily means bringing it back, re-visiting, and returning to an a prior context, an already interpreted relationship. It also necessitates a strategic methodology to justify such an ambitious and arguably unnecessary undertaking.

Theoretical strategies

The critical epistemology of the negative will be seen to pivot essentially around two key conceptual themes: thinking (Bion), on one hand, and playing (Winnicott), on the other. Underlying these themes are a number of key analytic concepts which I shall frequently allude to. These were developed in the 1950s such as Bion's 'The Imaginary Twin' (1950), 'Attacks on Linking' (1959), 'A Theory of Thinking' (1962), and Winnicott's 'Transitional Objects and Transitional Phenomena' (1953 originally hypothesised in 1951). These concepts will be systematically presented in a later chapter. Suffice to say here that these dual notions enable us to re-conceptualise the role of the archaic maternal object in Beckett's writing since, for both Bion and Winnicott, 'the absent other marks the place, names the conditions which allow thought, playing, or vitality to move forward; or inversely, becomes the graveyard or the void of the subject, where attacks on linking (Bion 1959), unintegration (Winnicott 1963) reign' (Sekoff 1999, 114).[10] What is common to Bion, Winnicott and Beckett, is a fundamental drama of absence being thought or played out. The elucidation will be seen to work both ways.

However, neither Bion nor Winnicott's concepts will be 'applied' to Beckett. The issue at stake is perhaps no longer that of the application of psychoanalysis to literature, but, rather, of their interimplication in each other. Reading Beckett's negative through Bion and Winnicott amounts then to an interexplanation of texts and concepts, and involves both a critical transference and a counter-transference.[11] Freud saw the transference as an ambiguous phenomenon, but one meaning he assigned to it was that of a playground. However, as analyst, Freud placed himself outside the playground leaving himself with either/or choices. There is either the illusion of transference or the reality of historical and material truth. In such a location he cannot account for the creative aspects of the transference or of the analyst's constructions (Schwartz 1978, 7).

As regards methodology, the study could be loosely described as an exercise in textual performativity due to its critical reappropriation and deployment of Klein, Winnicott and Bion's theories. In my description of the textual process of Beckett's negative, I wish to put greater emphasis on the dialogic aspect between text and theory and combine, as it were, my subjective response and my attempts to be objective about Beckett's writing. More than just a distant 'observer' reading or 'hearing' of Beckett's text, I shall endeavor to somehow 'participate' in the writing in order to re-present the Beckett negative to and through my reading. Reading is not a one-way imposition on my part, that is, theory to text, but rather a two-way imposition involving 'parts' of both text and theory, including possibly, reversals of roles. The aim is to learn to read, think and play the negative as fully as possible. The work of interpretation is not to exchange text for theory, illusion for reality, but to establish a flexible boundary between Beckett and psychoanalysis and to bridge these simultaneously (Gunn 1988, ix–x).[12]

The readings proposed of the trilogy and *Godot*, broadly trace the development of what could be loosely called an aesthetic of absence, originating in the mother–child relationship, which is thematised in the trilogy and takes a more abstract or 'blank' form on stage.[13] An analysis of Beckett's reinvestment and re-enactment of earlier maternal metaphors of separation and reunion, loss and repetition, shows that these metaphors are substitutes for the ultimately unthought or unthinkable bringing us thereby in the distinctly aesthetic direction of unnamability, formlessness or the indeterminate. Beckett's concern with blankness and emptiness on stage obliges us, therefore, to reconceptualise his space of writing in terms of mental or abstract space thereby allowing us to think anew Beckett's aesthetic concern with form and structure: 'To find a form that accommodates the mess, that is the task of the artist now' (qtd in McMillan, 14). The concluding chapter leaves the basic corpus chosen for this study to focus on Beckett's later 1975 production of *Warten auf Godot* placing this in the context of the shorter texts of the 1970s such as *Footfalls* and *That Time*.

A subsidiary theme in all of this concerns the relationship between novel and play, page and stage, theatrical notebook and performance. Where some Beckett critics are guilty of either excluding one genre in order to favour another, or even neglecting essential differences between the two genres, I have chosen to read *Waiting for Godot* firstly in relation to the trilogy, since it was written *between Malone Dies* and *The Unnamable* (Ross 1998) and secondly as an irreducibly different and separate discourse from the novels, hence my interest in Beckett's ulterior productions of his own work.

As 'there cannot be a theory without an experience, without a subjective discovery, without a dynamic "understanding"' (Rabaté 2001, 4), it is only fitting that we should begin our exploration of Beckett's literary creation by re-locating the negative in the decisive events of his life prior to his emigration.

1
Setting up Shop in the Void

It is a truism to argue that Beckett became Beckett when he had finally settled in Paris and decided to write in French *and* in English. But this shouldn't diminish the importance of that other truism that even the most uncompromising radical writer must start out from somewhere. And Beckett was no exception. Hence the necessity in this opening chapter to return to the Irish Beckett and to review the following issues: the importance Beckett's mother took in his life and work, as if he needed to find ways of using her 'savage loving' for aesthetic purposes; the subsequent analysis with Bion, following the sudden death of Beckett's father and the son's ultimate choice to leave Ireland and to embrace France. Beckett's self-acclaimed vision he had in his mother's room is read here as the formal acknowledgement of the importance of the negative, as if Beckett is making friends or peace with his life-long scepticism and obsession with failure. The return to Beckett's Irishness, then, is necessary even if it is to acknowledge that to all intents and purposes the writing must remain irreducible to any original state of affairs. The other strand of such a paradox lies in the fact that Beckett's search for the void and emptiness – 'no man's land, Hellespoint or vacuum' (*D* 70) – was propelled by his earlier experience.

Making absences present

A cynical view of Beckett's Irish relations would be to say that even if the writer had not experienced insurmountable personal difficulties and conflicts, the wider Irish cultural and political environment would have proven to be sufficiently persecutory and debilitating as to necessitate exile and rupture. Notwithstanding, Beckett seemed to have always been glad of his persecutors be they religious, cultural or political. While his writing career did not really flourish until he had left Ireland and adopted the language and culture of France, when asked how a small country like Ireland could have produced so many great writers since the last half of the nineteenth century, Beckett replied:

> It's the priests and the British. They have buggered us into existence. After all, when you are in the last bloody ditch, there is nothing left but to sing. (Bair 1978, 241)

In an interview with Tom Driver, Beckett claimed that Irish Catholicism was not seductive but was more profound than Protestantism. Yet, he humorously undercuts these sentiments by saying:

> When an Irish bus passes a church all hands make a quick sign of the cross. One day, the dogs in the street will do likewise, perhaps even the pigs. (Driver 1961)

Such mockery cannot of course be simply seen as some sectarian anti-Catholicism on Beckett's part. It must be seen as Beckett's dismay with the lack of a wider intellectual freedom in the Irish Free State. It is this dissenting dismay which had incensed him into writing the article: 'Censorship in the Saorstat' in 1935. The article decries the act of 16 July 1929 which established a board of censors to determine what books should be allowed into the Republic of Ireland. Beckett dismissed the bill as panic legislation revealing how sterilised the Irish mind had become (*D* 87).

The Irish artist, writer or poet who in the early decades of independence chose to remain in Ireland, had two roles available to him. He could either furnish the new conservative order and essentialist ideology of the state through self-conscious nativism, an idyllic celebration of the rural folk tradition, or he might seek to define his artistic identity in terms of opposition and dissent (Brown 1981, 312–13). If he was Protestant, as Beckett was, he would have probably found himself in an artistic vacuum of a sort or an internal cultural exile to all intents and purposes. As the Anglo-Irish literary critic Vivian Mercier showed, alienation and the search for identity were serious problems for Irish Southern Protestants:

> The typical Anglo-Irish boy ... learns that he is not quite Irish almost before he can talk [...] later he learns that he is far from being English either [...] 'Who am I?' is the question that every Anglo-Irish man must answer. (Mercier 1977, 25–6)

Expatriation, whether physical or spiritual, was easy, according to Mercier, for Southern Protestants since they formed a minority group that drew its ideas and general culture from outside its native country.[1] It was Beckett's cultural background which explicated his status as a writer. Mercier asserts that the novels and plays cannot therefore be consistently interpreted as versions of pastoral or pleas for the down-trodden. Instead they link up with an Anglo-Irish literary tradition. Even if Vladimir and Estragon of *Godot* were not born into the landed gentry, it is reasonable to argue that 'they came from the professional classes, prone in Ireland as in England, to ape the manners of the aristocracy while possessing a better education than they' (Mercier 52). Despite Beckett's initial radically negative image as a Parisian dramatist, Mercier sees his self-imposed exile not as a rupture from Irish theocratic society on Beckett's part, but as a symbolic continuation with an Anglo-Irish Protestant cultural tradition. It follows that the Beckett who was initially linked to French existentialism is, in disguise, the Irish Protestant Beckett. In fact, for Mercier, Beckett's Irish cultural identity crisis antedated his so-called existential problems of self-identity that Martin Esslin was to later explore in his *Theatre of the Absurd*:

> When we remember that the [Beckett] is a very special kind of Irishman [...] Protestant, suburban, middle-class, but brought up and for the most part educated in what is now the Republic [...] the special kind of universality he seems to communicate to the world at large is more readily understood. To employ two modern clichés, alienation and the search for identity are both serious problems for an Irishman of that heritage. (Ibid., 25)

Mercier argues, then, that Beckett's fundamental identity as a writer can be better understood as an Irish Protestant sociological conflict within Irish Theocratic society. As Beckett's sardonic quips, which I have already quoted, testify, the conflict concerns the incompatible relations between Protestant artists/intellectuals and Irish Catholicism with the former proving to be radically superior and intolerable to the limited *Weltanschauung* of Irish Catholic society. Consequently, by replacing Beckett's radicalism within his 'original' context of Irish Protestantism, Mercier is recuperating Beckett's radical reputation back into a more domesticated and parochial form of radicalism. In doing so, he tries to hold onto a paradoxical position, for by claiming that Beckett's radical appeal lies in his capacity to transcend his original context ('the special kind of universality he seems to communicate to the world at large'), he is equally claiming that Beckett's appeal can be better understood within the very issues which Beckett actually transcended, that is, his Protestant, suburban, middle-class universe.

Mercier's line of enquiry has been taken up by recent 'Irish Beckett' critics who, in different ways, show that Beckett's exclusion as a Southern Irish Protestant has proven to be a decisive factor in his search for a poetics of solitude and solipsism. Speaking of the Beckett family, Kiberd underlines the keen sense of estrangement felt by the Beckett family for they were neither Empire loyalists nor Irish Republicans. Quoting Mercier, he writes:

> They [the Becketts] lived in something akin to a cultural vacuum: 'Foxrock deliberately avoided much of Irish popular culture, while providing regrettably little English culture, high or low, to put in its place.' It is hardly surprising that their son should have eventually set up shop in the void. (Kiberd 1996, 531)

Indeed Beckett's 'home' was, Kiberd continues, quoting *More Pricks Than Kicks,* 'nowhere so far as I can see'. But such a 'nowhere', Kiberd goes on to argue, proved to be an artistic blessing for Beckett. It made him the 'first truly Irish playwright, because the first utterly free of factitious elements of Irishness' (ibid.). Similarly, in Sinead Mooney's terms the 'willed solitude and solipsism of [Beckett's] mature work [...] [is] a writing of extreme introversion and puritan self-scrutiny' (Mooney 2000, 228). She goes on to argue that Beckett's Irish Protestant sense of marginality and exclusion from a theocratic cultural mainstream provides the bedrock for Beckett's increasingly puritan probing of the quintessentially Protestant themes of examination of conscience and autobiography and iconoclasm:

> It is this Irish Protestant sense of the marginal and excluded, the spiritually-hyphenated, the less-than-complete assent to an identity, a coercive cultural heritage, a literary tradition perceived as unmediated pressure rather than incitement, which provides, so to speak, the bedrock for Beckett's henceforth increasingly puritan probing of the quintessentially Protestant activities of examination of conscience, autobiography and iconoclasm. (Mooney, 225)

In these readings of Beckett's Irishness, his texts have clearly been repossessed for an interpretation – among others – governed by a reading of Anglo-Irish society. By stressing the consensual relationship between Beckett's writing and his home culture, it seems to be that Beckett's Irish commentators not only seek to restore Beckett's texts to Irish culture(s) but they *'mistakenly return Beckett to contexts from which he is in flight'* (Milne 2000, 281, my emphasis). I would claim that the radical force of Beckett's writings is being recuperated for the here and now of the present and for the romantic nostalgia of the past in Ireland. Declan Kiberd goes further when he argues that Beckett's Irish legacy consists of a supremely religious artist who 'three hundred years from now [...] will be remembered more for his prose than his plays:

> In an Ireland whose institutional churches had for centuries policed spirituality, he [Beckett] confronted some of the great themes of the puritan conscience: work, effort, reward, anxious self-scrutiny, the need for self-responsibility, and the distrust of artifice and even of art. (Kiberd 1996, 454)

Even if Beckett's constrained conditions at home proved to be an artistic blessing, and on this point I am in total agreement with Kiberd, it has to be said that Beckett's Irish commentators practise a thoroughly traditional sociological view in regarding Beckett's texts as representative and conformist to the established order of southern Protestant cultural discourse, the narrative of the Irish Protestant Beckett constituting a narrative of 'Irishness' that David Lloyd, in a different context, qualifies as 'self-evident, normative, truthful' (Lloyd 1993, 6).

At the other end of the Irish critical spectrum, Beckett's Irish environment is seen to be the debilitating factor, the very thing he had to repudiate and evacuate in order to become the writer he actually became. The 'Irish Modernist Beckett' is virtually synonymous with a radical separation with all matters Irish – 'the rupture of the lines of communication' – (Kearney 1984, 15), making exile into a fetish. Richard Kearney, for instance, places Beckett's exile in a counter-tradition of Irish authors like Joyce, MacGreevy, Coffey and Devlin, who all embraced a modernist Continental literature of self-reflection (Kearney 1984, 16). Like Beckett these writers began with their own nothingness and wrote about the impossibility of ever translating this nothingness into something else. Theirs was an art of '"pure interrogation". Question without answer' (ibid.) As Beckett had put it in relation to Joyce, 'language ceased to be *about* something and became *that something itself*' (Kearney 14, 1984, Kearney's emphasis). David Lloyd is even more adamant when he reminds us that 'there can scarcely be a writer more devoted than Beckett to the thorough and elegant elaboration of the insurmountable contradictions of identity' (Lloyd 1993, 4), identity here meaning Irish identity. Anna McMullan, in her essay devoted to the Irish Beckett debate and the issue of post-colonialism, astutely points out that 'the unstable and multiple modes of identification embodied in [Beckett's] work were incompatible with existing categories of "Irish writing"' (McMullan 2004, 90), Beckett thereby challenging 'both the historical and the cultural boundaries of what was being constructed as a national tradition of Irish writing' (ibid., 91).

While at the risk of schematising and caricaturising the different readings of Beckett's Irishness, the Irish Modernists do leave us with the impression that one day Beckett left home, booked a one-way passage to no man's land, thereby silently crawling away from the 'historical island of Hibernia, towards the metaphysical island of inwardness' (Kearney 1988, 61), swapping en route a tight-fitting genteel Irish Protestant identity for a looser fitting identity of modernism. Thankfully, things were not so depressingly simple as we shall see in this book. While the first Beckett Irish critics had the merit of granting to Beckett's texts some cultural specificity, I would argue (and will illustrate later) that Beckett's exile was a radical gesture of cultural expropriation and self-dispossession. If anything, Beckett's Irishness was a crucial factor in the elaboration of a poetics paradoxically predicated to the negation of any would-be overriding Irish identity. Where Beckett's Protestant commentators make 'absence' present, my aim in this book is to revert this and show how Beckett's Ireland is and was, for Beckett the writer, his 'primary absence' but a necessary one at that.

Beckett's other postcard from the homeland

Samuel Barclay Beckett was the second son of an upper-class Protestant Anglo-Irish family. Originally named 'Bequet', the Becketts were French Huguenots who moved to Ireland for economic and religious freedom. When Beckett finally left Dublin in 1937 to live permanently in Paris, he was reversing the migration which had brought his ancestors to Ireland. Beckett's childhood seems to have been a lonely one. He claims they were brought up 'like Quakers' by a puritanical mother, May Beckett, who exerted a suffocating grip on both sons, but particularly on him (Bair 1978, 22). His childhood seems to have been one long battle of wits, with May determined to conquer Samuel's stubborn refusal to be reached and his determination to maintain his independence from May's domination (ibid., 23).[2] Years later, in 1937, Beckett was to evoke in a letter to MacGreevy what he called his mother's 'savage loving'

(Knowlson 1996, 22) that crushed him and demanded conformity to her own rigid standards and values:

> I am what her savage loving has made me, and it is good that one of us should accept that finally. As it has been all this time, she wanting me to behave in a way agreeable to her in her October of analphabetic gentility, or to her friends ditto, or to the business code of father idealised – dehumanised ... the grotesque can go no further. It is like after a long forenoon of the thumb screws being commanded by the bourreau to play his favourite song without words with feeling. (*LSB*, 552)

James Knowlson aptly captures the constant tension and threats that fraught the mother–son relationship *chez* the Becketts:

> Everyone who knew them spoke of the fierce bond of affection that seemed to bind them together, but also of the stormy conflicts that would blow up between them, sometimes, apparently, over nothing at all. In this conflict of wills, even as a young boy, Sam struggled hard not to be dominated. (Knowlson 1996, 21–2).
> [...]
> It was not that Beckett disliked his mother or did not care what she thought of him. Rather he loved her almost as strongly and cared for her too much. So conflicts of will became heart-rending struggles with that loving side of himself as well as with his mother, as he saw her determinedly and diametrically opposed to him in her judgements or her expectations. (Ibid., 22)

By all accounts Beckett had considerable affection for his father. Professionally a quantity surveyor, Bill Beckett was, in Beckett's own words, 'absolutely non-intellectual' (ibid., 10). Tremendously energetic, large in figure, excellent at swimming, tennis and golf, Bill Beckett was very much a 'man's man' (ibid.). And it was for his straightforwardly affectionate, uncomplicated, chummy relationship with his two sons that Beckett best remembered his father (ibid., 12) who seemed to have been an important counterweight to his domineering, demanding mother (Connor 2008, 9). 'They sort of understood each other', remarked Sheila Page, a family friend (Knowlson 1996, 12). Certainly the childhood memories in *That Time* pick up on Beckett's love of walking with his father into the Dublin mountains, particularly to Three Rock Mountain on Sunday mornings. As Beckett himself recollects, 'there were three rocks. The further one beyond that is Two Rock' (Knowlson 2006, 13). He remembers his father being tired and leaving him to go ahead which is not unlike the memory related in *Company* where the son waits for him in the lee of a rock (*COM* 13). In *From an Abandoned Work*, the fictive son, speaking of his father, says: 'One day I told him [the narrator's father] about Milton's cosmology, away up in the mountains we were, resting against a huge rock looking out to sea, that impressed him greatly' (qtd in Knowlson 2006, 13).

Beckett's education was that of a typical upper-class Irish Protestant: Portora Royal School, in Enniskillen, county Fermanagh, and later in 1923, Trinity College, 'the educational and spiritual hope of the Protestant Ascendancy' (Bair 1980, 40) where he read French and Italian. In 1927, Beckett graduated from Trinity with a First Class degree and a Gold Medal. After teaching briefly in Campbell College in Belfast in 1928, he took up an appointment as *lecteur* in English at the Ecole Normale Supérieure in Paris. After his years of promise and freedom at the Ecole Normale, during which time he came to know Joyce and begun to make out a reputation and literary career for himself, Beckett had suffered a series of reverses. The terms of his fellowship required him to return to teach at Trinity College Dublin; Beckett loathed teaching and quickly sank into his characteristic condition of shabby apathy and depression before resigning his fellowship at Trinity in December 1931 (Connor 2008, 9). However, James Knowlson tells us that Beckett did feel remorse for letting his father down by resigning from his post (Knowlson 1996, 157–8). Intriguingly, as a guilty son, he was able to find someone with whom he could identify and that was, of course, Joyce whose father died in December 1931. When Beckett resumed his friendship with Joyce in the first few weeks of 1932, he was to be struck by Joyce's beautiful and moving poem 'Ecce Puer', written to celebrate his grandson's birth but also to acknowledge the remorse that he felt at having 'forsaken' his father, John Joyce (Knowlson 1996, 157). The last two lines: 'O Father forsaken/Forgive your son', not only epitomised Beckett's guilt at having 'forsaken' his family. The fact that Beckett was still able to recite part of the poem, as late as his eighty-third year, suggests that he still felt remorse some fifty years after his resignation (ibid., 158).

During the following year, in June, his father died of a sudden heart attack. Beckett's reaction was unsurprisingly touching. In a letter to MacGreevy, he wrote: 'I can't write about him, I can only walk the fields and climb the ditches after him' (*LSB* 165). In a letter written just months previously, he lovingly evokes a walk he went on with his father poignantly realising that he'll 'never have anyone like him' (ibid., 154, Knowlson 1996, 170). According to Steven Connor it may be that Beckett experienced this as a confirmation of the loss of his second father, Joyce, who had broken angrily with him after Beckett's abortive affair with Lucia, who was herself sinking more and more inexorably into illness (Connor 2008, 9). But the death of Bill Beckett also meant that Samuel Beckett had to cope with his bereaving mother which fostered an undesired compliance on his part. After Bill Beckett's death, the family home became like 'a mausoleum' (Knowlson 1996, 172). They were, wrote Beckett, several weeks after the funeral, 'up to the eaves in the vile worms of melancholy observance' (ibid.). He was stifled by this 'ostentatious display of prolonged reverence and suffocated by the atmosphere in the "blank silent house"' (ibid.).

While Beckett was later to acknowledge that he 'will always be depressed' (Bair 1980, 299), it is conceivable that he had identified with his mother's depression much earlier on. This is what André Green calls the 'dead mother complex' (Green 1986). The latter is a revelation of the analytic transference which usually comes late in the analysis of patients who do not usually present with depression as a primary feature. Green calls it a 'transference depression' which is the repetition of infantile depression acquired in the presence of a person absorbed in bereavement. Insidiously, as Green writes: 'what comes about then is a brutal change of the maternal imago, which is truly mutative. Until then there is an authentic vitality present in the subject, which comes to a sudden halt' (Green 1986, 149). Green's full statement is:

> The dead mother has taken away with her, in the decathexis of which she had been the object, the major portion of the love with which she had been cathected before the bereavement: her look, the tone of her voice, her smell, the memory of her caress [...] She had been buried alive, but her tomb had disappeared. The hole that gaped in its place made solitude dreadful as though the subject ran the risk of being sunk in it, body and possession. (154)

In a biographical context, we know too that life in Cooldrinagh stopped dead after the death of May Beckett's husband and Beckett found himself at the mercy of a deadened mother. He described his desperation in terms of an arrested movement:

> After my father's death I had trouble psychologically. The bad years were between when I had to crawl home in 1932 and after my

> father's death in 1933. I'll tell you how it was. I was walking down Dawson street. And I felt I couldn't go on. It was a strange experience I can't really describe. I found I couldn't go on moving. So I went into the nearest pub and got a drink just to stay still. (Knowlson, 1996, 172–3)

His depression expressed itself in endless unshiftable colds and flu, boils and cysts and panic attacks accompanied by palpitations and sensations of suffocation. He was persuaded by his friend Geoffrey Thompson that his symptoms might be of psychosomatic origin and managed to persuade his mother in turn to let him come to London in late 1933 specifically in order to undertake analysis (Connor 2008, 9). Shortly after Christmas 1933, he began therapy at the Tavistock Clinic with Wilfred Bion (Knowlson 1996, 174–81).

Reaching the deeper coils

When Beckett finally went for analysis, thanks to the help and advice of Geoffrey Thompson, he presented himself to Bion with severe anxiety symptoms which Beckett himself described as follows:

> a bursting, apparently arrhythmic heart, night sweats, shudders, panic, breathlessness, and at its most severe, total paralysis. (Knowlson 1996, 176)[3]

If Beckett remained doubtful about and hostile towards psychoanalytic theory and procedure, Bion seems to have had the intelligence and breadth of cultural awareness to gain Beckett's respect. As James Knowlson outlines, Beckett liked Bion, calling him 'the covey'. Off the job, Beckett found Bion, 'pleasant but against a background of TocH and Tank Corps that makes [me] tremble' (Knowlson 1996, 176).

Contrary to what Deirdre Bair tells us, Bion was not a Kleinian psychoanalyst at the time of working with Beckett (Bair 1978, 155–6). It is perhaps not inconceivable, as Steven Connor shrewdly suggests, that Bion became a Kleinian partly because of first having to have been, for a short while, a Beckettian (Connor 2008, 15). He was a trainee therapist, who was himself undergoing analysis with J.A. Hadfield, whose work and influence were dominant in the Tavistock at this time.[4] Bion, six years Beckett's senior, had fought with distinction in the First World War. He served in the Royal Tank regiment, winning the DSO at Cambrai. After taking a degree in history at Queen's College, Oxford, he taught for a short time at a minor public school (his own) and subsequently undertook six years of medical training at University College, London with a view to becoming a psychoanalyst. He met and was impressed by Wilfred Trotter, an outstanding brain surgeon who had also written the famous *Instincts of the Herd in Peace and War* in 1916, based on the horrors of the First World War. This was to prove an important influence on Bion's interest in group behaviour. It should be noted that Bion recounted some of his own traumatic wartime experiences with humour as well as horror in his autobiography *The Long Week-End, 1897–1919* coining enigmatic notions such as 'nameless dread' or 'withoutness'.

After qualifying as a doctor in 1930, Bion joined the staff of the Tavistock Clinic in 1932. In 1938 he began a training analysis with John Rickman, but this was brought to an end by the Second World War. He joined the RAMC in 1940 and worked in a number of military hospitals including Northfield Hospital where he initiated the first Northfield Experiment. The entire group at Tavistock had in fact been taken into the army, and were working on new methods of treatment for psychiatric casualties (those suffering post-traumatic stress, or 'shell shock' as it was then known). These ideas on the psychoanalysis of groups were then taken up and developed by others such as S.H. Foulkes and Rickman. As his interest in psychoanalysis increased, Bion underwent training analysis, between 1946–1952, with Melanie Klein. He joined a research group of Klein's students (including Hannah Segal and Herbert Rosenfeld), who were developing Klein's theory of the paranoid-schizoid position, for use in the analysis of patients with psychotic disorders. He produced a series of highly original and influential papers (collected as *Second Thoughts*, 1967) on the analysis of schizophrenia, and the specifically cognitive, perceptual and identity problems of such patients.

During the forties, Bion produced a series of brilliant papers on group dynamics (collected as *Experiences in Groups*, 1961). Later he attempted to understand thoughts and thinking from a mathematical and scientific point of view, believing there to be too little precision in the existing vocabulary. Later he abandoned the complex, abstract applications of mathematics, and even the Grid, and developed a more intuitive approach, culminating in the *Memoir of the Future*. (A more thorough account of Bion's concepts will be developed later).

Returning to Beckett, in a 1976 Irish Television broadcast, Geoffrey Thompson was to say that the key to understanding Samuel Beckett was to be found in his relationship with his mother, a re-echoing of Beckett's much earlier acknowledgement to MacGreevy that it was his mother's 'savage loving' that made him what he was. While Deirdre Bair rashly claimed that the analysis didn't help Beckett to arrive at any understanding or acceptance of his relationship with his mother (Bair 1980, 176), James Knowlson tells us that the ongoing analysis crystallised, if anything, the 'fierce tug-of-war that seems to have been going on between an almost umbilical dependence on and a desire for independence from his [Beckett's] mother' (Knowlson 1996, 178). Beckett's letters at the time make it quite clear that he was concerned about the progress and nature of their relationship (ibid., 179).[5]

Beckett's actual memories of his analysis and feelings about it are ambivalent to say the least. If we turn to his letters written at the time, we see that Beckett counted the sessions: 'On Monday I go for the 133rd time' (*SBL*, 247), clearly feared that the analysis 'is going to turn out a failure' (240), and at a moment of despair likened it to torture:

> Bion in his last acknowledgment of the filthy 'trusted I had by now taken up my work with pleasure and satisfaction', as he was sure I must 'even though not entirely freed from neuroses'! Mother's whole idea of course is to get me committed to life here. And my travel-courage is so gone than ever frightened by the prospect of effort, initiative & even the little self-assertion of getting about from one place to another. Solitude here, perhaps more sober than before, seems the upshot of the London Torture. Indeed I do not see what difference the analysis has made. (Letter to MacGreevy 16 January [1936], *SBL*, 299–300)

Yet the analysis with Bion goes on – 'I go on with Bion' – for there is no reason 'why it should ever come to an end', Beckett managing to evoke what he wittily calls 'the intolerable symptoms of an improvement' (Letter to MacGreevy 20, February 1935, *SBL* 253).

While in reality the analysis lasted two years, Beckett in a late interview with James Knowlson remembered it having lasted only six months (Knowlson 2006, 68). Although he stopped it because he felt it wasn't doing him any good and that he was using his mother's money that she could ill afford, notwithstanding Beckett acknowledged that it probably did help:

> I think it helped me perhaps to control the panic. I didn't have that feeling of panic or dizziness or something. I think it all helped me to understand a bit better what I was doing and what I was feeling. I certainly came up with some extraordinary memories of being in

> the womb, intra-uterine memories. I remember being trapped, of being imprisoned and unable to escape, of crying to be let out but no one could hear, no one was listening. I remember being in pain but being unable to do anything about it. (Knowlson 2006, 68)

Despite the ambivalence, the analysis seems to have provided Beckett with lucid self-enlightenment about what he called his 'diseased condition' that began in a time which he could not remember (ibid., 180). With poignant self-insight into his own arrogant feelings of superiority and his tendency to withdraw and isolate himself, Beckett, in a letter to MacGreevy (10 March 1935), saw his way of living as 'a negation of living':

> For years I was unhappy, consciously and deliberately ever since I left school & went into T.C.D., so that I isolated myself more & more [...] But in all that there was nothing that struck me as morbid. The misery & solitude & apathy & the sneers were the elements of an index of superiority & guaranteed the feeling of arrogant 'otherness', which seemed as right & natural & as little morbid as the ways in which it was not so much expressed as implied & reserved [...] It was not until that way of living, or rather negation living, developed such terrifying physical symptoms that it could no longer be pursued, that I became aware of anything morbid in myself. In short, if the heart had not put the fear of death into me I would be still boozing & sneering & lounging around & feeling that I was too good for anything else. (*SBL*, 258–9, qtd in Knowlson, 179–80)[6]

Late in 1935, Beckett announced and subsequently carried out his intention of terminating the analysis at the end of the year. He had begun *Murphy*, his first masterpiece, during analysis; breaking off from analysis seems to have enabled him to complete the novel in the following year. As some have suggested, this is a pattern which is repeated later and in different ways: the breaking off from psychoanalysis produces a complex, non-analytic, but nevertheless reparative response in Beckett's own writing. As to the influence of Beckett's analysis on his writing and the wider question of Bion's influence on Beckett, I propose to defer these issues until later.

The lure of exile

The ultimate turning point of Beckett's career, if we exclude the very important relationship Beckett enjoyed with Joyce during his earlier two-year Parisian stay (1928–30) and the undoubted beneficial and creative effects of his London analysis with Bion (1934–36), was his emigration to France and his decision to write bilingually.

In a sense, the only relations that ever mattered to Beckett were foreign relations, foreign languages, not only French but also Italian and German. He carried out an important number of translations from French and Italian, not forgetting his translation of Anna Livia Plurabelle and the publication of his critical essays and reviews in the influential journal *transition: An International Quarterly for Creative Experiments*.[7] While Beckett's French connections turned out to be the most telling ones, one must also be mindful of his interest in Italian and German literatures and languages.[8]

German painting and music literally form a leitmotif running through his works, going from the broken German that provides so much wordplay in *Dream of Fair to Middling Women*, to the haunting use of Schubert's music in *All That Fall*, one of whose songs (Lieder) was to give Beckett a German title for one of his last short plays, *Nacht und Träume*, not forgetting the bleak Baltic scenery that figures in Krapp's memories (*Krapp's Last Tape*) and the references to Theodor Fontane's novel, *Effie Briest*. More importantly, James Knowlson has shown that through Beckett's unknown diaries of 1936–37, a period Beckett spent touring Germany and her museums, one discovers an extraordinary interest on Beckett's part in painting, classical and modern and, in particular, the German Expressionist painters that had been banned by the Nazis (Knowlson 1996, 237–40). Beckett was to later develop a tremendous admiration for the work of the romantic painter Caspar David Friedrich whose *Two Men Observing the Moon* provided inspiration for the image of Estragon and Vladimir waiting at the tree for Godot (Knowlson 234, 254, 258, 378).

The sort of commuting that goes on between countries, cultures and languages, and literary styles in a text as early as *Dream of Fair to Middling Women* was certainly also Beckett's during the thirties.[9] But while we know more today, thanks to Knowlson, about where and how Beckett spent his exiling years before making his home in Paris such knowledge still doesn't purchase much when faced with those nebulous and ghostly zones the writings gladly inhabit.

Obviously, there can be no fast, easy or definitive explanations for Beckett's exile. Any re-legitimisation of an 'Irish Beckett' must begin then by taking into consideration and for granted what I term the exiling, negating and estranging forces of Beckett's texts. To quote from Beckett's tribute to Henri Hayden: 'everything is recognisable, but in order to be misunderstood' (*HH* 10). Beckett's work was certainly part of the symbolic resolution of a lived exile from 'that unfamiliar native land of mine' (*BT* 288). Adorno once said that for a man who no longer has a homeland, writing becomes a place to live. Nothing could be truer about Samuel Beckett.

The space of self-transfer

I have elsewhere argued that Beckett's self-transfer to France and to French was not so much an escape from a problematic cultural heritage as a positive search for a 'transitional' or 'potential' space (Ross 2004, 29–37; Bryden 2004, 157). This space, to follow Winnicott's theory, is 'at the interplay between there being nothing but me and there being objects and phenomena outside omnipotent control' (Winnicott 1971, 118). This third area of human living is one that is neither inside the individual nor outside in the world of shared reality or, in other terms, an intermediary zone between the dreamlike unconscious and the social world, between what Winnicott termed 'me' and 'not me'. Paradoxically the space negates the idea of separation between the baby and mother but its very existence depends on there being a clear separation between the two.

Winnicott shows that for a child to have the possibility of play – fantasy, illusion – there must be paradoxically an illusory space which is neither subjective nor totally objective (Winnicott 1971, 1–7). Winnicott describes an invisible terrain of maximally intense experience which arises between mother and child. It is a terrain between the child's me-extensions and the not-me, at the interplay between there being nothing but the child's 'me' and there being objects and phenomena outside his omnipotent control. Play belongs to this intermediate space since the latter antedates any established reality-testing and is fundamentally illusory. Play then can be used to master the differences between the 'mother-world' and the 'non-mother-world'. The play-space or transitional space which arises can be seen as both the child's separation and denial of this separation from the breast. The me's relation to the not-me is neither symbiotic nor separate, but both; and the me's illusory omnipotence and disillusionment follow the same paradoxical pattern (Moorjani 2004a, 181). The relevance of Winnicott's concept does not stop here. For Winnicott, the potential space does not – indeed must not – disappear. It yields to cultural experience in general and to the art-work in particular.

Winnicott's theory of development is by definition a story of a struggle against compliance with the environment, compliance because of the fact of dependence. The infant relies on the mother's attentiveness for his survival. Winnicott explains how the individual grows, through dependence, towards a personal way of being and how the early facilitating environment makes this possible. In his theory of human development, it is the mother, as the first environment, who actively adapts to the needs of her infant. This allows the infant the opportunity for the illusion that her breast is part of the infant. It is, as it were, under the baby's magical control (Winnicott 1971, 13). The latter uses the mother ruthlessly for the recognition and gratification that his development requires. But the mother's task is gradually to disillusion the infant but, as Winnicott stresses, has no hope of success unless at first she has been able to give sufficient opportunity for illusion (ibid).

To return to literature, the Beckett who famously said he preferred warfare in France to peace-time and tea-time at Cooldrinagh chose to be in exile, that is, to find himself or to place himself outside the familiar and the homely, outside any given 'system of representation', but this in order to explore the interplay between me-extensions and the not-me.[10] Hence, in my view, the need for Beckett to be on the margin, that is to be neither wholly in or wholly out of either one's own culture or that of one's adopted culture. Beckett's exile was both a taking into the space of writing representations of the mother and, also, of other objects in his home environment and at the same time a break with expectation and a courting of absence. His investment was into the 'no-place' of the mind, not quite here or there, a relentless engagement with negativity and with what Steven Connor terms 'separative art':

> It separates itself from the world, from meaning, from reference, from every 'occasion', and centres upon the processes of negation, reduction, purification, discarnation, the stripping away of every kind of excrescence, superfluity or contamination. (Connor 1992, 100)

The in-between, the ambiguous, the composite

'The artist who stakes his being is from nowhere, has no kith', Beckett once said in a homage to Jack Yeats (*D* 149). It is reasonable to assume that Beckett never saw his home culture as whole, unique, irreplaceable; it was exchangeable for other part-objects in the same way that religion had 'no more depth than an old school tie' (Junker 1995, 22).[11] It is equally unreasonable to assume that Beckett managed to evacuate his original environment by beginning with his own nothingness and writing 'about the impossibility of ever translating this nothingness into something else' (Kearney 1985, 16). That Beckett's work does not flow seamlessly into some hypothetical Irish world but has a separate identity, hardly requires defending or rehearsing here. But to recast this in Winnicott language may be helpful.

In the state of primary identification, the baby is unaware of himself as a separate, autonomous human being: he does not realise where he begins and ends, or that he begins and ends. Subjectively, he feels completely merged in with the mother-environment. Gradually and progressively given a facilitating environment, the baby becomes dimly aware of the otherness of the mother, of the fact that he himself does not flow seamlessly into the world, or into her (Fuller 1988, 202).

To return to Beckett, one could conceivably argue that the negative of France was more real for him than the positive of Ireland.[12] Within this perspective, I would re-place Beckett's Ireland as bearing the sense of a 'primary absence'. Intimately familiar and worryingly strange, Beckett's Ireland provides so much of his work with its energy and pathos. In a way, Beckett's Ireland forms a strange love-affair, a strange postcard from the homeland (*NOV*, 15) and yet there can exist no real picture or full text of home.[13]

Beckett's Irish identity can only be seized by glimpsing in which the peculiar manner Beckett 'threw it all away, and chose to write from an abandoned Irish culture' (Ross 2010, 200). While the radio play, *All That Fall*, one of Beckett's most explicit Irish texts, may inaugurate a 'return' to Irish Protestant subject matter, it is more fruitfully read as the repetition of an inaugural separation from home, that is, the re-abandoning by Beckett, the dramatist, of his home Protestant culture, which is no other than a radical gesture of cultural expropriation and self-dispossession. What is important here is to see *All That Fall* as a figment of the imagination, a drama of haunting, hence Beckett's insistence on it being a radio text for voices, not bodies. As Beckett said to Everett Frost, who produced the American première of *All That Fall* in 1986, it all depends 'on the whole thing coming out of the dark' (qtd in Frost 1994, 191) and as Frost astutely remarked, 'the "whole thing depends" not only "coming out of the dark" but also on returning to it' (207).

As to the conception of play, we learn that Beckett 'heard' it in his head, 'in the dead of t'other night [got] a nice gruesome idea full of cart-wheels and dragging feet and puffing and panting which may or may not lead to something'. He modestly dismissed it as 'boyhood memories [with] the Devil tottered in the ditch',[14] 'ancient works' with which he had lost contact (Frost 215). Where critics like John Harrington see in *All That Fall* 'an explicit extension of Beckett's poetics of futility and a regression to a precisely identified Ireland' – a 'pointed application of Beckett's exposure of sustaining, positivistic illusions of a modern, partitioned Ireland' (Harrington 1991, 185–6) – I would rather insist on the importance of Beckett's experiments with what one could call an out-of-body voice. If anything, Beckett de-materialises place, body and person, stripping place of any familiar co-ordinates as his characters dream of other roads, other lands and other homes (*ATF* 32–3). The play has the strange power of extinguishing the world it seeks to see by animating and re-animating voices, sounds and memories. Although the author put in considerable effort to provide a full range of acoustic material and effects with which the listener might construct Boghill and its inhabitants, Boghill, for all its hints at an Irish setting sinisterly turns out to be an indeterminable *topos*, a space that resembles nowhere in particular. Maddy may be able to register the local world around her, with its hills, its racecourse and its station, but such a place doesn't compare to the things she has seen 'and not looked away ... this is *nothing ... nothing*' (23 and 24, my emphasis).

From a foreign land, from a constitutional exile (the modernists had legitimised exile and universalised it as it were), it is indeed easier to talk of unnameable domains, things, secretive unreachable horizons of love and desire, which no precise image can ever manage to encompass. Things are so necessarily lost so that the subject might speak and write. Like Molloy, Beckett, too, vanished happy in that 'alien light' which must once have been his (*BT* 40). Indeed, there is rarely anyone at home in Samuel Beckett's work or, at least, no one stays at home, even if there were such a thing, such a place. One thinks of the imaginary house of Mr Knott, a not-house, the 'ruinous old house' in *All That Fall* (*ATF* 7), the dangers of returning home in *Molloy*, returning to discover chaos and havoc as Moran does. Beckett's writings, particularly in their idiosyncratic and cryptic use of places and names, such as the Cackon Country in *Waiting for Godot* (*G*), Turdy and Hole in *Molloy* or Boghill in *All That Fall*, indicate, among other things, that these are strange places to be, places not to be, non-places of a sort. As Paul Davies astutely remarks, 'Beckett's art is precisely the art of a consciousness *finding itself in non-location*' (Davies 2001, 400). Such immemorable places apart, something of Beckett's foreign trajectories makes itself be felt through the writings whether it be some free-floating metaphor of spatial indeterminacy, uprootedness, unnameable loss, unthinkable origins. One thinks here of some of the most obscure and quasi poetic moments in his work where rare moments of personal nostalgia creep into the narrative as when Malone, musing about the grotesque Mol, imagines what it is to be abroad and 'what it is to have been what we have been, and sink together, in an unhappiness that has no name' (*BT* 240).

Far from sponsoring a would-be ahistorical or apolitical view of Beckett, I would argue that the works are awash with the flotsam and jetsam of Irish culture, literature, names, speech, codes and conventions – ranging from the explicit literary parody of the Irish Renaissance in *Murphy* to the Yeatsian intertext in *... but the clouds ...* passing by Beckett's celebrated exploitation of 'cod-Irish surnames' (Mooney 2007, 18) and Gaelic place-names in the trilogy (Ballyba, Shit, Shitba, Turdy, Turdyba, etc.). I would also argue that these sub-texts function as dynamic structure and not as a self-presentation. Not unlike the play of multiple voices and inter-texts in Eliot's *The Wasteland*, Beckett's Irish references too resist any fixed boundaries or facile categorisation.

For example, there is a personal dimension to Beckett's interest in stone, for, according to Gottfried Büttner, as a child, Beckett would pick up stones from the beach and carry them home, where he would build nests for them and put them in trees to protect them from the sea, describing his relationship to stone as 'almost a love relationship' (Büttner 1984, 163, n. 200; Knowlson 1996, 29; Rodriguez 2004, 105). Malone's night-time stone, for instance, has all the making and trappings of a transitional object: it is the hard object he happens to find, arbitrarily collected, which becomes one of his night-time comforters. He tells us how he loved to fall asleep holding in his hand a stone, a horse chestnut or a cone, and he would be still holding it when he woke (*BT* 227–8). Knowlson and Eoin O'Brien claim that Beckett was familiar with the stone relics at Glen Druid – 'the Cromlechs located in the countryside near Foxrock' (Knowlson 1996, 669). Mary Junker, for example, sees in the imagery of stones in Lucky's speech in *Waiting for Godot* an evocation of ancient Irish stone-relics and stone oratori (Junker 1995, 50–1). I shall return to the stone motif later in this book.

Sieges without, sieges within

Together with the French stories, Beckett's post-1945 French writings illustrate very well how deeply the approach that Beckett dated from his 'revelation' in his mother's house after the war affected his writing. And they reveal how his attitudes had changed with respect to the use of personal or erudite material since his pre-war novels and poems (Knowlson 2006, 371).

Having returned to Dublin at the end of the war to see his mother, Beckett found it difficult to return to France. So he volunteered to work as an interpreter, storekeeper and ambulance driver for the Irish Red Cross Hospital in St-Lô in Normandy, which had been destroyed by allied bombings and shellings after the D-Day landings (ibid., 2006, 345–50). Indeed Beckett's wartime experience in St Lô cannot be underestimated. It was vital in terms of the content of his post-war writing (350).

In 1946, Beckett wrote a short script *The Capital of the Ruins* which was to be delivered on Irish radio but in fact never was. The text grew out of Beckett's experience in the town of Saint-Lô where he had spent from August 1945 to January 1946 serving as interpreter and store keeper in the Hôpital de la Croix-Rouge Irlandaise,[15] the Irish Red Cross Hospital. As James Knowlson points out, it meant that he saw real suffering at first-hand. It was there that 'he witnessed real devastation and misery; buildings [...] reduced to rubble; possessions blown to pieces [...] people in desperate need of food and clothing, yet clinging desperately onto life; a hospital created out of nothing on fields that became churned into a sea of mud' (ibid.). One of Beckett's medical colleagues in the hospital, Dr Jim Gaffney, in letters home to his sister, spoke significantly not about Beckett's quiet, introspective manner, his sullenness or his moods of despair, but of his positive helpfulness, general kindness and thoughtfulness towards others (Knowlson 2003, 27).

To briefly summarise and paraphrase the text, Beckett first takes his audience on a guided tour of the hospital before shifting to a different plane. What was more important than the material details was the Irish staff's encounter with what Beckett calls 'the rare and famous ways of spirit that are the French ways' (*AST*, 22). More important than the penicillin brought to France by the Irish medical team was their discovery of shared human values there, or as Beckett put it:

> the occasional glimpse obtained, by us in them, and, who knows, by them in us [...] of that smile at the human conditions [...] the smile deriding, among other things, the having and the not having, the giving and the taking, sickness and health. (23–4)

Finally, after evoking the bombed town and returning again to the Irish Hospital wooden huts, the piece ends on a philosophical note when Beckett spells out in a memorable phrase the impact of the experience of working in war-ravaged France:

> a vision and sense of a time-honoured conception of humanity in ruins, and perhaps even an inkling of the terms in which our condition is to be thought again. These will have been in France. (27–8)[16]

Unsurprisingly, Beckett critics have picked up on this atypical glimpse of Beckett's alleged humanism. Lois Gordon stresses Beckett's experience of 'the human capacity both for destructiveness and for stoical forbearance, courage, humanity and even humour in the face of brutal forces' (Gordon 1996, 193). Beckett's experience in Saint-Lô provided him with a long-awaited equanimity giving him a sense of balance of what in *Godot* he would call the 'tears' and 'laughter' of the world (Gordon, 192–3).[17]

Between these crucial experiences, something else occurred that enabled Beckett to see negativity as the matrix of his literary creation. While staying in Foxrock with his mother, towards the end of the war, he had a vision or a revelation in his mother's room and not on Dun Laoghaire Pier as was commonly assumed (Knowlson 1996, 771 n. 52). To Ludovic Janvier, Beckett stated that the 'dark he had struggled to keep under' was ultimately to become the source of his creative inspiration (Bair 1980, 298). 'What comforts me', Beckett stated to a friend, 'is the realization that I can now accept this dark side as the commanding side of my personality. In accepting it, I will make it work for me' (ibid., 299). Beckett's revelation was to fuel the romantic mystical experience evoked by Krapp in *Krapp's Last Tape* (*KTP*), his 'vision at last':

> What I suddenly saw then was this, that the belief I had been going on all my life, namely [...] clear to me at last that the dark I have always struggled to keep under is in reality my most (*Krapp curses, switches off, winds tape forward, switches on again*) – unshatterable association until my dissolution of storm and night with the light of the understanding and the fire. (Qtd in Knowlson 1996, 352)

When Beckett explained to James Knowlson who, in 1987, was preparing an edition of Beckett's theatrical notebook of *Krapp's Last Tape,* that the dark was in reality Krapp's 'his most precious ally', his 'true element at last and key to the opus magnum', we are certainly not far away from Beckett's own visionary experience where light is rejected 'in favour of darkness' extending to 'a whole zone of being that includes folly and failure, impotence and ignorance' (ibid.). But what had been 'the vision at last' for his creature Krapp, was for Beckett less a matter of vision, and, as John Pilling astutely points out, more a matter of recognition. It is perhaps no exaggeration to say that Beckett became Beckett by beginning *Molloy* in May 1947 for it was only then that Beckett began 'to write the things' he felt (Pilling 1997, 2; Anzieu 1992, 95). With this respect, James Knowlson tells us that the stories to come revealed how

Beckett's attitudes had changed with respect to the use of personal or erudite material since his pre-war novels and poems.

What the stories of the trilogy usher in and how the trilogy be seen in the light of Beckett's turning to theatre, is a way of giving the negative a history, an individual subject however impoverished:

> He [Beckett] would draw henceforward on his own inner world for his subjects; outside reality would be refracted through the filter of his own imagination; inner desires and needs would be allowed a much greater freedom of expression [...] In future, his work would focus on poverty, failure, exile and loss; as he put it, on man as a 'non-knower', and as a 'non-can-er' (i.e. someone who cannot). (Knowlson 1996, 352–3)

It is also reasonable to argue that Beckett's vision looks back as much as it looks forward. It was, among other things, a retrospective recognition of how much Beckett was indebted to James Joyce:

> I realised that Joyce had gone as far as one could in the direction of knowing more, [being] in control of one's material. He was always adding to it; you only have to look at his proofs to see that. I realised that my own way was in impoverishment, in lack of knowledge and in taking away, in subtracting rather than in adding. (352)

I am also tempted to see this admission as a re-working of Beckett's early German letter to Axel Kaun where he had developed the idea that literary language must negate itself, that is, be self-destructive and that literature must in fact be turned against itself. In that letter, Beckett had abstractly opposed a literature of the *Unwort* – 'Unword' – to Joyce's 'apotheosis of the word' Beckett likening (his own) language to 'a veil which one has to tear apart in order to get to those things (or the nothingness) lying behind it'. He continues:

> Since we cannot dismiss it at all at once, at least we do not want to leave anything undone that might contribute to its disrepute. To drill one hole after another in it until that which lurks behind, be it something or nothing, starts seeping through – I cannot imagine a higher goal for today's writer [...] At first, it can only be a matter of somehow inventing a method of verbally demonstrating this scornful attitude vis-à-vis the word. In this dissonance of instrument and usage perhaps one will already be able to sense a whispering of

the end-music or of the silence underlying all. (*LSB*, 513–14, qtd in Pilling 1997, 154)[18]

The vision in the room is also a vision that repeats and works through the earlier views that the younger Beckett had cherished with regard to the negative role of writing.[19] In his early Proust essay Becket assumed that art had to enact a labour of radical negation: 'the undoing of every (pseudo-) relation, the destruction of every surface' (Weller 2005, 45). But the vision also points forward to what Beckett was to term, in his discussion of Bram van Velde's painting, namely 'a nonrelational art, an art that ruptures relations' (Gontarski 2006, 3). I am referring here to Beckett's letter of 9, March 1949 to Georges Duthuit, which preceded the French exchange that was finally published in English in the December issue of *transition* as 'Three Dialogues: Samuel Beckett and Georges Duthuit' (to which I shall return). By relation Beckett means not just 'what proposes itself [to the artist] from outside, but also and above all those which, within him, provide him with lines of flight and recoil, variations of tension' (18). For Beckett Bram's painting 'is new because it is the first to repudiate relation in all its forms. It is not the relation with this or that order of encounter that he refuses, but *the state of being quite simply in relation* full stop, the state of being in front of' (19) – 'mais l'état d'être en rapport tout court et sans plus, l'état d'être devant' (16).

I would tentatively suggest, then, that Beckett's newly found fidelity to his inner darkness may have inspired his views on art and the role of the artist expounded in *Three Dialogues with Georges Duthuit*. There in his discussion about Van Velde's painting, Beckett aphoristically reminds us that 'to be an artist is to fail, as no other dare fail, that failure is his world' (*P* 125). But the artist's 'fidelity to failure' is anything but negative despite Beckett's rhetoric of negatives and nothings as he reminds us that there is nothing to express, nothing with which to express, etc. (*P* 103). Where Beckett's salutary vision could be said to provide him with a matrix for literary creation, equally artistic failure contains creative potential, novelty insofar that it is 'an expressive act, even if only of itself, of its impossibility, of its obligation' (ibid.).

Beckett's salutary vision virtually crystallised his attitude towards seeing his writing as a 'negative object' with his ethics of failure. In other terms, we could say he had formally decided not to conquer the negative, but to use it. John Pilling tells us that for Beckett negation was 'a kind of compositional principle, and an unusually productive one, given its potentially destructive effects' (Pilling 2005, 171).[20] As Pilling goes on to show, Beckett's growth as a writer was a perilous balancing act between endorsing negation as a principle of composition and fending off destructiveness. Even at the height of his fame, Beckett's writing – 'that bitter folly' (*BT* 276) – always left him with an incurable and irreducible feeling of frustration, disappointment and fundamental failure. As Pilling again outlines:

> Nor could he ever rid himself of the knowledge that with every achievement (insofar as he could permit himself to think of it as such) went a sense of failure. Even with *Molloy*, *Malone Dies*, *The Unnamable* and *Waiting for Godot* written, Beckett can be found, in the third of the *Three Dialogues* with Georges Duthuit, saying: 'There are many ways in which the thing I am trying in vain to say may be tried in vain to be said'. (Pilling 1996, 2)

Inventing the French Beckett

The French trilogy and *En attendant Godot*) are almost certainly Samuel Beckett's most enduring works if not his first mature works. They belong to Beckett's period of 'creative turmoil', which gave rise to an extraordinary 'frenzy of writing' of novels, poems, short-stories and two plays (Knowlson 1996, 376, 358). Beckett also likened the period to 'the siege in the room' (Bair 1980, 294) conjuring the image of the writer withdrawn from the world, writing in his mother's room, as Molloy does, and considered 1945 and 1946 as the years which conditioned his subsequent development as a writer (Pilling 1997, 1). It is of course the period when Beckett implemented French as a new writing language and theatre as a new medium. It is no exaggeration to say that Beckett re-invented himself or in John Pilling's words, 'Beckett, in his own eyes, became Beckett' (ibid., 2). Let us now briefly review some of the criticism on this question.

Didier Anzieu argues that Beckett's most productive period from 1946 onwards was the result of a decisive break from his mother tongue and culture and that Paris provided him with a space of play – a Winnicottian 'transitional' space – of which he had earlier been deprived by the suffocating influence of his mother and of the Irish cultural context (1983, 85), an issue that I have also addressed elsewhere (Ross 1998; 2004, 185–8). Anzieu argues that the process of writing the Trilogy both recapitulated and brought to completion the truncated analysis with Bion of 1934–5, the inner space of creation being externally facilitated by Beckett's cultural and personal freedom from Ireland and France's newly-found freedom from Nazi persecution.

Deciding to write in French was certainly a means for Beckett to rethink his relationship with his mother tongue. Patrick Casement, also using Winnicott's theory of play, stresses Beckett's search for space and play, either through the wider foreign cultural environment of France which facilitated Beckett's choice to write bilingually, and the inner environment of the exiled writer. Casement argues that, in Beckett's case, we have the possibility not to simply see Beckett's exile and his adoption of French as a simple rupture or separation from the past. The French writings are both a separation from and a reunion with the past. Casement argues – albeit reductively and heavily relying on Bair's controversial biography, – that through French, Beckett was able to play out something of his own unresolved internal relationship to his mother alongside the new phenomenon of the 're-created mother of his literary art' (Casement 1982, 39) which Casement saw as reflected by the appearance of the theme of play and playfulness in *Malone Dies*: 'Now it is a game, I am going to play. I never knew how to play, till now. I longed to, but I knew it was impossible.' (The question of play and playing in *Malone* will be re-assessed in a later chapter.)

Leslie Hill, critical of the fact that both Anzieu and Casement rely too heavily and reductively on Bair's biography in order to substantiate their readings, argues that what the shift into French achieves for Beckett is 'the creation of productive distance or difference between his writing and the stresses at work in *Watt*:

> As Beckett the bilingual writer is written into French as a displaced person, he is forced to confront there, once again, the event of birth. To wish to be reborn, into another language, into the words of others, as another, does not allow Beckett simply to annul his genealogy. Incorporating a foreign language does not resolve the enigma of birth. Rather, in the foreign tongue, Beckett is obliged to re-enact and repeat the process of birth itself and reinscribe, albeit from a different position, the confrontation with language and birth as such. Beckett's emancipation from English is a submission to French, and his self-expulsion from the mother tongue a re-enactment of birth itself. (Hill 1990, 36)

Equally important in Beckett's newly found bilingualism is the rediscovery or recovery of wit and humour. Beckett had admitted to his biographer that writing in French was simply easier for him for it amounted to writing without style. It was a means of stripping and evacuating his Irish English or what he called his 'Anglo-Irish exuberance and automatisms' [...] 'to cut away the excess, to strip away the colour' (Knowlson 1996, 357). It was ultimately the perfect alibi to dispense with any fixed sense of place. For example in the English translation of *En attendant Godot,* Beckett, choosing to avoid any literal translation of place-names such as the Vaucluse (a region where Beckett had spent part of the War years as a refugee) playfully displaces the sense of place onto the maternal body, in particular onto evocative images of digestion and evacuation:

> J'ai coulé toute ma chaude-pisse d'existence ici, je te dis! Ici! Dans la *Merde*cluse! (*EAG*, 86)
>
> I've puked my puke of a life away here, I tell you! Here! In the *Cack*on country! (*G*, 62 my emphasis)

Another example of the manner Beckett subverts all sense of there being a dichotomy between the original and the translation can be had from Molloy and the passage concerning Lousse's parrot. In a novel that was supposed to be first written in French, we read:

> Il disait de temps en temps, Putain de conasse de merde de chiaison. Il avait dû appartenir à une personne française avant d'appartenir à Lousse. Les animaux changent souvent de propriétaire. Il ne disait pas grand'chose d'autre. Si, il disait aussi, Fuck! Ce n'était pourtant pas une personne française qui lui avait appris à dire Fuck! (*BT* 49)

As Alain Astro points out, it is indeed strange to read that while the parrot's repertory is in French slang ('Putain de conasse de merde de chiaison'), the narrator clumsily alludes to 'une personne française'. This comes across as poor French on the part of the 'Irish' Molloy who with his '*a french person*', is clearly thinking in English (Astro 1990, 753). So much for there being a 'French' original or even an original Irish Molloy, as Beckett apparently refuses 'to decide whether he is writing a French-language text about an English- (or Hiberno-English) language reality, or vice-versa', to quote Sinead Mooney (Mooney 2007, 17).

The change of languages also ushers in a sharper self-reflexivity in the writing as the following contrast shows. If we compare a sentence from

L'Innommable: 'Peut-être que cette fois-ci encore je ne ferai que chercher ma leçon' (*INN* 27) to the English version: 'And perhaps now again I shall do no more than seek my lessons, to the self-accompaniment of *a tongue that is not mine*' (*BT* 281, my emphasis), the latter comes across as being more elaborate and self-reflexive, Beckett reflecting on the sheer otherness, foreigness of his 'mother' tongue. By the time Beckett got to writing *The Unnamable,* the sense of returning to some maternal original is beyond all reach, even if the place-names in the trilogy are all given a pseudo-Irish 'original' with Gaelic variations: Bally, Ballyba, Ballybaba, Shit, Shitba, Shitbaba, Hole (the gaelic 'baile' means 'town'). Between the two languages, we are simply elsewhere. As Bruno Clément remarks, the French already serves to situate the Beckett narrator elsewhere. His address has disappeared and a sense of strangeness remains (Clément 1994, 246–7).

Space within space: from page to stage

The siege in the room was temporarily suspended when between the second and third novels of the trilogy – *Malone Dies* and *The Unnamable* – Beckett spontaneously wrote *En attendant Godot* in a very brief time.[21] It was 'to get away from the awful prose I was writing at the time', and 'from the wildness and rulelessness' of the novels' (qtd in Bair 1980, 323). The play came to be canonised as the founding text of Beckett's post-war career, and enshrined as a turning point in Beckett's writing. As John Pilling points out, the variety of modes, registers and genres in Beckett's work observable between 1929 and 1946 is a mark of how difficult Beckett found it to make progress confronted as he was with what he called 'the problems that beset continuance' (Pilling 1997, 3).

Waiting for Godot comes in at a time when Beckett had been essentially writing first-person voiced prose. The 'We' with which Vladimir and Estragon speak, stressing a marked 'mutual interdependence' (Pountney 1988, 7), can be seen as part and parcel of 'the shift toward "relationship"' (Pilling 204) in Beckett's oeuvre. When asked how he started to write for the stage, Beckett replied:

> When I was working on *Watt* I felt the need to create for a smaller space, one in which I had some control of where people stood or moved, above all of a certain light. I wrote *Waiting for Godot.* (McMillan 1988, 15)

During rehearsals of *Endspiel* in Berlin in 1967, Beckett told Michael Haerdter: 'theatre for me is a relaxation from work on the novel. You have a definite space and people in this space. That's relaxing' (ibid.).

Many critics have commented on the switch over from prose to drama, from subjectivity, stories of 'I', to drama of couples. Janvier goes as far as suggesting that Beckett finds communality, fraternity on stage hitherto inexistent in his work: 'La structure fondamentale est, au theatre, Moi plus l'Autre' ('The fundamental structure in theatre is Self and Other') (Janvier 1986, 50). Similarly, discussing the origins of *Godot* in relation to the earlier novel, *Murphy*, and in particular the pursuit of Murphy's 'nothing', Dougald McMillan, the American critic, reminds us that where Murphy seeks to achieve 'nothing', the characters on stage fail to do so since they 'have desires and entangling relationships' (McMillan 1988, 52, a point I shall return to in the chapter on *Godot*). The suggestion is that theatre allowed Beckett to set up and interrogate a social context, an alternative space. As his production notebooks for the Berlin *Godot* testify, he clearly wrote with a view to the audience and performance:

> When I write a play I put myself inside the characters, I am also the author supplying the words, and I put myself in the audience visualising what goes onstage. (McMillan, 16)

Where earlier in his life Beckett had seen the artist as being active, 'but negatively, shrinking from the nullity of extracircumferential phenomena, drawn into the core of the eddy', and 'art [as] the apotheosis of solitude', theatre is very much about alternative worlds and the existence of others. Perhaps more than the blank page of prose writing, the stage and the concomitant 'we' provides the possibility of transaction between psychic reality and external reality, page and stage. This is the borderland inhabited by Vladimir and Estragon and one of the central issues that will be addressed in this book.

2
Beckett's Negative Sublime

In this chapter a critical overview of the classical Freudian and Kleinian aesthetics will form the background against which I shall situate and introduce my theoretical model of the negative.[1] As regards my use of concepts, it might be useful to explain the methodological strategies involved: André Green's notion of 'the work of the negative', with its positive and pathological forms, will be seen to form a general framework for theorising Beckett's writing. It also forms a useful link with both Bion and Winnicott since there is a clear resonance between all three post-Kleinian analysts' respective approaches to primary narcissism as a structure and not a state. Seeing that I am specifically interested in the manner and mode by which Beckett's texts produce a void, which is not without critical implications for thought processes, I shall first begin by looking at Bion and his theory of thinking after briefly presenting Melanie Klein. But, as we shall see, there is nothing cut and dried about Beckett's negative. And to get a sense of what could be loosely called the achievement of the work of the Beckett negative, its playfulness, its vulnerability, not to say its primary creativity, I will be turning again to Winnicott's theory of playing and potential space. If thinking for Bion performs the 'work of the negative', it will be equally seen that 'playing' does that too. Beckett, Bion and Winnicott, write, think and play in the void.

Beckett and the negative at work

By Freud's definition, the psychoanalytic situation is both a space and a relationship or series of relationships between two people.[2] The analysis is designed to encourage regression and verbalisation simultaneously to make apparent to all involved the dynamic relation between words and things in the patient's experience of his world. As Murray Schwartz makes clear, the instruction to free associate is, in effect, an instruction to define oneself by not defining oneself (Schwartz 1978, 6). One repeats oneself primarily in words and the Freudian interpretive process was to convert repetition into remembering and thereby recover or reclaim repressed material transforming the latent into the manifest. As Freud put it, draining the unconscious was not unlike the draining of the Zuider Zee. The patient recovers and reclaims his past, or the history of his subjectivity and learns to *separate* the past from any would-be inappropriate projections onto the present relation with the analyst in the transference. The end of analysis, following this simplified model, is the reconstruction of historical truth, the 'real life' that was unconsciously enacted in the present and that the analyst relegates once more to the past, its proper place (ibid.).

Beckett's early post-war writings complicate and problematise such processes. Obviously in the case of *Molloy* there is nothing to recover or reclaim since Moran ultimately doesn't care about ever finding Molloy. Beckett comically subverts the classical psychoanalytic model of memory as a reconstruction of historical truth and conversion of the repetition of infantile experience into remembering. The loss of memory and ultimately the loss of the faculty of thinking is in fact a benefit to the Beckett character – Malone tells us he lived in a coma and for him his loss of consciousness 'was never any great loss' (ibid., 169); Vladimir and Estragon jubilate in always finding things to do in order not to have to think; and, to temporarily leave behind the 1940s, while in *Company* (1980), Beckettian mental activity is playfully reduced to a minimal state, that is to say somewhere between thinking and remembering. The narrator acknowledges that while there is no escape from displaying some mental activity, 'the lower the order of mental activity the better the company' (*C* 15).

The Beckett character playfully refuses to reveal the history of his subjectivity, to separate the so-called past from its projection into the narrative present. Whether on the page or on the stage, the confrontation is less with the burden of a repressed past as with its emptiness where, more often than not, memory often fails to function. The loss of memory is literally thematised in *Godot*, functioning in the cases of Estragon and Pozzo as contact barriers between their inner void and the outside, time being made something accursed and abominable (*G* 89).

Beckett's world is simply 'out too far' to be reached, or too far away to be brought closer to some sense of a recovery, whether it be a recovery of body, self or time. For example, the negation of the body is something

Beckett lavishes on with his deliberately provocative, extravagant imagery. Moran's mind swoons when he thinks of his paralysis. While he exults in his incapacities he nonetheless dreads that death might bring about a regeneration of a sort (*BT* 129). One aspires towards non-existence, as it were, through the expression of an ideal, a self-sufficiency which is progressively reduced in the direction of self-annihilation (Green 1986, 56).

It's difficult then to talk of a *self* or an ego let alone a Reality Principle in Beckett's writing, since 'standard' functions such as thought, conscience, attention or judgement would seem to be grotesquely absent. For the Beckett character, religion, education, emotion and culture are all unassimilable and incomprehensible facts. So Malone, in speaking of his past, acknowledges having been unable to evolve in the field of affection, for otherwise he would have been reduced to the society of nice people or to the consolation of religion (*BT* 56).

Indeed, the relentless negative charge of Beckett's imagination is always uncomfortably there with its relentless topology of decrepitude bodies and minds, enclosed in jars, dustbins, urns, cells, rotundas, mounds. The 'self-portraits' of Molloy and Malone as 'degenerates' read literally as a dark caricature of the inhuman, a parody of a humanity on its dying legs. Whether it is between its last convulsions or its first gasps of breath, we may never know for, in Beckett, beginning is always a way of ending. The Unnamable fancies he is the last of humankind (*BT* 233) yet the same person reassures us that there are no human creatures in his world (ibid., 271). Mahood is alive with life belonging to others. Malone is delighted to be the old foetus he is, hoar and impotent (207), but is not beyond engendering a little creature (72). Molloy would have made love to a goat to know what love was (54). Neither man nor beast, he likens himself to a monster on the move worthy of extermination. He swings 'low in the dark over the earth, along the little empty country roads' (62) saying to himself that there is little likelihood of his being molested. It is indeed the 'nature' of his creatureliness or his fictive creaturehood – that lawless law of fiction – that frequently becomes the object of Molloy's ponderings and interrogations. 'Son of that poor uniparous whore', Molloy is the last of 'his foul brood, neither man nor beast' [...] 'the old bitch, a nice dose she gave me, she and her lousy unconquerable genes' (75).

Conquering the negative or using the negative?

In psychoanalytic criticism of Beckett, the question of negativity is frequently brought to bear on the idea of primary narcissism, the trajectory of the Beckettian hero usually being described in terms of an increasingly marked separation from exterior reality (Beausang 1982). But the withdrawal of investment equally affects, in Beckett's work, inner reality as well as outer reality. This is an important point because the phantasm inherent in the creation of the Beckettian character, examples of which we have just seen, is the result, in my opinion, of primary processes having being destroyed rather than the expression of what these processes are supposed to be. At the risk of stating the obvious, if there is an underlying logic to be derived from Beckett's image of humans and their relationships, it is not one based on desire or pleasure, but rather one of unpleasure and ultimately despair. As André Green reminds us:

> the logic of primary processes was a logic based on the idea of a couple of opposites formed by desire, on the one hand, and prohibition on the other [...] In this perspective, the logic of primary processes is a logic of hope; a case opposite to what I have called the logic of despair. Here the object is in the forefront, not the wish, not the prohibition. (Green 1986, 23 and 24)

In other words, 'the search for pleasure has substituted itself for the search for displeasure, and the avoidance of displeasure has become avoidance of pleasure [...] it is as if the subject says "Yes" to displeasure and "No" to pleasure' (ibid., 22). This logic of despair, Green goes on to explain, has one constant goal: to produce evidence that the object is really bad, incomprehensive ('incompréhensif', Green 1990, 49) and rejecting because of the extent to which they entreat rejection by others' (Green 1986, 23; Anzieu 1992, 206). But underpinning Green's notion of negative logic is his wider concern with what he calls the negative counterpart of a conception of narcissism taken as structure and not only as state, making room therefore for the negative element which he considers as essential. In simpler terms, negative narcissism, for Green, is a process that tends not towards the One, as narcissism does in its Freudian version, but towards nothing. The negative must be understood here not as the inverse of the positive, but as a return to nothing. To understand this important construct, a brief return to Freud is necessary.

Freud had seen negation as a clearly defensive procedure, an intellectual substitute for the repressed. Inadvertently, negation freed thinking from repression and was a way of taking cognizance of what is repressed but, as Parsons explains, only one consequence of the process of repression is undone – 'the fact, namely, of the ideational content of what is repressed not reaching consciousness' (Parsons 1999, 236). In other words, with the intellectual function being separated from the affective process, negation allows ideational content but not affect into consciousness. While Freud wondered to what extent can one succeed in 'conquering the negation as well, and in bringing about a full intellectual acceptance of the repressed' (ibid.), this is a one-sided view of the double function of negation according to Parsons. As the latter points out in his discussion of Green's theory, the double function shows that it is not so much a question of conquering negation as of how it is being used in the first place (Parsons 70). Indeed, negation can be used in different, opposing ways, and the use to which the act of negation is being put, is what determines whether psychic reality or symbolism is being used defensively or constructively (69).

Green addresses and explores such issues. He divides the 'negative' into normal and pathological. The normal work of the negative shows itself as the indirection instituted by repression and other defences to protect the mental apparatus from becoming overwhelmed. Through such indirection individuals spare themselves the psychic truths that analysts help their patients retrace to their unconscious roots. The structuring form of the work of the negative is constructive insofar as it involves bearing loss, deprivation and absence. It follows that 'all exploration of reality, all movement towards new experiences or new ways of being, all creativity and any kind of symbolic functioning [...] implies an ability to negate ordinary reality in favour of psychic reality' (Parsons, 71–2).

The work of the pathologically negative is destructive in that it involves the radical withdrawal of investment in the object world. Such destructuring use of negation might be exemplified by another important concept of Green's, 'The dead mother' (1983), which we have already referred to in relation to Beckett and his coping with his mother's bereavement. Here the truth of loss and absence cannot be faced and negation can only be used to contradict the reality that cannot be borne. The classic case involves the death of a child in infancy – a leitmotif in Beckett's writing. As Michael Parsons points out, the child's life and the mother's relationship with the living child have been negated by death. But the mother cannot allow that, she can only use the function of negation to contradict the truth of it. So she becomes frozen into a relationship with the negative of the child's existence. As Green points out, in relation to Bion, this is a relationship to a 'no-thing' (Green 1993, 18). The dead mother makes a relationship to the 'no-thing' that is constituted by the absence of the dead child.

Another term used by Green for this is 'negative hallucination' which he further instances by referring to the patient described by Winnicott (1971, 23) who said to Winnicott about her previous analyst: 'the negative of him is more real than the positive of you'. The negative element is formed through and by introjecting the negative hallucination of the mother during her absence (Green 1986, 55) meaning concretely that the individual perceives not an absence of representation but a representation of the absence of representation (Oppenheim 2003, 80).

To return to Beckett, the 'work of the negative' can be likened to John Pilling's apt description of Beckett's earlier pre-war writing and its compositional principle of negation which is 'at once generative but degenerative, organic but disabling, and dynamic but dysfunctional' (Pilling 2005, 171). The world Beckett paints in the trilogy and in *Godot* is manifestly and literally a world of useless uniformity, blankness, sameness, indifference where all links and relations seem to have been irredeemably severed and ruptured. Bodies hardly function or move; memory no longer remembers, thought no longer thinks; desire no longer operates; names no longer name. Molloy fails to make sense of his namelessness (*BT* 31), his words only serving to fill in the holes of words (ibid., 14).

Before going any further in our theoretical explorations, one preliminary conclusion can be drawn about Beckett's work of the negative: it cannot be 'divided' either one way or another. It 'works' defensively *and* constructively (Parsons 69). It is both 'a fixed state to be held on to', and a 'mobile and flexible activity', a 'provisional suspension of [...] reality to be moved on from when it has served its purpose' (71). But what or which purpose one is inclined to ask?

As we shall develop later in our study, the sense and quality of emptiness encountered in Beckett can be precisely understood as that particular experience which suspends existence in a state of non-existence. As Winnicott has remarked, emptiness can be likened to a past state which cannot be remembered and corresponds therefore to a primary narcissistic organisation of the self before 'it begins to fill up', emptiness being 'a prerequisite for eagerness to gather in' (qtd in Kohon 1986, 181). In and through his work, Beckett explores this experience which seems to be simultaneously the 'goal' and structure of his literary discourse. That is to say that not only does emptiness structure object relations, as we shall discover, in the trilogy and *Waiting for Godot* – the withdrawal of the self from libidinal investment, detachment from the outside world – but we can notice that Beckett's void is characterised by states of unanticipated conservation, inert tension-free equilibrium and suspension. In other words, the void in Beckett's work cannot only be reduced to the representation of a phantasy. It is a structural and structuring principle.

But it is not only in terms of space that the question of Beckettian emptiness must be formulated. Radical disinvestment – the aspiration to non-being – also affects time by the capacity to suspend experience and create 'dead time' where nothing can be symbolised (Green 1986, 56). As we shall later see, the suspension of time, its past and its memory, is not just specific to *Godot*, but forms the very basis of Beckett's novels.

Good or bad: the Kleinian object

Initiated by Melanie Klein, with the insights of Anna Freud's version of child analysis, and later contributions from the work of John Bowlby and Donald Winnicott, the British School of Object Relations Theory translated psychoanalysis from a theory of sexual desire into a theory of emotional nurture (Glover 2004; Kohon 1986, 24–50). The principle idea of object-relations is that the ego-self exists only in relation to other objects, which may be external or internal. The internal objects are internalised versions of external objects, primarily formed from early interactions with the parents, essentially the mother. In other words, as Gregorio Kohon explains, 'it is not only the real relationship with others that determines the subject's individual life, but the specific way in which the subject apprehends his relationships with his objects. It always implies an unconscious relationship to these objects' (Kohon 1986, 20).

According to Melanie Klein, what is central to psychic life is neither sexuality nor language but, rather the 'object': not the mother but the breast which itself is 'divided' into two central phantasies: the good breast (idealised as all giving) and the bad breast (witholding counterpart). The infant only recognises the mother as a *whole person* at what Klein calls the 'depressive position' (Klein 1935).

The paranoid-schizoid position is characteristic of the first four months of life. In it, violent and sadistic impulses, especially towards the breast, coexist with positive and libidinal impulses, and result in a splitting of the breast into a good object and a bad object. The bad object becomes the source of persecutory anxiety and threatens the destruction of the ego. In this stage, the ego can tolerate anxiety only by replicating the violent division between good and bad objects in its own self-constitution, taking in the good and disgustedly, anxiously, disavowing or expelling the bad. The psychotic patient recapitulates the disintegrated condition of the paranoid-schizoid stage. After about four months, the depressive position may be attained. In this, the mother may begin to be grasped as a whole person, in whom the good and the bad are combined. The anxiety here is not of imminent destruction by the aggressive bad object, but of the loss of the mother

According to Klein, the depressive position is reached when the infant realises that his or her love and hate are directed to the same object, the mother and her body (Skelton 2006, 269–71). The child thus begins to experience ambivalence and also his own effects upon another object. Klein was the first to point to the importance of the unconscious impulse to repair objects felt to have been damaged by destructive attacks of hate. This is inherent in depressive feeling. Klein believed that anxiety originated in aggression – and she regarded this as fundamentally innate and grounded in the projection of the death instinct outwards from the self. This emphasis on anxiety, internal danger threats and the workings of the death instinct, were to have important consequences for her formulation of the concept of phantasy and also for her understanding of the nature of creativity.

Klein suggested that true artistic and creative activity were both rooted in anxiety and the urge to make good the destructive and sadistic phantasies set in motion by the death instinct. In a later work, *Envy and Gratitude* (1957) Klein was to approach the problem of creativity from a new angle. Here she postulates that the first object experienced as manifesting creativity is the feeding breast, and she also describes the detrimental effect of excessive envy on creativity. The concept of the inner world remains a major theme in Klein's work, and lies at the heart of a Bionian approach to art and aesthetics.[3]

Thinking with Bion

Certain simplifying assumptions must be first made. My principle aim here is to present Bion's theories and to indicate in what way I may be able to use them in this book as part of a theoretical model of negativity. As we have seen, there has been a considerable amount of commentary about Bion in Beckett criticism. However, I prefer to draw the wider theoretical picture concerning Bion's ideas, which, hopefully, will help us to formally situate the Beckett–Bion critics already alluded to. Afterwards, I shall outline the direction I would like to take.

Beckett's former analyst developed Kleinian theories about the role of envy in the interpersonal relations to encompass the idea of the intolerable link and the hatred of learning from experience. Central to Bion's account of mental processes is the mechanism that Melanie Klein called 'projective identification', which Bion defines as 'a splitting off by the patient of part of his personality and a projection of it into the object where it becomes installed, sometimes as a persecutor, leaving the psyche from which it has been split off correspondingly impoverished' (Bion 1967, 37).

The evolution of Bion's work begins with his early papers on schizophrenia in the fifties where he described the attacks on the ego itself, which represented the experiences that Klein (1946) had regarded as the effects of the death instinct arising from within – the feeling of falling to pieces. Bion emphasised, in particular, an attack on the awareness of internal reality. It is the *links between mental contents* which are attacked by the schizophrenic:

> In fact, not only is primitive thought attacked because it links sense-impressions of reality with consciousness but, thanks to the psychotic's over-endowment with destructiveness, the splitting processes are extended to the links within the thought processes themselves. (Bion 1967, 50)

Although Freud had also outlined this process when he studied severe obsessional neurosis, Bion emphasised its violent quality. The result is that the schizophrenic lives in a fragmented world of turbulence, with unusable, primitive ideas in his mind – ones that cannot be used for thinking:

> All these are now attacked till finally two objects cannot be brought together in a way which leaves each object with its intrinsic qualities intact and yet able, by their conjunction, to produce a new mental object. (Ibid.)

The result is that splitting processes and projective identification are seen to operate not just on thoughts but also on words as in the example of the patient splitting the word 'penis' first into its syllables and then into its component letters, in a way that is indistinguishable from splitting of the ego that contains these functions (Meltzer 1978, 24). It follows that the destruction of these connections and conjunctions leads to the patient feeling threatened by the raw, unprocessed sense data which cannot be assimilated and symbolised by the ego as 'food for thinking':

> Further, since that-which-links has been not only minutely fragmented but also projected out into objects to join the other bizarre objects, the

> patient feels surrounded by minute links which, being impregnated now with cruelty, link objects together cruelly. (Bion 1967, 50)

It must be understood here that Bion employs the term 'link' in order to emphasise the relationship with a function rather than with the object that subserves a function such as language, thought, the senses, memory, judgement, etc. Bion in his influential paper, 'Attacks on Linking' (1959) reports on patients who display in their attitude towards the analyst and the analytic session a hostile inability to tolerate the possibility of emotional links:

> These attacks on the linking function of emotion lead to an over-prominence in the psychotic part of the personality of links which appear to be logical, almost mathematical, but never emotionally reasonable. Consequently, the links surviving are perverse, cruel, and sterile. (Ibid., 108–9)

Attack on linking means the thing attacked when the person seeks to destroy his capacity for thought and emotion or, in Beckett's case, for memory. The Bionian attacks on linking are assaults on 'anything which is felt to have the function of linking one object with another' (93).

This hypothesis is literally borne out by manifest themes in Beckett such as loss of memory, loss of sight, loss of hearing (central to *Waiting for Godot*) loss of thought, loss of bodily functions, and loss of time (all essential to the novels). Simply put, in getting rid of memory, Beckett's text is getting rid of that-which-joins: the capacity for articulation, methods for synthesis, the possibility of linking two periods of time. For example in *Molloy*, Moran cannot forge any meaningful links with the messenger Gaber who is comically lacking in memory and undecipherable to all but himself (*BT* 98). It is thus the negative value or counterpart of the capacity to join or to link which matters in Beckett, meaning that any joining that does take place – remembering, thinking, seeing, feeling, communicating, making love – is done with a vengeance or hatred. Feelings of hatred are therefore directed against the emotions which stimulate memory including memories of hate itself. (More on this in a later chapter.)

Other Beckett critics have equally underlined the importance of Bion's concept. For instance, Oppenheim (2001, 775–6) and, as we have already seen, Connor (2008, 20), maintain that Beckett's often-quoted 1937 letter to Kaun (already quoted in this book), with its own programmatic assault against words, recalls a Bionian attack on verbal thought.

It will be remembered that in this letter Beckett articulated his hostility towards language and intention and, if anything, wished to build an art around its systematic molestation or negation. Yet, as Moorjani argues, Beckett's 'unwording the word' through words, is a process precariously posed between a failure to destroy and a failure to create links (Moorjani 2004a, 180).

Returning to our presentation of Bion's work, the schizophrenia papers of the 1950s – 'The Imaginary Twin' (1950), 'Differentiation of the Psychotic from the Non-Psychotic Personalities' (1957) and 'Attacks on Linking' (1959), lay the basis for a theory of thinking which is intrinsic to Bion' understanding of creativity.

Bion conceives the thinking apparatus as the 'container-contained' operated upon by the dynamic influence of the paranoid-schizoid (PS) and depressive positions (D), plus the 'selected fact' – akin to a catalyst. This process he termed 'PS↔D' with the double arrow suggests an ongoing oscillation between the two positions. However, any potential creativity will be thwarted if the destructive forces manage to fragment positive links to objects which will result in an impoverishment of psychic life. Bion's understanding of the creative process supplements the view of traditional Kleinians, like Segal, by using Klein's concept of the paranoid-schizoid and depressive positions in order to place value on the essential *interdependence* of processes of fragmentation and integration, which he regarded as essential to all creative thinking. Where Klein emphasised the negative aspects of the paranoid-schizoid position and had placed the depressive position at the heart of successful development, Bion saw the fragmentation and splitting in the paranoid position as a necessary aspect of human experience.

Bion's theory of thinking and creativity marked a big step forward in psychoanalytic theory for not only does it provide psychoanalysis with its first account of thoughts (the 'contained'), and the thinking apparatus created to think them (the 'container'), and their relationship to the thinker, it also radically re-orientates psychoanalytic theory into the mainstream of western epistemology. Bion moves away from Freud's mechanical causal system, aimed at explaining deviations in normal development (Meltzer 1978, 113), into a philosophical sphere, invoking the pre-determinism of Kant and Plato. He supplemented Freud's instinct theory with Plato's theory of inherent forms or pure thoughts and Kant's a priori assumptions or things-in-themselves, what Bion called 'thoughts without a thinker' (Bion 1967, 165).

Essentially, Bion wants to describe a mythical apparatus which could perform the function of processing 'emotional experiences' (which may occur in either the waking or sleeping state) in such a way as to generate 'dream thoughts' which can be stored as memory or used for thinking (Meltzer 39). For Bion, the thinking apparatus evolves in response to the pressure of thoughts:

> I repeat – thinking has to be called into existence to cope with thoughts. It will be noted that this differs from any theory of thought as a product of thinking, in that thinking is a development forced on the psyche by the pressure of thoughts and not the other way round. (Bion 1967, 111)

This begins when the infant projects his uncontainable fear, discomfort and anxiety into the mother, who acts as a container for the child's fears. The mother is able to receive these projections and modify them so that the infant can introject the fear but in a 'detoxified' form.

Accordingly, Bion's model of the mind as a thinking and learning apparatus is concerned with understanding (rather than gratifying) the emotional experiences that impinge upon it. The latter correspond to three major functions: love (L), hate (H) and knowing (K). But Bion's attention is mainly with K, knowing, and later Un-knowing (minus K or –K). As with love and hate links, K-linkage involves mental pain which may be accepted, modified or evaded, the truth and the lie emerging as the food and poison of thought and growth of the personality (ibid.). In short, the growth of the capacity for thinking about emotional experiences enables the individual to learn by becoming a different person with different capabilities from the person of the past. On the contrary, failure 'to use the emotional experience produces a comparable disaster in the development of the personality [...] that could be described as death of the personality' (qtd in Meltzer 1978, 48). So how does one think?

Bion introduces the terms: 'alpha function', 'alpha elements' and 'beta elements' to designate certain dynamics of this mythical machinery of the mind (Skelton 2006, 55–60). *Alpha function* refers to the ability to *create meaning* out of raw, unprocessed sensory data. Bion calls the whatever-it-is that appears in the mind when alpha-function fails to operate by the un-name, *beta-elements*. It is the continuing alpha-function turning out a membrane of thought which will function as a 'contact barrier' between conscious and unconscious, while, when it operates in reverse it will throw out a beta-screen which prevents such differentiations (Meltzer 39). The mother's 'reverie' is her alpha function, and represents the ability to modify her child's tensions and anxieties. The mother and the child form a 'thinking couple' which is the prototype of the thinking process that continues developing throughout life.

According to Bion, the alpha function works on the unprocessed beta elements and transforms them into alpha elements in a way similar to a chemical transformation – Bion compares it to the digestive process, thinking being 'alimentary'. The 'beta elements' (which are fit only for projection and splitting) are so modified that they become absorbable and quite literally, *food for thought.* The alpha element represents the link between our innate preconceptions (intuitions) and raw experience of the external world. They form the building-blocks of thought upon which more complex systems can be built. Ultimately, Bion saw the psychotic experience as the result of a failure by the mother to contain her infant's fear of dying. Perhaps the mother was psychotic herself or depressed and unable to contain and modify her child's fears. In this situation, all the infant's anxiety is projected into the mother and instead of being contained and modified by her, the fears are returned to the child but now in a heightened form. The establishment of the alpha function is impeded and thinking seriously impaired.

Bion limits the term 'thought' 'to the mating of a preconception with a frustration' (Bion 1967, 111). Mythologically, the first thought consists of thinking the mother's absence. The infant's 'expectation of a breast is mated with a realization of no breast available for satisfaction. This mating is experienced as a no-breast, or "absent" breast inside' (ibid.). 'If the capacity for toleration of frustration is sufficient the "no-breast" inside becomes a thought and an apparatus for "thinking" it develops' (112). The distressed baby has a set of inherent empty ideas or preconceptions about the mother which meet a realisation (term meaning experience) that is approximative enough to give rise to a conception of the mother, in other words, there is interplay between the mother's absence and her presence. These empty thoughts or general schemes, in turn, can transform experience into visual images, dreams, memories. The system of conceptions may become gradually organised into concepts and a deductive system for experiencing the world. Dream thoughts grow in complexity, sophistication and abstractness into a scientific deductive system under the dominance of love of the truth. An apparatus, modelled on the mother's capacity for reverie, is developed in infancy for the purpose of transforming these experiences into thoughts which can be used for thinking, that is for manipulation with a view to increasing their level of abstraction and sophistication. Thought, then, is not a defence mechanism, but rather a mechanism for modifying the truth about oneself so that it can be thought.

Remapping the (mental) void

The later Bion gradually shifted away from a scientific to a more aesthetic and mystical conception or vertex of the psychoanalytic experience. In *Attention and Interpretation* (1970) he postulates mental space as 'a thing-in-itself' that is unknowable but which can be represented (subject to certain limitations) by thoughts. He developed what one could call a mystical conception of inner space concerning the *inner* world, one which arises from of what he calls 'Ultimate Reality' or 'O' which:

> stands for the absolute truth in and of any object; it is assumed that this cannot be known by any human being; it can be known about, its presence can be recognised and felt, but it cannot be known. It is possible to be at one with it. That it exists is an essential postulate of science but it cannot be scientifically discovered. No psycho-analytic discovery is possible without recognition of its existence. (30)

By putting tolerant knowledge in the place of negativity and intolerance of frustration, Bion is trying to give formlessness a form (Connor 2008, 31) (not unlike what Beckett was attempting to do in directing *Warten auf Godot* in Berlin in 1975).

Bion's mental space is multi-dimensional, vast and infinite, with no direct correspondence with sensuous reality. It is therefore quite a move away from Klein's account of the inner world which is, prototypically, based on the child's phantasies concerning the mother's body and its contents. However, unlike Winnicott's account of the space *between* mother and child, the psychic experience of this *inner* space has potentially persecuting and threatening aspects, in that it can be perceived (during mental disturbance, for example) as an alien, hostile void or emptiness. For example, the threat of being engulfed by this space is akin to the feeling of 'falling forever' or of having no boundaries to contain anxiety or fear, and the result is a psychic catastrophe – what Bion calls 'catastrophic chaos' or 'nameless dread' (Bion 1967, 116). In such cases the process of projecting parts of the self (which Klein termed 'projective identification') takes place in a mental space which has *no* visual images to fulfil the functions of a co-ordinate system. There is no conception of containers into which projection and introjection could take place and the mental representation of space is felt as an immensity so great that it cannot be represented at all. Under these circumstances the very notion or thought of 'space' becomes terrifying, or terror itself. Bion quotes Pascal: 'Le silence de ces espaces infinis m'effraie' (Bion 1965, 171) The 'O' earlier referred to – Ultimate

Reality – can only be apprehended when there is no memory, desire, knowledge or understanding.

Another term for this state of mind is 'negative capability'. Here Bion fastens onto a formulation of John Keats who in a letter to his brother, described the capacity to tolerate uncertainty as the 'negative capability' – 'without irritably reaching after fact and reason' (qtd in Meltzer 1978, 109).[4] Unsurprisingly it is the religious mystics, according to Bion, who have probably come closest to the experience of O. From a literary and philosophical perspective, he likens it to Milton's 'void and formless infinite' (Bion 1965, 151), Plato's 'Ideal Forms' (138), and Kant's unknowable 'Noumena' (12).[5] As we shall see later, the negative, persecutory aspect of inner mental space as described by Bion, is highly relevant for our understanding of the peculiar quest for knowledge and truth that takes place in the Beckettian void not to mention the spatial dynamics of Beckett's writing in general.[6]

Winnicott and Beckett: making the negative play

One major criticism of Klein was her exclusive emphasis on the *object* almost to the exclusion of the actual *relationship* and that not enough attention had been paid to the fact that in the phrase 'object relation' the word 'relation' was the most important. Where Klein privileged the object, and Bion, as we have just seen, the internal processes, Winnicott studies the interaction between the internal and the external. He directs our attention to what lies *between* these terms, which are united by actions, or between the effects of different actions. For Winnicott it is the *space* of thinking that takes precedence over the object (Green 1986, 286).

While Winnicott took a lot of ideas from Klein – the importance of the internal world and its objects, the elaborate and pervasive power of phantasy, the central notion of primitive greed and ruthless love – he developed his own idiosyncratic positions. For example, he claimed that from the very beginning, the infant sought contact with a person, not simply instinctual gratification from an object. The child clamours for relatedness, not simply satisfaction. 'It is not instinctual satisfaction', that makes a baby begin to be, to feel that life is real, to find life worth living' (qtd in Phillips 1988, 9) It was maternal care, Winnicott believed, that made it possible for the infant self to be enriched, as opposed to be overwhelmed, by instinctual experience (ibid.). The child's play arises in response not to the libidinally exciting 'object mother' but to the quietly supportive 'environment-mother' (ibid., xiii).

Winnicott's most well-known concept of the transitional object, already alluded to, which is neither an internal nor an external concept, but one that transcends both inner and outer reality and occupies a 'potential' or 'transitional' space, marks a new way of understanding symbol-formation, creativity and the aesthetic experience. It is also my contention that it allows us to have a fresh look at Beckett's concern with things negative.[7] But let's first delve into what André Green aptly calls Winnicott's 'intuition of the negative', which is the title of his article (Green 1999).

As Green astutely remarks, Winnicott's defining the transitional object as a 'not-me' possession is a way of defining the object as 'a negative of me' (Green 1999, 206). Equally when Winnicott insists on holding the paradox (of the transitional object) without resolving it through a 'flight to split-off intellectual functioning', for 'the price of this is the loss of the value of the paradox itself' (1971, xii), he is insisting on the need to tolerate and to contain the negative. As Winnicott says: 'it's *not being* the breast (or the mother), although real, is as important as the fact that it stands for the breast' (ibid. 6, my emphasis).

The clinical material that Winnicott uses in his seminal paper, 'Transitional Objects and Transitional Phenomena', reveals the prime importance of absence in the psychopathology of the transitional area, which Green sees as 'the inner representation of the negative, 'a representation of the absence of representation' materialised by the the absent negative bond (Green 208). For example, Winnicott presents the particular case of a woman who was evacuated during World War II. Her case is characterised by her multiple absences: absence of memory, absence in the mind, absence of contact, absence of feeling alive. As Green remarks, Winnicott's approach to the 'negative side of relationships' brings us closer to a theory of lack where for this particular patient, the only reality is the reality of that which is not there, that which makes one suffer by its very absence: 'the only real thing is the gap; that is to say, the death or the absence or the amnesia' (Winnicott 1971, 26), 'the negative is the only positive' (28).

Working on the negative side of relationships led Winnicott to formally recognise the role and importance of emptiness stating in his paper, 'Fear of Breakdown' (1974), that 'emptiness is a prerequisite to gather in [...] It can be said that only out of non-existence can existence start' (qtd in Kohon 1986, 182). As Green remarks, this invites us to reconsider Freud's metapsychological hypothesis of *primary absolute narcissism* as a tendency to come as close as possible to the zero degree of excitation rather than as a reference to unity (Green 1986, 54). Green reminds us, in passing, that Bion famously and provocatively recommended to the analyst to attain a state without memory or desire, a state of the unknowable but yet a starting point for all knowledge (ibid.). It is indeed the confrontation with emptiness which is probably the most intolerable of states, feared by patients (ibid.). Similarly, in another remarkable paper, 'Communicating and non-communicating leading to the study of certain opposites' (1963), Winnicott stresses that this lack of communication is in no way pathological, that is to say, negative, since it strives to protect that which is most essential to the self and which must never be communicated.

It is clear from these examples, that Winnicott, perhaps inadvertently but certainly implicitly, is postulating what I would term a 'potential self'. The first relationship, in Winnicott's account, is one of reciprocity rather than overwhelming conflict or submission. Compliance is a crucial issue for Winnicott, and, as we shall see, for Beckett too, because of the fact of dependence. Beckett's literary art could very well be likened to a search for a radical way of communicating that is not compromised by 'concession to the object' (Phillips 1988, 145). In philosophical terms, we could say that for Winnicott, 'man can only find himself in relation with others, and in the independence gained through acknowledgment of dependence' (Phillips 7). While 'at the start' there 'is an essential aloneness' (Winnicott 1988, 132), paradoxically, this aloneness can only take place under maximum conditions of dependency. Winnicott later reformulates this when he writes: 'at the centre of each person is an incommunicado element, and this is sacred and most worthy of preservation' (Winnicott 1965, 187). For the Winnicott who famously declared that 'there is no such thing as a baby', the notion of a solitary self is of course highly paradoxical. But this is part of the point.

Typically enough, Winnicott used the concept of the Self in a deliberatingly idiosyncratic and sometimes mystifying way writing, for example, that 'a word like 'self', naturally knows more than we do; it uses us and can command us' (qtd in Phillips 3). Permanently non-communicating, inarticulate and ultimately unknowable, Winnicott's 'Self', not unlike Bion's O, is at his most idiosyncratic when he is at his most anonymous, since compliance is 'what we have invented personality for. Desire, aliveness, "creative living" require something quite different' (ibid., xi). In a letter to Bion in 1955, Winnicott stressed the need to be on the side of what he called 'the more subtle communication which is the only basis for communication that does not violate the fact of the essential isolation of each individual' (qtd in Phillips xi–xii).

So as it is hopefully clearer now, Winnicott's account of the constructive role of negativity in the establishment of a sense of self, is the inverse of the process which Bion describes. In *Playing and Reality* (1971), he clearly adopts a more tentative and ambiguous posture than Bion, certainly when it comes to his accounts of his patients' experiences of formlessness, their activities of indeterminate outcome (71), their states of unintegration, or what Winnicott calls their 'neutral zones' (75). One other clinical example which deserves mentioning, comes from the case of a female patient who 'cannot bear to be' (72) and remarkably has recourse to poetry, – Rossetti's 'Passing Away' and Hopkin's 'Carrion Comfort' – to communicate her incommunicable inner void:

> but what is so awful is existence that's negatived! There was never a time when I thought it a good thing to have been born. It's always that it would have been better if I had not been born – but who knows? [...] Don't make me wish to be. (Winnicott 1972, 72)[8]

Finally, as regards his view of art and literature, Winnicott complained that psychoanalytic aesthetics had directed too much focus on the art product and its content rather than on the creative impulse itself, and in *Playing and Reality* he explicitly separates the idea of creation from actual works of art. According to his theory, everything that happens to a person is creative except insofar as the individual is not ill or hampered by ongoing environmental factors which stifle the creative processes. He believed that the *creative impulse* is something that can be looked at as 'a thing in itself' and is necessary 'if an artist is to produce a work of art' (ibid., 80). Analytic writers who focus on specific art works and/or questions of why a particular individual was a great artist, miss the main point – the creative impulse itself – since 'the creation stands *between* the observer and the artist's creativity' (81 my emphasis). But one is tempted to retort here and say that, for example, Beckett's text is 'all' we have and necessarily stands *between* the author's creativity and the observing critic.[9]

The central feature of this approach to art and creativity, then, is the focus on the creative *process* rather than on the art *product*. This diverges somewhat from Freud's account of the writer's relationship to his creation. Freud sees the writer or artist as turning away from reality as he is oppressed by powerful instinctual needs (Freud 1985). However, unlike most people, the writer knows how to shape and work over his day-dreams in ways which make them acceptable to others. Crucial to this shaping and softening, is the power of artistic form which affords the reader or viewer fore-pleasure, and relaxes his defences against others. This enables the artist to lift his repression for a brief moment and take forbidden pleasure in his own unconscious processes of creation.

By publishing his writing, the writer 'returns' to reality from his fantasies, his creation being a compensation for his neurosis. However, writing neither 'cures' nor does it allow the writer to adapt himself to 'reality' (Freud 1985).

While Winnicott also continues to insist on its infantile origins, art has nonetheless an integrity as an autonomous human activity. Like play, art provides a lifelong refuge to which we can turn as we negotiate our precarious oscillations between illusion and reality and culture as a *thing-in-itself*. As Peter Rudnytsky explains in his introduction to *Transitional Objects and Potential Spaces: the Literary Uses of D.W. Winnicott* (1993), the contention here that art is real in itself and cannot be reduced to sublimation or instinctual gratification, converges with Kant's theory of the disinterestedness of aesthetic experience in *The Critique of Judgement* (1790). Both Kant and Winnicott exempt aesthetic experience from reality-testing. If the creative impulse is an inexplicable thing-in-itself, one wonders to what extent, in a study of Beckett's negative, can we see the latter also as an irreducible creative impulse, a thing-in-itself, a playing process rather than an end-product?

The space of absence

By bringing Bion and Winnicott together in order to read Beckett's negative, one may be tempted to say that I am articulating two very different even incompatible models of inter-personal relationships. For example, for Bion, the relationship between container and contained may be violent, parasitic or mutually crushing, whereas for Winnicott the 'holding environment' is positive and growth-producing. Similarly, Winnicott's theory of the 'potential space' is essentially a benign concept of the interaction between child and mother, benign because, as we have seen above, unlike the Kleinians, Winnicott did not believe in the existence of an innate instinctual clash between love and hate. Indeed, he saw no unconscious phantasy operating from birth.[10]

However, what resonantly reunites Winnicott and Bion (and, in France, André Green and Lacan) is the fundamental problem of absence. Indeed, according to Jed Sekoff, to constitute absence may be among our most vital tasks (Sekoff 1999, 114). For Bion, thought, love and transformation exist only in relation to their negatives. In this perspective, the absent, that is to say, to be without memory or desire, is somehow a call to the potential emergence of the positive. As we have seen, Winnicott treasures the place not to be communicated, the solitude that allows self-emergence and the creative non-verbal silences in analytic treatment. For both Bion and Winnicott, the non-object is the object, the non-object meaning not the representation of the object but the non-existence of the object (Green 1986, 291). Epistemologically, the matrix of the negative and its tributary forms – the void, emptiness, blankness, death – is a prerequisite common to both Bion and Winnicott for acceding to truth, understanding and knowledge.[11] Bion, Winnicott and Green are seen, then, by Sekoff as 'the explorers par excellence of what might be called the *negative sublime* (Sekoff 1999, 114, Sekoff's emphasis). If absence conjures the sublime, it is because the sublime is a beauty that inspires awe and evokes both reverence and dread. Psychoanalysis, Sekoff continues, offers us an engagement with the 'terrible beauty' of our absences (ibid.).

I would complete this reflexion by turning to Kant who located the sublime not in the object looked at, but rather in the mind of the beholder or more precisely in the abyss separating Reason and Imagination. If the sublime is to be found anywhere, writes Kant, 'it is to be found in a formless object', represented by a 'boundlessness' (qtd in Ross 2006, 462). I would suggest that the sublime of the negative resides more crucially in the peculiar way absence tends to elude representation, symbolisation and defy expression. Ironically the more deconstructionist and linguistically oriented approaches to Beckettian negativity almost come to a similar conclusion even if their concern is hardly with beauty or the sublime.

Using Derrida's ground-breaking essay 'How to Avoid Speaking: Denials' ('Comment ne pas parler. Dénégations'), which appeared in *The Languages of the Unsayable: the Play of Negativity in Literature and Literary Theory* (Budick & Iser 1989), Marius Buning defines negation or more broadly, negativity, as a form of discourse that attempts to articulate the unsayable – that which has been excluded by what is sayable (Buning 1999, 34). Like Derrida, he takes into consideration the theology of negation and the wider tradition of negative theology defined as 'knowledge of God obtained by negation' (ibid.). As epistemology, and exemplified by the writings and teachings of Pseudo-Dionysius, Meister Eckhart or St John of the Cross, it speculates on the value of negating the given revelation and ponders over the question of non-being. The mystical way of negative theology operates on the assumption that it is only by divesting God of all attributes and by divesting our human selves of all desires, fears and hopes, that we may experience the *mysterium tremendum et fascinans* of God.

As Buning affirms, the affinities between negative theology and Beckett's negative practice are striking: both are aware of the inability to express ultimate reality; both are concerned by the need to give voice to the ineffable; both also emphasise solitude, detachment, dispossession and the negation of the self as indispensable to concentration and contemplation (Buning 38). According to Beckett, as we have seen, the artist is active, 'but negatively, shrinking from the nullity of extracircumferential phenomena, drawn into the core of the eddy', and art is 'the apotheosis of solitude' (*P* 65–6). But, as Buning correctly remarks, Beckett is no mystic, no John of the Cross, but, as he put it in *Dream of Fair to Middling Women*, a 'dud mystic', a 'John of the Crossroads' (qtd by Buning 38).

Less theologically and more rhetorically, Buning shows us how Beckettian negativity manifests itself in and by its absence – implications, cancellations, equivocations, and denials. Such gaps or lacunae function to form the unwritten and unwritable as well as the unsaid and unsayable base of the utterance (34–5). Where Shira Wolosky's study, in the same volume (Budick & Iser 1996), on Beckett's obsessive attempts 'to avoid speaking', argues for a discourse that constantly privileges negation over affirmation and absence over presence, Buning suggests that an 'other' reality is at least hinted at, although it cannot be put into words (37). He concludes by claiming that in some texts Beckett reaches some kind of equilibrium between presence and absence, resistance and resignation, voice and silence (ibid.). It is between such polarities that Buning locates 'the play of the negative text' (39):

> It is this constant interplay between absence and presence, between maximum negation and minimum affirmation, that constitutes the play of the negative text. This kind of negativity is basically an enabling structure and far from negative (in a pejorative sense) in its effects, for it lures absence into presence, but by continually subverting that presence, turns it into a carrier for absence of which we, as readers, would otherwise not know anything. (Ibid.)

Interestingly, in all three models of negativity – post-Kleinian, theological and deconstructionist, the negative is an 'enabling structure' giving rise to a dynamic interplay between absence and presence. The essential difference, however, between Buning's account of the negative and our post-Kleinian aesthetic model, lies in the fact that one has, on one hand, a theory of language, of communication, and, on the other hand, a theory of inter-personal relations. The 'cause' of the negative is different even if the effects may seem to be similar. However, in my view, Beckett's text is more than an indeterminate interweaving of linguistic traces and I would argue that an analysis of the role of object relations is indispensable for understanding the particular states, affects, tones and subtleties of Beckett's negative universe.

We need to know *why* and *how* Beckett's negative works. For example, Bion's conceptualisation of the interdependence of the processes of fragmentation and integration may help us to see why there is a renowned spiral of assertion and denial in *The Unnamable*, or more precisely affirmation-negation-affirmation as in: 'you must go on, I can't go on, I'll go on' (*BT* 382). Concepts such as 'attacks on linking' or 'thinking' might prove fruitful in helping us understand why, in the trilogy, Beckett's writing launches attacks against the integrating and linking function of language and thought. The value of Winnicott's theory is that it leaves room – a potential intermediate space – for accounting what Beckett 'creates' in the void or how one 'continues to be' in such an unnamable zone or state. With Winnicott we are always in the paradoxical realm of illusion that is neither inner nor outer, neither 'presence' nor 'absence' but rather the intermediate state or space *between,* – the 'interplay', to quote Buning.

For example, to enter into the paradoxical not to say almost nonsensical world of Beckettian relationships, one remarks that one exists sufficiently in order to have the sentiment of not existing; one remembers sufficiently in order to have the impression of not having had any memory, any past. It is the negative – as in photography – of a past, a memory which has no memory and which can't be remembered, the apparent absence of 'real' childhood which matter. Malone reminds us that he must have lived, once, out there from which there is no recovering (*BT* 203). The Beckettian negative is potentially positive: the negative of remembering, speaking, and loving is about the only 'real' thing in Beckett's work. The Godot that is not there is more real than the Godot who might eventually come.

In this project of theorising Beckett's void, the critical epistemology of the negative will be seen to pivot around thinking and playing. These dual notions will enable us to re-conceptualise mental space as a space of writing. It is not that Beckett writes with his head, but he writes rather against the head, against thinking and thought. Pushed to the extreme, one could argue that the 'object' for Beckett is emptiness, blankness, void, vacuousness. Yet the stories of the trilogy and the voices in *Godot* can be seen as playful attempts at sounding the unknown and the unknowable, reinventing and reconstructing absence, giving shape to 'the place where something was' (Bion qtd in Ross 1995, 63). Can Beckett's negative be said to have an aesthetic value? Beauty? A sense of the sublime? My tentative reply is yes as we shall see later in this book.

3
Family Matters

> 'there is no being but being conceived'
> (*The Unnamable*)

The story

A critic once said that the material of *Molloy* is so bizarre that the reader is forced to ask for the reality underlying the text. A brief presentation of the novel will hopefully make it easier to follow the subsequent analysis.

Part one of *Molloy* deals with Molloy's mother as the object of his quest. Molloy tells his story in his mother's room; he has taken her place; he resembles her; he may even have a son. His story is essentially about how he set out by bicycle to visit her. On his way, Molloy kills a dog belonging to a woman called Lousse who adopts Molloy and keeps him *chez elle* for a while. Then terrible things happen to Molloy; he ponders suicide and his body gradually gets paralysed. He eventually makes it to the coast where he describes how he sucks sixteen stones distributing them between four pockets. Virtually paralysed, Molloy makes it into a forest where he ends up crawling, going round in circles before ending up in a ditch.

The second part of the novel essentially dramatises a father–son relationship between the Morans: Jacques Moran is proud of his well-ordered existence and the tyrannical relationship he has developed with his son Jacques. One Sunday, Moran gets strange orders from a messenger, Gaber, to go and track down Molloy (the 'obidil'). His mission is to wait for a mysterious Youdi beside a tree for news or a message concerning Molloy. Just as Molloy undergoes a regressive collapse in part one, equally Moran experiences some sort of annihilation on having a vision of his birth or someone's birth. Gaber finally returns but with no news of Youdi. Moran is ordered home where he discovers his hens and bees dead and still wonders if he will meet Molloy. If Moran has been obeying Youdi's orders to track Molloy, he has also been obeying a voice that tells him to write his report: 'Does it mean I am freer now than I was?', he wonders at the end.

Bridging the gulf between Molloy and Moran

The general purpose of this chapter is to reread the Moran–Molloy relationship and rethink *Molloy*. If critics have compellingly pointed out the double Oedipal structure (Baker 1997, 39) – a 'mother–father palimpsest' (Moorjani 1991, 61) – of the novel with its double story of Molloy's obsessive quest for his mother, in the first part of the novel and in the second, of Jacques Moran's tyrannical relationship with his son, Jacques, they have also pointed out the spoofing of the oedipal scenario or the ironic distance Beckett takes from it. Much of the debate has been about the relation between the two parts of *Molloy*, many adopting Edith Kern's contention that Molloy's part follows Moran's chronologically (Kern 1959, 188–9) and that Moran represents an earlier version of some sort of Molloy-effect, Moran becoming Molloy in fact. Recent studies have shown how the two parts of the novel strategically oppose and complement one another, offering us two antithetical versions of the same story, where within each part, the doubles mirror and replicate. Angela Moorjani, for one, argues that the Molloy segment is contained within the Moran text in the manner of the unconscious within the conscious (Moorjani 1991, 54; Moorjani 1982, 39–46, 108). My reading will take this thesis on further.

The basic strategy of my reading is to maintain and 'hold' the undecidability of the meaning of the Molloy–Moran relationship. Just in the same way that both Molloy and Moran jubilantly meditate on the ultimately indeterminable meaning of various enigmas such as Molloy's saw-horse and Moran's dance of the bees, I shall be confronting 'the puzzle's insolubility' rather than trying to resolve it, (Katz 195). I wish therefore to look at what happens or doesn't happen *between* Molloy and Moran since Beckett's provocative and playful staging of their non-meeting or missed union is highly significant.

The place 'in-between' – the space between' – Molloy and Moran is a notion I propose to hypothesise as a mental space, and the Molloy–Moran relationship as a mental container of a sort. The way the two halves of *Molloy* communicate or fail to communicate is tantamount to saying that it is the link between the two parts of *Molloy* corresponding precisely to the internal parent couple, or the combined parent figure that is being attacked or destroyed.

My theoretical reference for getting through the Beckett labyrinth will be Bion's conception of the thinking apparatus as the 'container-contained' operated upon by the dynamic influence of the paranoid-schizoid (PS) and depressive positions (D), plus the 'selected fact' – akin to a catalyst. From the previous chapter, it will be remembered that Bion suggests an ongoing oscillation between these two positions, ultimately placing value on the essential *interdependence* of processes of fragmentation and integration, which he regarded as essential to all creative thinking. That Moran and Molloy cannot be brought together in a way that leaves each character intact and yet able, by their conjunction, to form a relationship, or what Bion would call, 'a new mental object' (Bion 1967, 50), will be taken to be the structuring leitmotif – the 'selected fact' – of my reading. For Bion, the 'selected fact' is the name of an *emotional* experience insofar as it describes a process whereby the patient uses one object or element to harmonise and give a pattern of meaning to both the chaotic elements and the fact selected. I have therefore chosen to see the Molloy–Moran relationship as a drama of linkage and 'inchoation' in terms of a complex psychical interplay of container and contained. The function of projected identification will be seen in terms of Moran's failed attempts at thinking Molloy, his secret imaginary twin or complementary double (Moorjani 2004a), that is to say, at fitting meaningless or malevolent contents into a container (Cousineau 1996, 76–7).[1]

I shall first look at the formal interplay between meta-narrative and narrative before looking at the general psychic structures that 'contain' the narrative. I'll then focus on the novel's epicentre of mental turbulence, which for me is in Moran's mind.

'Oh the stories I could tell you'

A lot of narrating in Beckett could be described as permanently non-communicating and this is how I would situate the role of metafiction or metanarrative in Beckett's writing, where the narrative act is often subject to assault by negation and the 'progress' of the narration is continually interrupted by irresistible wishes to regress. These are facilitated by the frequent use of ellipsis, repetition or aporia. For all its downright repudiation of family relationships and interconnected issues such as dependence, affects, emotions, *Molloy* is a vicious, sarcastic text, and doesn't lend itself to literal meanings: 'what tenderness in these little words, what savagery' (*BT* 76), as Molloy states. To echo Leslie Hill's analysis, if there is a family drama or genealogical fable to be unearthed within the fictional content of Beckett's trilogy, 'it is present only in cryptic, displaced fashion' (Hill 1990, 80), existing 'only to the extent that it is also full of omissions and indeterminacies, gaps and suppression, repetitions and displacements' (81). In other words and more concretely, the Molloy son–mother relationship, for example, is simply not available 'in any fully complete version' (ibid., 80).[2]

The deceptiveness of the second part of *Molloy* lies in the way Moran, the writer, builds caricature and comedy into his account of his own mental catastrophe. For example, although conspicuousness is the A B C of his profession, Moran is at his most ridiculous when he chooses for his secret mission a 'get-up' comprising a shooting-suit with knee-breeches, stockings to match, and a straw boater together with a ludicrous umbrella (*BT* 114). He makes ready to go without knowing where he is going, without consulting a map or a time-table. Indeed it is no surprise that critics see Moran as 'a tremendous comic creation' (Baker 1997, 45). However, I do have reservations about seeing Moran's breakdown as being 'relatively good-natured and sympathetic, without the clawing bitterness it assumes in *Endgame*' (ibid., 46). For me the comedy and caricature are Beckett's means of containing and manipulating Moran's experience (more about this later).

If one story in *Molloy* is about Moran the character-narrator who is particularly possessed, obsessed and inhabited by one character in particular, that is, Molloy, another story is about Moran the writer whose head is filled 'with all the others': 'Oh the stories I could tell you if I were easy. What a rabble in my head' (*BT* 126). Moran's distinctive rational style, with his unfeeling, almost blank narrative voice is at odds with the tumultuous metamorphosis he finally undergoes. And, typically enough, there is no shortage of tongue in cheek in the way Moran skirts the issues. Either he can't come to the point, or when he does, he reminds us that he is writing it all down 'with a firm hand weaving inexorably back and forth and devouring my page with the indifference of a shuttle' (122). Consequently, the unemotional Moran finds distance from painful events through his artful manipulation of language, with the striking use of abstract nouns and definite articles. For example, justifying his recourse to ellipsis and summary, Moran chooses not to tell us what he grandly calls 'the misdemeanours of *the* son, [or] 'the disintegration of *the* father' (145 my emphasis); the journey home is reduced to the clichéd rhetoric of 'furies and treacheries' (153).

Even when Moran dreams of having no memory or desire anymore and no body worthwhile talking about, the language is shot through with the lethal liveliness of cliché: for example, he is as blind as a bat and deaf as a post (192).[3] Yet, for all that, Moran is at his most vicious when dealing with his own sufferings. As he grows weaker and weaker and is on the point of losing consciousness altogether, Moran is enchanted with his performance as he crawls out to have a good laugh at the lights of Bally (150), his laugh being the sinister equivalent of an uncontrollable fit that shakes his body (149).

For all its formal structure, shape and intricate system of symmetry, *Molloy* is a novel in bits and pieces and may be seen to be always falling apart. Formally speaking, the missing details in Gaber's report concerning Molloy double up as the lacking element in the writer's plot (125). Indeed one of Moran's rare meta-fictional thoughts as he is left thinking in the void, concerns the possibility of meeting up in heaven not only with the fictive cast of *Molloy*, but also with the characters of preceding Beckett novels such as 'Murphy, Watt, Camier and the rest' (154).

Family relations

If *Molloy* is about family matters and family relations, Beckett's radical psychoanalytic stance is that of a writer who wrenches the individual and literature free from the pull and power of family as institution and structure (Moorjani 1991, 64). In many ways, *Molloy* is about the negation of freedom, agency and spontaneity with Self finding itself invariably shackled and fettered by parental authority and power: Molloy by his harrowing persecutory mother, Moran by Youdi and the obligation of the report (see Cousineau 1999). Insofar as one may talk of a self in Beckett's writing, the Molloy–Moran couple points to separate selves with their unlinkable parts that resist integration and union. In a strange way they are in constant rebellion not so much with the world, in the social or political sense of the word, but with the earth at large: 'With time, and nothing but my teeth and nails, I would rage up from the bowels of the earth to its crust [...] I would dig through the rock with my bones' (*BT* 144), fumes Moran. The space 'in-between' Molloy and Moran is to be read more widely as the space between self and world, the space of a rupture with the world, the rapture of the self sounding the unthought, with its intimations of nothingness or self-dissolution. If there is a world or if there was a world in *Molloy*, it is a world of fleeting illusion with its dead time and dead places where nothing can be symbolised. One's anguish of return is perhaps that of returning to absence: 'then the anguish of return, I won't say where, I can't, *to absence perhaps*' (40 my emphasis), says Molloy.

One of the overriding ironies of *Molloy* is that for all its over-determined structures, Beckett creates a text with characters that remain irreducible to such fatal or traumatic events. Indeed so much of the writing carves out the space of another story that Molloy hints at when he wonders if his living so long has been due to his solitude, his persecution, his long silent screams and the daily longing for the earth to swallow him up (74). Hence the mystery, the uncertainty, the confusion around Molloy's description of 'the thing in ruins' (38), not knowing what it is or what it was. Yet parental structures there are with their indelible fatal relations and hated linking functions.

The prototype for all links, Bion reminds us, is the breast or penis. However, Bion's concern is not only with the breast, or penis, or verbal thought, but with their function of providing the link between two objects (Bion 1967, 93–4). In order for communication and mental activity to proceed, envy needs to be manageable enough for a link between two minds to be tolerated. The attack on the link between two internal mental objects is also an attack on the internal parental couple. Because of the connotations of the oedipal couple, the conjoining of two mental objects is felt not only to arouse envy, but to be the basis for internal mental creativity.

Molloy is structured around a powerful phantasm of destroying meaningful family links and yet somehow surviving these.[4] If the maternal realm and the paternal domain serve to provide structure and archetypal form for *Molloy*, the mother's breast for Molloy's quest, on the one hand, and on the other hand, the function of the father for Moran's story, this structure of containment is itself subject to assault. In between the lines, in between Molloy and Moran's stories, the Beckett parental couple are eviscerated of their functions and attributes. Not unlike the violent thumps Molloy gives on his mother's skull, Beckett too hammers pitilessly on the maternal and paternal imagos that structure his novel.

Through the pitiless parody of Molloy's excessive identification with the mother, Beckett turns on its head one of the most potent cultural and psychic myths in modern Irish literature: the filial pieties of sons towards mothers, with stories of attachment and their images of the 'strong' mother. The reader's initial shock or surprise derives from the manner Beckett explicitly shows the unerring sense of a symbiotic fusion, or a oneness between the mother-world and the non-mother-world of *Molloy*. Despite Molloy's opening intimations that his story will be about a union with his mother, paradoxically, we get more the impression that he is already re-united with his mother albeit in spirit if not in body. Indeed, Molloy lies and writes in her room, imagines having taken her place, pisses and shits in her pot. Resembling his mother more and more, he even surmises that he has a son somewhere (9). Beckett's mother and son have already become 'a couple of old cronies [...] with the same memories, the same rancours, the same expectations' (18). But as Leslie Hill remarks, in Molloy's relation to his mother, 'attraction and repulsion match one another in a movement of reciprocal deferral' (Hill 1990, 86).[5] For instance, the Oedipal scenario is recycled, in inverted fashion, for it is the mother who sees her son as a replica of his father, calling him Dan (*BT* 18). Furthermore, Molloy sneeringly champions his mother's madness and grotesqueness. On one hand, he is the only one who understands his mother's 'clattering gabble' (18), her incapacity to think enabling him to maintain his identification with her. Yet the same description of her ruined mind is repulsively aggressive as Molloy tells us how he entered into communication with her by knocking on her skull (ibid.) ultimately making her responsible for his state of mind and body (19). Let us first look more closely at what Molloy calls his unreal journey (17).

Indeed, one wonders if Molloy goes anywhere? Has he been anywhere? Has he ever left his mother? This is another way of expressing Beckett's peculiar way of playing with the mother–son relationship.

The ambiguity of the son–mother relationship has already been mentioned with its mixture of dread and attraction, but not enough has been made of Beckett's creativity and the way his narrative makes room for its own play-zone where Molloy's mother is both dead and alive, persecutory and salutary. Molloy wonders if she was already dead when he came or did she only die later (9). This makes her very much a dead-alive or a living-dead mother, always there to harrow and prompt Molloy to get on with his journey and his story. The suggestion made is that Molloy was born to a 'dead mother', in Green's sense of the notion – psychically dead or critically absent when he was born – but on actually dying, she has managed to remain sinisterly alive. For example Molloy wonders if she wasn't buried alive: 'Ah the old bitch, a nice dose she gave me, she and her lousy unconquerable genes' (75).

The journey to mother is always the journey from mother. Molloy is unable to abandon his mother for fear of being abandoned by her. He is harried by the dread of waking far from her, with his two legs as still as his crutches (74). Rhetorically and elliptically, Molloy's journey, far from being unique or singular, is really only a repetition of many previous ones. The eponymous hero realises that he had always been going to her with the purpose of establishing his relationship with her 'on a less precarious footing' (80). If there is or was a matter to be settled, and however dim that matter grew, it never completely vanished, remarks Molloy (60). However, even if his visits and stays have been to no effect, Molloy is always on his way to her hoping that he'll do better the next time (80). Even when he tries to abandon his maternal quest and busies himself with something else, in reality he finds himself hatching plans to see her again (ibid.). As in the case of the Molloy–Moran missed or missing encounter, not to mention Vladimir and Estragon's non-meeting with Godot, the significance of the double visit/journey motif linking son and mother, may be said to lie more in the fundamental absence of such an encounter rather than in one ever actually taking place. Molloy's mother is somehow still waiting to 'really' meet her son but when Molloy realises that he may be in the same town where his mother had waited so long and perhaps was waiting still for him, his haste is always to leave it (60). The absence of the other is always preferable to any would-be form of presence.

In this mother-controlled narrative with its vertiginous separation-abandonment game, it is Molloy who is directed and steered on by his mother, whereas in the second part of the novel, it is the son who steers the Morans' bicycle, the paralysed father being transported on the carrier. Rather than a son visiting his mother, we have more the sense of a mother who is always *in* Molloy, in his mind, visiting him, as her harrowing image prompts him into movement and action. For example, Molloy realises that he is not free to stay in the forest for if he had stayed there he would have had the feeling 'of going against an imperative' [...] even 'committing a fault, almost a sin' (79). Accordingly, Molloy's physical and narrative progress may be more likened to a series of interruptions or stops where Beckett sets up a clear rhythm between movement and stasis, mobility and immobility, separation and abandonment, purpose and purposelessness. Molloy's 'real' movement may be said to be that of a regression to immobility and stasis, where stopping is his way of progressing (72). Beckett may be suggesting that Molloy's journey is about an arrested relationship, a relationship that had stopped before it even started.

Significantly, Molloy's final position is in a ditch, as if his journey and discourse were ways of ditching the mother quest. It is an image that suggests abandonment or failure, but it reads both ways: Molloy abandons his mother and is abandoned by his mother. But like much in Beckett, meaning hangs on voice. The indifference of the anonymous voice we hear at the end, that of an implied author perhaps, might also be suggesting that there is more than just a story of a quest being ditched, but also its central character and subject since Molloy could stay, where he happened to be (84).

Turning to the second part of the novel, Beckett literally makes Moran into a paranoid tyrant and authoritarian figure. Although helpless and hapless in relation to Youdi and the enigmatic commanding voice that tells him things, above all to write his enigmatic report (162), Moran can only impose himself on his son through fear and terror. For example, Moran's paternal 'character' or 'stamp' is literally ridiculed by the textual motif of a prized stamp collection; Moran senior giving his son, Jacques Moran junior, one of his rare stamps – the Timor.[6] As Phil Baker points out, the primary significance of this stamp lies in the word 'Timor', Latin for 'Fear', which is appropriate giving the way Moran, the tyrant father, terrorises his son: 'I was sometimes inclined to go too far when I reprimanded my son, who was consequently a little afraid of me' (qtd in Baker, 37). But the fearsome father doubles up as a fearful son. Just as Molloy cannot distinguish his name from his mother's, equally Moran cannot distinguish himself from his offspring, his son sharing the same name. As Moran despairs in the forest of ever seeing Molloy or seeing his son again, it is 'the terrified son in Moran the father' who dreams of his son returning to him or even Molloy coming to him, becoming his friend and helping him do what he had to do, so that Youdi would not be angry with him and would not punish him (149).

That Moran is a failed rationalist of a sort strikes us even more poignantly in the way Beckett affords his character with a cruel invulnerability, a radical indifference or even a repressive distance from matters emotional. While Moran forbids his son to call him papa, or show him any signs of affection in public, if he did not want to get one of those clouts he so dreaded (115), he himself comes within a hair's breadth of kissing his son (112). In another episode when Moran's son gives free vent to his grief (101), following a dispute over the stamp albums, Moran rationally concurs that purging one's emotions is salutary. In the bedroom scene just before the Morans leave in search of Molloy, as the son screams with anger and defiance (116), the moralising rational Moran coldly responds by saying that anger is a luxury he cannot afford (ibid.) and finally calms down by hacking madly at an old chopping-block (117). Such rational repression of anger and rage leads Moran father to gloat over the spectacle of his son ravaged by a 'thwarted and impotent rage towards the father' (Baker 42).

Moran's idea of literally attaching his son to him by means of a long rope ridicules there being emotional attachment between father and son. Beckett may be playing with the negation of the Name-of-the Father, not so much a paternal knotting as a subversive 'notting', a no-thing, a not-father or a no father (see Ross 2004, 146–55).[7] Moran's phantasy of the chain is more than just a negative image of attachment. It suggests that the relationship between contained and container is mutually constrictive, crushing, even parasitic. Unsurprisingly, Moran is incapable of having any guiding influence on his son. This is parodied in the forest scene when it is the paralysed Moran who is transported on the back of his son's bicycle (144–5) with the father incapable of influencing or directing his son's bicycling (148).

Rethinking the Moran–Molloy link

The double paternal/maternal story of our novel encourages us to view Moran's journey as that of a father in search of a son, not unlike Joyce's Mr. Bloom in *Ulysses,* with Moran, as a father figure, being commanded to track down the maternally mollified Molloy or the mother Molloy (103). Consequently, Moran's problem would be ultimately determined by a wish to solve the riddle of the mother's desire, the 'Molloy affair' becoming the 'mother Molloy affair'. This is certainly one instance of the way Beckett cunningly provides reductionist meanings *within* his narrative. The text tells us that Moran finds himself 'inscribed, on the threshold of the Molloy affair, the fatal pleasure principle', and is at a loss to explain how a man like himself 'so patiently turned towards the outer world, as towards the lesser evil' should let himself be 'haunted and possessed by chimeras' (105). Another reductive and simplistic answer, contained in the text, is that Moran is found lacking to institute the requirements of the Reality Principle. But curiously, in his room before he sets out on his journey, Moran already acknowledges and concedes 'defeat' in not being able to have any custodianship over the threatening mother-fixated Molloy. In his enigmatic third person, he says: 'for where Molloy could not be, nor Moran either for that matter, there Moran could bend over Molloy', recalling Freud's celebrated description of the psychoanalytic project: 'where id was, there ego shall be' (qtd in Baker 6–7). Beckett, in parodying Freud's dictum, disqualifies it, as it were, as a plausible working model for reading the Moran–Molloy relationship, which might encourage us to read for an interplay of two psychical agencies or a two-way mapping with the Ego and its attributes – thought, reality – as they attempt to come to terms with the Id.

The Moran/Molloy relationship can also be brought literally closer to the psychoanalytic discourse, Molloy being the patient and Moran the analyst. For example, Molloy's definition of the purpose of his story comes close to summarising the issue of a personal psychoanalysis for 'it bore on the same question, that of my relations with my mother, and on the importance of bringing as soon as possible some light to bear on these and even on the kind of light that should be brought to bear and the most effective means of doing so' (*BT* 80). While Moran presents himself as a secret agent or a detective of a sort – he works on behalf of an anonymous cause (105), he also doubles up as a psychoanalyst. I am referring here to an interesting slip made by Moran when he lets us hear: 'I lost interest in my patients, once I had finished with them' (126). In defining his mission as bringing people (like Molloy) to a certain place at a certain time (ibid.), Beckett may be remembering the work of Bion and his way of proceeding. At the time that Beckett underwent his analysis, the work of J.A. Hadfield, Bion's own analyst, was dominant at the Tavistock Clinic (Bléandonu 1990, 37–41). Hadfield insisted on a rather reductive notion of analysis as the identification and uncovering of traumatic events in the life of the patient (Connor 2008, 13–14). In this view the analysis itself was an instrumental and not a constitutive procedure; thus the effects of transference and counter-transference in the analytic session itself were regarded as at best a kind of distracting noise. To extend these remarks, we could say that it is the counter-transference between Beckett's fictional analyst and patient – Moran and Molloy – that causes the turmoil and disturbance and this is what I wish to explore here.

It might therefore be more fruitful to approach the Moran/Molloy relationship – 'the inexplicable object and the equally inexplicable organism' to quote David Hayman (in Friedman 1970, 156) – not so much as a story of searching, mastering or controlling the other, but rather as a story already haunted by absence and otherness, a story preceded by an unsaid, or unspoken discourse belonging to the void that separates the two halves of the novel. After all, Moran, for no evident reason, has *already* mentally identified with the unknown and unknowable Molloy making him into his 'opposite', his not-me (104). To come to the basic question I set out to answer – what happens *between* Molloy and Moran – the simple answer is: Moran is required to think Molloy or, more accurately to make sense of his thoughts about Molloy. More darkly, the Molloy motif is the troubling element that plunges us into the depths of Moran's mind making the very foundation of the novel shake. Molloy's troubling 'presence' in the second part of the novel is similar to the opening up of a vertiginous and deepening void, a heart of darkness that Moran's thoughts seek to penetrate. This is not a simple case of the return of the repressed. It is my view that the Molloy motif functions more like an uncontainable or unthought message/meaning that defies verbalisation, eludes representation or symbolisation and attacks the very possibilities of thought and thinking. So as to why the appearance of Molloy in Moran's universe represents a disaster for Moran's mental life, not to mention his body, we have to explore the fundamental trope of mental operations in the text which may be likened to a container-(un)contained configuration.

Mental agents and thinking relations

Moran could be likened to an absurd mental agent of a sort. The dominant trope in the Moran story is very much the unfathomable mind, 'now beacon, now sea' (97). When planning his mission to track down Molloy, Moran wonders if his instructions he gives his son will 'stand the test of second thoughts' (95). His mind is a maze, empty and full, familiar and strange as he hears distant cymbals (97). There is an irresistible temptation to play here on sounds for one wonders what are Moran's cymbals symbols of? Originally meaning a hollow vessel, the cymbal is a percussion instrument consisting of a concave plate of brass or bronze, which is struck against another or with a stick to produce a ringing or clashing sound (Brown 1993, 582). To a certain extent the Moran–Molloy affair is about violent ringing sounds clashing around the thinking apparatus of Moran. But lest we think that the mental clanging that persistently goes on in Moran's mind where Molloy 'was forever on the move' (104), simply serves to sabotage our secret agent's capacity for thought and thinking, it must be remembered that before the Morans even set out on their mission, the Molloy affair is set up to symbolise mental deterioration of a sort, a damaged or porous mental container. By his own admission Moran was already losing his head (91) as he continued to shirk 'the kernel of the affair' (90), resulting in his confusion and immense uneasiness ever since the beginning of the Molloy affair (103). If Moran the psychoanalytic detective/thinker doesn't make any progress in tracking down Molloy, what *does* progress is his gradual or cumulative breakdown, caricatured as 'the disintegration of the father' (145). Any would-be spiritual or mystical recuperation of Moran's psychic catastrophe is undermined by Moran's rare thoughts

(153) before he goes on to recite an Our Father in the negative – 'the pretty quietist Pater, Our Father who art no more in heaven than on earth or in hell' (154). All this culminates in an ultimate assault on self, Moran likening himself to a turd waiting for the flush (149).[8] Ultimately unrecognisable, Moran has the impression that his body is no longer his. Yet in spite of its deep lesions and the wounds with which it is covered, he has a clearer sense of his identity than ever before (156–7). His circular journey, then, enacts a *via negativa* of a sort, a re-possession of self through a radical dispossession, a clearing out of self, a self-evacuation of a sort – 'This time a year ago I was setting out. I am clearing out' (161).

In looking at the repercussion of the Moran–Molloy affair on thought and thinking, I am arguably more interested in looking at the effects of the Moran–Molloy relationship rather than its causes. The latter are simply not available or if they are, they are rhetorically figured as the missing link or the incomplete, lacking element not unlike Gaber's incomplete report. One of the major effects of the Moran–Molloy relationship that particularly interests me and will guide my reading, is its peculiar mode of resistance to meaning and elucidation. But before continuing with our psychoanalytic reading, I want to return to some biographical details concerning Beckett's own activities during the war as a Resistance agent and first propose a historical reading of Moran's 'intelligence service'.[9]

James Knowlson tells us that Beckett's role in 'Gloria', the Intelligence service, consisted of liaison work and secretarial work. Although Moran tells us that 'we agents never took anything in writing' (97), Beckett's work consisted of collecting information (about the German military movements) on 'various bits, scraps of paper' and compiling reports. These would be microfilmed by a photographer and secreted away by a courier in one form or other (Knowlson 1996, 307–8).

Moran's sparse account of Youdi's intelligence service with its directorate, messengers, agents, vast organisation, where everyone is working 'on behalf of a cause which [...] was in its essence anonymous' (105), does have a resemblance, albeit parodied, with Gloria and its world of secrecy, codes, cover stories, clandestine activities and constant danger. If Moran and Gaber think themselves as 'members of a vast organization' (99), Gloria was equally 'vast' in that it recruited its agents as wide as possible and incorporated members from many different professions and social strata (Knowlson 308–9). Such anonymity and secrecy is parodied by Beckett when he has Moran wonder if he and Gaber were not operating in a void of a sort: 'for I had never seen any other messenger than Gaber nor any other agent than myself' (*BT* 98). Just as Moran comes to down the existence of the nebulous Gaber, one is prone to suspect the integrity of the Youdi network and its doings. Using Bionian metapsychology, one could see the Youdi network as an alternative agency of 'truth' whose function would be to break down contacts and destroy ties rather than pinning down ties. As we have seen, Moran defines his mission as a form of definition or localisation, his mission consisting of bringing people to a certain place at a certain time (126). Citing the 'Yerk affair', he tells us that it 'was over on the day I succeeded in possessing myself of his tiepin and destroying it' (ibid.) or that 'establishing contact was the least important part of my work' (ibid.). The theoretical ramifications of this detail are illuminating: alongside the Love ('L') and the hate ('H') impulse or links, Bion draws attention to the epistemophilic impulse, which he calls 'K', knowledge. This third link forms the basis of relationships to objects (including the relationships and cross-fertilisation of ideas in the mind) which establishes meaning and respect for the integrity of these objects. Youdi and his gang are clearly working against these 'positive' ties (parodied as the destruction of the tie-pin) suggesting they could represent what Bion would term negative or '−K' anti-links. The agents and messengers' activities might be seen as working to annihilate and corrupt meaning and psychic reality. The corrupt figure of Father Ambrose with his unconsecrated bread comes to mind as does the 'unspeakable punishment' Moran evokes as instances of Youdi's destructive effect.

Containing the uncontainable Molloy

If anything, *Molloy* is a comedy *about* faulty containers where nothing can be fully or completely retained, remembered or registered. We have already seen the example of Molloy's mother whose capacity for thinking is sadistically reduced to a system of knocks and blows. The corresponding figure of such mental blankness in Moran's story is of course the memory-less Gaber, already referred to. Gaber's sole reliable container for 'holding' the Molloy case is his notebook since it contains the mysterious written instructions concerning Molloy which Gaber reads to Moran (87). While Youdi's messenger certainly has the Irish 'gift of the gab' indulging in comments and observations of which Moran had no need (87), it is the silent incommunicable content of Gaber's notebook – the 'contained' Molloy – that becomes the fulcrum of Moran's quest, which at times resembles more a re-reading of Gaber's undecipherable message: 'I was looking for what was wanting to make

Gaber's report complete' (125). If Gaber cannot 'communicate' his Molloy message, it goes without saying that Moran cannot take anything 'in'. Unsurprisingly, Moran comes to doubt the existence of Gaber himself (99), with his 'corpse fidelity to the letter of his messages' (106). If Gaber is anything at all, he is a link with absence, the sole liaison for the absent figure of authority, Youdi.

If the containing functions of speech, memory and thought are highly unstable what about the relationship of the contained to the container (the container here being Moran's thinking apparatus)? Here one is tempted to hypothesise that, intrapsychically, Gaber's role as container has been irredeemably 'damaged' by the uncontained or uncontainable Molloy. But we also have to watch that we don't arrive like Gaber at the most extravagantly false conclusions (98). Rhetorically and psychically, the contained 'Molloy' may be said to figure and signify something that remains uncommunicated, unthought, or unthinkable – a Kantian thing-in-itself. Notwithstanding, such mystery or menace is at the same time undermined by the text when we are told that for Moran the Molloy affair seems childishly simple, or even a kind of nonsense (87). As always with Beckett, we are at the limits between unspeakable unrepresentable trauma, a recapitulation perhaps of the disintegrated condition of the paranoid-schizoid stage, and/or some contrived nonsense.

The container-contained configuration for thinking the Molloy–Moran affair continually defies its own representation. We have more a sense of containers within containers: Moran within Gaber, Gaber within Youdi, Moran within Youdi, the Youdi–Molloy affair subsequently becoming the Molloy/Moran affair. But Moran is ultimately under the mental command of Youdi, he is his mental agent, as it were, obeying a voice, which if it is not Youdi's voice, could be seen as introjected thoughts of the Other: 'for it (the voice) is within me and exhorts me to continue to the end the faithful servant I have always been, of a cause, *that is not mine* (121, my emphasis). If Youdi is the absent thinker of Moran's thoughts, what about Molloy? To what extent does Molloy come to represent 'thoughts' that require thinking and the presence of a thinker?

That Molloy may be simply lost or missing is one of the first hypotheses that attracts Moran's thoughts, hence Moran preferring the name Mollose since his mind has a weakness for this ending (ose, or lose) (103). However, Moran soon realises that Molloy is rhetorically and psychically present and absent, everywhere and no one place in particular. The Molloy–Moran container may be said to swing from an intrusive, threatening 'presence' to an unbearable absence or void, with the inaccessible Molloy dynamically wavering in and out of Moran's mind.

Like thoughts that exist to be thought, finding Molloy in Moran's mind is a way for Moran to find Molloy again, invent him and create him. He wonders if he hadn't invented him, or found him ready-made in his head (103). Indeed Molloy is a stranger who is not a stranger, having played a part in certain 'cerebral reels' (ibid.). Not that Molloy ever totally disappears from Moran's mindscape, for no amount of thinking will ever think away Molloy who, in another way, has yet to appear to Moran: 'perhaps I shall meet Molloy' (161). Equally, no amount of journeying to the Molloy country – 'that narrow region' (123) with its 'strangled creek' (ibid.), and 'its curious bitter blue grass' (124) – will ever find Molloy. As Angela Moorjani astutely remarks, Moran's mock journey to the Molloy country, is a journey that 'stops' at the borderline of Molloy's territory, the zone between consciousness and the unconscious (Moorjani 1982, 116).

The least we can say about the Molloy–Moran pair is that they are not a thinking couple. When Moran tries to enclose Molloy within his mind, he is crushed by the pressure of his own thoughts, which I would re-term as 'Molloy being thought'. Ever since Moran receives 'the order to see about Molloy' (85), he fails to 'think' the Molloy affair since, one, Molloy cannot be conceived as a full or whole person and, two, for the rational Moran, he already exists as a source of persecutory anxiety, most of which remains unthought or unthinkable. But even if Molloy matters nothing to Moran, it is the return of those evacuated parts of Molloy that makes Molloy uncontrollable and menacing, independent of Moran and yet persecutory: 'And let us not meddle either with the question as to how far these five Molloys were constant and how far subject to variation' (106). Moran believes, however, that the fragmented and expelled bits of the Molloys (mollose, mother Molloy) have entered a real Molloy. But Molloy's return in Moran's thoughts, is not only the Molloy who Moran was ordered to see about, the day when his last moments of peace and happiness slipped away (85), it is also the return of those evacuated parts belonging to the object, that is, those which are the most uncontrollable, independent, threatening and persecuting for Moran. The image of Molloy's intrusion into the thought of Moran is not only violent, but is equally the projection of all the frustration and pain felt by Moran at the time of the attack: 'He had only to rise within me for me to be filled with panting [...] Then I was nothing but uproar, bulk, rage, suffocation, effort unceasing, frenzied and vain. Just the opposite of myself' (104).

Molloy is experienced, then, by Moran as an intrusive, threatening presence and yet an unbearable absence, a void. But never being absent, the 'object' Molloy cannot be thought and as a result mobilises a permanent counter-cathexis on the part of Moran forcing him to 'get rid' of the different Molloys by expulsive projection, his 'own' Mollose and the other Molloy of the enquiry (104). Speaking of his hopes of ever finding again either his son, Jacques (who mysteriously abandons his father in the forest) or Molloy, Moran says he let them spring within him and grow in strength, before sweeping them away 'with a great disgusted sweep of all my being' and surveying with satisfaction 'the void they had polluted' (149). Such is an example of Moran's 'thinking', which is achieved by a sweeping away of internal objects, a process of evacuation. We have more a sense of evasion by evacuation, the very opposite to 'thinking', that is, thinking the absence of the other. A thought, according to Bion, is the union of a preconception and a frustration; we cannot think without a sense of absence (absent breast inside). If the capacity for toleration of frustration is sufficient the 'no-breast' inside becomes a thought and an apparatus for thinking develops differentiating between sense-impressions and emotions. With Beckett's Moran, however, we have more the impression of someone turning with increased hatred and anxiety against the various Molloys that have shown their power to exist. Moran atomises them, as it were, not so much as a means of searching for his identity or rejecting Molloy, but rather as a struggle to maintain an inner identity always under threat from an exterior but inassimilable object. However, any reparation of the ego becomes impossible. Sweeping Molloy away is also a sweeping away of Moran's being.

Thoughts in labour

The pressure exerted by Molloy on Moran's mind takes its toll and there is no better place to see this than in the forest shelter where Moran is literally left grappling with words to describe his visionary experience. A premonitory advance on all this is already signalled by the temporary switch in the narrative voice from first to third person: 'And it was not so much Moran as another, in the secret of Moran's sensations exclusively, who said, No change, Moran, no change' (135–6). Despite these desperately defensive remarks, the subsequent vision or effort of thought (137) – is ironically one that ushers in change, or in Moran's word, 'a further index of the great changes I had suffered' (ibid.) and culminates in Moran's 'growing resignation of being dispossessed of self' (ibid.). In any event, it is probably at this moment in the text that one realises that Moran's journey is neither a search for his own identity nor for Molloy's for that matter, but rather a self-exposure to otherness, a mental *mise en scène* which could evoke what Bion calls a 'catastrophic change', a notion I shall return to. Equally prior to the vision, Moran tells us that he had been poring on himself, the English here being more evocative than the French – 'on myself too I pored, on me so changed from what I was' (136) ('je me penchais', *M* 247). Here we have again an advance on the imminent vision, Moran already giving us an image of an uncontained self, a psychic flux, that pours and flows, with no clear limits or demarcations. But before going any further, let's quote the decisive passage:

> And what I saw was more like a crumbling, a frenzied collapsing of all that had always protected me from all I was condemned to be. Or it was like a kind of clawing towards a light and countenance I could not name, that I had once known and long denied. But what words can describe this sensation at first all darkness and bulk, with a noise like the grinding of stones, then suddenly as soft as water flowing [...] and nothing to show if it was a man's face or a woman's face, a young face or an old face. (136–7)

In his attempt at naming his experience, Moran crosses the literal and figurative boundaries of language repeatedly with his recourse to approximative images: 'was more *like* a crumbling', 'a *kind* of clawing', 'a noise *like* the grinding of stones', 'as soft *as* water flowing'. In Bion's terms, we could see such a description as Moran's search for concrete images, for units of thought. But what spills over here is the irreducible uncontainable force of a new thought that is felt by Moran's psyche as potentially disruptive and shattering. The 'catastrophic change' I already alluded to, lies in Moran's inability to tolerate this upheaval, verbalise his sense of disaster (137) and thereby withstand fragmentation, anxiety and doubt.[10] Even if he is bereft of mental functioning, Moran is nonetheless cognisant that these 'poor figures' (137) have turned out to be poor inadequate 'containers', if that indeed is their function, since on this point Moran isn't even sure: 'But I confess I attended but absently to these poor figures, in which *I suppose* my sense of disaster sought *to contain* itself' (ibid.). The syntax of the sentence just quoted is significant. The 'I' takes on the role of experiencer: 'I suppose', instead of the role of agent. This curious syntax of Moran's lends itself to a different meaning or at least a different emphasis, which could be refigured as: 'my disaster tried to think itself or contain itself in the absence of an I-container'. The point is that his disaster is everything but self-contained. In the absence of an 'I' or even a 'me', it is uncontainable. Saying that he 'attended but absently' ('Je ne prêtais qu'une attention distraite à ces pauvres figures', *INN* 248), is tantamount to saying that Moran is not only unable to make links, but is indifferent to the state of his own destroyed capacity for linking[11] (see also Hunkeler 1997, 228–9).

What is it that Moran 'sees'? The text denotes 'a little globe', 'a face, with holes for the eyes and mouth and other wounds' (*BT* 137. We get more the impression that Moran's thinking on the mysterious face with holes, gives up half-way through its own mental elaborations for, finally, all had been for nothing (*BT* 137). Indeed, Moran's mental strategy is one of evasion or even abandonment as he 'flees to other cares' and when he thinks again of Molloy, we are told that Moran turns 'in haste towards other unknowns' (ibid.). But what is it that he abandons?

Moran qualifies his thinking as a labour or an inadequate labouring, – 'and that I didn't *labour* at them [figures] more diligently was a further index of the great changes I had suffered' (my emphasis) – which picks up on the suggestive imagery of an embryo 'swaying up slowly from the depths'. In French, we get more the literal sense of work: 'et le fait de ne pas y travailler davantage' (*INN* 248). Beckett, who read Rank's *The Trauma of Birth*, may be intimating not so much an act of birth in the form of a definite expulsion from the womb, but a hallucinatory vision of intra-uterine psychic life, a Rankian 'prenatal and posthumous timelessness fused in the mind'. As Angela Moorjani remarks, for Rank, 'this phantasy in which a progression towards death is identical to a regression to the womb, or where the future after death is also conceived as a return to a past before birth, is an attempt as healing the trauma of separation at birth' (Moorjani 2004a, 173; see also Baker 1997, 64–105).

To return to *Molloy*, insofar as we may see Molloy and Moran as inverted spectral doubles or twins ironically linked by having the same journey and quest – 'their journeys [...] are but one journey staged at different psychic levels' (Moorjani 1982, 96) – one possible 'content' for Moran's space of unborn thought or unthinkable birth would be to suggest the double scene or double projection of a foundational or originary event. I say 'double' since what might bring Moran and Molloy into a relationship of identity would be the traumatic experience of birth. Moran's wife died in childbirth and, as we know, Molloy never forgave his mother for having him and for not having aborted him. Of course, Moran doesn't actually see Molloy, as the face remains unidentified and unidentifiable. It is nonetheless conceivable to imagine that Moran's vision of 'birth' is also a vision of Molloy's trauma.

To paraphrase the key-quotation already given above, as a secret sharer, Moran had long protected himself from this trauma, something he long knew and denied. He re-lives then a dangerous moment of identification, a possible merging with Molloy and Mother Molloy – 'a scurf of placenta, her stamp' (103). In this specular moment of inversion where Moran is son and resembles Molloy, it is Molloy who thinks his birth trauma through the container-less Moran. But, contrary to what many critics argue, Moran doesn't become Molloy and the 'thought of trauma' (which is my interpretation or my projection) is quickly abandoned or, split off, to use the theoretical language of psychoanalysis. Indeed, as already alluded to, Moran cannot 'labour' any further and, as a result, the figure doesn't come to life; it isn't fully born in his mind; it is neither inside nor outside the body, but rather somewhere between water and light – 'or if its calm too was not an effect of the water trembling between it and the light' (137). If Moran's vision eludes representation, it is perhaps closer to the unknowable, the unknowable object, and literally becomes one of Moran's many unknowns who, as he says, will soon be 'in haste towards other unknowns'.

Unsurprisingly, then, and paradoxically, what Moran does 'contain' and, equally Molloy, are figures of the unfigurable: in Moran's case his bees and in Molloy's his sawing-horse (56). Indeed, as he stares into a gaping spiritual void that he tries to fill by listing his 'rare [theological] thoughts' (153), the 'nearest things to comfort' for Moran – his Keatsian 'beauty and joy for ever' – is 'the thought of [his] bees and their dance': 'I was more than ever stupefied by the complexity of this innumerable dance' (156). As Angela Moorjani rightly claims, Molloy and Moran study the figures that will continue to baffle them and engage in multiple bids at understanding cryptic texts against a horizon of unknowingness (Moorjani 1991, 53). Molloy realises that 'to be beyond knowing anything, to know you are beyond knowing anything, that is when peace enters in, to the soul of the incurious seeker' (59). He is under the rapture of the unknowable: 'and I said with rapture, Here is something I can study all my life, and never understand' (156). While Moran is resigned to never knowing anything about the mysterious figure of the unborn child in the forest, on his way home, he exults in the realisation that the unfigurable dance (of thought) exists to out-manoeuvre and out-think him. This echoes back the opening image we get of Moran, as that of someone who watched *absently* the coming and going of his bees. Perhaps it is here through the intermediary images of the unfigurable bee dance or the disturbing child form, that Beckett articulates the 'relationship' of self to its absence by giving it a 'form', an unfigurable object. One is indeed tempted to see *Molloy* as a novel that follows 'an infinite chain of regression to the unknowable (Moorjani 1982, 118), where regressing to the unknowable would amount to regressing to the 'unborn'. One wonders who might fill the space of the unborn figure. But this is making absences present, that is, filling in what is a necessary void, an ineffable experience – theatrical animism of a sort – that lies beyond the realms of word or thought. My tentative conclusion on this and to which I shall return later, is that by creating a space for the unknowable or unknowingness, Beckett is, by the same sleight of hand, carving out a space for absence, an impenetrable space. Indeed, not much 'remains of the representable' in *Molloy*, the essence of the Molloy–Moran link being to 'elude representation'.[12]

An aesthetic encounter

It goes without saying, as Angela Moorjani has remarked, that as regards the Molloy–Moran configuration, 'there is no resolution of conflicts but an endless to-and-fro between contradictory forces within. All that these writers/narrators might hope to do is unwrite themselves in the direction of anonymity and dissolve the contraries into silence' (Moorjani 1991, 64). As Richard Begam astutely points out, Beckett leaves us in an 'an interstitial zone, the space of an in-between that not only refuses to resolve itself into either of these two terms but renders impossible their very articulation' (Begam 1996, 156). The least we can say about the space of the in-between, separating and joining Moran and Molloy, is that it hollows out its own void, its own unthinkable dark centre, where one might 'locate' the unsymbolisable Molloy–Moran affair. Molloy and Moran seek out an encounter not where one character bests another but where both characters are bested by otherness.

The experience of the *Molloy* reader is perhaps more than anywhere else 'between the phrases, in the silence, communicated by the intervals, not the terms, of the statement', in 'the memory of an unspeakable trajectory' (*DFMW* 137). Like all great texts in literature, *Molloy* dwells darkly on the reader's experience, with its expectations, longings and frustrations. Unlike Moran who was getting to know the language of his voice better, to understand what it wanted (162), we may never know what this novel wants us to understand unless it is to be in awe of the incomprehensible and the unfigurable. Understanding that the Molloy–Moran link is beyond understanding is still understanding.

Molloy is fundamentally about writing and writers, the non-encounter coming to designate an aesthetic encounter of a sort. What Moran gets out of his mission is a message from Youdi via Gaber, a recycling of the line from Keats that life is a thing of beauty and a joy for ever, wondering if Youdi meant human life (151–2). Indeed, Keats's most well-known poetic dictum that all we need to know, and all we can know, is that 'Beauty is Truth and Truth Beauty', tells us that truth has an aesthetic dimension, since the love of knowledge, together with love itself are one and the same. Of course there is hardly anything overtly Keatsian about Moran's search for knowledge and truth concerning Molloy. Yet for all that, the Molloy affair is enigmatically available only to aesthetic intuition, as Moran has been irremediably distorted by Molloy and there is no longer any point in looking for links or meanings, 'truth' or 'understanding'. In the face of destruction, loss and disintegration, Moran only has his writing. Where Keats linked truth with the question of justifying good and trusting to it in the face of destructive and evil elements that abound (Glover 2004, 24), writing for Beckett is ultimately devoid of any justification or fundamental cause, least of all family matters. By negating his sentences as Moran does when he finally sits down to write the report about Molloy, Moran certainly appropriates the freedom to lie, to play and to invent (Gunn 1988, 162; Moorjani 1982, 46).) But it is also a freedom to simply write: 'does this mean I am freer now than I was? I do not know' (*BT* 162). To write in the absence of truth and above all, to write in the absence of Molloy.

4
Playing, Dying and the Art of Being Absent

The story

Written as a pseudo autobiography, *Malone Dies* deals with the minutiae of Malone's existence in his room, like dropping his pencil or his dwindling amount of writing lead. He is slowly getting ready to die and while waiting he sets out to tell stories about his possessions such as his exercise book, brimless hat and pencil. He alternates between writing his own situation and that of a boy named Sapo. When he reaches the point in the story where Sapo becomes a man, he changes Sapo's name to Macmann, finding Sapo a ludicrous name. Eventually, Macmann falls over in mud and is taken to an institution called St John's of God. There he is provided with an attendant nurse, an elderly, thick-lipped woman named Moll, with crosses of bone on either ear representing the two thieves crucified with Jesus on Good Friday, and a crucifix carved on her tooth representing Jesus. The two eventually begin a stumbling sexual affair, but after a while she does not return, and he learns that she has died. The new nurse is a man named Lemuel, and there is animosity between the two. At the end of the novel, Lemuel is assigned to take his group of five inmates on a trip to a nearby island organised by a Lady Pedal. They leave the grounds of St John's and take a boat to the island to picnic and see Druid remains. Lemuel runs amok with a hatchet killing several inmates but the scene of carnage is uncannily comical with the tone of 'guignol' or a Punch-and-Judy show. The novel closes with an image of Lemuel holding his bloodied hatchet up. Malone writes that Lemuel will not hit anyone with it or anything else anymore, while the final sentence breaks into semantically open-ended fragments.

Is Malone at the end born into death or does he die to be born? No resolution of the conflict is provided.

Clearing a play space for rereading *Malone Dies*

Perhaps no other Beckett text is as literally concerned with absence, playing and death as *Malone Dies*. Yet criticism tends to isolate and privilege one of these terms without seeking to interrelate them. For example, Malone's 'death' or 'birth' has been singled out to be the crux of the novel, a moment of self-possession as much as it is a moment of self-dispossession (Hill 1990, 101). As Richard Begam points out, 'if the nexus is clear – womb, room, tomb – its significance is less so' (1996, 139). He goes on to argue that the crux dramatised and performed by Malone is no less than that of writing itself which is figured throughout as game, invention: 'live and invent'. Leslie Hill, too, argues that Beckett's playing with language and fiction is a means of exploring the limits between the fictional and the real, self and other, order and disorder, identity and difference. To play is also to be 'the child again and to repeat the moment of birth by restaging, as though in a game, the process by which already, in earlier childhood games, the self was first constituted' (102). Hill goes on to explain Beckett's playing in the light of the relationship between 'the procreative father and the procreated child' (ibid.) the theme of playing being 'an attempt by the narrator to compensate for the non-event of birth and give birth to himself' (ibid.).

Using Winnicott's theory of the transitional object and transitional phenomena, and his conceptions of play, paradox and space, already alluded to, I wish to look at a different conceptual model for approaching Malone's playing and to place the emphasis rather on the mother–infant relationship or, more generally, on the dynamic play of spacing between presence and absence, subject and object. In doing so, I shall be building on what Angela Moorjani has already said regarding the importance of paradoxality in this particular text:

> Malone thus paradoxically must either die in order to be born, or be born in order to die, a paradox that all the former games and pastimes have played through and on which Malone will concentrate [...] Is Malone at the end born into death or does he die to be born? As in the other novels, no resolution of the conflict comes about; the end [...] the birthing/dying of the narrator from the womb of writing is endlessly postponed. (Moorjani 1982, 121)

My particular contribution to this debate is to place the interplay between Malone's dying and being born in an intermediate area of play. My hypothesis is that a space develops between Malone's inner and outer worlds and is contributed to by both.[1] This intermediate space between presence and absence, dying and living, is, theoretically, in direct continuity with the play area of the small child who is 'lost' in play (Winnicott 1971, 15). By using Winnicott, it is hoped that we may get a different insight into the peculiar relationship between absence, death and playing in this particular novel, and, underlying these issues, the vexed relationship between Malone's past and his present. It is also the occasion to displace the importance of the play content in *Malone Dies* and focus more on the *playing* as a thing in itself.[2] For me, Malone's playing is more than a question of his relationship with his possessions, nor is it just a narrative ploy. More widely it can be seen in the way he seeks to stay somewhere *in-between* his descriptions of himself in the room, his stories and his meta-narrative discourse, and thereby orchestrate the boundaries and lines of demarcation between his first-person narrative and his third-person narrative, between his past and his present.[3]

Taking the playful interweave between Malone's past and his present as a central theme, I wish to show that the present can be read as a re-actualisation or a re-enactment of Malone's traumatic past in at least three distinctive interrelated ways:

1. Through playing with his transitional possessions as a means of creating a potential presence and asserting self-autonomy.
2. Through the Sapo–Macmann–Lemuel narrative which, I argue, is a fantasised doubling of Malone's history, that is, the trajectory of the withdrawn self with its blank holes and impaired thought leading to madness and murder.
3. Through the enigmatic birth–death enactment. Here I see Malone's articulation of absence as a repetition of a psychic death. The birth–death crux in *Malone Dies* will be re-approached, then, in terms of the born-unborn, living-unliving dialectic. Malone's playing may be seen as traversing the various gaps, splits and caesuras of his existence in order to re-establish a permeable caesura or an 'articulating caesura' (Skelton 2006, 94) that allows dialogue and even an experience of continuity. His playing is a search for an earlier state of aloneness. I also argue throughout that if the present is a re-visiting of the past, it is also at attempt at inventing and at providing a form and a figure for the unbearable formlessness of experience: 'The forms are

many in which the unchanging seeks relief from its formlessness' (*BT* 181).

Present state, past state and the space in-between

Where *Molloy* is logically structured by two divided maternal and paternal stories and explicitly over-determined, *Malone Dies* presents the reader with an apparently shapeless and even desultory interweaving of stories that are continually interrupted and deferred by Malone, least of all the one about his forthcoming death, for he shall soon be quite dead at last in spite of all (ibid. 165). As Thomas Trezise points out, the description of Malone's experience distinguishes itself from that of Moran's, Molloy's and the Unnamable's by the relatively greater emphasis it places on indecision and especially on inaction or *désoeuvrement*' (1990, 109, Trezise's emphasis). In addition, whether they are about himself, Sapo, Macmann or Lemuel, Malone's stories don't seem to have any other function than to occupy him, deal with the tedium, fill in the void and thereby to distract him as he approaches his death. The stories about his 'creatures', Sapo and the birds, Moll and the peasants, are scotched as being a mere pretext for not coming to the point (*BT* 254). Behind this posture of playing and inventing – for Malone shall never do anything any more from now on but play (ibid. 166) – hides another posture, one of detachment, calmness, almost resignation, as if Malone has no longer any family scores to settle.

Fancying himself as the last of human kind (232), Malone is delighted with his death-like quietus of emptiness and inertia from which he can re-tell his stories, these being as lifeless as their teller (165). Even if words and images run riot in his head, beyond this tumult there is a great calm and a great indifference, as if Malone will never be troubled by anything again (182). There is a telling parodic moment in the room when Malone starts sucking the pillow and declares that his search for himself is now over, culminating in a sense of solace and peace: 'I suck. The search for myself is ended. *I am buried* in the world' (182, my emphasis). If we strip away the layer of self-parody here, Malone's burial – buried self – is one which might be said to have ancient origins, psychically speaking, the remnants of a 'catastrophe [...] in the ancient sense', Malone notes before adding rather stoically: 'to be buried in lava and not turn a hair' (233).

However much Malone must establish the present before he is avenged, it is a present state that is very much a past state, but a past state which cannot be remembered and corresponds therefore, in Winnicott's terms, to a primary narcissistic organisation of the self before 'it begins to fill up' (qtd in Kohon 1986, 181). Malone cannot remember how he ended up in the room, surmising that he probably lost consciousness somewhere and unwittingly benefits by a hiatus in his recollections. Beckett's hero is, at it were, re-creating dead times where no symbolisation can take place or could have ever taken place: 'dead world, airless, waterless' (*BT* 185). What is hated here is the attempt to bridge sense impressions and consciousness. The embryonic thought or state evoked must remain meaningless. Significantly Malone has the impression that he has returned 'after a long absence' (ibid. 228). Yet, however bereft of memory Malone may be, he hasn't forgotten those that have abused him ever since he was born (165), for he forgives nobody (166). As Steven Connor adroitly tells us, only a kind of consciousness can embrace the unthought (Connor 1992, 3) or in Malone's case, only a kind of memory can remember the unremembered.

Significantly, the most vivid memories of Malone's are those filled by shades and shadows, reminiscent of his absence than of any lively presence:

> What I sought when I struggled out of my hole, then aloft through the stinging air towards an inaccessible boon, was the rapture of vertigo, the letting go, the fall, the gulf, the relapse to darkness, to nothingness. (*BT* 179)

The choice of the word 'boon' in the above passage, is not without interest with regard to Bion. In the French original, Beckett enigmatically used 'inaccessibles nourritures' (*MM* 34) (literally 'inaccessible food') suggesting a modelling of Malone's thought on a digestive system. If we link the two texts, the French original and the translation, one could deduce that Malone's return to darkness and nothingness forms an original – originary – thought of a non or empty breast. Similar images of a derisory death-like breast occur in Malone's allusions to his dish and pot or his two basic poles of nourishment and evacuation, since eating and excreting are Malone's bodily coordinates (*BT* 170). While the mysterious present-absent female figure may be moved with regard to Malone (171), she is equally capable of killing Malone with her 'nourishing muck' (178), starving him or even poisoning him thanks to large quantities of poisoned soup (234). But the 'reality' of the 'same' breast is constantly subject to macabre speculation and doubts as Malone wonders if she is dead, having pre-deceased him (171) (see Ross 2004, 99–100).

The void of the present: Malone's room

With his pots, bed, stick, cupboard, pencils and exercise books, Malone seems to have found a new playground, different to the one he knew as a child. For a significant theme in Malone's autobiographical story is precisely the absence of creativity and playfulness where playing was passively if not painfully endured: 'I couldn't play ... For I was already in the toils of earnestness. That has been my disease' (*BT* 179). Ironically the void that Malone escaped to from the playground of his childhood turns out to be his new playground in the shape and form of his secluded room. Emptiness being 'a prerequisite for eagerness to gather in', to quote Winnicott (qtd in Kohon 1986, 181), to a large extent, *Malone Dies* is about a man's response to emptiness in a room.

Malone talks, thinks, remembers, writes and plays in the void of his room which serves as a refuge and a stage for playing absence and playing with absence. He is inventing a world that is not 'there'. Indeed, a good part of Malone's narrative is precisely about staking out a space devoid of 'definitional boundaries' (Begam 1996, 142) precariously suspended between subjective and objective, me and not-me, past and present, possession and non-possession, love and hate. This reclamation of illusion and illusoriness – an indeterminate zone – is in stark contrast with a childhood memory evoked by Malone, concerning a walk with his mother where she failed to adapt to his need for illusion. We are given the fictionalised image of a 'moment of illusion' that is not shared between mother and son, the illusion not being allowed to form. If anything we have the absence of any interchange or illusion:

> One day we were walking along the road, up a hill of extraordinary steepness, [...] I said, The sky is further away than you think, is it not, mama? It was without malice, I was simply thinking of all the leagues that separated me from it. She replied, to me her son, It is precisely as far away as it appears to be. She was right. But at the time I was aghast. (*BT* 246)

As Winnicott explains, 'from birth, therefore, the human being is concerned with the problem of the relationship between what is objectively perceived and what is subjectively conceived of, and in the solution of this problem there is no health for the human being who has not been started off well enough by the mother. *The intermediate area to which I am referring is the area that is allowed to the infant between primary creativity and objective perception based on reality-testing*' (1971, 13, Winnicott's emphasis).

To come back to Malone and his room, we may venture the Winnicottian paradox as regards creativity, that 'what was wanted was created and found to be there' (Skelton 2006, 101). Malone finds himself in a plain private room (*BT* 168). It is what it isn't: it is not a room in a hospital, or in a madhouse, nor is it in a house of rest (ibid.). It nonetheless becomes a resting-place – a potential space – for Malone who is engaged in the task of keeping inner and outer reality separate yet interrelated. So he imagines he is at the 'edge of an abyss' (191) or in a vault, a tomb, where there may be other vaults deeper than his (201). Unsurprisingly there is no 'real' light in Malone's room but rather a leaden light that makes no shadow where the dawns are also his dusks (202). For someone who claims he never really learned to play as a child, Malone is at his most playful when he cannot decide where he is in relation to the room or where the room is in relation to him. For example, the outside, as much as the inside, remains subject to endless speculation. If Malone sees from his window the roofs and the sky but doesn't see any fields or hills, he wonders if the latter are near (169). If he doesn't see the sea either, Malone nonetheless 'hears' it when it is high (ibid.). Indeed, a lot of Malone's musing and introspections could be described as 'playing' at the frontiers and limits between inside and outside, illusion and reality. For example, musing on night, Malone writes:

> For in the room it is not night, I know, here it is never really night [...] but often darker than now, whereas out there up in the sky it is black night, with few stars, just enough to show that the black night I see is truly of mankind and not merely painted on the window-pane, for they tremble, like true stars, as they would not do if they were painted. (218)

Whether there is an 'external world' outside and beyond Malone's room is in a way irrelevant. It is the rich interchange *between* Malone and his perception of the outside, the other world, that matters. Malone is someone who has to 'look long and fixedly and give things time to travel the long road that lies *between me and them'* (ibid. my emphasis).

Malone for the most part contents himself, then, with measuring the gulf between mind and world, self and other. For example the sounds he hears testifying to the presence of others in the apartment-block – cries, steps, doors, murmurs – literally come and go leaving him to enjoy the occasional silence even if silence is not what it seems to be. Like all the other sinister sounds of childhood that intrigue Malone, the cries of nearby children (203) or bawling babies (200) may cease in his mind, but in reality they never cease (203).

Obviously such a room could also be seen as a metaphor of Malone's body and mind, or more precisely, of the maternal womb, as just about every Beckett critic has noticed, that is to say, the work's 'matrix from which Malone will either die, be born, or both' (Moorjani 1982, 120; and see Katz 2006, 14–15). This is a point I shall return to at the end of the chapter, when I deal with Malone's reputed 'death'. But for the moment I wish to stress another aspect of the inter-uterine trope, generally overlooked by critics, which would be to see the room as a metaphor and metonymy of mental space or rudimentary mental functioning. As Bion reminds us, feelings and thoughts need a 'mind' to think them. Malone's mental musings may suggest an embryonic mind, which would be first that of the mother and then that of the infant. For example, sense impressions dominate the 'room' of our narrator's mind. Malone as foetus 'hears' noises, cries, steps and murmurs (*BT* 203). There is 'a kind of air' that circulates which Malone can hear 'beating against the wall and being beaten back by them' (ibid.). Even silence can be 'heard' as 'the faint sound of aerial surf' (ibid.). If Malone can manage to bridge impression and consciousness, it seems to be to suggest a void of a sort as when he wonders if there is a vacuum in the skull (203–4). Similarly when his bed is being tossed like a straw by the swirling eddies, and he in it, he has the impression that he is caught in someone else's mental maelstrom (204). While Malone acknowledges that it is all in his head, as to which head he is in remains open to speculation: 'but thence to conclude the head is mine, no, never' (203).

Malone's playroom: from loss to re-attachment

Malone presence *in* the room is mediated by the objective reality of the room's contents, that is the objects that surround him and intrigue him. The room is after all what he finds there, that is his dish and pot (170). Paradoxically, for a writer so much devoted to self-dispossession, Malone is concerned with his possessions. They have allowed him to lull himself as he rummages through them, sorting them out and drawing them over to him (180). Indeed the whole discussion about the inventory of his possessions seems to hinge on determining which ones constitute meaningful extensions of self and which ones don't.[4] For example, as Malone makes clear, the pots are not 'his' even if he says 'my pots' as he says 'me' (231–2). While Malone wants his inventory to be free from all trace of approximativeness (180), the task of the inventory gradually turns out to be a case of artful blurring of limits and boundaries, me and not-me, as Malone becomes gradually unable to account for the changing aspect of his possessions (230) and no longer knows what is his and what is not his. But viewed as transitional phenomena, Malone's possessions are paradoxically *both* Malone's 'me' and his 'not-me'. They are his imaginary presences he uses as a buffer zone between himself and his anxiety-provoking stories: 'quick quick my possessions. Quiet, quiet, twice, I have time, lots of time, as usual' (226). Having lost his stick and wondering if it is time to see how Macmann is getting on, Malone writes: 'why this need of activity? I am growing nervous' (234). Adversely, and as we shall see later in this chapter, the story is a necessary defence mechanism against the threatening emptiness of the room.

Apart from his dish and pot, which are the objects that represent his bodily existence in the room, Malone finds a whole range of objects – 'treasures' – that serve to occupy him and even represent him in some way such. These include: his stick, the bowl of a pipe, a boot, a brimless hat, the cape of a bicycle bell, the top half of a crutch ('a baby's crutch', 232), his photograph, his stone, his scrap of newspaper or his buttons, not to mention his two privileged and precious possessions that become inseparable from Malone, namely his pencils and his exercise book. Malone's possessions contribute to his 'autonomy' for they are under his control in a way that his body and mind are not. They also provide a temporal link with his earlier symbols of separation, solitude and aloneness – his not-me possessions – that he lovingly remembers, such as the bowl of his pipe or 'other little portable things in wood and stone' that he would stoop and pick up and put them in his pocket often with tears (227).

Indeed one of the special qualities in the relationship between child and transitional object, as Winnicott outlines, is that it must seem to the infant to give warmth, or to move, or to have texture, or to do something that seems to show it has vitality or reality of its own. Malone loved to finger and caress the hard shapely objects that he found in his deep pockets. It was his way of talking to them and reassuring them (227). As he says of his night-time stone already alluded to (in the first chapter), he would be still holding it when he woke, his fingers closed over it (227–8).[5] The usual fate of the transitional object 'is to be gradually decathected' since 'it is not forgotten and it is not mourned. It loses meaning', Winnicott writes (1971, 6).[6] When Malone wearied of his objects, his tactics of dealing with separation and loss, consisted of abandoning them, literally throwing them away, hiding them or even burying them. What is particularly striking in Malone's account, is how his objects come to symbolise a zone of non-contact, a space of self-isolation, by occupying the place not to be communicated, a secret hermetic space only known to Malone and accessible to him: 'And those of which I wearied, or which were ousted by new loves, I threw away, that is to say cast round for a place to lay them where they would be at peace forever, and no one ever find them short of an extraordinary hazard, and such places are few and far between, and I laid them there'.[7] The ambiguity of the detail concerning the rotten string – 'But many a wooden friend too I have sent to the bottom, weighted with a stone. Until I realized it was wrong of me. For when the string is rotted they will rise to the surface' (228) – lends itself to be understood as an image of faulty attachment and of Malone's failure to deal with separation. Attachment is denied or negated and, despite Malone's efforts, will always remain and will return ('will rise to the surface').

In a way, Malone finds new substitutes in his room, new objects of attachment. In the spatial configuration of his newly found play-space, the bed and stick seem to function as boundaries separating subjective from objective, me and not-me, self and world, the groaning of the bedstead being part of Malone's life (171). The hooked stick allows Malone to control the threatening void of the room, that is, to control the furthest recesses of his abode (170). It 'becomes a tool for marking a boundary between what is still "him" and what is "without"' (Katz 2006, 13). But, ironically, the object that allows Malone to divide and distinguish between me and not-me is very much an object that was not 'his' in the first place. Malone 'only' found the stick when he came to the room, but in finding it, he magically creates it, making it his own: 'the stick, which I did not have either when I came here, but which I consider mine' (*BT* 226). The stick, then, allows Malone to shift and sort out the past from the present, presence from absence. As he goes through his cupboard, opening doors, drawers and rooting everywhere, he is, as it were, playing games of retrieval and re-possession (181).[8] The stick magically 'communicates' with other objects; the message flows along the stick making Malone desire to do things such as hooking the desired object and bringing it over to the bed (229).

Just as he can play with the presence of the stick to envisage escaping from the room by using it as a punt-pole (233), its absence or loss equally gives Malone opportunities for illusion and potential alternatives. For example, later having lost his stick, Malone realises what it is he has lost and all it meant to him for it would have introduced a little variety into his decomposition (234). Yet, Malone's sense of possession or possessiveness falters as his sense of self-dispossession increasingly dominates: 'for all I ever had, has been taken from me, except the exercise book', (248) (Moorjani 1982, 124; Hill, 102). We have the impression that as Malone nears his death, his moment of self-dispossession, he needs to 're-posses' his self which is tantamount to saying that the stick, his pencils and his exercise-book become Malone: they are his and he is they.

Significantly, Malone tells us of an incident where having lost the pencil, he finally recovered it after 48 hours of intermittent efforts, two days 'of which nothing will ever be known' (*BT* 204). This constitutive void brings us to the very blank centre of *Malone Dies*, for Malone tells us that these two blank days brought him 'the solution and conclusion of the whole sorry business' (ibid.) and likens the 'unutterable' vision to a crumbling away of two little heaps of finest sand, or dust, or ashes and leaving behind them, each in its own stead, 'the *blessedness of absence*' (ibid. my emphasis). This is not unlike his meta-narrative comment on his actual writing where 'the subject falls far from the verb and the object lands somewhere in the *void*' (215, my emphasis). If Malone 'exists where he most thoroughly *is not*' (Gunn 1988, 163), as a corollory *Malone Dies* is about a nothing that happened when something might have happened, an unknown gap that cannot be filled in.

Malone and his narrative possessions

The business of Malone is also the business of the other (*BT* 204), the concern is not with him, but with another (179). I propose to read the playful doubling between the Malone, Sapo, Macmann and Lemuel stories as Malone's attempt at playing at imaginary self-representations whose function is to escape from the void in the room by paradoxically reinscribing the void of self. Malone can only 'show myself' when he is the point of vanishing (180). In this playful overlapping between the self and other, there is simply no room or place for reality testing. As in the case of the Moran–Molloy relationship, it is the space created between Malone and Sapo that is significant: 'Nothing is less like me than this patient reasonable child' (178).[9] 'I slip into him', writes Malone in reference to Macmann, 'he is mine now' (208).

Malone oscillates between exerting magical omnipotent control over his narrative possessions, his me and not-me, and in turn being submitted to their 'control', as his imaginary puppets acquire a threatening realness, leaving the shifting boundaries between Malone and his others all too fragile. In other terms, the narrative functions as a 'barrier contact' for Malone in that it both provides the point of contact and separation between self and other, narrator and character.[10] For example, Malone seeks to protect contacts with self from being disturbed by emotions coming from 'inside', that is from the other. Meta-narrative comments illustrate this point.

Malone interrupts the narrative to tell us that he is threatened by the thickening darkness in his Sapo story, a darkness that is liable to burst and drown everything (175). Malone's defence against persecutory depression is, however, a slender one. Elsewhere, his sinister foreboding of the rack letting loose its black unforgettable cohorts scattering away 'the blue for ever' (181), suggests he is still prisoner of depressive anxiety. Such black imagery of depression in the novel can be related to Malone's hate, but is arguably only a secondary product, a consequence rather than a cause of a 'blank' anxiety which, according to André Green, expresses a loss that has been experienced on a narcissistic level (1986, 146). Unsurprisingly, Malone needs a rest, 'for safety's sake' (*BT* 177), from telling us of Sapo's silent ways (176). But there is no getting away from the invisible presence of Sapo's gull's eyes that remind Malone of an old shipwreck and Democritus's '*nothing is more real than nothing*' (177). One has the impression that Sapo becomes more and more Malone's 'object' that he brings to life, manipulates, making him present or making him absent: 'I stop everything and wait. Sapo stands on one leg, motionless, his strange eyes closed' (179). Similarly, Malone grows nervous as regards Macmann (234) and feels 'delirium' (236) in relation to Mol who he finally decides to kill (242). Paradoxically, as much as the presence of his narrative possessions is salutary for Malone, their ultimate destruction is even more desirable as if Malone sets out to create and preserve a void at all costs. And it is hatchet-happy Lemuel who is finally left in charge not only of the fateful excursion, but of the ending of the novel to which he belongs.

Many critics have fastened onto the symbolism inherent in Lemuel's various weapons – a hatchet, a hammer, a stick, a fist and a pencil linking this not so much with Malone as with Beckett himself.[11] Lemuel's savage killing would be equivalent to 'the act of writing' as 'a process of self-inflicted injury [...] or of controlled belligerence directed against the world and language' (Hill 1990, 107). Moorjani sees the boat and stick along with the clubs, umbrellas, fists, hammers, and crutches 'as symbolic writing vehicles [...] emphasising writing as a route into the psyche-womb, as the blow of death' (1982, 126). Yet, Moorjani adds, it is 'a conflict never resolved in favour of one or the other conception. Malone's Venus [pencil] is, of course, an instrument of both life and death' (ibid.). She reads the undifferentiated mass of inmates as 'fragments of the writer's psyche sinking into the dark and silent womb in which they remain still unborn' (123).

My contention is that the pencil–hatchet couple functions more like a play-thing that has the power to create and destroy, produce presence and at the same time hollow out absence. The point of it is not so much its symbolic value as its actuality, its realness. As Winnicott reminds us with regard to the relationship of the transitional object to symbolism, 'its not being the breast (or the mother), although real, is as important as the fact that it stands for the breast (or mother)' (1971, 6).

If read as 'playing', the final murder scene does suggest that Malone has lost all 'control' over his narrative objects, as he and we drift towards a narrative effort of dissolution, a drifting away, where there is 'never anything, there' (*BT* 264), a narrative void of a sort. The novel ends precisely on a dramatic present-absent or dead-alive image where action and agency are suspended. Whether it is because the narrator finally dies and cannot finish his story about the inmates drifting in their boat or whether it is because Lemuel and his men perhaps expire at this moment, we are left to wonder. Lemuel raises his hatchet on which the blood will never dry (263) and the subsequent series of negatives and negations bring about a freezing of the moment. Assuming Malone is still alive somehow, the narrator's use of 'will' does suggest an attempt to regain 'control' over his play-space, as if it is time to stop playing such aggressive games and that this particular excursion has gone too far, too 'far out in the bay' (263):

> he *will* not hit anyone, he *will* not hit anyone any more, he *will* not touch anyone any more. (Ibid., my emphasis)

Yet, Lemuel has only done what Malone has been doing all the time with his imaginary objects, that is, controlling them by either attacking them, destroying them or evacuating them. The meta-narrative comments made about the writing in progress illustrate this point. For example, Malone fantasises making a little creature in his image and seeing what a poor thing he has made, he shall eat it (207). His writing notes tend to annihilate all they purport to record (238) and he sinisterly finds a bloody club in his room that is already an advance on how the Lemuel story will end: 'it is stained with blood but insufficiently, insufficiently' (228). At a particular moment of confusion, Malone wonders how many characters has he killed, whether hitting them on the head or setting fire to them (217). He can hear them clamouring after him down the corridors, stumbling through the rubble, beseeching him to take them with him (ibid.). It is no surprise, then, that Malone likens the writing to a violent mental evacuation, a self-attack of a sort: 'for in my head I suppose all was streaming and emptying as through a sluice ... until finally *nothing* remained' (205 my emphasis) or, in the fashion of Moran's manner of thinking, to a pitiless sweeping away of internal objects. For example, Malone mentions being under the control of an impersonal hand, the uncontrollable other who already inhabits the writer Malone:

> I feel it plunged in me up to the elbow, but gentle, and as though sleeping. But soon it stirs, wakes, fondles, clutches, ransacks, ravages, avenging its failure to scatter me with one sweep. (206)

It is writing that becomes Malone's container, his inseparable me/not-me object, and by extension, his life. He enjoys harpooning the exercise book with his stick, as he likens himself to a big child and bitterly realises that it has taken him a long time to resign himself to that (252). His pencil is an old acquaintance and he hopes it will see him out (192), Malone punning here on writing as being durable – 'from the point of view of durability' (204) – that must survive if it is to 'accompany' him to his death and the inmates 'out' to their fateful end. Comically, the writing as material trace may not survive since the dwindling – dying? – pencil obliges Malone to write as lightly as he can lest nothing remains but a fragment too tiny to hold (ibid.).

Absent minds made 'present'

Using the idiom of Malone's own description of his life, the long secondary narrative is concerned with 'shapelessness and speechlessness, incurious wondering, darkness, long stumbling with outstretched arms, hiding' (166). The 'self' is enmeshed in the other: 'be another, in myself, in another', as Malone says. What enmeshes Malone is Sapo–Macmann's radical inarticulacy, the inherent darkness and the bottomless pit. Where Richard Begam tells us that 'this M-alone is quite simply inenarrable, a self that cannot be rendered in the form of a story' (Begam 1996, 128), I would counter this by saying that it is in the potential space of narrative play that Malone creates forms or figures of inarticulacy even if these are 'at the limits of apprehension' (ibid.). His story with its last outpouring of misery, impotence and hate, is his way of seeking 'relief' from its formlessness: 'The forms are many in which the unchanging seeks relief from its formlessness' (*BT* 181). In the interspacing between

Malone and Sapo–Macmann Beckett draws the contours of an embryonic mind, where being is non-being, knowing is not-knowing: 'Either you know all or you know nothing, and Macmann knows nothing' (213), Malone tells us quite emphatically.

At the risk of over-schematising, the 'objects' of the interpersonal relationships dramatised by the story may be said to hover about the same issues: the psychic death in reaction to the mother's failures and mistakes, the breakdown in mental functioning culminating in ultimate violence and madness, and the gradual evacuation of curiosity, knowledge and desire, darkly parodied by the Macmann–Mol relationship. Let us now explore these 'objects' in detail, but, first, some theoretical guidelines.

It will be remembered from an earlier chapter, that the notion of the mother (and specifically her breast) as a 'container' which the child himself takes in, is the prototype of all thinking and creativity. Through the activity of the mother's reverie, the infant's split-off anxieties or projections are contained, de-toxified, as it were and returned to the infant, who introjects them, but now in a modified tolerable or thinkable form:

> The establishment internally of a projective-identification-rejecting object means that instead of an understanding object the infant has a wilfully misunderstanding object – with which it is identified (Bion 1967, 117)

The mother figure in *Malone Dies* is identified with and identifies with a wilfully misunderstanding object such as Mme Louis, whose mind is a press of formless questions, mingling and crumbling limply away with its sinuous links and whose mental tasks are never finished (*BT* 199). Thus, Saposcat, we are told, was sorry he had not learnt the art of thinking (177). His mind was always elsewhere, or blank (172). It was all the more remarkable since his teachers failed to get anything into it (175). Yet it is precisely this incapacity to think which is strangely desirable for Malone. Between being in someone's else's mind, or being assailed by rudimentary consciousness, the impression is one of defencelessness in face of persecution: 'Somewhere in this turmoil thought struggles on [...] It too seeks me, as it always has, where I am not to be found. It too cannot be quiet' (171).

Our hero clearly mirrors himself in Sapo's silent ways (176), in his graveness and expressionlessness, (189) and is mystified by Sapo's troubling look with 'eyes as pale and unwavering as a gull's' (176).

His ignorance of the natural world and the strange joy it gives Sapo, is also another plus point for Malone (ibid.). Where at least Sapo had the 'strength and courage in knowing what manner of being he was' (177), Malone tragically acknowledges how he had lost his head, fled to his shadows as to a sanctuary. After the fiasco, the solace, the repose, Malone 'began again, to try and live, cause to live, be another in myself, in another' (179). The cross-identification with the flight of the hawk is also pertinent here, Malone being fascinated by such extremes of need, of pride, of patience and solitude (176). Malone's story of Sapo's void and nothingness attracts him yet disturbs him, but, paradoxically, it is in the telling of the story that Malone shows his capacity to 'receive' Sapo's mental chaos, the 'babel raging in his head, the doubts, desires, imaginings and dreads' (177) – and to sound its dark depths.

In his creation of Macmann, Malone delivers a fatal psychic blow to the psyche as he cruelly reduces the aim of mental life to something equivalent of semi-coma where all mental tensions become a kind of stuporous comfort, a good half of Macmann's existence being spent in a motionlessness akin to that of stone (223). Hence, 'the black joy of (Macmann's) solitary way, in helplessness and will-lessness, through all the beauty, the knowing and the loving' (255). For instance, Macmann only rose again when the struggle of life began to prod him in the arse again (223). Where Molloy at least actively manipulates stones to some effect, Macmann grovels and wallows in his supine stone-like state thanks to his cast-iron vegetative system that he has received 'from his numerous forbears, through the agency of his papa and his mama' (ibid.). It is as if Macmann yearns to stay in his stony kingdom, at one as it were with the dumbness and silence of stone, that 'absolute mode of being', as Eliade wrote (Eliade 1996, 107)[12] or in Freud's terms, a 'particular stratum of living matter' (Freud 1961, 32).

But during the violent rainfall that surprises Macmann, the latter finds himself propelled into 'thinking' his mineral inertia which has overtaken more than just his body – 'a motionlessness at first skin deep, but which little by little invaded, I will not say the vital parts, but at least the sensibility and understanding' (*BT* 223). If the rain is an image of a destructive instinct, it is because it tests Macmann life-preservative instinct, that is whether to lie down on the ground or continue his course in as straight a line as possible (221). Of course this is more than a simple dual conflict between life and death, love and hate or creativeness and destructiveness. The persecutory rain is also Macmann's primary masochism, his primary self-destructiveness which he endeavours to think in terms of guilt, sin and punishment even if he is still 'ill-fated for pure reason' (223).

It is significant, then, that Macmann's withdrawn self finds home or space in an asylum, since, paradoxically, that is where he had always been, plunged within (234–5). The least we can say about Malone's asylum (after all it is Malone's story) is that it is violently quiet. While it is both a space of mental isolation that spells a disaster for mental life – 'it is we shall think and act for you' (235) – where violence and madness prevail in the destructive figure of Lemuel, it is also a place strangely synonymous with solitude, absence, isolation, as, for example, in Macmann's perception of the grounds of the asylum and its inmates:

> and the trapped huddled things changed and died each one according to *its solitude.* (255, my emphasis)
>
> Little by little the haze formed again, and *the sense of absence*, and the captive things began to murmur again, each one to itself, and it was as if *nothing* had ever happened or would ever happen again. (256 my emphasis)

As regards its mental violence, *Malone Dies* is a novel about blows to the head in more than one sense of the word. Just as Malone enjoys hitting his characters over their heads, in phantasy destroying their minds, he in turn receives a violent blow on the head from the mysterious visitor, sinisterly dressed in black (247). This visit comes just after the description of Lemuel's self-attack, using a hammer from an inner pocket. It is not so much that Macmann's new keeper clearly represents destroyed or impaired thought – 'flayed alive by memory, his mind crawling with cobras, not daring to dream or think and powerless not to' (245) – but he actively seeks to destroy any possible mental activity, his targets being that of the mind and consciousness itself: 'the seat of the shit and misery' (ibid.). Here we have an advance on the hatchet attack that takes place during the excursion.

The word 'excursion' literally means a pleasure trip where people are brought to a particular place with the intention of returning to the starting point. Malone's excursion story is however closer to the other etymological meanings of the word 'excursion': a running out, a going beyond limits or a going to extremes, a transgression of a sort (Brown 1993, 876). What sets out to be an outing for the insane, through scenery renowned for its beauty or grandeur (*BT* 257), organised by Lady Pedal, who is assisted by other ladies sharing her way of thinking and similarly blessed in means and leisure (ibid.), turns out to be an expelling of the mind, a radical rupturing of the mind/self relationship.

Lady Pedal's charitable gesture of deciding 'to let them loose' on the secluded island which of course gives rise to Lemuel running havoc with his hatchet, comes across more as a strategy of control than an authentic gesture of liberation.

As Frederik Smith interestingly points out, 'like the eighteenth-century aristocrats who toured Bedlam for entertainment's sake, Lady Pedal is incapable of comprehending the Saint John of God inmates as anything more than charitable *toys* [...] my creatures, she calls them' (Smith 2002, 37, my emphasis).[13] The journey from the asylum to the island is tantamount to a trajectory of self that travels inexorably towards its point of radical separation, an incommunicable mental gulf of a sort. Here I want to underline the image of the island as a *mise en abyme* of the asylum. Equally significant is the fact that the island with its (archaic) 'Druid remains', is threatened to break up into 'two islands', where 'it is difficult to talk of man under such conditions' (*BT* 262). As a place of radical separation from land and the living, it is a place threatened by further splits, division and gulfs: 'One day nothing will remain of it but two islands, *separated by a gulf*, narrow at first, then wider and wider as the centuries slip by, two islands, two reefs' (ibid. my emphasis). Might we have here an image of Beckett's mental zone of non-contact? An incommunicable void? Between the asylum, the island, the mutiny and the future gulf we are left to reflect on a series of incommunicable zones, one embedded within the other, a spiralling void of a sort. Silhouetted against night and water, the 'ship of fools' is indeed 'far out in the bay' (263) their embarkation being their last with no promise of a return to any other world: 'Silent, dim, perhaps clinging to one another, their heads buried in their cloaks, they lie together in a heap, in the night [...] Lemuel has shipped his oars, the oars trail in the water' (263).[14]

'The great cunt of existence'

There is nothing irreversible or fatally regressive about 'all this ballsaching poppycock about life and death' (206). If anything there is much more continuity between living and dying than the impressive caesura of Malone's act of 'birth–death' would have us believe. Narrative time appears at once progressive and regressive, leading us simultaneously forward and backward, paralleling an approach of Malone's death that literally approximates his rebirth. If anything Malone's concern is with self-invention, self-origination where he can inhabit the potential space *between* birth and death, a liminal state of a sort. Such a permeable caesura or an 'articulating caesura' (Skelton 2006, 94) allows fantasy and dialogue between the unborn and born aspects of self. The intera-uterine imagery and tropes speak for themselves. Malone, an old foetus, shall 'never get born and therefore never get dead, and a good job too' (*BT* 207).

At the same time, Malone 'did get born' and acknowledges having lived 'and wandered in the towns, the woods and wildernesses' (ibid.) 'wishing night would never end and morning never come' (ibid.). But birth and death as originary moments of self-dispossession, cease to have significance for Malone:

> But what matter whether I was born or not, have lived or not, am dead or merely dying, I shall go on doing as I have always done, not knowing what it is I do, nor who I am, nor where I am, nor if I am. (Ibid.)

Here Malone is hinting at a fundamental rupture between self and world, a being that is a non-being, a knowing that is a not knowing: '*if* I am' (207 my emphasis). The last quote gives us an image of a silent self or what Winnicott calls 'an isolate, permanently non-communicating, permanently unknown in fact unfound' (qtd in Green 1986, 289). To return to Malone, his world is blotted out, as he remembers being 'tarried by the seas in tears before the islands and peninsulas where night lit the little brief yellow lights of man and all night the great white and coloured beams shining in the caves' where he was happy (*BT* 207).

Where death might be seen as a dissolution of fundamental boundary lines between past and present, the animate and the inanimate, presence and absence, Malone imagines death as a boundary or borderland, a potential source of playfulness. The sheer theatrical quality of Malone's narrative – its liveliness – keeps us alert to the fact that Malone's death is already happening before it 'really' happens in the narrative. He is potentially dead, with already 'a foot in the grave' (215), is proud of his capacity for being dead: 'I could die today', he says, 'if I wished, merely by making a little effort', and he can even imagine the arrival of the undertaker's men: 'so my head bangs against the jamb, it's inevitable [...] Bang! Easy! Right! The door! And the room is vacant at last and ready to receive, after disinfection' (216), and his future grave: 'here lies Malone at last' (249). But when it comes to the crunch, and it is time to die, the 'dying' Malone prefers to play at being a struggling foetus, suggesting perhaps that there is more continuity between death and birth than one may suspect, that is, between the silence of death and the unrepresentability of birth (Hill 1990, 53, Gunn 1988, 163). But the point that needs to be stressed here is that Malone is playing. His side commentaries and his humour suggest that he is as concerned with the representational status of his birth–death as he is of the event itself:

> I am swelling. What if I should burst? The ceiling rises and falls, rises and falls, rhythmically, *as when* I was a foetus [...] I am being given, *if I may venture the expression*, birth to into death, such is my impression. The feet are clear already, of the great cunt of existence [...] *favourable presentation I trust*. (260 my emphasis)

If psychic reality is constituted by finding ways of representing our experience to ourselves, 'the point of a representation (being) that it is not the thing itself', to quote Michael Parsons (Parsons 1999, 62), similarly, Malone's 'birth to into death' doesn't refer to any thing in particular. If anything it is almost foregrounded as expression, a figure of speech ('if I may venture the expression') and remains very much a subjective impression. If the 'great cunt of existence' is certainly Malone's damning of the vagina and the mother's procreative function, it also plays on the other meaning of the word 'cunt', signifying a very unpleasant person. It is existence that is a cunt. Either way, Malone both dies (he is clear now of existence) and is born (he is out clear of the vagina). He literally dies alive: 'Play at last and die alive' (*BT* 192). If the birth–death couple can be bracketed off or curtained off as 'playing', then it is clear that Malone never dies and, for that matter he never 'lives' or has never 'lived': Malone could 'neither live nor suffer the sight of others living' (179).

To probe further into the meaning of Malone's paradoxical death, I wish to refer to Winnicott's article, 'Fear of Breakdown' where he explains that the clinical fear of breakdown is the fear of a breakdown that has already been but not experienced. In other words, the patient must go on looking for the past detail which is not yet experienced (qtd in Kohon 1986, 176 and 177). In an interesting application of this theory, Winnicott talks about the fear of death, quoting Keats' most well-known line 'half in love with easeful death'. Winnicott comments Keats' line by saying that the poet was 'longing for the ease that would come if he could remember having died; but to remember he must experience death now' (ibid. 179).[15] Similarly Malone could be said to have the need to remember his past death for the first time in the present, that is to say, in the transference of playing. Lost 'in forests of high treshing ferns or whirled far out on the face of wind-swept wastes', Malone wonders if he had not died without knowing and had gone to hell or been born again into an even worse place than before (*BT* 208). For Malone, dying, as playing, is a form of remembering, a repeating and a re-playing of that memory, a lifting of repression. Like the inmate who is 'dead young' (258), to die for Malone means to be born again, or to be born for the first time. Malone may not remember having died, but he remembers having been born 'somewhere': 'it was there somewhere he was born, in a fine house, of loving parents' (262). This is of course the narrator's view of the hills on the coast as the boat approaches the treacherous island. Here the identification between Malone's death and Samuel Beckett's birth is hinted. Malone consistently predicts that he will die in April or May – 'then it will be the month of April or of May' (165) – the two months variously given for Beckett's birth (Begam 1996, 141).[16] That Malone's death is foregrounded by resurrection imagery of Easter week is hardly insignificant. On the morning of the ill-fated excursion, we are told that 'the sun was dragging itself up, dispatching on its way what perhaps would be, thanks to it, a glorious May or April day, April more likely, it is doubtless the Easter week-end, spent by Jesus in hell' (257).

By a sleight of hand, Malone's birth–death is neither the beginning nor the end of anything in particular, but rather the repetition of what he always was, a re-enactment of his liminal state. As we have seen, he shuts himself up and off in his room, insulating himself as it were from the universe as if he is searching for some personal non-existence or some primary state of being from which Malone may hope to start again as a different M-Alone or Me-Alone.

Winnicott reminds us that if there is no capacity of the infant (or foetus) to be concerned with death, there must be, however, a capacity in every infant for concern about the aloneness of pre-dependence since this has been experienced. This state would be 'an essential aloneness' that can only take place 'under maximul conditions of dependence':

> The state prior to that of aloneness is one of unaliveness, and the wish to be dead is commonly a disguised wish to be not yet alive. The experience of the first awakening gives the human individual the idea that there is a peaceful state of unaliveness that can be peacefully reached by an extreme of regression. Most of what is commonly said and felt about death is about this first state *before aliveness*, where aloneness is a fact and long before dependence is encountered. (1988, 132, Winnicott's emphasis)

Malone Dies, then, is about aloneness, a 'me-alone' being in a room, in the absence of others or in the presence of no one. It is also about the precarity of presence, of 'self'-presence. 'The true prayer', remarks Malone, 'is the one that asks for nothing' (*BT* 254). Nothing happened when something might profitably have happened, might be Malone's principal objection to the world. Throughout his life and his narrative, Malone does not know what may have happened, and so cannot experience anything except to note that something may have been: 'Whence that child I might have been, why not?' (191).

Malone who cannot bear to be, can only be glimpsed perhaps through the fissures of his own strange poetry, a poetry of silence and solitariness: 'a little breath of fulfillment revives the dead longings and a murmur is born in the silent world, reproaching you affectionately with having despaired too late' (254). In a dream-like atmosphere very reminiscent of the islands and peninsulas of Malone's childhood (Moorjani 1982, 123), it is perhaps here in the 'absurd lights, the stars, the beacons, the buoys, the lights of earth and in the hills the faint fires of the blazing gorse' (*BT* 263), that Malone can communicate with what is deepest in himself, and with what is most solitary. For it is only then that he is potentially present when absent.

5
Incomprehensible Damnation

The story

The Unnamable energetically defies summary, synthesis, simplification and understanding. The text consists entirely of a disjointed monologue of a sort coming from the perspective of an unnamed (presumably unnamable) and immobile protagonist. There is no concrete plot or setting. Whether the other 'characters' (Basil, Mahood, Madeleine, Worm) actually exist or whether they are figments of the narrator's mind is debatable. The protagonist also claims authorship of the main characters in *Molloy* and *Malone Dies* and Beckett's earlier novels *Murphy*, *Mercier and Camier* and *Watt*. The novel is a mix of recollections and musings on the part of its narrator, many of which pertain specifically to the possibility that the narrator is constructed by the language he speaks. Other characters serve as the passive recipient of the dialogue and in many places (as the narrator suggests) the dialogue's genesis. The novel builds in its despairing tone until the ending, which consists mainly of very long run-on sentences. It closes with the phrase 'I can't go on, I'll go on'.

Introduction

Beckett famously remarked about *The Unnamable* that 'there's complete disintegration, no "I", no "have", no "being". No nominative, accusative, no verb. There's no way to go on' (qtd in Hill 1990, 121–2). It follows that any critical reading of the novel is tantamount to recuperating and restoring some order to Beckett's self-fashioned chaos and formlessness, integrating meaning where there is none. At the same time, there are dangers in accepting Beckett's view since it endorses a misleading and oversimplified teleological approach to the trilogy, and to the numerous short prose texts written since the trilogy, the danger being to reduce Beckett's writing to exercises in 'controlled disintegration' (121).

Where commentary has greatly concentrated on verbal language and its 'disintegration', our concern in this chapter is to analyse the place of thought and thinking in the novel's economy of negativity, or its *via negativa*, using such Bionian tropes as engulfment, expulsion, thinking and the interplay of the container and the contained. Beckett's narrative 'work of the negative' takes the form and function of reverse thinking which consists of 'using' thinking to attack and undermine all forms of self-awareness or consciousness, a way of setting up a mental void, as it were. It is the narrator's 'negative capability' (Meltzer 1978, 106, 108) that allows him to paradoxically accede to knowing as un-knowing, to thinking as un-unthinking, or to understanding as mis-understanding.[1] However, the particular relevance of thinking for the novel is seen in the way it functions as a symptomatic operator in the relationships between the unnamable voice, or self, and his multiple others: the question of thinking is invariably the question of the other. The thinking relations analysed here are seen as persecutory battles of minds that are both mirrored in and mirrored back by the Mahood/Worm stories. One common denominator in all of this is the central tension between the desire to produce psychic chaos, on one hand, and, on the other hand, the need to control, manipulate and contain such perturbations. In terms of linking and linkage, the writing espouses a dialectical movement of attacking, destroying or dispersing links, relations and contacts – 'presence' – and, at the same time, seeks to contain these by thinking them.

The critical strategy deployed in this chapter is to stake out some hypothetical middle-ground between the negative stereotyping among the earlier psychology and psychoanalytic critics who dismissed the novel as pathological case-study (Bajomée 1969, Hoffman 1962, Alvarez 1973) and the more recent deconstructionist and post-structuralist critics who, in different ways, have highlighted its patterns of oscillating incorporations and rejections, its endless potential differentiations which resist all stable determination (Hill 1990, Trezise 1990, Begam 1996, Katz 1999). Among the more specialised psychoanalytic critics, I shall endeavour to dialogue with Steven Connor's illuminating remarks about the 'Bionian' dimension of *The Unnamable* that lies in the psychic interplay between the container and the contained (Connor 2008, 25). Another important reference is Stephen Barker's Lacanian inspired reading of the novel's concern with thinking the nothing (Barker 1991).

In the void between thinker and thought

Where, as we shall see, *Waiting for Godot* brings Beckett's characters to the last refuge of the unspeakable and the unspoken, the unthinkable and the unthought, *The Unnamable* seeks to go even further as its eponymous voice spirals a way through 'the nullity of extracircumferential phenomena', drawing itself and us into 'the core of the eddy' or in the words of Richard Begam 'toward a literature that seeks to free itself from representation and expression' (Begam 1996, 155). But where Vladimir and Estragon can somehow show us the mystery of their condition by just standing and waiting, the Unnamable, 'in obedience to the unintelligible terms of an incomprehensible damnation' (*BT* 282), is obliged to 'speak' his way towards his dream silence (381).[2]

The experience described in *The Unnamable* may be likened to taking a leap into the dark void and somehow surviving there where 'there's nothing here, nothing to see, nothing to see with' (345), and, through a miraculous act of faith, deciding to go on: 'You must go on, I can't go on, you must go on, I'll go on' (381). As in *Godot*, it is the beam of darkness, of obscurity and of unknowingness that paradoxically 'lights' the narrative way with the dim intermittent lights (268) or faint fires (269) where 'all is clear' and 'no, all is not clear' (ibid.). Where Malone at least had a 'ready-made' room to talk and muse about, the Unnamable struggles to find even the vaguest sense of place – 'the place where one finishes vanishing?' (269) – if it is not that of a bottomless pit: 'the place is no doubt vast [...] are there other pits, deeper down [...] other places set aside for us' (268), or the sense of a mysterious pre-existing empty womb: 'did I wait for this place to be ready to receive me? Or did it wait for me to come and people it?' (271). Like a black hole in space the Unnamable's 'world' is hypothetically there, but not 'really' there 'by any definitive measurements known to conventional physical science', to quote Sydney Homan (Homan 1984, 194). 'If only I could describe this place', pants the Unnamable, 'it could be black dark' (*BT* 367), 'perhaps it's the abyss' (377), 'open on the void' (378). Yet the impossibility of designating limits between outer/inner, same-different, past-present, thinking/non-thinking, is apprehended by the narrator as a problem of elocution and knowledge: he wants to know why he doesn't know. He wants to see 'into' the dark: for 'how can one be sure, in such darkness?' (267) 'and this black, of which I know nothing either' (278).

So given this omnipresent haunting black void where 'only I and this black void have ever been' (278) and the unmistakable Miltonic quality of the sheer hellishness suggested by the unchanging 'eternal' present that doesn't pass – 'nothing comes right, nothing, nothing, this will never end. I'll never stir, I'll never know peace' (350) – how are we to 'think' the text's darkness?[3]

Let us first perhaps describe the dynamics of mental space where the function of thinking might be more clearly seen as an important operator within the novel's wider mode of negativity. And let us keep in mind Bion's fundamental thesis, already alluded to, namely that thoughts exist before the capability of thinking and that thinking has to be called into existence to deal with thoughts (Skelton 2006, 457). Commenting its own strangeness, the voice quips 'it's coming to think of it that is strange' (*BT* 371). In a way, I would like to take up the challenge of thinking the novel's strangeness or to see what is so strange about thinking in this novel, what Daniel Katz coins as 'the nightmarish aspects of the Cartesian cogito for Beckett' (Katz 1999, 96).

Thinking is essential to the awareness of internal and external reality, the attempt to think being tantamount to bringing under control and integrate any would-be expelled particles of the psyche. The role of hatred has to be underlined since as Freud pointed out, such hatred is extended to all aspects of the psyche that make for awareness of it (Bion 1967, 37). The mental siege of *The Unnamable*, for example, might be said to consist of one long onslaught not so much on thinking as on a hated state of mind, and of all that 'goes on' in that mind. Just as Lemuel gladly hammers in his head – 'the seat of all shit and misery' (*BT* 245), Beckett's unnamable narrator gives his hatred free reign to all forms of perception or awareness. Some of his 'self' descriptions lend themselves to being understood as a destruction of his aptitude to think, that is, we are witnessing an inaptitude for being conscious and for being unconscious. At times the narrator is incapable of being aware, suggesting that his unconscious is equally incapable of functioning. He can neither be aware or unaware of things. The divisions between conscious–unconscious, bodily state/mental states are, as it were, suspended, with an inaptitude to reject or ignore the slightest mental or sensorial excitation in the narrator's universe:

> But I who am here, who cannot speak, cannot *think,* and who must speak, and therefore perhaps *think* a little, cannot in relation only to me who am here, to here where I am, but can a little, sufficiently, I don't know how. (276, my emphasis)

To affirm, as the narrator does, that he cannot situate himself within his 'own' thinking discourse, or that he no longer knows where he is, is to imply that language is not to be found 'inside' thought and that Beckett's text, in its turn, does not allow itself be caught within thinking, that is, present to itself and to thinking:

> I feel nothing, know nothing, and as far as thinking is concerned I do just enough to preserve me from going silent, you can't call that thinking. (281)

If one can't 'call that thinking', one might call it a form of blank thinking. The least we can say about our narrator's 'thinking' is that he is actively thinking nothing. Feeling nothing, knowing nothing, he nonetheless grapples to situate his physical state between immobility and restlessness, quietude and change. It is the void of his thinking that paradoxically functions as a prerequisite for thought – 'an active renaming of the néant' (Barker 1991, 140) – which amounts to saying that thinking is a notion that does not explain the phenomenon it designates and connotes, but is a part of it.[4] Being its own metaphor, it can only be the figure of a figure, the thought of a thought, the thought of the effacement or emptiness of thought: 'And now let us think no more about it, think no more about anything, think no more' (*BT* 309).

If thinking can be said to be anywhere, it is 'non-localised in space' (Davies 2001, 403–4), circulating as an object expelled from sense and meaning, never 'available' except as absence – or as an object damaged or destroyed depriving the voice any mastery over things. 'Has my head lost all feeling? Or did I have a stroke, while I was meditating? I don't know', wonders Mahood in the head-in-the jar story (*BT* 317). Like the name, thinking cannot be grasped for itself, as a coincidence of body and mind, voice and writing. It is irredeemably elsewhere:

> it is some considerable time now since I last knew what I was talking about. It is because my *thoughts* are elsewhere. I am therefore forgiven. So long as one's *thoughts* are somewhere everything is permitted. (296 my emphasis)[5]

If in *The Unnamable*, it is impossible to say nothing and it is equally 'impossible to stop trying' (Barker 1991, 139), I would add that it is the persistence of thoughts of non-being that make the narrator think and repeat his thinking. One might be inclined to see the end 'result' of submitting thought to attacks as a means of achieving some redoubted mindlessness or irretrievable madness that precisely defies thinking. But, as we shall see later, this is not quite the case. However mind-bending the Unnamable's narrative may be, there is still a mind to talk of or at least a mind behind the mindlessness (Takahashi 2001). This is all the more noticeable in the novel's remarkable self-reflexivity that serves to displace any of the story's pathos allowing us thereby to see the 'comedy', albeit dark, of the situation. For example, while Beckett's narrator has us believe he is prone to anxieties – 'all change to be feared, in comprehensible uneasiness' (*BT* 271) – by a sleight of hand, he also rubbishes such self-indulging pathos: 'what rubbish all this stuff about light and dark. And how I have luxuriated in it' (280). In other words, Beckett thinks thinking paradoxically and not at all negatively: a thought cannot exist without being and not being a thought. Thinking only exists if it is perceived as both being possible and impossible 'elsewhere' and 'somewhere' which amounts to saying that 'all thinking is "thinking other"' where there is 'no stability, no coming to rest, and, most important, no supreme system that can be known' (Barker 1991, 138).

The anatomy of a thought thinking thought

'*I have never thought for myself*', wrote Beckett in his unpublished German diary, and went on to add: 'I have switched off the incipient thought in terror for so long that I couldn't think now for half-a-minute if my life (!) depended on it' (2 February 1937, qtd in Knowlson 1996, 252). Similarly, in one of his more lucid moments, the Unnamable reflects on what makes him think, which may be seen as an attempt at 'thinking thought'. More than just leading to 'time-abolishing joys of impersonal and disinterested speculations', thinking is rethought as a form of terror, an emotion that is triggered off 'by another's thoughts':

> I only think, if that is the name for this vertiginous panic as of hornets smoked out of their nest, once a certain degree of terror has been exceeded, etc. Does this mean I am less exposed to doing so, by the grace of inurement? To argue so would be to underestimate the extent of the repertory in which I am plunged and which, it appears, is nothing compared to what is in store for me at the conclusion of the novitiate. These lights gleaming low afar, then rearing up in a blaze and sweeping down upon me, blinding, to devour me, are merely one example. My familiarity with them avails me nothing, they invariably give me to reflect. Each time, at the last moment, just as I begin to scorch, they go out, smoking and hissing, and yet

> each time, my phlegm is shattered. And in my head, which I am beginning to locate to my satisfaction [...] the sparks spurt and dash themselves out against the walls. And sometimes I say to myself I am in a head, it's terror makes me say it, and the longing to be in safety, surrounded on all sides by massive bone. And I add that I am foolish to let myself be frightened by another's thoughts, lacerating my sky with harmless fires and assailing me with noises signifying nothing. (322)

In this passage, the narrator and us are uncomfortably confronted with a paradox: one is not always there where one thinks one is, there where one thinks that one is thinking ('And sometimes I say to myself I am in a head'); nor are one's thoughts necessarily one's 'own' thoughts ('frightened by another's thoughts'). Equally alarming is the narrator's inability to make sense of his terrified thoughts. At best he can make *nothing* of his mental experience, but it is precisely this nothing that generates his need to think – 'my familiarity with them avails me *nothing*, they invariably give me to reflect'. What determines the functioning of the narrator's thoughts is outside his control: it is the pressure and terror of the unthought or the unthinkable – 'this vertiginous panic' – which gives rise to the act of thinking. We could say that it is the concrete yet hallucinatory image of thoughts as angry or aggressive hornets that prevents the narrator from thinking and yet necessitates an act of thought.

The 'hornets being smoked out of their nests', and the 'devouring lights' provide apt illustrations of what Bion calls the raw materials of thoughts, which are equivalent, for him, to emotional facts or experiences indigestible by the mental apparatus – beta elements. These cannot be thought but only accumulated or evacuated – 'smoked out' to refer to our quote. Although the 'lights gleaming low afar' would suggest that the narrator has located his apparatus for thinking thoughts – 'they invariably give me to reflect ... And in my head, which I am beginning to locate to my satisfaction' – like the hornets the violent lights have the quality of bizarre objects of hallucination or concrete modes of thought where words are treated as things in themselves: 'blaze', 'sweeping', 'the sparks spurt and dash'. But the essential point is that thinking is not to be considered as a simple product of the act of thinking, but is a development of the psyche which is carried out under the pressure of these thoughts and not the other way around. If anything thinking turns out to be both the possibility and the impossibility of using itself as a defence against itself: 'Does this mean I am less exposed to doing so, by the grace of inurement?' The narrator's 'terror thought' paradoxically exceeds the distinction the thinker makes between terrifying and non-terrifying, his thinking being both full of terror and completely devoid of any content. He has been assailed 'with noises signifying nothing'. The hornets, and the terror they inspire, are not only the origin of thought but also its end or *telos*. It is the devouring lights (the lights of reason?) which seem in fact to pre-exist his thoughts and his vulnerable hypotheses ('what is in store for me'); it is they who constitute the 'certain degree of terror' and yet leave him in a state of not knowing or unknowingness. It is this empty state that gives rise to the need to think.

The siege in mental space

What the passage just analysed particularly problematises is the place or presence of the other in relation to the thinking subject: 'I am foolish to let myself be frightened by another's thoughts.' The idea that one is only thinking, or is thought by, the thoughts of an other, or that one is living within the mind of an other, is a central theme in the entire trilogy, examples of which we have already seen and also in *Waiting for Godot* as we shall see in the next chapter. It is also a central concern in some of the later shorter plays like *Footsteps* or *Eh Joe* with their haunting voices and haunted minds. (This point will be developed in the last chapter of this book.) But for this section, we shall limit our endeavours to tackling the following question: how can one situate the (im)possibility of thought, that is, 'presence', in relation to its impossible target, that is, absence?

In his deconstructionist study of the novel, Thomas Trezise links 'the undecidability or, indeed, the unnamability of the authorial or artistic subject ... 'to the spatial indeterminability or "between" of intersubjectivity itself' (Trezise 1990, 115–16). I would like to develop this insight and argue that the indeterminable 'in-between' that Trezise invokes is very much the effect and cause of what I would term the novel's mental cacophony. In other words, there are no clear-cut 'thinking' relations to speak of, no means of differentiating between one's thoughts and those thoughts belonging to another or between one's words and those words coming from another: 'No matter, rest is one of their words, *think* is another' (*BT* 307 my emphasis). If what our narrator is doing is 'being done without a minimum of mind', adding that it is certainly 'not mine' (285), then whose, one might ask?

The persecutory presence of others in the mind of the Unnamable and the associated threat of annihilation by these, contains the most telling images and features of what one might term a reworking of the paranoid-schizoid phase. The reader will hopefully remember from our introductory chapter that this phase is characterised by an open, uncontrolled process of splitting, together with the preponderance of destructive impulses that swing to sadism. Central to all of this is the use of projective identification, that is to say, the splitting and projection of mental functions such as consciousness, attention, judgement, perceptions, etc. in order to rid oneself of the awareness of reality (Skelton 2006, 379).

For instance, the Unnamable splits parts of his self and projects them into others, such as Basil, Mahood and Worm, who provisionally become his 'threatening twins' of a sort or, to refer to the text: 'If we are *twain*' (*BT* 289 my emphasis), which is Beckett's translation of the French: 'si nous sommes deux' (*INN* 47). This is echoed later on by the phrase: 'one may experience the need of such creatures, assuming they are *twain*' (*BT* 342), which is Beckett's translation of: 'en admettant qu'elles soient deux' (*INN* 141).

Paul Stewart adroitly sees the Unnamable's creation of characters as a process 'of making the internal external, the better to view it (Stewart 2006, 124) adding that 'the lines of communication between the creator and created [...] are unknown' (ibid. 125). However I would suggest that the lines of communication may be detected in the space of the in-between – the space between self and other, between something and nothing, between the narrator-thinker and his mental 'creations'. The in-between is perhaps more of a dynamic spacing than *a* space per se, insofar that it is liable to be emptied or filled according to the needs of the voice. The latter, 'tired of being pawed and pummelled endlessly in vain' (*BT* 319), is torn between ejecting intolerable parts of self and reintrojecting 'the voices and thoughts of the devils who beset me' (ibid.). These are the Unnamable's tyrannical figures of punishment such as Basil and the Master. It is they who make the Unnamable 'perform' his 'pensum' (285), act out, as it were, his 'punishment for having been born perhaps' (284). In his vivid description of his tormentors, we have the impression that the voice has 'replaced' his unconscious by what Bion would term a 'dream furniture', that is to say, 'real' bizarre objects in the form of a persecutory superego in whose state of mind the voice feels imprisoned (1967, 51). Hence the hallucinatory presence of the 'college of tyrants' (*BT* 284), 'their pockets full of poison' (273), 'a meeting of deputies' who 'assemble to discuss me' [...] 'the fact of my continuing' (287). One demon in particular, who gets special mention, is the hated figure of Basil described as 'fastening on me his eyes like cinders with all their seeing [...] changed me into what he wanted me to be' (273).

As Stewart reminds us, 'the delegates are a part of the Unnamable and apart from the Unnamable' (124). Confused by their language, their mind and their reason, he dreads the thought that they might 'represent' him or worse, 'understand' him. For example, the narrator's initial rueful reflections on his recourse to his 'troop of lunatics' (*BT* 282) to represent him 'in the midst of men'? (272), double up as a meta-narrative reflexion from the fictional writer that the Unnamable is. Instead of coping with the burden of solitude and absence, instead the voice has to deal with the presences of others. He has been 'floundering through a ponderous chronicle of moribunds in their courses' (282–3), where, with a nod at Molloy, tells us that the 'innate knowledge of my mother [...] was one of their favourite subjects of conversation' (273). The need for their subsequent mental evacuation or disidentification is urgent. They are his past puppets he is going to scatter 'to the winds': 'All these Murphys, Molloys and Malones do not fool me [...] Let them be gone now, them and all the others, those I have used and those I have not used, *give me back the pains I lent them* and vanish, from my life, my memory, my terrors and shames' (267, my emphasis).

But it will take more than a radical disowning of his puppets to get finally rid of his 'manikins' (280). As Steven Connor insightfully remarks, 'No matter how many layers of *inauthentic* accretion and surrogacy are scoured away, there are always further calcifications of "vice-existers" to be dealt with' (Connor 2008, 18, my emphasis), as if the narrator's thinking is always unable to bring under control the split-off parts of self. Thus, he has to deal with new 'disturbers of my peace' (*BT* 274). He describes Mahood's voice, for example, 'as though interwoven into mine' [...] 'when he was away I tried to find myself again' (283) and 'to take advantage of his absence to unravel my tangle' (289). While there is a constant dissociation of links between the narrator and his 'two fomenters of fiasco' (310), the Unnamable nonetheless tries to establish and even maintain relations with what he has expelled from himself and thus acknowledges his expelled others. It is they who have allowed him to think of himself as being 'somewhere on a road, moving, between a beginning and an end, gaining ground, losing ground, getting lost' (288, my emphasis). Despite his 'search for the means to put an end to things [...] to banish [...] the beings, things, shapes, sounds and lights with which my haste to speak has encumbered this place' (274–5), the self can only succeed in proliferating – evacuating by splitting – more and more others, the 'I' becoming a version of 'they' and of the 'things' that 'they have crammed me full of to prevent me from saying who I am, where I am, and from doing what I have to do ... How they must hate me! Ah a nice state they have me in, but still I'm not their creature, not quite, not yet' (297–98).

Mahood's story of truth, lies and poison

Thinking, then, cannot contain the narrator in a space of his own without expelling him from the space of thinking by transforming him into another, into the residue of language and the unthought: 'for what I am doing is not being done without a minimum of mind. Not mine perhaps, granted, with pleasure, but *I draw on it*' (285 my emphasis). In terms of the relations between contained and container, the Mahood stories might be theorised as the return of the pulverised ejected contents of the psyche that are now seeking a narrative form or receptacle (Connor 2008, 27). However, as we shall see, the 'new' container proves to be as persecutory as its re-introjected 'contents.

The first Mahood story, with its thought of lies, poisoning, incomprehension and falsification, is a probing instance of 'these stories of a being whose identity he (Mahood) usurps' (*BT* 285). The state of tension and conflict between the narrator and Mahood can be likened to the relationship between the thinker and his thoughts. This takes the form of a duel between truth and lies, knowing and un-knowing. Seeing that the one concrete detail we have about the story is that the narrator's family was 'carried off by sausage-poisoning, in great agony' (292), the duel may also be said to be between psychic nourishment and lethal poison.

It might be useful to remember what we have already said with regard to Bion's theory of emotional links, notably the function of knowing (K). The K-linkage involves mental pain which may be accepted, modified or evaded, the truth and the lie emerging as the food and poison of thought and growth of the personality (Bion 1967, 111). In other words the lie remains mentally indigestible as a bizarre unthinkable or unthought object of hallucination. Although the operative trope in the Beckett story might appear to be the physical breast given the image of lethal food-poisoning – 'incommodated by their shrieks, then by the stench of decomposition, I turned sadly away' (*BT* 292), I would argue that it is the lying discourse around the story – story as lie – that launches a wider attack on the maternal container's thinking, knowing and understanding functions (Skelton 2006, 287).

If anything, the story has the opposite effect and function than that first imagined by Mahood. The narrator imagined his first story as having the task of setting 'about the truth again', making him think he was 'a free agent' (*BT* 284). But, as Begam points out, it is never clear where we should situate Mahood with respect to his narrative nor is it very clear what that narrative is (Begam 1996, 160). In fact we are left to think about three contradictory versions. One, that Mahood arrives home but turns back after discovering that his family has been poisoned to death. Two, that Mahood actually trampled underfoot the unrecognisable *remains* of his family – 'here a face, there a stomach, as the case might be, and sinking into them with the ends of my crutches, both coming and going' – fantasising on having spent the last day of his long voyage 'in mother's entrails' (297, my emphasis). Three, that he was never there or that he had never left his home in the first place. But 'to tell the truth', if the Unnamable doesn't know what he is talking about or where his thoughts ever 'were', it is because his thoughts have always been elsewhere (ibid.). What is lived again in the remodelling of the story is the narrator's hatred of truth that serves as a stimulus for lying as well as a deterrent of thought:

> Let us rather consider what really took place, if Mahood was telling the truth And why should he have lied to me, he so anxious to obtain my adhesion, to what now that I come to think of it, to his conception of me? (296)

The particular point I wish to make here is that Beckett uses the narrative confusion and in particular the central image of the body, to make thinking run in reverse as un-thinking. Mahood gets rid of his thoughts much in the same way as a container rids itself of accretions of stimuli thereby dispersing any would-be contact barrier between conscious and unconscious elements. Mahood has 'filled' the narrator with lies which, being indigestible, can only but be violently vomited up as a poisonous residue:

> But I'll fix their gibberish for them. I never understood a word of it in any case, not a word of the stories it spews, like gobbets in a vomit. *My inability to absorb*, my genius for forgetting, are more than they reckoned with. Dear *incomprehension*, it's thanks to you I'll be myself, in the end. *Nothing* will remain of all the lies they have glutted me with. And I'll be myself at last, as a starveling belches his odourless wind, before the bliss of coma. (298 my emphasis)

Beckett's thinking is closer then to an 'action' than to a 'discourse' as it tries to violently 'spew' up its accumulated excitations and stimulations. The lie emerges then as the poison of thought and produces a state of unknowing – non-knowledge – the narrator's unknowing amounting to reducing all activity of understanding to a body state of being glutted with untruths. The narrator's strategy of keeping abreast from his others is precisely to 'un-think', to 'mis-understand' and to deny what their thinking may represent of him or for him: 'but enough of this nonsense. I was never anywhere but here' (297). This is very similar to what Bion says regarding the space of what he calls the condition of –K, or non-knowledge, in analysis. Contrasting K 'space' in classical analysis where 'classical transference manifestations become "sense-able"', Bion describes –K space as 'the place where space used to be. It is filled with no-objects which are violently and enviously greedy of any and every quality, thing, or object, for its "possession" (so to speak) of existence' (Bion 1965, 115). Similarly in Beckett, later on, when the voice reflects back on Mahood's story, the latter denies having ever suffered when he was Mahood – 'like true thinking flesh' (*BT* 325), since this would have assumed that he had the mental capacity to think or in the vicious cynical terms of the voice 'bubbling with the pus of reason' (ibid.). In this drama of self-entrapment and shacklement, the sole ally of the Unnamable is his stupidity or should one say his capacity for non-knowledge: 'they'll never get the better of my stupidity' (317).

In the jar of the dwindling mind

The second story offers us an account of Mahood's 'confined, stranded or islanded consciousness' (Davis 1994, 53) with its imprisoning jar. It's a story that may be seen to 'come' from another split part of Mahood, not necessarily the same Mahood who told the first story, both 'Mahoods' being arguably split off parts of our unnamable speaker: 'I may therefore perhaps legitimately suppose that the one-armed one-legged wayfarer of a moment ago and the wedge-headed trunk in which I am now marooned are simply two phases of the same carnal envelope' (*BT* 303). This time the voice comes to us from a mutilated body in a jar, the narrator being deliriously conscious of everything: his 'organs of digestion and evacuation', he tells us, 'though sluggish, are not wholly inactive' (306). He is comically unable to be unconscious of the least sensorial sensation: his eyes (are) 'still open to impressions, and one ear, sufficiently, and the head sufficiently obedient, to provide [him] at least with a vague idea of the elements to be eliminated from the setting in order for all to be empty and silent' (307).

Commentary on this story has unsurprisingly focused on the image of the imprisoning jar, made equivalent to the Cartesian *cogito*. 'The external world is *ruled out'*, explains Paul Davies:

> From there it is a short step to being *shut out*. And what must come of this is less than a step away: the very moment the external world is shut out, the 'cogitator' is *shut in*. The enclosure is complete, the jar, its perfect symbol, is in place, with its victim inside. (Davies 1994, 52, Davies emphasis)[6]

However, I propose to place the emphasis more on the peculiar interdependence between Mahood and his maternal benefactress, Madeleine, who, ambiguously, also goes under the name of Marguerite. Strangely, both need each other. Mahood needs Madeleine to physically protect him. But, he is also her 'undeniable asset', not only because his jar serves as 'a kind of landmark, not to say an advertisement' (*BT* 301) for her restaurant, but, more importantly, because Mahood allows her to fill the void in her: 'she loves me [...] she needs me [...] there is in her a void that I alone can fill' (316). My contention is that such reciprocal interdependence needs to be understood as the outcome of thinking, or mental interplay, since communication between the two is exclusively that of two silent but uncomprehending minds – 'this woman has never spoken to me, to the best of my knowledge' (ibid. 316). Given that the containing jar rapidly becomes the object of Madeleine's maternal care, we cannot but notice a parodied reworking of the mother/infant mental bond. Casting the bond in terms of the container-contained configuration, the infant's rudimentary consciousness is mediated by the mother's reverie, that is the mother's capacity to receive and contain feelings or thoughts from her child (Bion 1967, 116). This is how I propose to read the Mahood–Madeleine couple, the latter being figured as a psychic translator or container of the former's thoughts or desires.

It is certainly not difficult to see that Madeleine's adaptability to respond intuitively to her 'infant's' needs is clearly scored. She empties the narrator's receptacle, 'punctually and without complaint' (*BT* 301), feeds him with 'a marrow-bone' (301), festoons his jar (301–2) and makes sure he is 'snug and dry' (301). Her protectiveness is best captured by the image of the tarpaulin with which she covers Mahood when it gets cold: 'No other form of filthy weather lets loose in her the maternal instinct, in my favour' (302).

But, for all that, this never quite warrants any sense of gratitude from our 'wedge-headed trunk': 'Besides I realised darkly that if she took care of me thus, it was not solely out of goodness, or else I had not rightly understood the meaning of goodness, when it was explained to me' (ibid.). Since she is the sole link between Mahood's jar-like imprisoned mind and the outside world, Madeleine is more of a psychic asset to Mahood than the latter is ready to admit. As proprietor of the chop-house, her food is more than just the symbol of a nourishing breast and may be likened to that of a thinking breast, thinking in the 'alimentary' sense of the word.[7] Bion reminds us that 'beta elements' (which are fit only for projection and splitting) can be so modified that they become absorbable and quite literally, *food for thought*. In Beckett, although parodied as 'food for delirium' (307), Madeleine's food at least allows Mahood to have clear ideas and, as a result, may be seen to form a link between Mahood's innate preconceptions (intuitions) and his experience of the external world: 'a turnip, I know roughly what a turnip is like, a carrot too, particularly the Flakkee, or Colmar Red. I seem to grasp at certain moments the nuance that divides bad from worse' (302–3). The food and what the passers-by say about it, form the building-blocks of thought upon which more 'complex' systems can be built. For example, it is Madeleine's menu, attached to the jar, that provides the narrator with 'spiritual nourishment' – 'turnips in gravy, carrots in gravy [...] the gravy has not varied' (302) – since it is written in a 'kind of language I can almost understand, these the kind of clear and simple notions on which *it is possible for me to build*' (ibid. my emphasis), insists Mahood.

With Madeleine's menu attached to Mahood's jar, we might be given hints of a thinking couple. Yet when it comes to communicating mentally, Mahood and Madeleine, not unlike Molloy and his frantic mother, equally 'made a balls of it between us, I with my signs and she with her reading of them' (302–3). For example, when Mahood fails to make her understand that he wishes to be shrouded more often – 'dashing my head angrily against the neck of the jar, that I should like to be shrouded more often' (302) – it is tantamount to saying that he fails to project the feeling of dying into Madeleine or that such death-like projections are not easily tolerated by the ever so busy Madeleine, who is 'always thinking of something new to relieve' (313) Mahood. It is my view, then, that we witness a gradual breakdown in the interplay between Mahood's rudimentary consciousness and what one may call Madeleine's maternal reverie. While the restaurant proprietress may be, in Mahood's words, the woman 'wanting me in vain to live' (317), her reverie or her alpha function increasingly fails to modify her own tensions and anxieties in seeing Mahood slowly sink and disappear:

> I have dwindled, I dwindle. Not so long ago, with a kind of shrink of my head and shoulders, as when one is scolded, I could disappear [...] for the woman, displeased at seeing me sink lower and lower, has raised me up by filling the bottom of my jar with sawdust which she changes every week. (304)

Of course the other 'player' in this space of uncontained and uncontainable anxiety is Mahood himself whose malicious 'little game' (305) consists of mentally manipulating his distraught benefactress. This is all the more comical given Mahood's notorious physical incapacities: 'And I move my head in and out, in and out [...] and often at dawn having left it out all night, I bring it in, *to mock the woman and lead her astray'* (304 my emphasis).

The container-contained drama of thinking that Beckett stages can be seen, then, in terms of Madeleine's efforts at containing Mahood's sense of imminent self-annihilation. As Madeleine's life-drive continues to protect Mahood physically – 'from chills. It's snug' (313) – Mahood's dream-thoughts are concomitantly one of being engulfed, swallowed up by nature – 'If only the earth would quake! The shambles swallow me up!' (313). Madeleine fends off, then, the unthinkable anxiety of 'losing' her asset by frantically redoubling her attentions – her 'thoughts' – and checking Mahood 'every few minutes to see if [he is] still more less imaginable in situ' (315). While Mahood apparently doesn't know 'what to think of the redoubled attentions she has been lavishing on' [him], (ibid.), it is clear that he senses this as an argument against his existence, a radical doubting of his presence (Katz 1999, 120). By a sleight of hand he is also suspecting that something has broken down in her capacity for reverie or mental protection. For instance the remark: 'there is no getting away from it, this woman is losing faith in me' (*BT* 315) might be seen to double up as: 'it is me who is losing faith in her'.

The Madeleine story, which is left off at this point (305) and taken up again later (313) is, unlike the first story, a precondition for thinking the persecutive presence of 'they'. On the brink of 'assembling the world at last' ('just at the moment when the world is assembled at last', 307), the narrator is susceptible of being 'bundled in [his] shroud and whisked away, out of sight and mind' (ibid.). Even the search for non-thinking or the space of the unthinkable, which forms a new idea in the discourse at this point, must reckon with the fact that 'think' is one of 'their words' (ibid.). So in taking up the strands of the narrative again, Mahood narrows everything down to thinking his 'independence' or his 'separation' from Madeleine. This amounts to his thinking his capacity for thought itself and where the distinction between death and life, presence and absence, thinking and being thought by the other, becomes increasingly untenable.

In his attempt to think his 'presence' – 'I must be still thinking' (115), or his absence since no-one notices him: ('how is it that no-one notices me?, 313) one finds, for the first time, a systematic series of 'thoughts' applied to Mahood's problem of continuity: 'How is it the people do not notice me? I seem to exist for none but Madeleine?' (313). Ignored, excluded and *unthought* by the other, Mahood is no more than a pure physical attraction for the dogs that come pissing against his abode and the flies that vouch for him: 'can it be out of discretion, and a reluctance to hurt, that they affect to be unaware of my existence?' (314).

Our hero, then, is practically unable to 'be', unable to be without the 'attentions' of his maternal other. This is tantamount to saying that for Mahood 'thinking' can only mean 'thinking that the other thinks me' or 'I can only exist in and through the thoughts of the other':

> Attention such as hers, the pertinacity with which she continues to acknowledge me, do not these sufficiently attest my real presence her, in the Rue Brancion [...] Would she rid me of my paltry excrements every Sunday, make me a nest at the approach of winter, protect me from the snow, change my sawdust, rub salt into my scalp [...] would she have put me in a cang, raised me on a pedestal, hung me with lanterns, if she were not convinced of my *substantiality*? (315, my emphasis)

Mahood's conclusion or summing up ('I shall now sum up', 316) – his 'cogitation' – leads not to the conclusion 'I am', but as Daniel Katz rightly outlines, 'doubts as to whether one exists, doubts which are founded on the lack of recognition from all but the caretaker ... Madeleine' (Katz 1999, 119).[8] The meaning of Beckettian thinking could be formulated as follows: even if the totality of what I think is contaminated with madness, falseness or 'the same set of hallucinations' (*BT* 305), I think I am while I am thinking, or I think while I am not.[9] But Mahood's thinking experiments culminate in a confrontation with an uncontainable nothing that immediately heralds the 'end' of Mahood's stories:

> Nothing has happened ... (316) ... Hours have passed, it must be day again, nothing has happened, I hear nothing ... For this feeling of being

> entirely enclosed, and yet nothing touching me, is new. The sawdust no longer presses against my stumps, I don't know where I end. (317)

Mahood's rediscovery of a 'new' sense of void ('nothing touching me, is new') suggests the definitive absence of Madeleine or Marguerite. She may have come and gone without his having noticed her (316). Both benefactress and client 'return', as it were, to the original voids from which they respectively emerged.

Worming back into the void

The orbit of awareness in *The Unnamable* spirals pitilessly and inexorably inwards or backwards as the voice increasingly generates fantasies about boundaries and thresholds bringing us closer to the genesis of all or any mental activity. This is how I propose to re-read the Worm motif, that is, as an intuition of feeling-thoughts in search of a mind to think them. By intuition I refer here to Bion's use of the term 'intuit' which he preferred to 'observed' or 'heard' or 'seen' as it does not carry the penumbra of sensuous association (Bion 1967, 134). This is in line with Bion's view that psychoanalytic experience or discourse refers to and uses 'non-sensuous realisations' or experiences (Skelton 2006, 253).

Worm cannot be 'realised' or represented by either language or thought, and resembles more an embryonic mind searching for itself in the depths of the unknowable. It is as if the search for the unthought leads our Unnamable voice further and further away from the concreteness of experience expressed earlier in his formulations of the Mahood experience. Where ignorance and stupidity are Mahood's assets in his battle with his others, Worm's 'only strength' is 'that he understands nothing, can't take thought: with what could he take care, with what could he form the faintest conception of the condition they are decoying him into, with their ears, their eyes, their tears and a brainpan where anything may happen' (*BT* 331).

The Worm motif brings us into a world of anti-thought, a perilous glimpse of an unformed and unformable being: 'his senses tell him nothing, nothing about himself, nothing' (318). We are tempted, maybe encouraged, to see Worm as the figure of some secret inaccessible self whose existence is paradoxically balanced on inexistence or on the existence of his persecutory others. For example, Worm 'exists nevertheless, but not for himself, for others, other conceive him and say, Worm is, since we conceive him, as if there could be no being but being conceived' (318). 'Feeling nothing, knowing nothing, capable of nothing' (320),

Worm can neither be delivered by birth nor claimed by death: 'unborn, abiding there unliving, with no hope of death' (318). If he is to have a mind, a 'thinking' apparatus, it is to contain his rage and terror: 'in it nothing but rage' (327). The suggestion here might be that Worm's rage has evacuated all traces of a would-be embryonic mind, for in constructing Worm's head in terms of violence, the Unnamable is attacking the very existence of thinking in Worm and in himself: 'No he can't think anything, can't judge of anything' (328).

Not unlike Malone's birth–death, Worm's 'delivery' is likened to an irretrievable loss, a violent ejection into the world of the other where 'an eruption is needed, to spew him into the light [...] it's like slime, paradise [...] life trying to get in [...] there's no air' (335). Giving form to the primeval mess that Worm is – 'nothing but a shapeless heap' (328) – necessitates the tragic breaking of inner silence for 'silence once broken will never again be whole' (336). The condition of being or the modality of being can only be figurative, 'where all assertions are made in the subjunctive' (Begam 1996, 165). For example, in evoking Worm's transit from darkness to light (*BT* 329), the narrator can only speak *of* Worm in resolutely hypothetical terms: '*as if* he were alive, *as if* he could understand, *as if* he could desire' (239, my emphasis). Worm 'is there, as it were, as it were' (334), always beyond reach, 'too far for them to reach him even with the longest pole'... 'that tiny blur, in the depths of the pit, is he' (329). An image of the void itself perhaps, for to quote a later text of Beckett's, *Worstward Ho*, like the void Worm is 'most when almost' (*WH* 42).

Whether the 'I' is now Mahood or Worm – his two fomenters of fiasco (310) – becomes a pure problem of rational speculation and a cause for inexhaustible play – playing at self-differentiation in relation to the other. At times the 'I' manages to be the negative of his others, their 'other' as it were, the one 'who will never be caught, never delivered' (*BT* 311). The only place where he can incarnate his own irreducible otherness is in the nothing, a sacred sanctuary of a sort, the place of the 'nowhere' and the 'no time' of thought: 'the essential is never to arrive anywhere, neither where Mahood is, nor where Worm is, nor where I am [...] what a joy to know where one is, and where one will stay, without being there' (ibid.).

The (dis)continuity game of being and of not being

We have now come round full circle in our analysis of the novel's mental void. We have seen how the 'I' alternates between 'intake and discharge' (Connor 2008, 26) temporarily investing the void by 'thinking' the presence-absence of others as it tells us of the sieges and battles pitted against him. We now need to look at one last battle, 'the battle of the soliloquy' as Beckett described it (qtd in Connor 33) and to see if the 'I' can be said to survive its own 'catastrophic changes', a term I'll explain further on.

More than just a series of disavowals and invalidations of a speaking subject, the disruptive and shattering effects of language and thought that characterise the latter part of *The Unnamable* give us more the sense of a mental machinery of destructiveness that unleashes confusion and chaos. Such mental explosions or eruptions leave in their wake a pulverised, discontinuous 'self' (for want of a better word), at least a 'void' in self, where one can only 'be' present by being actively absent: 'there I am the absentee again' (*BT* 380). For example the unnamable must somehow withstand and survive his own self-fragmentations as he finds himself 'one minute in a skull and the next in a belly, strange, and the next nowhere in particular' (324). Indeed the massive splitting and fragmentation of the 'I' increasingly reaches almost parodic proportions as in his comments on his bodylessness:

> that's why I can't stir, that's why I don't feel a body on me, I'm not suffering enough yet [...] not suffering enough to be able to stir, to have a body, complete with head, to be able to understand, to have eyes to light the way. (379)

and his mindlessness where he finds himself cut adrift from all understanding or self-awareness:

> What would I understand with, that's what I'm asking, how I manage to understand, oh not the half, nor the hundredth, nor the five thousandth, let us go on dividing my fifty, nor the quarter millionth, that's enough. (357)

In Bion's parlance, the narrative might be said just here to undergo an unstoppable series of 'catastrophic changes' (Meltzer 106). These occur whenever any new thought is felt by the psyche as potentially disruptive and shattering. The ability to tolerate this upheaval and re-form a new set of views and theories will result in growth, but it is a painful process that is dependent on the individual's capacity to withstand fragmentation, anxiety and doubt, a test of 'negative capability'. But, to return to Beckett, in the unnamable narrator's alien and hostile void, there are no boundaries to contain his apparently dissolving or dispersing 'self', his 'me' or his 'I'. The container surreptitiously becomes the 'contained', which, in turn, erupts, explodes or overflows, becoming, by extension, the 'uncontainable' container:

> I'm in words, made of words, others' words ... I'm the air, the walls, the walled-in one, everything yields, opens, ebbs, flows, like flakes, I'm all these flakes, meeting, mingling, falling asunder ... nothing ever but me, a particle of me, retrieved, lost, lost, gone astray, I'm all these words [...] no ground for their settling. (*BT* 355–6)

As Steven Connor remarks, the voice is 'split agonisingly between the condition of a content which wishes to be free of its oppressive container and the process of containment itself' (Connor 2008, 27). Yet if the writing 'seems to erupt out of its containment', it still paradoxically manages to 'contain': 'It is this paradox which allows those wonderful manoeuvres, executed, as it were, in ontological mid-air, in which language suddenly knits together the process of its unravelling' (28). I would like to bring Connor's remarks to bear on the increasing tensions that set in between what we might term a chaos-proliferating voice or mind[10] – the 'labouring whirl' (*BT* 370) – and the potential containment of such 'chaos'. While the novel might be said to formally stage or contain a 'painfully disintegrating drama' (Connor 28), a self-dissolution of a sort, a gradual going to pieces, I would argue that it provides its own internal dynamics of containment in the form of on going to-and-fro movement between disintegration and potential continuity. I am picking up here on what Bion considered to be essential to all creative thinking, namely the *interdependence* of the processes of fragmentation and integration. Glover's account of this issue merits quoting:

> In the creative process, Bion shows that thinking involves the dismantling of previous views and theories, allowing the formation of new ideas. In changing one's way of thinking, the container has to be dissolved before it is reformed. [...] Creative effort can therefore be viewed as an on-going process, on a small scale, of movements to-and-fro between the paranoid-schizoid and depressive position. (Glover 2008, chapter 4, 6–7)

It is also at this point that I would like to bring in Winnicott's important distinction between disintegration and unintegration, the former term being defined as 'an organised defence against the tremendous pain of various anxieties associated with the fully integrated state' (Winnicott 1988, 119). But at the theoretical start, writes Winnicott, 'is an unintegrated state, a lack of wholeness both in space and time. At this stage there is no awareness [...] awareness [only] becomes possible [...] because there is a self to be aware' (116).

My thesis is that the novel's ultimate state of irresolution with regard to its undetermined and *unintegrated* 'I' is an achievement of containment, the drama being sustained by the strong tensions *between* chaos and continuity and their essential *interdependence*. For example, despite all the phantasmatic self-annihilating chaos surrounding him, the Unnamable still has the instinctual urge and the creative impulse to invent even if his 'creations' can only be bits and pieces of a hypothetical body-self or mind-self: 'I'll make myself a head, I'll make myself a memory [...] I'll have eyes' (*BT* 379).[11]

The role of the void in all of this needs to be stressed yet again, since, being unknowable, it is experienced as the symptom needing to be 'thought' or 'understood' by the 'I'. We started this chapter by describing the abysmal depths of the novel's inner void. What I want to add here is that the void might be seen as the irreducible third or transitional term that provides an alternative to the psychic dualism the narrator is struggling to move beyond: thinking/un-thinking, containing/contained, disintegration/integration, chaos/order, etc. Where Stephen Barker argues that Beckett, in *The Unnamable*, 'is concerned with transcending the dialectics of "nothing and something" to isolate the threshold of the nothing's appearance, the undisclosable "moment" of deferral and distance' (Barker 129), I would argue for an essential *interdependence* between 'nothing' and 'something'.[12] For example, the only ground where the narrator's whirls and eddy of sensations and impulses might be said to 'settle' is a groundless one – 'no ground for their settling' (*BT* 356), which is imagined as 'a wordless thing in an empty place', 'a hard shut dry cold black place, where nothing stirs, nothing speaks' (ibid.). The space *of* the nothing is the space *for* the nothing, a nirvana of the unthought and anti-thought, a nebulous zone between speech and thought, being and non-being:

> But how can you think and speak at the same time, without a special gift, your thoughts wander, your words too [...] *between them* would be the place to be, where you suffer, rejoice, at being bereft of speech, bereft of thought, and feel nothing, hear nothing, know nothing, say nothing, are nothing, that would be a blessed place to be, where you are. (344, my emphasis)

But whether the 'I' 'is' 'something' or 'nothing' – some *one* or *no* one – is arguably beside the point. The 'I' is perhaps more 'at home' when finding himself near thresholds, boundaries, borders, frontiers – the zones of the in-between – as in the much commented tympanum passage, where he 'belongs' both to one side and the other and, of course, to neither for he feels 'nothing of all that' (352 my emphasis; Ross 2004, 274–6).

What matters, then, is the voice's attempt at preserving a space for the nothing, its 'inappropriable site of difference' to quote Luce Irigaray (2006, 44). The same critic goes on to sketch out the more positive role of the space of the nothing in the constitution of personal interrelationships. For example, Irigaray sees the nothing as permitting the articulation between the worlds of self and other, even pointing to a path leading toward the Other:

> Calling into question one's own world, so as to preserve the existence and the access to the world of the other, allows and needs to bring about a nothing that will permit the articulation between the two worlds. This nothing implies both a 'no longer anything of one's own' and a 'nothing yet in common' [...] to preserve a space for the nothing [...] between us puts into question the values of a subject, provides limits to its world, and allows us to go out of our own borders in order to meet with the other. This nothing, or this negative, between us will remain forever insurmountable. (Ibid.)

The insurmountable 'nothing' of Beckett's writing of course reverts these assumptions since, as we have seen, the self, although disavowing having anything 'of his own' or having anything in common with others, rather clings to its precarious border-line *between* merging and separateness, awareness and unawareness, annihilation and survival.

The Unnamable dramatises, then, a psychic catastrophe that remains 'incapable of resolution into quiescence', to quote Connor's quoting of Bion (Connor 2008, 13; Bion 1967, 101). The playful motif or refrain of 'you must go on/I can't go' (*BT* 381) suggests less a fatal endgame as a continuity/discontinuity game: going on or not going on being or, perhaps, going on *and* not going on. If there is a hint here at a birth process, it is one that is liable to be interrupted or arrested. In Winnicott's parlance, the 'continuity of the going on being of the individual' is the very condition of mental health (qtd in Phillips 1988, 94) where, curiously, 'birth can be the prototype for the impingement or interruption of the infant's *going-on-being*' (ibid., my emphasis). The Beckett unnamable voice has been reluctantly 'going on' since the 'beginning' as he finds himself in a state that is neither life nor death: 'a sperm dying, of cold [...] a drying sperm' (*BT* 349) who remains unsurprisingly envious of those people 'born of a wet dream and dead before morning' (ibid.). He wonders in the event of his dying, whether 'death in itself could be regarded as evidence, or even a strong presumption, in support of a preliminary life' (314–15). Evidently enough, he has been looking for his mother to kill her, something he should have thought of a bit earlier, before being born, he reminds us (360). For all that the Unnamable must go on for 'it's a question of going on' (372).

The Unnamable seems to 'end' by 'going on' but, in a way, it fails on both accounts. It closes on a potential opening or a beginning, as the voice brings us to the threshold of 'my own' story (382), 'unimaginable, unspeakable' (380). We find ourselves at 'a mythological gateway back to the beginning' (Hill 1990, 82). Yet the final 'I'll go on' (*BT* 382) does not mean that the Unnamable finally 'goes on'. As Leslie Hill points out, 'the quest becomes its own end and a means of suspending its own end' (Hill 83). And the Unnamable's ultimate 'going on' equally remains unresolved since the question as to whether he will 'go on going on' necessarily remains unanswered. We are brought, then, in front of an enigmatic door that might and might not 'open' onto the I and its mythical silence. It is as if the preceding narrative had been a long prologue, a clearing ground for self, with the 'unintelligible' (282) presence of fiends and devils that necessitated thinking. Having had to tell 'other' stories – the stories of and about others – here we have the promise of a re-appropriation of story, the I re-appropriating 'his' story, the one of silence, the one about silence – 'it will be the silence' (382). By the same token the story of that other potential life 'that might have been mine' (366), which we'll never hear, is the one that we have been hearing in absentia – 'there I am the absentee again' (380). The I, then, has been unwittingly tracing the archaeology of its silence – 'the story of the silence that he never left' (ibid.) – in the interstices between self and other, between I and they, between his unthinkable terrors and his miraculous dream of crawling 'between the thwarts, towards the new day that promises to be glorious, festooned with lifebelts, praying for rack and ruin' (311).

6
The Void on Stage

The plot

Waiting for Godot consists of two acts, the second virtually repeating the first: two friends, Estragon and Vladimir, wait uncertainly for a mysterious Godot. In each act they are visited by another couple, Pozzo and Lucky, a master and his slave, who then move on, leaving them alone and longing for night to fall. At the end of each act, a young boy arrives with a message from Godot that he will not come that day but surely the next. After the departure of the boy, night falls, the moon rises and the couple decide to go, but enigmatically do not move. As a critic once wrote, nothing happens twice.

Introduction

In turning to theatre, Beckett found on the stage an alternative space, a zone of indeterminate outcome and at least a way of suspending, albeit temporarily, the siege in the room of the trilogy. Indeed, between the violent ending of *Malone Dies* and the frantic beginning of *The Unnamable*, *Godot* comes as a calm moment between two storms. This is testified by the manuscript's heading: 'storm sudden calm lull/certain wreck brings threat' (Cohn 1973, 139). Yet, in many respects, *Godot*, written on a child's notebook, takes up where *Malone Dies* leaves off since it is literally about playing in the absence of the other thanks to the availability of a self-created psychic playground. Like *Malone Dies*, *Waiting for Godot* relies heavily on the availability of objects such as tree, boots, hats, carrots, cords as supportive companions against the threatening emptiness. From the claustrophobic interiority of the siege in the trilogy room, Beckett invents an outside, a hypothetical 'country road' which is equally unlocatable and indefinable: 'you recognise the place?' (*G* 15).

Structured by a central principle of absence that is not without generating anxieties of separation and abandonment, loss and isolation, *Godot* lends itself to a dark parody of the Fort-Da game Freud interpreted in *Beyond The Pleasure Principle*, the game staging the infant's symbolic mastery of its mother's absence. Yet, Beckett's classic is not simply about loss and separation where Godot might be seen as the original lost object necessitating and justifying Estragon and Vladimir's presence on stage, as if the latter were impelled to pursue substitutes for this lost arrangement in the 'endless metonymic movement of desire' (Eagleton 1996, 161). If anything, the play insists on the 'ineluctability of loss [and] absence' (ibid.), the ultimate absence of Godot being the condition *sine qua non* of the characters' world, that is the absence of any source, essence or locus. In doing so, Beckett's play insists on Vladimir and Estragon's need to witness, testify to and think such absence.

Against claims made by critics such as Peter Boxall, for whom Beckett appears to represent on stage 'nothing' at all (2003, 11), presenting 'us with a stage that is perpetually falling into the void left by its relentless negation of its own meaning' (ibid., 12), I would rather underline and emphasise the creative force and positivity of Beckett's theatrical void. For as we shall see, the negative is always positive. The real thing is the thing that is not there: the negative of remembering, thinking or knowing is about the only real thing in Beckett's play. The Godot that is not there is more real than the Godot that might eventually come. Where other critics tend to convert such 'negativity' into positivity, my aim in this chapter is to work dialectically with Beckett's negativity by examining the functioning of playing and thinking in the production of such a theatrical void. *Waiting for Godot* is a play that oscillates between, on one hand, an inclination to protect and conserve its void and, on the other hand, to modulate and transform it by operations of remembering, thinking and playing.

The general purpose of this chapter, then, is to reread the Estragon–Vladimir relationship and the relationship of this relationship to the absent Godot. This necessitates therefore rethinking the figure of Godot and emphasising the space or gulf of the 'in-between' that structures the Vladimir/Estragon relationship to the absent Godot. If Godot has left a void for Estragon and Vladimir to inhabit, or may be said to be the void, it follows, then, that their task of waiting is no more and no less than a call to think Godot, that is, to think in the empty place left by the absent other. Where Beckett clearly insisted in the original production of

En attendant Godot on the physical connectedness and physical complementarity of Estragon and Vladimir (Bradby 2001, 60), my reading shall be looking at their interdependence in terms of their mental connectedness or a hypothetical 'thinking' relationship. It is as if by thinking the void – the silence, the emptiness – that they may avoid the terror of finally uncovering an unthinkable vacuum or unknown. I shall be developing Steven Connor's interesting hypothesis that Beckett appears to have turned to the concreteness of the drama in an attempt to supply for himself that necessary containment which his fiction had learned so terrifyingly to dissolve (Connor 2008, 29).

My reading is limited to the standard 'unrevised' dramatic text of the English *Godot*. Considerations of performance and Beckett's production of the 1975 Berlin *Godot* (*Warden auf Godot*) will be treated in the final chapter.

Beckett's theatrical work of the void

We shall begin our analysis of the void by first providing a general description of the play's 'nothing'[1] before looking at specific activities such as remembering and sleeping. I argue that the sense of an irreducible otherness is gradually generated *between* the two couples.

Waiting for Godot postures itself as a depthless, de-historicised even decathected play where 'there's no lack of void' (*G* 66). The least we can say about the play's 'nothing' is that it is both the condition *sine qua non* of the characters' present situation on stage – a pre-existing void – and the metaphor and metonymy of their lives. The no-thing, the ever repeated and repeatable 'nothing to be done' (9) is everything but a negation – a '*not* doing anything' – but rather a constitutive action, a *doing* nothing statement. For example, Estragon replies to Vladimir's question: – 'what did we do yesterday evening?' – by reminding him that they blathered about 'this and that ... nothing in particular ... yesterday evening we spent blathering about *nothing* in particular' (66, my emphasis). Yet there is a significant gradation to be observed in the way the nothing functions.

Initially it works negatively insofar that it signifies an invisible limit or barrier that can only be observed but never transcended. For example, 'nothing to be done' is repeated three times by Vladimir at the beginning of the play to underline their inherent condition of impossibility. His verbal discourse is simultaneously counterpointed by a series of 'absence' gestures. For example, Vladimir *finds nothing* (11, my emphasis) in his hat and equally Estragon has nothing to show Vladimir (ibid.). However the nothing slowly becomes Vladimir and

Estragon's privileged means of defence. By suspending or deferring action, it is as if the couple tries to conserve some inert tension-free equilibrium. For example, the discussion about hanging themselves in the first act is 'resolved' by the desire to do nothing since it is safer (18). Unsurprisingly, Estragon prefers to be stuck there doing nothing (71) or earlier, in the first act, when Estragon and Vladimir are being 'entertained' by Pozzo, Estragon breaks a silence with 'in the meantime nothing happens' (38). If Estragon is always beaten although he wasn't doing anything (60), Vladimir reminds him that doing nothing is always a question of style and manner: it is the way one does things that counts, if one wants to go on living (60).[2] Consequently, the 'we're waiting for Godot' motif comes positively synonymous with an emphatic, 'there's nothing we can do':

ESTRAGON: Ah! (*Pause. Despairing.*) What'll we do, what'll we do!
VLADIMIR: There's *nothing* we can do.
ESTRAGON: But I can't go on like this! (68)

Similarly, as Estragon tries to escape from his imaginary intruders – 'they're coming there too!/we're surrounded!' (74) – he quickly realises that there's nothing to do (74). The subsequent 'watch' gives rise to a play within a play, a *mise en abyme* of waiting for nothing and seeing nothing:

ESTRAGON: Do you see anything coming?
VLADIMIR: (*turning his head*) What?
ESTRAGON: (*louder*) Do you see anything coming?
VLADIMIR: No.
ESTRAGON: Nor I.
(*They resume their watch. Silence.*) (74–5)

For a play that is traditionally reputed to be devoid of action, Vladimir and Estragon are characters dynamically engaged in creating a void of their own, the danger being they are liable to fall into it at any moment. Even Estragon realises that the 'nothing happening' that gradually takes over *Waiting for Godot* is not without inducing fear and anxiety: 'nothing happens, nobody comes, nobody goes, it's awful' (41). But the paradoxical fact of the matter is that Estragon and Vladimir uphold blankness and emptiness as their supreme condition of being as they actively suspend any particular sense of time or place. Before looking now at the role of time and memory in the play's economy of void, the reader may need to understand more precisely what is meant by the term 'memory'.

As Bion tells us, memory is seen as something limited and limiting since memory is born of, and only suited to, sensuous experience. To remain 'without memory' is to leave the mental space open for the reception of something new, something which is not known. What is already known functions as pre-existing contents which belong to the past, and, as such, obstructs contact in the present and the intuition-discovery of something new (Skelton 2006, 306). The same applies to desire. Memory and desire must be precisely understood as past and future 'senses' (analogous to the mathematical concept of sense and applying indifferently to time or space of the same thing). Desire is like a 'future' memory since it refers to an event that has not yet happened. Like memory, it is an obstacle or a defensive barrier against the intrusion of 'thoughts': 'memory and desire obstruct the patient's relationship to an absent breast or penis on a level of mind, or at a time of life, which such an object would be so important as to evoke feelings analogous to what would in an adult be religious awe' (Bion 1967, 144–5).

Returning to the theatre, whether it is in relation to the horrors of wartime in St-Lô, Normandy, or in a more abstract sense, to the horrors of time, *Waiting for Godot* is predicated on an active forgetting of the past, time, history, or to conjure Joyce, the nightmare of history. Instead it takes a mind-boggling jump into the free air of temporal and spatial indeterminacy:

> ESTRAGON: (*very insidious*) But what Saturday? And is it Saturday? Is it not rather Sunday? (*Pause.*) Or Monday? (*Pause.*) Or Friday? (15)
>
> [...]
>
> POZZO: It's indescribable. It's like nothing. There's nothing. There's a tree. (87)

The active suspension of remembering, of thinking and, indeed, of knowing is for most part the 'work' of Estragon who either forgets immediately or never forgets (61). Any object that may serve as a temporal link between present and past is quickly emptied of meaning such as the 'unknown' tree that seems to function as a thing-in-itself, a place-in-itself that is unknowable but can be represented by phantasies, dreams, memories:[3]

> ESTRAGON: Was it not there yesterday?
>
> VLADIMIR: Yes, of course, it was there. Do you not remember? We nearly hanged ourselves from it. But you wouldn't. Do you not remember?
>
> ESTRAGON: You dreamt it.

VLADIMIR: Is it possible that you've forgotten already?
ESTRAGON: That's the way I am. Either I forget immediately, or I never forget. (60–1)

Or Pozzo and Lucky:

VLADIMIR: And Pozzo and Lucky, have you forgotten them too?
ESTRAGON: Pozzo and Lucky?
VLADIMIR: He's forgotten everything. (61)

Despite the play's scanty geographical references, it is clear that Vladimir and Estragon's country road cannot be mapped out or given coordinates. Estragon for one cannot have any sense of place unless he has some sense of its sheer emptiness which is reflected by his own internal void: 'there's no lack of void' (66).

Relevant to understanding Estragon's feelings conveyed by space, in particular the hatred and anger that are generated, is Bion's suggestion that geometric conceptions of space are derived originally not from a realisation of three-dimensional space, but from the realisations of emotional life, from the experience of the place where something was (Bion 1970, 10). Bion reminds us that there is an essential difference between the geometer's space and that characteristic of *mental* images. In the latter, an infinite number of lines may pass though any one point (multidimensionality) but if one attempts to represent such a visual image by points and lines on paper, there would be only a finite amount of lines. This 'limiting quality' that inheres in all representations of three-dimensional space approximates to the points, lines and space of the geometer, does not inhere in mental space until the attempt is made to represent it in verbal thought. To illustrate these notions, let us turn to the memory of the Macon country episode.

As Vladimir tries to remember grape-harvesting in the Macon country, this unleashes anger and hatred on Estragon's part. We may wonder why?

ESTRAGON: Recognize! What is there to recognize, All my lousy life I've crawled about in the mud! And you talk to me about scenery! (*Looking wildly about him.*) (61)

Estragon's anger is not just being targeted at a particular place, but perhaps at Vladimir's attempt to represent it and 'limit' it by fixing a precise mental image:

But we were there together, I could swear to it! Picking grapes for a man called ... (*he snaps his fingers*) ... can't think of the name of the

> man, at a place called ... (*snaps his fingers*) ... can't think of the name of the place, do you not remember? (62)

However precise Vladimir tries to be in his evocation of the Macon country where everything is red (ibid.), Estragon treats place and, indeed, space, as indistinguishable from things-in-themselves such as 'the mud', 'the muckheap' and 'the worms' (61), from which he has never stirred, his life being one long evacuation of waste: 'I've puked my puke of a life away here, I tell you! Here! In the Cackon country!' (62). His discourse consists, then, of violently evacuating Vladimir's conceptions of place and this in order to annihilate all sense of space. The Macon country being perceived as being identical with a bad object is destroyed and becomes a no-place, another compartment in Estragon's void: 'I didn't notice anything' [...] 'I didn't notice anything I tell you'. By erecting a barrier against the intrusion of memory into his inner state of void, Estragon seems to be intent on destroying and abandoning memory as a means of recovering time, experience and granting, thereby, coherence or even a sense to the present situation of waiting. But when the object of memory is a death-drive or death-instinct, then Estragon has no difficulty in restituting and reconstructing it as when he remembers the time he tried to drown himself in the Rhône, a memory that is evoked only to be put back to rest since 'all that's dead and buried' (53).

If remembering, then, can only be a way of dreaming – 'You dreamt it' (61) – it is therefore no better than a form of sleeping. Indeed, Estragon's sleeping and dreaming seem to assist him across the void of waiting, described by Vladimir as 'straying in the night without end of the abysmal depths ... [where] ... in an instant all will vanish and we'll be alone once more in the midst of nothingness' (81).

Sleep, unconsciously, can be a form of potential death since it interrupts time, separating day from night and above all the mother from the child. And as Grolnick reminds us, this is where dreams as a transitional object come in, since they allay the separation anxiety signalled both by sleep and later by the idea of death (Grolnick 1978, 381). They are 'stepping stones across a void' (ibid., 382). However, in Estragon's case, he sleeps in order not to wake up, floating between a unfamiliar state of sleepiness and an immemorial waking state. But in order to sleep, Estragon needs the presence of Vladimir whose lullabying in the second act, serves to allay the separation anxiety by accompanying the latter on his journey into the threatening territory of sleep. Notwithstanding, Estragon's sleeping is 'sabotaged' by one of his 'personal nightmares' (*G* 16), one that he can finally tell Vladimir in the second act, where he finds himself falling even further down into an empty pit – 'I was falling' (70).[4] Where in the first act, Estragon just needed to tell Vladimir his dream, here the latter is required to 'hold' Estragon from 'falling for ever' (Winnicott 1988, 176): *'Vladimir runs to him, puts his arms round him.* There ... there ... Didi is there ... don't be afraid ...' (*G* 70). It is Vladimir's 'holding' and 'handling' of Estragon's 'primitive agony' (Winnicott 1988, 176) that proves to be more important than it being communicated or even expressed:

> ESTRAGON: I was on top of a –
> VLADIMIR: Don't tell me! Come, we'll walk it off. (*He takes Estragon by the arm and walks him up and down until Estragon refuses to go any further.*) (*G* 70)

Such spacing between waking and dreaming is echoed by Vladimir's dream-like soliloquy towards the end of the play: 'was I sleeping, while the others suffered? Am I sleeping now? Tomorrow, when I wake, or think I do, what shall I say of today?' (90). Not unlike a visual or an invisible hallucination, the monologue roams the void in search of signs of presence, concrete memories of a testifiable past:

> That with Estragon my friend, at this place, until the fall of night, I waited for Godot? That Pozzo passed, with his carrier, and that he spoke to us? Probably. But in all that what truth will there be? (Ibid.)

Closer to a dream state, Vladimir finds himself between a timeless memory of waiting and a time with no memory, between a hallucinated present and a persecutory past. It is not a state out of which he is liable to wake: 'At me too someone is looking, of me too someone is saying, he is sleeping, he knows nothing, let him sleep on' (ibid.).

Like Vladimir, Pozzo cannot dissociate between waking and sleeping as he wonders if he is not still asleep (86). Unlike the amnesiac Estragon, Pozzo in the first act is time ridden, even time obsessed, and is terrified by the thought that time may have stopped: 'Whatever you like but not that' (36). But when he returns inexplicably blind in the second act, Pozzo, not unlike Estragon, is solely concerned with blanking out time, destroying all links with personal memory, his mental void exclusively filled with the paradigmatic death-like memory of birth:

> Have you not tormenting me with your accursed time! It's abominable! When! When! [...] they give birth astride of a grave, the light gleams an instant, then it's night once more. (89)

Waiting for Godot, then, is a play plunged in its own otherness as it mirrors it own fundamental sense of absence. This can be seen in the way the mirror relations *between* the two couples *and* between the Estragon–Vladimir couple and the boy, turn insidiously into a dark comedy of misperception and misrecognition.[5] For example, Vladimir and Estragon first become enmeshed in an identificatory relation set up by Pozzo:

> 'you are human beings none the less ... of the same species as myself [...] of the same species as Pozzo' (23) ...'Yes, Gentlemen, I cannot go for long without the society of my likes (*he puts on his glasses and looks at the two likes*), even when the likeness is an imperfect one' (24).

The likeness to Pozzo and the fact that Pozzo recognises them as 'human beings none the less' ultimately brings about a collusion of a sort between Vladimir, Estragon and Pozzo in their oppression of Lucky: 'What do you prefer? Shall we have him dance, or sing, or recite, or think, or' [...] (39). However, Vladimir and Estragon can never attribute to Pozzo and Lucky a stable fixed sense of 'they', that is 'they' really being 'they'. The suggestion made by Beckett's troubling text is that there are many 'different' Pozzos and Luckys which makes Vladimir and Estragon wonder, after the departure of the second couple, if they're 'not the same' (48) – repeated three times. Equally and predictably enough, Vladimir and Estragon remain 'unrecognised' by the other and 'unrecognisable' to others: 'and then nobody ever recognizes us' (ibid.). Whether they are eventually 'seen' or 'not seen' ultimately hardly means much – 'that means nothing' (ibid.).

Vladimir and Estragon struggle, then, to mirror themselves, to think anew their 'likeness', but the portrayal of mutual observation that comes in the moonlit scene at the end of act one enables Estragon to 'rejoin' their collective image only asymptotically, that is, never. Here Estragon remembers part of Shelley's 'Art thou pale for weariness / Of climbing heaven, and gazing on the earth', which is reduced to: 'Pale for weariness / Of climbing heaven and gazing on *the likes of us*' (52, my emphasis).

The boy's role in the overall production of a mental void merits mentioning. This can be seen by Vladimir's anxiety at first not being seen by Godot and ultimately at never having been seen by the boy, as though the actual encounter between the couple and the boy (which we can see) never really happened. Since both Vladimir and the boy are mirrored by their ambiguous relationship to Godot, they equally mirror one another, for Vladimir's discovery in both acts of Godot's non-arrival (thus the boy's arrival) coincides with nightfall, a metaphor of death and abandonment, loss and separation. Repetition however in the play does not suffice to constitute a 'memory-base' for Didi and Gogo. The boy who repeatedly comes for the 'first' time has no memory of our couple. Only his eyes, reduced to inducing a visual hallucination, may serve as a sign of reciprocal existence and a link for them and for him:

> VLADIMIR: Tell him .. (*he hesitates*) .. tell him you saw us. (*Pause.*) You did see us, didn't you?
> BOY: Yes, sir. (52)
> [...]
> VLADIMIR: Tell him .... (*he hesitates*) ... tell him you saw me and that [...] (*he hesitates*) that you saw me. (*with sudden violence.*) You're sure you saw me, you won't come and tell me tomorrow that you never saw me!' (92).

If the static image at the end of each act suggests a suspended world of memory and action, it also suggests that Godot will always be potentially 'present'. It is time now to analyse the mode and modality of such 'presence'.

Godot: a transitional object in the void[6]

If the 'real' thing is the thing that is not there – the void – this *no-thing* also demands to be mastered, to be given a content, a form, or at least calls to be 'filled in' with activity and repertory. In one sense, *Waiting for Godot* is precisely about finding ways of dealing with the void, using it, manipulating it in order to play with it. Where criticism has dwelled on the more obvious modes and forms of play and playing in *Godot*, drawing on literary and theatrical conventions (Kern 1970; Busi 1980; Cohn 1980), the approach I wish to follow here is to see the void as the prerequisite for playing and creativity. This would give 'Godot' the role of a transitional object in Estragon and Vladimir's void as they confront absence and night: 'will night never come?' (*G* 36). But before looking at the development of a transitional play space, and in particular the way thinking is played with, first, let us look at the relationship formed between Estragon, Vladimir and the absent Godot.

The structural and thematic resemblance between Beckett's imaginary Godot and Winnicott's 'transitional object', whose original hypothesis was formulated in 1951 (Winnicott 1971, 1) but first addressed in

1945 (Skelton 2006, 468), is so striking that one is attempted to read Winnicott's celebrated concept in the light of Beckett's universal imaginary figure. As in Winnicott's concept, there is equally a paradoxical tension at the heart of Beckett's theatrical aesthetic of absence. Similar to the pre-existing void, Godot, being absent, can be said to pre-exist both Vladimir and Estragon and yet, like the tree, Godot is both 'found', created, taken up by Estragon and Vladimir and used:

> ESTRAGON: You're sure it was here?
> VLADIMIR: What?
> ESTRAGON: That we were to wait.
> VLADIMIR: He said by the tree. (*They look at the tree.*) Do you see any others? (14)

By virtue of being an object of play, Godot is irreducible to any one 'reality' or 'meaning' and this probably because Beckett himself always wanted to direct attention away from Godot to the act of waiting.[7] Such irreducibility, however, is not an autonomous one nor is it a mere effect of language. Using Winnicott, I want to show that it is constituted by an undifferentiated intersubjective *playing* between Vladimir and Estragon spanning two types of 'reality' concerning Godot, namely, an inner Godot, a personal or idiosyncratic one, which would correspond to Vladimir's point of view and an outer Godot as represented by the boy. For example if Godot can be made into a transitional object, it is because he can represent very different things that need not be explained or 'resolved'.

Thus, the free associations made around Godot are never differentiated, but rather held or fused in the illusory or potential space that Godot's absence affords. This 'fusion' is generally expressed in the performance by the interplay between the multiple images of Godot. For example, Vladimir jocularly paints the picture of a business man with a family who said that he'd see, in the quiet of his home, consult his family, his friends, his agents, his correspondents, his bank account, before making a decision (18). The same male figure is imagined to have a horse (19), to be maybe Pozzo (22) and even to resemble a wicked God straight out of the Old Testament. The fact that Godot may be 'really' a 'shepherd', biblical or otherwise, who, according to the first boy, minds sheep and beats young boys (92–3), takes nothing away from the role he plays as a transitional object or figure in Estragon and Vladimir's relationship. Equally, insofar that it is definitely not the same boy who returns at the end of the second act – 'This is your first time/Yes, sir' (91) – the 'second' Mr Godot may not necessarily correspond to the first boy's Mr Godot. What we can say with a reasonable amount of confidence, is that Godot's paradoxical present-absence and absent-presence is mirrored by the boy or boys. The latter represent Godot's potential presence and his 'definitive' absence.

Through their playing, whether it is Vladimir playing with Estragon and vice versa or the couple Estragon/Vladimir playing 'with' the absent Godot, the characters stake out a 'neutral area of experience that will not be challenged' (Winnicott 1971, 14), an intermediate area which antedates and defeats any reality testing. For example, if Godot is unknown and unknowable for Vladimir and Estragon – 'a kind of acquaintance' (*G* 23) – he remains all the more unknown and unknowable to anyone outside the playing circle, such as Pozzo and Lucky: 'what happens in that case to your appointment with this ... Godet ... Godot ... Godin ... anyhow you see who I mean' (29). Not knowing who Godot 'is' seems to be more important than knowing who he 'really' is even if such a thing were possible. Estragon and Vladimir imagine that they have magically created Godot because the Godot motif is presented to them at the time of their needing it. As companions, Godot has brought them together and by resisting their desire to separate and leave, Vladimir and Estragon unwittingly remain attached to 'their' inseparable Godot, possessing him to some extent, just in the same way as he has possessed them:

> VLADIMIR: How do you mean tied?
> ESTRAGON: To your man.
> VLADIMIR: To Godot? ... Tied to Godot? What an idea! (20–1)

It follows that Godot gives 'meaning' not so much to the characters' presence as to their decision to continue waiting: 'Let's go/We can't/ Why not?/ we're waiting for Godot' (14). Without wanting to overstate the positive effect their imaginary companion has on their relationship, we may nonetheless make the cautious claim that Godot helps the couple to develop their capacity to discover and adapt to their reality, even contributing to their autonomy, despite all the mutual threats of separation and abandonment:

> ESTRAGON: I wonder if we wouldn't have been better off alone, each one for himself. (*He crosses the stage and sits down on the mound.*) We weren't made for the same road.
> [...]

VLADIMIR: We can still part, if you think it would be better
ESTRAGON: It's not worth while now. (53–4)

Arguably, everything that happens in the play is predicated to the maintenance and survival of the Estragon/Vladimir relationship. Around the Godot matrix of inseparability, with its links of separation and abandonment, Beckett seems to highlight their interdependence to such an extent that all theatrical event is secondary to this particular relationship: *they remain motionless, arms dangling, heads sunk, sagging at the knees* (19). They have both come into the play or into the world 'on [their] hands and knees' (ibid.), with no rights ('we got rid of them', ibid.). Estragon's emotional dependence on Vladimir forms a sub-plot of a sort oscillating between the fear of separation and yet the desire to abandon the other: 'I'm going [...] you'll never see me again' (71). If Estragon often projects separation as a solution to their predicament, it is nonetheless Estragon who comes 'crawling back' (59), because he doesn't know how to defend himself. Invariably Estragon's wants nothing, desires nothing and just wants Vladimir to stay with him: 'stay with me' (58). Not dissimilar to the Fort-Da game, earlier alluded to, the constant desire to separate and the subsequent undoing of that separation, is always Estragon and Vladimir's way of throwing Godot away – 'let's go' – and simultaneously retrieving him – *they do not move*:

ESTRAGON: Well, shall we go?
VLADIMIR: Yes, let's go. (*They do not move*). (54)
[...]
VLADIMIR: Well? Shall we go?
ESTRAGON: Yes, let's go. (*They do not move*). (94)

In the space of play

If Estragon and Vladimir to some extent 'create' Godot, it would be interesting to see now to what extent do they also create a potential space of play within the wider waiting zone in which they find themselves, a third area which may be said to arise *between Godot* and his dependent couple, or more precisely *between* the inner Godot and the outer Godot. First, let us take a general look at how Vladimir and Estragon develop a transitional playing space *between* them before looking at one particular playing sequence in detail, the one concerned with thinking.

Waiting is a form of playing and quickly becomes a thing in itself. It is significant that the 'we are waiting for Godot' motif or cause actually disappears or is forgotten for long stretches only to return when the playing reaches its saturation point:

> ESTRAGON: Let's pass on now to something else, do you mind?
> VLADIMIR: I was just going to suggest it.
> ESTRAGON: But to what?
> VLADIMIR: Ah! *Silence. ...*
> ESTRAGON: And now?
> POZZO: Help!
> ESTRAGON: Let's go.
> VLADIMIR: We can't [etc.] (84)

Playing is another way for Vladimir and Estragon to suspend the Godot motif and thereby free themselves from the strain of relating inner to outer, absence to presence, dream to reality. For example, they avail of anything they find on the empty road/stage – the tree, their boots, hats, cord, carrot, radish, the contents of their pockets – not only to pass the time, but also to master the differences between the Godot world and the non-Godot world, that is to say, their subjective perception of Godot and the objective reality of the same absent figure. Everything is drafted in to allay the separation anxiety by passing time and filling in the threatening space, the improvised content giving form to the formlessness, and a sense of control and balance: 'let's just do the tree, for the balance' (76).[8]

If the major theatrical sequences that structure the play lend themselves to be read as a series of play-objects or separate playing moments enabling the couple to occupy and inhabit their void, it is because they are ends in themselves, self-contained and self-containing episodes, with a sense of closure being operated on every gesture and movement: the bible-reading discussion (12–13), the sleeping scenes (15–16, 70), Lucky's dance and 'think' (40, 42–5), the 'terrible to have thought' sequence (64–5), the exchange of hats (71–2), Vladimir and Estragon's playing at Pozzo and Lucky (72–3), the trade of insults (75), Vladimir's imitation of the tree (76), the 'movements', 'elevations', 'relaxations', 'elongations' (ibid.). For example, on Pozzo and Lucky's departure from the stage in the first act, Vladimir opines: 'That passed the time', only for Estragon to remind him that 'it would have passed in any case', but, as Vladimir reminds his friend, 'not so rapidly' (48). Similarly, the long exchange about 'thinking' finishes up with: 'that wasn't such a bad canter' (65). (This is a sequence I shall return to later.)

It is precisely because there is nothing that Vladimir and Estragon can 'really' do – 'there's nothing we can do' (68) – that their reality can be constantly transformed and reinvented by their limitless playing. In the second act putting on a pair of shoes fills them with their own sense of child-like omnipotence for it would be 'a relaxation/a recreation/a relaxation':

VLADIMIR: What about trying them?
ESTRAGON: I've tried everything.
VLADIMIR: No, I mean the boots
ESTRAGON: Would that be a good thing?
VLADIMIR: It'd pass the time. (69)

Playing with the shoes provides them with a life-line as it gives them the impression that they exist – 'Yes, yes, we're magicians' (ibid.). It is perhaps only in the most insignificant and unremarkable of human activities that Valdimir and Estragon can actually find a way of going on being: 'this is becoming really insignificant/Not enough' (68).

The danger of ever thinking (again)

One of the subtler points made by Estragon and Vladimir's playing is not so much that their experience may defy expression and thought, but that thought defies itself and is more to be dreaded than desired. To get a sense of the paradoxality that underpins the characters' playing and to see how thinking is played with, let us look at the 'thinking' sequence in detail. (This will provide a useful link with our next section which is devoted to the question of thought and thinking.)

The sequence follows a circular pattern of proposition, negation and contradiction. As often with Beckett, the 'thinking' sequence tends to search for a balancing effect, even a neutralising one, between, on one hand, the desire to exclude and evacuate thinking and on the other, the need to acknowledge and invoke thinking. Not unlike the paradoxically absent yet present Godot, thinking is wished absent, but found to be 'present'. For example, our couple begin the sequence by 'opening up' and performing all sorts of alternatives, where speaking becomes a weapon against thinking and falling silent:

VLADIMIR: You're right, we're inexhaustible.
ESTRAGON: It's so we won't think.
VLADIMIR: We have that excuse.

ESTRAGON: It's so we won't hear.
VLADIMIR: We have our reasons. (62)

However, far from excluding or rejecting thinking, Vladimir and Estragon make thinking paradoxically possible despite its inherent impossibility. Yet such a possibility is just as quickly negated:

VLADIMIR: When you seek you hear. [...] That prevents you from thinking.
ESTRAGON: You think all the same.
VLADIMIR: No, no, impossible. (64)

Just when Vladimir and Estragon begin to feel 'safe' from the threat and challenge of thinking – 'we're in no danger of ever thinking any more' (ibid.) – their dreaded object is taken up again and 'inspected' since, despite everything, 'thinking is not the worse' (ibid.).

When articulated with the past, thinking is mysteriously evoked as being synonymous with death, corpses, skeletons and charnel-houses. Vladimir's tragic reminder – 'what is terrible is to *have* thought' (ibid., Beckett's emphasis) – is more than just his regretting having ever been endowed with mental faculties in the past (emphasis being on *to have*), which Estragon typically denies ('Did that ever happen to us', ibid.). Vladimir seems to be suggesting that to think is to notice what has died or what remains dead in the mind. The death imagery: 'we must have thought a little/At the very beginning. A charnel house! A charnel house!' (ibid.), does suggest a mortified mind with its death-like contents: 'where are all these corpses from?/these skeletons' (ibid.). Is Vladimir evoking the death of an embryonic mind ('the very beginning'), which would be first that of the mother and then that of the infant, his own thinking apparatus being no more than a glorified mental vault or tomb? If he is, it provides us with yet another variation on Beckett's 'death in birth' trope which we have already seen in Malone and which we find later in both Pozzo and Vladimir's monologues: 'they give birth astride of a grave' (89) [...] 'astride of a grave and a difficult birth' (90). The thinking canter ends, then, with the reluctant recognition that to be still saddled with a mind constitutes a necessary evil of a sort: it's not the worst to have thought even if they 'could have done without it' (65).

Thinking, however, is more than a theme or an object in Vladimir and Estragon's play zone, it may even said to constitute one of their weapons used to prolong their waiting and to go on being. Waiting for

Godot is, after all, waiting to be able to recognise and accept Godot's absence, that is, Estragon and Vladimir's 'Godot', someone who is never forgotten nor ever mourned. It is time, then, to consider more fully the mental dimension to the Godot/Estragon/Vladimir play-space.

To think or not to think Godot?

What does it mean to think in *Waiting for Godot*?

Thinking can only take place in the necessary absence of the other, which inevitably implies that thinking means thinking the thinking breast that Godot is and, consequently, thinking absence. But looking more closely at this question, one cannot but wonder if there is any coherent internal world in *Waiting for Godot* that could be said to be the product of thought operating on the perception of emotional experiences? (Meltzer 1978, 92) Hardly, one is inclined to answer, but a closer look at the play's mental dynamics might yield unsuspected proof of a thinking experience that might be best qualified as oscillating between being able and unable to think. Our earlier analysis of the thinking sequence already points to this.

Thinking, it will be remembered, begins in infancy when the infant can sufficiently tolerate the frustration of the mother's absence who is able to contain the infant's normal or realistic projections of dread (Skelton 2006, 58). Thinking for Bion has to be called into existence to cope with thoughts thus differing from any theory of thought as a product of thinking. It is modelled on the digestive system since the function of all thought for Bion is to digest emotional experience. The mental apparatus needs truth as the body requires food. Bion limits his concept of a thought to the bringing into contact of a pre-conception with a realisation that approximates to it. The conception, for Bion, is initiated by the conjunction of a pre-conception (or empty *a priori* thoughts) with a realisation (or experience.) It follows then that conceptions 'will be expected to be constantly conjoined with an emotional experience of satisfaction' (Bion 1967, 111). Adversely, and what is particularly pertinent for our play, 'if the capacity for toleration of frustration is inadequate, the bad internal no-breast [...] confronts the psyche with the need to decide between evasion of frustration or it its modification':

> What should be a thought, a product of the juxtaposition of pre-conception and negative realization, becomes a bad object, indistinguishable from a thing-in-itself, fit only for evacuation [...] The crux

> lies in the decision between modification or evasion of frustration. (Ibid., 112)

On the other hand, if the capacity for frustration is sufficient the 'no-breast' inside becomes a thought and an apparatus for 'thinking' develops. From this, Bion postulates mental space as a 'thing-in-itself' that is unknowable but which can be represented by thoughts. Memory and desire are thus seen as forces which impair the process of thought.

Thinking is one of the main 'objects' under attack in Beckett's art of absence. As we have already seen in our analysis of the trilogy and of playing in *Godot*, Beckett's characters dread, fear and ultimately hate thinking where 'thoughts' become objects of sadistic violence and destruction. However, in *Godot*, even if thinking is something terrible, catastrophic and devastating, particularly in the shape and form of Lucky's 'think', Beckett's play can be seen to 'think', or, at least, it aspires to a minimum of self-reflexivity against the beckoning threat of self-extinction and nothingness. There are two main mental developments in the play I wish to examine here: the first is the development of thoughts and thinking in the Vladimir–Estragon relationship. These require an apparatus to cope with them. The second development is that of the apparatus itself which I tentatively call 'thinking Godot', a synonym for 'waiting for Godot'. First we shall compare and contrast the play's two main couples in terms of their capacity for reverie, thought and patience.

In the centre of the play's thinking space is the Vladimir–Estragon relationship, one that is characterised by Estragon's mental helplessness and emotional dependence on Vladimir, which, in turn, reflects the couple's mental helplessness and dependence on Godot. Such a relationship is more than a question of emotional support or protection; it is primary for thinking insofar that Vladimir and Estragon derive from their experience thoughts that may be used for thinking. While Godot may not be 'available' for satisfaction, meaning here to 'save' Estragon and Vladimir, the question that really matters is how do our two characters tolerate such a state of affairs and gradually symbolise it? This is where one may situate Vladimir's 'alpha-function', his maternal 'service' to Estragon since the former clearly espouses an empathetic and communicative role in their dyad.

Symbolically, it is hardly a coincidence that it is the maternal Vladimir who 'feeds' the violently hungry Estragon – (*violently*). 'I'm hungry' (21). As Jean-Michel Rabaté reminds us, 'if the relation between the infant and the mother is lacking in truth, the result is a premature weaning or starvation: this internal object starves its host of all understanding that is made available' (Rabaté 1996, 27). If Estragon is hungry for 'truth' about Godot, it is hardly surprising then that Vladimir's food (a miserable carrot) is aggressively rejected by Estragon as 'muck': 'the more you eat the worse it gets ... I get used to the muck as I go along' (*G* 21). In the second act the nourishing 'breast', in the sinister form and function of a black radish, is turned down and returned to Vladimir: (*Estragon gives it back*) (68).

On the emotional front, it is Vladimir who reminds Estragon of his dependency on him: 'all these years [...] but for me', Estragon 'would be nothing more than a little heap of bones at the present minute' (9). He resorts to memory – 'we were presentable in those days' (10) – to satisfy his desire, and Estragon's desire, for security evoking thereby the resistance-proliferating elements in Estragon. In other words, Vladimir stimulates Gogo's desires and memories ('the tree, look at the tree', 60) and his understanding, (taken in the everyday sense).[9] For example, Estragon's wish to immediately evacuate the waiting experience by destroying the self – 'let's hang ourselves immediately' (17) – is considerably modified to wishing to do nothing: 'don't let's do anything. It's safer' (18). This is met by Vladimir's decision to tolerate the frustration rather than to evade it: it is he who creates thoughts that are necessary for the manipulation in a process to be called thinking and eventuating in waiting: 'let's *wait* and see what he says' [...] 'let's *wait* till we know exactly how we stand' (18, my emphasis). Equally it is Vladimir who reminds his partner that there's 'nothing' they can 'do' (68). Even if they are happy, they still have to wait for Godot: 'What do we do now, now that we are happy?' [...] (60) 'Wait for Godot' (63). Notwithstanding, even if Estragon's split-off 'unmentalised' elements of experience – anxieties, visions, nightmares – are not always contained, de-toxified and returned to him by Vladimir in a modified form – 'I dreamt that/ DON'T TELL ME' (16, Beckett's emphasis) – waiting for Godot becomes nonetheless increasingly bearable for Gogo:

> POZZO: What is he waiting for?
> VLADIMIR: What are you waiting for?
> ESTRAGON: I'm waiting for Godot. (*Silence.*) (87)

Against Estragon's limited capacity to tolerate the frustrating and increasingly threatening situation, and his wish to expel the 'no-Godot' – 'let's go' – Vladimir transforms such impulses by gradually inculcating a state of mind, if not of security, at least of patience: 'we have kept our appointment, and that's an end to that. We are not saints, but we have kept our appointment' (80).

The Godot link functions, then, like a mental membrane, a barrier which structures the mental phenomena of the play, turning the couple's emotions into 'thoughts', allowing them to defer action and modify frustration rather than evade it. It is precisely such a structural and structuring membrane that is cruelly missing in the mental universe of the play's other couple. But first, let's turn to a revealing exchange between Vladimir and Pozzo concerning the identity of Godot.

Pozzo and Vladimir's discussion about who Godot is and how they came about to know Godot is significant. If Godot can be thought by Vladimir and eventually by Estragon, but not known, in the case of Pozzo the Godot membrane operates in reverse throwing out a beta screen, a Un-knowing (minus K or –K), a psychic blindness which prevents such differentiation:

> POZZO: Who is Godot?
> ESTRAGON: Godot?
> [...]
> POZZO: Who is he?
> VLADIMIR: Oh, he's a ... he's a kind of acquaintance.
> ESTRAGON: Nothing of the kind, we hardly know him.
> VLADIMIR: True ... we don't know him very well ... but all the same (23)
> [....]
> POZZO: What happens in that case to your appointment with this ... Godet Godot ... Godin ... anyhow you see who I mean, who has your future in his hands ... (*pause*) at least your immediate future. (29)

The discussion revolving around Godot – knowing (K) or un-knowing (–K) – is not so much about the identity of an unknown person ('a kind of acquaintance'), but rather about what is unknown about the thought of a Godot or a Godot idea ('we don't know him very well'). The figure of Godot and the relations constituted through and by it, do not constitute a finality or any truth. Even if Godot holds Vladimir and Estragon's future 'in his hands', the couple's K link is nonetheless prospective and turned towards the future. On the contrary, Pozzo's un-knowing link (–K) is synonymous with what has been lost. But what has Pozzo lost?

The Pozzo–Lucky dyad with its cruel physical bondage has connotations of a destroyed mental bond, not unlike a container-contained relationship that is clearly disjoined or denuded of all emotion and reduced to an inanimate object. The mental link or bond between the two men may be seen in the light of their reciprocal dependency as thinkers. Pozzo, who is not '*particularly* human' (29, my emphasis), poses as a pseudo-thought master always searching for effects, as he does after his rhetorical set-piece on the fall of night (37–8) – 'how did you find me?' (38). The unemotional Pozzo 'thinks' without any real thoughts or feelings that might generate thought. For example, on realising that Lucky has stopped crying, Pozzo continues with his empty abstractions about the tears and laughs of the world (33). Yet for all that, Pozzo cannot quite divest himself mentally or physically of Lucky, his delirious tragic other: 'Guess who taught me all these beautiful things (*Pause. Pointing to Lucky.*) My Lucky! [...] But for him all my *thoughts*, all my *feelings*, would have been of common things' (ibid. my emphasis). His plan to get rid of Lucky can be read as Pozzo's violent method of coping with Lucky's 'thoughts' or 'thinking'. But before such menacing thinking can be effectively expelled or evacuated from Pozzo's mind, it has to be endured by Pozzo himself. This must be one of the subtlest ironies in the play's mental dynamics. First Beckett has Pozzo suffer at the very memory of Lucky's ways of thinking in the past, Pozzo's blanked memory being paradoxically capable of recalling the way Lucky had persecuted him:

> I can't bear it ... any longer ... The way he goes on ... you've no idea ... it's terrible ... He must go ... (*he waves his hands*) ... I'm going mad ... (34)

It is as if Pozzo is unable to be 'responsible' for Lucky's radical otherness, above all his thinking which has become increasingly disturbing: 'He even used to think very prettily once, I could listen to him for hours. Now ... (*he shudders*). So much the worse for me' (39).

While Lucky may have once been Pozzo's thinking master, now on stage we discover someone who has become a slave to knowledge, someone who is clearly no longer in 'control' of his 'thoughts', his famous 'think' coming *to* us or *at* us, or even *out* to us – 'for reasons unknown' – as a violent evacuation of *unthought* thought. It is as if Lucky's raw materials of thoughts are indigestible for his mental apparatus. Consequently they cannot be stored as memory, but only as an accumulation of nonsensical or fantastical facts such as 'the public works of Puncher and Wattmann' (42), 'the labours unfinished of Testew and Cunard' (43), 'the labours of Fartov and Belcher', or more realistically, 'the strides of physical culture' (ibid.). On closer inspection, Lucky's 'think' may be seen to be a farcical attempt at thinking not so much the tragic decline of humanity, where 'man' is seen 'to waste and pine waste and pine' (43), as the existence of infinity or a more cosmic sense of void. This is where Bion's notion of 'thoughts without a thinker' might be a useful pointer. The former compares thinking with the concept of infinity and, quoting Milton, writes:

> Thoughts exist without a thinker. The idea of infinitude is prior to any idea of the finite. The finite is 'won from the dark and formless infinite'. Restating this more concretely the human personality is aware of infinity, the 'oceanic feeling'. It becomes aware of limitation, presumably through physical and mental experience of itself and the sense of frustration [...] the thoughts which have no thinker acquire or are acquired by a thinker. (Bion 1967, 165; also qtd in Rabaté 1996, 27)

Lucky's 'think' seems to be dangerously aware of infinity, with its 'oceanic feeling' inexorably drifting towards images of a mineral universe 'in the great cold' where the earth is no more an 'abode of stones in the great deeps' (*G* 44). The monologue perhaps could be read as a yearning for the mineral kingdom, a yearning to return, not to the 'recent' traumatic rubble of war-time Saint-Lô or to the ancient stone walls of Connemara with their 'skull' – 'on the skull the skull the skull the skull in Connemara' (ibid.) – but to the quiescence of the inorganic world or the ideal of a mineral near-stasis: 'the stones ... so calm ...' (45). (The end of repetition within Freudian mythology – *Beyond the Pleasure Principle* – is the mineral state of death.) As James Knowlson tells us, Beckett's early fascination with the mineral, with things dying and decaying, with petrifaction, with stone and with bone was a tacit acknowledgment of Freud's view that human beings have a prebirth nostalgia to return to the mineral state (Knowlson 1996, 29).[10] However, it must also be remembered that Lucky's thought ends 'unfinished' (ibid.), as though there is more to come and more to be won from 'the great deeps' of his formless mind.

Significantly, Beckett gets us to experience Lucky's 'think' simultaneously as a breaking down of Pozzo's mind. The stage directions for Lucky's tirade include: '*Pozzo's sufferings increase* [...] *Pozzo more and more agitated and groaning* [...] *Pozzo jumps up, pulls on the rope*' (42). Where Lucky's body at least attracts comments from his onlookers – 'A running sore', 'goitre' (25, 26) – his 'think' provokes a furious struggle to seize his hat – his thinking apparatus – Pozzo finally mercilessly crushing

Lucky's hat with: 'there's an end to his thinking' (45). But that's not quite the end of Lucky's 'very fine hat' (71). It is 'restored' for playing purposes in the second act (71–2) with Vladmir actually wearing it for the 'play within the play' sequence when he impersonates Lucky. This time the impersonated 'think' – thinking 'like' the other – is reduced to a sinister silence:

> VLADIMIR: Tell me to think.
> ESTRAGON: What?
> VLADIMIR: Say, Think, pig!
> ESTRAGON: Think, pig! *Silence.*
> VLADIMIR: I can't. (73)

Godot's mental membrane

There is a necessary tautology in saying that continuing to wait for Godot signifies that Vladimir and Estragon are 'capable' of tolerating absence which is the very prerequisite for the elaboration of the thought 'we are waiting for Godot'. Yet it remains to be seen how the formation of the Godot mental membrane or barrier proceeds.

Godot is a drama about knowing and not knowing Godot, of understanding (rather than gratifying) the emotional experiences that impinge upon it: 'and if he doesn't come?/We'll come back tomorrow/And then the day after tomorrow/Possible' (14). Unlike Pozzo and Lucky, Vladimir and Estragon have at least an appointment, however unreliable, however unlikely it may be. The appointment with Godot serves as the fundamental problem to be solved, the symptom needing to be understood, as it were: how to transform the unknowable Godot – Bion's O – into thinking?

The appointment is the play's sole building block, the primordial empty thought or innate preconception that conditions the play and determines the structural interaction between Vladimir and Estragon. Such a thought can be conjugated as follows: that there is a Godot who 'said' that Estragon and Vladimir were to wait for him by the tree – 'he said by the tree' (14). If he comes Estragon and Vladimir will be 'saved'. The *a priori* thought also includes its negation or mode of denial. Vladimir tells Estragon that Godot didn't say for sure he'd come (ibid.). His time of arrival is equally fraught with doubt and uncertainty: 'he said Saturday. (*Pause.*) I think' (15). We have already within the structure of the empty 'Godot thought', the sense of a lack between wish and fulfilment, a potential appointment and its inscribed negative realisation.

To correlate from this, 'waiting for Godot' becomes synonymous with 'thinking about a possible or the possibility of Godot'. In any event, the Godot thought serves to transform the couple's experience into thoughts which can be used for thinking: they are waiting for Godot because they are attached to Godot and vice versa. 'Tied to Godot? What an idea!'

Against such inherent expectations and pre-conceptions of Godot, Beckett, as to be expected, leaves a trail of false conceptions of Godot, a multiplicity of illusory Godots that serve to temporally fill the void of Vladimir and Estragon's mental space. In other terms, Vladimir and Estragon, on imagining Godot, both evade the frustration of absence by hallucinating Godot or using projective identification. Such occurrences include:

> I thought it was he. Who? Godot (19)
> You're not Mr Godot, sir? (22)
> Who is he?
> Oh, he's a kind of acquaintance.
> Nothing of the kind, we hardly know him [...]
> Personally I wouldn't even know him if I saw him (23)
> It's Godot, we're saved (73)
> At last! Reinforcements at last !
> Is it Godot? [...]
> We are no longer alone, waiting for the night, waiting for Godot [...]
> Now it's over. It's already tomorrow. (77)

To such Godot 'conceptions', one may also add the notion of the lie, Godot being a lie in the 'first place'. Significantly, the first boy (the brother of the second boy?) is accused by Estragon of lying: 'that's all a pack of lies. (*Shaking the boy by the arm.*) Tell us the truth?/(*trembling*). But it is the truth, sir!'(50). Not unlike the Youdi outfit of agents and messengers in *Molloy*, the boy (and his brother?) could conceivably represent a rival organisation for creating lies that can only be used for creating delusions and bizarre objects concerning the whereabouts and fundamental identity of Mr Godot. Of course, whether true or false, there is no Godot to meet or to mate with Vladimir and Estragon's 'Godot conceptions', which, as we have seen, are partly fuelled by the boy's account of Mr Godot on whom Vladimir projects a figure of paternal persecution. If they abandon him: 'he'd punish us' (93). In terms of the play's mental economy of thinking, the boy's arrival formally completes the empty Godot thought by elaborating its fundamental lack. Godot can now be 'experienced' or intuited as an absent Godot, a 'no-Godot' inside. While there is some suspense with regard to the boy's message in the first act, it is clear that by the end of the second act, Vladimir intuitively 'knows' the message, the boy's role merely consisting of confirming Vladimir's conception of absence:

> VLADIMIR: You have a message from Mr. Godot.
> BOY: Yes, sir.
> VLADIMIR: He won't come this evening.
> BOY: No, sir.
> VLADIMIR: But he'll come tomorrow.
> BOY: Yes, sir.
> VLADIMIR: Without fail.
> BOY: Yes, sir. (91)

'In all that what truth will there be?'

Waiting for Godot, then, is a play about a conflict between thought and the impulse to action, where the waiting experience is *not* that of the thing-in-itself, but an abstraction and a representation of it (Meltzer 1978, 49). Simply put, thinking Godot is *like* waiting for Godot. For example, Vladimir grapples with representing the experience of waiting for Godot, which amounts to thinking the waiting experience, thinking the moment: 'waiting for the night, waiting for Godot, waiting for ... waiting' (*G* 77). Such attention to the moment is requisite to its very observation and perception (Meltzer 102), hence Vladimir's repeated insistence towards the end of the play on thinking the moment, without memory or desire – 'what are we doing here *that* is the question' (80, Beckett's emphasis). While *Waiting for Godot* takes occasional flights of fancy into an hypothetical future:

> *we'll* come back tomorrow (14) [...]
> Then *we'll* go together [...]
> *We'll* go to the Pyrenees.
> Wherever you like. (81 my emphasis)

it is a play essentially concerned with 'understanding' the present, or even intuiting the present. I am picking up here on what Bion says about the importance of the present in the psychoanalytic experience and the relevance of intuition.

Beckett's former analyst reminds us that psychoanalysis is not primarily concerned with what is sensorial, nor what had happened or what will happen, but with what is happening now; memory, desire and understanding hindering the intuition of the evolution of the non-sensorial psychical reality (Skelton 2006, 253 and 306). In this particular context, intuition means 'the direct and immediate vision or understanding of a reality or a truth, with no intermediate elements' (Skelton 253). As already alluded to in our analysis of Worm in *The Unnamable*, Bion uses the term 'intuit' as a parallel in the psychoanalyst's domain, to the physician's use of 'see', 'touch', 'smell' and 'hear'. This is related with the idea that the realisations of psychical reality cannot be touched, smelled or seen (Skelton 253). We are back again to Bion's use of Keatsian negative capability 'as a tool to investigate the utterly non-sensual world of the psychoanalytic experience' (Meltzer 1978, 99). 'By remaining without memory, without desire and without understanding', the analyst allows and aids 'the intuition of the dream-like psychical reality in evolution' (Skelton 306) or, in other words, 'to intuit an experience of "at-one-ment" with the analysand' (59).

We may conclude by saying that *Waiting for Godot* oscillates between seeking to understand and not being able to understand. Vladimir's monologues clearly embrace a desire to understand and even to remember what has been 'understood', but the most Vladimir can manage is to remain firmly in a state of uncertainty and lack of knowledge, for there is no psychic activity to discriminate between true and false, truth and lies, understanding and mis-understanding, a Godot or a no-Godot: 'Tomorrow when I wake, or think I do, what shall I say of today? ... But in all that what truth will there be?' (90). While Vladimir may admit the possibility of meaninglessness, he significantly has the intuition that there might be someone else (other than the sleeping Estragon) present looking at him, saying that 'he knows nothing' (91). Vladimir's reverie over the sleeping Estragon is receptive to another's reverie, who will think the same thoughts as Vladimir: that he also knows nothing, etc. It is as if Vladimir returns his fear to an absent Other, not necessarily Godot, but possibly Godot. Yet for all that, Vladimir and Estragon inexplicably wait on and stay on. Terminating their lives or abandoning their wait would have been hypothetically a way of attacking the growth of the 'Godot thought' that their waiting had gone into creating. Instead, the play ends by Vladimir and Estragon 'meeting' the 'new' thought of Godot's absence, the thought itself being the meeting of Vladimir and Estragon's 'Godot's pre-conceptions' of 'presence' and their negative realisation of these. The last static image makes us wonder if they have found sufficient psychic 'faith' required not to drop Godot and to return the next day to wait again,[11] as if they are intuiting an experience of 'at-one-ment' (Skelton 37) with Godot, that is, recognising and feeling that which cannot be known, a seeing 'into' the void. This raises the thorny question as to whether they 'feel' any mental pain concerning the 'truth' about Godot – that is to say, the continual absence of a figure that may stand in for friendship, love, or any other form of emotional dependence.

Perhaps the most reasonable thing to say about the way the play ends, is that we cannot know anything *about* this moment of the unknown. Insofar that Vladimir and Estragon may be said to be intuiting their unknown and the unknowable Godot, it is also at this moment that Vladimir and Estragon are at their most unknowable, their long silence being the last refuge of the unspeakable and the unspoken, the unthinkable and the unthought.

It now remains to see the relevance of such a reading for assessing the play in performance, namely Beckett's own production of *Waiting for Godot* in 1975. In what way does the theatrical performance of the void communicate differently from its written text?

7
Restyling the Ineffable Void

Godot in Berlin

In 1975 Samuel Beckett accepted the invitation by the Schiller-Theater in Berlin to stage his own production of his classic play *Waiting for Godot*.[1] Although this was not *Godot's* first time in Berlin, it was the first time Beckett assumed the full responsibility for his play which he directed in German. If French was Beckett's second literary language, then German must be ranked as the language he privileged for directing his work. After assisting with Deryk Mendel's 1965 German première of *Warten auf Godot* in Berlin, between 1967 and 1978, the Irish dramatist directed no fewer than seven of his stage plays in German, all in Berlin: *Endspiel* (1967), *Das letzte Band* (1969), *Glückliche Tage* (1971), *Warten auf Godot* (1975), *Damals* (1976), *Tritte* (1976) and *Spiel* (1978), *Warten auf Godot* marking the peak of Beckett's directing career in terms of both audience and critical reception (Garforth 1996, 171). As previously mentioned, Beckett had a life-long fascination with Germany and German, as testified by the unknown diaries of 1936–37, unearthed by James Knowlson, an influence that stretches back to the 'German comedy', *From Fair to Middling Women* (Pilling 1997, 62) and culminating in one of the later works, the mystical *Nacht und Träume* (1983), a piece greatly influenced by Schubert.

The purpose of this chapter is to see how the Berlin performance and Beckett's directing practice, at large, interact with the standard written text of the earlier *Godot*.[2] Our concern is not with the play as a whole, nor the performance as a whole – such an undertaking runs the risk of lacking any focus – but with those critical issues that have guided our study of the written text up to now, namely, the representation of the void and the role of thinking. If the void is something that is both feared yet desired, it remains to be seen how such a void 'performs' on stage and how Beckett's directing of the play reflects or, as the case might be, deflects, such psychic dynamics. In other words, we need to be able to account for the undoubted differences between performance and text and to see to what extent our reading of the staging of *Godot* may actually reshape and redefine our 'earlier' understanding of the void/thinking issues. If Beckett's directing can be said to be a way of engaging a dialogue with himself and his writing, equally our reading of the performance of *Godot* may also be seen to enter into a critical dialogue and perhaps a dialectical relation with our reading of the written text. But first some simplifying assumptions must be made.

The Berlin *Godot* belongs to a performance-orientated practice, which breaks considerably with Roger Blin's earlier tragi-comic conception of the first *Godot* and any residual expressionism. However, the production notebooks that Beckett used in Berlin cannot be simplified or thematically broken down to one overriding issue. That would be reductive. As James Knowlson reminds us, Beckett composed his notes 'with the practical aim of realizing the play on stage rather than with producing texts for public consumption' (*TN* xii–xiii). Directing the Berlin *Godot* literally necessitated many hundreds of changes and revisions, the end result being a revised text which may be regarded as a 'new version of *Godot*, shorter, tighter in structure, and visualized much more clearly in theatrical terms' (ibid., xii). Another commentator, McMillan, reports that Beckett, after breaking the main action of the play down into eleven sections in the *Regiebuch*, into another notebook he broke the action down further into 109 units which 'might be called 109 ways of waiting' for Godot (McMillan 91). However, all commentators agree that Beckett's basic concern was to give his play shape and pattern. Indeed, the general impressions and effects of Beckett's *Godot* is one of a graceful balletic play, with heightened moments of stillness and silence. Knowlson, for one, likens the directions set out in the Schiller notebook to 'a choreography performed to the "music" of the text' (*TN* xii).

It is my contention that such a general theatrical aesthetic of shape and effect – 'the balletic choreography' (ibid. xviii), does throw light on the play's major concern with representing absence and emptiness. More specifically, Beckett's theatricalisation of space, his radical dramatisation of place as unknowable and the importance of visualisation for Beckett, concretely confirm and reinforce the notion of the stage as mental space, an idea already explored in the previous chapter. My general hypothesis is that the theatrical void is performed as both place *and* passage, an inter-spacing between self and other, stage and off-stage where the object of the playing is to come to terms with the unknown and the unknowable. *Godot*'s opaque mental space or state is, however, a playful one, in that it may be seen as oscillating between the threat of engulfment or annihilation and the dream of succoured quiescence. My conclusion is to hint at a theatrical sublime of the void, a notion already alluded to in our discussion of the negative. But first let us look at the broader context.

All white in the whiteness

In revisiting his play, Beckett virtually revised it. Such 'revisionism' crystallises developments and changes in Beckett's dramatic practice going back to the early sixties, which heralded in what Stanley Gontarski calls in relation to *Play* the 'late style' (1997, 87). Gontarski argues that Beckett's experience of staging his own work had a double effect of altering his writing of new plays and offering him the opportunity to 'rethink, re-write, and finally re-create previously published work' (ibid.). Such a 'revisionist impulse' is no more than an instance of Beckett's 'creative process':

> From *Play* onward Beckett's stage images would grow increasingly de-humanized, reified and metonymic, featuring dismembered or incorporeal creatures. It became a theater finally static and undramatic in any traditional sense. It is a theater of body parts and ghosts, a theater striving for transparency rather than solidity. And the playing space is always delimited, ritualized, circumscribed, framed. (93)

But placed in the wider context of Beckett's general writing practice, the Berlin *Godot* is very much a 1970s text. In directing *Warten auf Godot*, Beckett subjects it to the scrutiny of a writer whom by the mid-seventies was quite immersed in what one could loosely call an aesthetics of blankness where space prevails over linear temporality, relationships a matter of horizontals and not of hierarchies. It is very much a world at the limits of the imaginable where white bodies lie in semicircles, emotions, if any, reduced to geometric figures in mathematical space (Ross 1997, 267–76). If the Berlin *Godot* is about silence and stillness, equally the shorter fiction and dramaticules are haunted by lifeless muteness, shapes and shadows, abstract diagrams that fix the neutrals, a whiteness devoured by whiteness:

> All white all known white planes shining white ping murmur only just almost never one second light time that much memory almost never. Bare white body fixed one yard ping fixed elsewhere white

> on white invisible heart breath no sound [...] white planes no trace shining white one only shining white infinite but that known not. (*PI* 150 and 151)

We have more a sense of architecture than 'writing'.

Intertextually, the German *Godot* may be said to unwittingly form a 'Ghost' companion with two plays written around the same time, *Footfalls* and *That Time*, which are equally concerned with void and ghostliness, imaginings of a sort. For example, one cannot overlook the closer connections between Estragon's stone, his mineral abode, which Beckett preferred over the original mound, and the childhood memory in *That Time* (*TT*), written in 1974: 'On the stone together in the sun on the stone at the edge of the little wood (228) ... you too still on the stone in a daze ... (229) ... all day long on a stone among the nettles' (ibid.).

If one were to gather the fragmented memories (recounted by three different voices) of the stone into one general childhood memory of stone – the gravestone of childhood – one could suggest that *That Time* develops the sense of an irreducible and unchangeable solitude and solipsism, the stone serving as a permanent locus, a metaphor and a metonymy of such a state of solitariness: 'the child on the stone among the nettles where none ever came' [...] 'with your picture-book':

> or by the window in the dark harking to the owl not a thought in your head till hard to believe harder and harder to believe you ever told anyone you loved them or anyone you till just one of those things you kept making up to keep the *void* out just another of those old tales to keep the *void* from pouring in on top of you the shroud. (230, my emphasis)

Unlike Estragon's 'universal' stone, the childhood stone in *That Time* is paradoxically ordinary and strange. As Knowlson acknowledges, at least it enjoys 'an Impressionist landscape of sunlight, blue sky "and wheat turning yellow"' even 'if the geographical is less important than the feelings of confusion, solitude, desolation and death that flood in' (Knowlson 1996, 601), and, I would add, the feelings of void.

Absence and ghostliness are very much the concern of *Footfalls* – the 'pacing play' (ibid., 614) – which, according to its author, should be played 'like one ghost speaking to another' (qtd in Pountney 1988, 67), the ghosts being May and her mother. As previously alluded to, May was 'Beckett's own poignant recreation of the girl who had never really been born, isolated and permanently absent, distant and totally encapsulated within herself' (Knowlson 1996, 616). In the same way that Beckett formally instills silence and darkness and mystery into *Godot*, each of the four sections of *Footfalls* is separated by a blackout and silence. Curiously the diagrams in the first manuscript of the play resemble those in Beckett's Schiller notebook in terms of precisions and detail. A similar sense of mental and physical restlessness and issueless repetition are to be found in *Footfalls* where May will never have done 'revolving it all ... in your poor mind' (*CSPa* 243). The very repetition of these words at the end of each section 'suggest an infinite cycle', even a 'spiralling into endlessness', writes Rosemary Pountney (67). Like the five characters who witness Godot's absence on stage, *Footfalls* is predicated to glimpsing absence albeit in the form of the ghost of May at Evensong even if Amy is adamant that she has 'observed nothing': 'For I observed *nothing* of any kind, strange or otherwise. I saw *nothing*, heard *nothing*, of any kind. I was not there' (*CSPa*, 243, my emphasis).

As Jean-Michel Rabaté remarks in his analysis of Beckettian ghostliness, the difference between a play like *Eh Joe*, written a decade earlier, where Joe is forced to imagine the ghost of the woman who had committed suicide, and the plays of the mid-seventies such as *That Time*, *Footfalls* (1975), *Ghost Trio* (1975), *... but the clouds* (1976) (and I would add Beckett's 1975 *Godot*), is that the latter actively seek out their ghosts, almost acquiring a mystical resonance (Rabaté, 1996, 37). While *Godot* is not literally about apparitions, it is about what 'happens' when nothing happens, not unlike the mysterious female figure in *... but the clouds* who 'busied [herself] with nothing, that MINE, until the time came, with break of day, to issue forth again, void my little sanctum' (*CSPa*, 261–2, qtd in Rabaté, ibid.). When Beckett decided to busy himself again with *Godot*, was it 'just another of those old tales to keep the *void* from pouring in' (*TT* 230)? Let us first look at Beckett's production notebooks and see how he went about revisualising his play or what Bradby calls Beckett's 'shaping work as director of his own play' (Bradby 2001, 109).

Beckett directing Beckett

> 'If this doesn't purge them, nothing will'
> (Beckett)

My purpose in reading Beckett's theatrical notebooks, – the paratexts – or what Gontarsky calls the 'ghost or grey cannon – letters, notebooks, manuscripts' – in opposition to 'the white canon (or the traditional canon)' (Gontarsky 2006, 143), is not to re-inscribe some presumption of authorial authority over *Waiting for Godot*, something which Beckett had always struggled to undo. It is well known that as an author, Beckett projected for himself an image of authorial impoverishment or impotence. A celebrated instance of this is his indignant response in 1954 to the English actor Ralph Richardson:

> who wanted the low-down on Pozzo, his home address and *curriculum vitae*, ... I told him that all I knew about Pozzo was in the text, that if I had known more I would have put it in the text, and that this was true also of the other characters which I trust puts an end to that star ... I also told Richardson that if by Godot I had meant God I would [have] said God, and not Godot. This seemed to disappoint him greatly. (Letter to Barney Rosset qtd in Knowlson 1996, 412)

Similarly as a director of his own work, Beckett actively strove to undermine or at least downplay any authoritative 'knowledge' over the meaning of his productions. His own musings about theatre, already alluded to at the end of our first chapter, are supreme exercises in critical detachment, even self-effacement or what Gontarski calls Beckett's resistance to theorising his own theatre, his 'resistance to self-reflection' (141). His oft quoted statement to Colin Duckworth: 'I produce an object. What people make of it is not my concern' (qtd in Gontarski 1997, 142), is illustrative of what Gontarski goes on to term Beckett's 'public posture of diminished authority' (143). Such a posture may be read as 'a performance inseparable from the mystique of the work' (ibid.).

To come to Beckett's German *Godot*, the content of which was never to be discussed during the rehearsals (McMillan 136), the voice of Beckett that we read in his *notebooks* and the rehearsal diary, may equally be said to be very much a performing voice. Beckett's reiterated concern is to safeguard the play's radical uncertainty and 'hold' the undecidability of the play's inner zones of mystery and unknowingness. As Beckett enigmatically acknowledged in a letter to Alan Schneider on returning from Berlin, 'Berlin wasn't too bad in the end. We were nearly there' (Harmon 1998, 324). Such a voice might be fruitfully 'read as fictive, the creation of his own ideal reader or spectator' (Gontarski 141) or even thinker.

Beckett wrote *Godot* because he had the need 'to create for a smaller space', and have some control 'above all of a certain light' (qtd in McMillan, 15). He was also extremely inexperienced in writing for the stage at the time, which explains why the play had not been 'visualised' to his satisfaction (qtd in Bradby 2001, 106).[3] In revisiting his play, Beckett strips away any undue facile familiarities by generally displacing the emphasis from the verbal onto the visual,[4] the purpose being to find a shape for the mess: 'Der Konfusion Gestalt geben' ('to give shape to the confusion') (*TN* xi), he said in German. This is an echo of an earlier public statement Beckett made to Tom Driver in 1961 about the need 'to find a form that accommodates the mess, that is the task of the artist now' (qtd in McMillan 14).

Beckett began, then, revisualising his play by expanding the initial stage direction, the description of Estragon 'sitting on a low mound' being changed to 'seated on a stone.' Where the original had begun with Estragon alone on stage, the Berlin *Godot* starts with Vladimir there from the start as well (ibid.). In his rehearsal diary, Beckett's assistant Walter Asmus wrote:

> Beckett says that Estragon is on the ground. He belongs to the stone. Vladimir is light, he is oriented towards the sky. He belongs to the tree. (Qtd in McMillan, 137)

Estragon's symbiotic bond with stone and mineral recalls Molloy, Malone and Macmann. But more than in the case of his fictional predecessors, his stone is his refuge, his intimate abode, it is there where he sleeps and dreams. In this new opening, 'the tramps appear from the outset as quite inseparable' (*TN* xiii). Indeed, Deryk Mendel recalls being corrected by Beckett for eliminating Estragon's stone from the set when he directed in the earlier 1965 *Warten auf Godot* in Berlin:

> When Sam saw this heap of twigs and branches he explained that it had to be a stone to go along with tree so that animal, mineral and vegetable would all be onstage. (Qtd in McMillan, 83)

The second major change in the 'new' version is that the opening moments of the play consist of a still, waiting tableau, identified as 'W1' in the notebooks or, a first *Wartestelle*, literally a 'waiting point'. Only after a long moment of silence and stillness does Estragon go on taking off his boot. The waiting motif is therefore given concrete form (*TN* xiii). I shall be returning to this important visual motif later.

Beckett broke the play down into eleven sections for rehearsal purposes, the purpose being to clarify thematic patterns. These are listed as A1–6 (pertaining to Act 1) and B1–5 (Act 2).

A-1 runs from the opening to just after Estragon's line 'People are bloody ignorant apes' (*G* 13). For this section Beckett noted: 'perpetual separation and reunion of V/E' (*Schiller nb.*, 5) and makes it clear that the function of the opening was to stress the couple's opposition and complementarity

A-2 goes from Estragon's first 'inspection of place' and 'approach by stages' to the arrival of Pozzo and Lucky (ibid., 7–9). The emphasis here is on exploring the place in which they are, but also on developing the theme of perpetual separation and reunion (Bradby 2001, 127).

A-3 covers the encounter between the two couples. It incorporates the third *Wartestelle* which follows Pozzo's line, 'Pan sleeps' (*G* 36).

A-4 goes from Pozzo sitting down to Pozzo's line: 'You see my memory is defective' (ibid., 38) culminating in the fourth *Wartestelle*.

A-5 begins with Estragon's 'In the meantime nothing happens' and covers the build-up to Lucky's 'Think' and the 'Think' itself. It ends with the departure of Pozzo and Lucky.

In A-6, Beckett's concern is with the lighting and with the boy's moves which was a variation of the theme of 'approach by stages'. The lighting effect he wanted was for the boy to emerge from deep shadow, and as Bradby notes, this was achieved in the Schiller-Theater (Bradby 2001, 128).

B-1 like A-1 defines the situation and goes from the opening to Vladimir's 'Ah! Que voulez-vous. Exactly' (*G* 65).

B-2 opens with Estragon's 'what shall we do now?'(*G* 60) paralleling A-2 by searching for activities to pass the time and continues up to the arrival of Pozzo and Lucky.

B-3 is a reversal of A-4: the once dominant Pozzo is now on the ground and it is Vladimir who dominates the scene with his rhetoric (McMillan 89). The fourth *Wartestelle* of Act 2 signals the end of B-3 and the beginning of B-4 after Vladimir's line, 'We are men' (*G* 82).

B-4 focuses on the rise of all four characters from their fallen state with the action concentrating on Lucky.

B-5 brings us from Pozzo and Lucky's exit to the end of the play.

In addition to these structural divisions, Beckett listed twenty units for special emphasis (*TN* 179). These are as much about the recurring themes or actions in play itself, such as Estragon's feet, or sleeps, as they are about giving further detailed stage directions for the coordination of lines and movement. There is no guiding principle behind Beckett's choices. If anything Beckett had no interest in distinguishing thematic concerns from practical details and problems such as how to organise all Lucky's paraphernalia (Bradby 131):

L's moves (in) A-3
L's think
E's feet

E's sleeps
Whip
V/E and tree
Inspection Place
W (*Wartestelle*)
Inspection hat/boot
Doubts confusions
Komm wir gehen (Let's go)
Help
Was sagte ich noch? (what was I saying?)
Sky
Sleep
Erinnern (Remembering)
Approach by stages
Divisions
Lighting
Tree

Three of these units particularly interest me since they constitute crucial visual motifs in themselves and, as regards the critical terms of our reading, they may be said to constitute the key elements that underline Beckett's theatricalisation of the void. These are: 'the Inspection place', 'Approach by stages', and the '*Wartestelle*'. I propose to present each one of these before giving a general description of the play's performance.

'Approach by stages' or 'calendar stops' concerns the pattern of movement Beckett wanted for his characters. The terms describe 'the separation of the action into segments of moving without speaking, a halt to deliver a line, then further movement, a halt for another line', etc. (*TN* 102). Such 'separating text from movement emphasizes the avoidance or attraction that is inherent in the action and allows verbal echoes to be heard and gestures and looks to be registered' (102–3). An example of this is when Estragon wonders what day it is. As he names three different days, his approach to Vladimir is in three stages or 'stops':

> And is it Saturday? (*Advances towards Vladimir.*) Is it not Sunday? (*Pause.*) (*Advances further.*) Or Monday? (*Pause.*) (*Advances further.*) Or Friday? (Ibid., 14)

Such a separation of speech and movement is not new as we have seen in our analysis of the 'let's go/we can't' motif' in the preceding chapter but, as Knowlson makes clear, it was to become 'a general principle of stage action in Beckett's productions and is not limited to the movement of characters towards each other' (1993, 102). Knowlson goes on to define the 'stops' as 'a pattern of movements that emphasises the *constant conflict* of approach and avoidance between and among the characters' (400, my emphasis). 'Approach by stages' constitutes, then, what Beckett called the ballet element of the play in that they embody the 'perpetual separation and reunion' of Estragon and Vladimir (102), Beckett 'agreeing in the Schiller rehearsals that it as was if they were connected by a rubber band' (ibid.).

To come to the two other important visual motifs, 'Inspection Place' and *Wartestellen,* these belong to a group of large structured stage movements which work as visual leitmotifs (McMillan, 97 and 98). The four inspections of place that actually occur are clockwise circuits around the perimeter of the stage exploring the physical possibilities confronting Vladimir and Estragon (ibid., 97) or to put it in terms of our psychoanalytic study, they may be seen as explorations of empty space. As Knowlson notes:

> Estragon's first circuit of the stage established the limits of their situation: *an unknown world offstage to which they cannot escape*; the path of the road which eventually brings Pozzo, Lucky and the Boy; the presence of the tree; the space downstage with the stone in which they wait; and the 'bog' of the auditorium in front of them. (*TN*, my emphasis 99)

The four systematic explorations of the stage at crucial moments all follow the same pattern and proceed in the same clockwise pattern: after the 'two thieves' discussion in A-1, after the first sleeping scene in A-2, at the beginning of Act 2 in B-1 just before the song and in B-4 just after the exit of Pozzo and Lucky. These inspections have predictably a run-down effect, since the final one is 'not properly inspection' (*Schiller nb.*, 73). At the end the 'limited scene is so well known that even the "restless" Vladimir is less eager to examine it' (*TN* 99).

The German term '*Wartestellen*' literally means points of waiting. The play is broken at twelve points by silence during which the action ceases as the characters assume unmistakable tableaux (McMillan 115), dramatically reminding us of the play's central motif: 'waiting', *Warten auf Godot* rather than *Wir warten auf Godot* (Garforth 1996, 156). Beckett saw the possibility of twenty 'waiting tableaux' but only twelve were used. The opening and closing tableaux of each act were considered separately by Beckett. The first of the series of four *Wartestellen* (*W*) for Act I, define the circumstances pictorially. For example, at Vladimir's suggestion that Godot might shout at his horse, the tramps freeze in position looking at each other (*TN* 19). The second, which comes after Pozzo's line, 'Pan sleeps' in A-3 presents the characters' physical condition – Estragon is asleep, Pozzo is sitting on his stool, Vladimir is upstage right and Lucky stands mid-stage still burdened with his luggage (McMillan 116). The third following Pozzo's 'my memory is defective' (*TN* 36), portrays confusion and disappointed anticipation. The fourth and last of the series in Act 1, which comes after Lucky's dance, 'presents a picture of a hapless victim and a conspiratorial master' (McMillan 117).

These frozen silences lead into different references to waiting, the first two defining specific expectations, the last two registering unfulfillment. For example, as regards the third *W*, when Pozzo's memory fails, Estragon complains because the diversion has ceased: 'In the meantime nothing happens' (*TN* 36). After Pozzo's explanation for Lucky's dance, a long section is cut so that Estragon's impatience erupts with: 'nothing happens, nobody comes, nobody goes, it's awful' (ibid., 38). As McMillan remark, the series establishes, then, 'the conditions, expectations, and disappointments that are central to the play' (117).

The four *Wartestellen* of Act 2 concentrate essentially on the ambiguous relationship between Vladimir and Estragon, presenting their 'contrasting temperaments and constant comings together and goings apart in alternating images of union and separation, stasis and activity' (ibid.). The first of this series presents the couple passive together on the stone, Vladimir's lullaby putting Estragon to sleep. In the second, in B-2, they are active and apart. Just after a moment of reconciliation leading to a 'waltz', they recoil and stand apart looking at each other for the line, 'How time flies when one has fun' (*TN* 160). The third *W* is signalled by Vladimir's answer – 'we are men' (ibid., 75) – to Pozzo's question 'Who are you?', the four fallen bodies of the characters forming a 'cruciform heap' (McMillan 118). The last *W* (excluding the final tableau) comes in B-5, just after the boy's exit. Estragon sits dozing on his stone and Vladimir stands near the tree, his back to the audience, as he contemplates the moon. McMillan adds that for a moment Vladimir and Estragon seem to lead separate existences, one inattentively passive, the other actively observant, neither one aware of the other (ibid., 118 and 119). To conclude, then, the series of *W*, used in Act 2, depicts all the possible modes of relationship at the disposal of the couples: reconciliation, repulsion, union without reconciliation, separation without rejection, solitude and separation; and finally, apart and alone (ibid.).

As to how Beckett instilled design in his actor's movements, commentators all concur on Beckett's use of the 'sonata form' of repetition and variation (Bradby 2001, 123), echoing Beckett's remark to Charles Marowitz in 1962:

> Producers don't seem to have any sense of *form in movement.* The kind of form one finds in music, for instance, where themes keep recurring. When, in a text, actions are repeated, they ought to be made unusual the first time, so that when they happen again – in exactly the same way – an audience will recognise them from before. In the revival of *Godot* (in Paris) I tried to get at something of that stylised movement that's in the play. (Qtd in Pountney 1988, 50)

The performed movements in Beckett's *Godot* form, in Knowlson's words, 'a whole pattern of moves in semicircles, arcs and chords, horizontals and verticals which created what may be termed a subliminal stage imagery' (*TN* 401, and Bradby 123–4). At several points in the play, Vladimir and Estragon take 'walks' that culminate in silent tableaux where they wait by the tree. In Act 1, two moves to and from the tree are followed by one ending at the stone. In Act 2, two patterns of movement leading to the stone are followed by one leading to the tree. More generally, the movements of Act 1 trace one half of a circle, those of Act 2 the other half. For example, Vladimir and Estragon move as if they are on a straight line. Beckett varies such a linear pattern by sometimes giving them a curved, semicircular trajectory (Bradby 124). While there is no single heading drawing the stage imagery together, McMillan contends that the interplay of arc and chord go to form two halves of a divided circle suggesting repetitiousness but also 'the duality in contrasting, complementary but unintegrated parts of a greater whole' (99).

Transforming *Godot*

What then are we to make of Beckett's theatrical strategies of shape and form? Taking up our psychoanalytic reading model, our suggestion here would be to see these as providing Beckett with a wider strategy of psychic and emotional containment for what he called the confusion and the mess. This would be one way of testing the relevance of one of the conclusions reached in our analysis of the play's written text, notably, the containing function of the absent Godot as thought that necessitates thinking. Within a Bionian perspective, Beckett's elaborate patterns of stage movement might be seen as his formal means of containment as they clearly allow for a sophisticated interplay of the container and the contained, these being virtually interdependent. An instance of this is the perpetual separation and reunion of Vladimir and Estragon whose movements to and fro were likened by Beckett to a rubber band as already mentioned. Discussion needs however to ultimately return to the quality of Beckett's 'stage container'. Is it constrictive, oppressive or is it perhaps a gateway to some 'higher' even mystical perception? The working hypothesis we will privilege, then, is that in order to experience the void, it has to be made thinkable, therefore, be given some formal container.

The least we can say is that in directing his play, Beckett trans*form*ed it. Here I want to make a tentative link between Beckett's directing work and Bion's development in the sixties. Bion moved away from an explanatory model of psychoanalysis towards a descriptive, more evocative and aesthetic conception of the psychoanalytic experience. In the same way that Beckett turned to music, film and painting analogies to 'describe' his work, Bion also used analogies from the visual arts and literature, stressing that it was the visual sense which lies at the core of unconscious phantasy (see Oppenheim 2001, 770–1, 775).[5] For example, Bion, in *Transformations* (1965), tells us that when he thought he grasped his patient's meaning, it was often 'by virtue of an aesthetic rather than a scientific experience' (52), suggesting that the form of art, like the analytic encounter, captures meaning which lies outside its own boundaries.

Bion strikingly uses the example of a painter who transforms a landscape (the experience or realisation) into a painting (the representation) for public viewing. Bion supposes that 'despite the differences between a field of poppies and a piece of canvas, despite the transformation that the artist has effected in what he saw to make it take the form of a picture, *something* has remained unaltered and on this *something* recognition depends' (Bion 1965, 1, Bion's emphasis). The elements that go to make up the unaltered aspect of the transformation are what Bion calls 'invariants' (ibid.). If the painter is able to transform a landscape (the realisation) into a painting (the representation), 'he does so by virtue of invariants that make his representation comprehensible: The invariants depend on the technique he employs: thus the invariants in an impressionist painting are not the invariants of a painting by a member of, say, a realist school of painting' (5).

The psychoanalyst equally effects a transformation by transforming the facts of analytic experience (the realisation) into an interpretation (the representation): 'an interpretation is a transformation; to display the invariants, an experience, felt and described in one way, is described in another' (4). A transformation, then, is more than a change in form: it is the representation or abstraction of an unknowable experience – a thing-in-itself (12) – denoted by the sign O, which gives the experience a possibility of growth and accretion of meaning. This growth, remarks Meltzer, 'increases the *generality* of the mental formulation but thereby increases the *specificity* of the uses to which it can be put' (1978, 73, Meltzer's emphasis). It follows that the capacity for transformation and abstraction is a means of tolerating conflict and negativity:

> Confronted with the unknown, 'the void and formless infinite', the personality of whatever age fills the void (saturates the element), provides a form (names and binds a constant conjunction) and gives boundaries to the infinite (number and position). Pascal's phrase 'Le silence de ces espaces infinis m'effraie' can serve as an expression of intolerance and fear of the 'unknowable' and hence of the unconscious in the sense of the undiscovered or the unevolved. (Bion 1965, 171)

To return to *Waiting for Godot*, the long history of the play's productions might be likened to a group of transformations, where even if the different 'end-results' hardly bear any resemblance either with Beckett's 'original' personal experience – O – or with Roger Blin's inaugural *Godot*, the least we can say is that the play's 'reality' depends on its invariants being somehow 'common' to the original *Godot* (O) and the various theatrical representations (T) (see Bradby 45–134). To restate Beckett's directing of his own play in terms of the theory of transformation, one obvious question to be addressed is, what is O and how does Beckett go about transforming O? I am hence equating Beckett's directing activity to an emotional experience that can be represented by T. In other words, O can be made comprehensible and thinkable but cannot be known.

Approaching *Godot*

On reading Beckett's theatrical notebooks, one senses a tension, on one hand, between Beckett's desire for formal containment and, on the other, his desire for greater emotional complexity and reflexivity. Outwardly, Beckett in his desire for greater and greater abstraction seemed intent on transforming the play's potential emotional content by the regularly spaced pauses – the *Wartestellen* – and the cyclic patterning of movement and gesture, geometric precision and mathematical concision – in other words, 'the "thought" of space, line, point to be matched with a realization that is felt to approximate to it' (Bion 1967, 106).

For example, half-way between gesture and thought, the 'approach by stages' – approach work – resembles more a choreography of the void, a search for stepping-stones to best approach or avoid the other, thereby anticipating *Quad.* Although one moves warily and defensively towards the other – Lucky is protected by his rope which, in the first act, forms a half-circle around him – the self-reflexivity and the sheer sophistication of the manoeuvrings through space, touch on self-parody of a sort with a nod perhaps at Pascal's: 'le silence de ces espaces m'effrayent', quoted by Bion.

The stylisation indeed affords the characters an undue invulnerability, an affective indifference in this theatrical playground where everything comes down to 'gaming', otherwise everything, as Beckett explained himself, becomes only an imitation of reality (McMillan 140). These remarks needs to be balanced by the fact that during the rehearsals Beckett was worried that his actors would lapse into 'a mechanical way of speaking' (ibid. 143), and wanted certain passages such as 'where are all these corpses from', delivered with 'more colour' and feeling (ibid.). In the same light, Knowlson reminds us that Beckett's stylisation of gesture and movement 'did not dehumanize the tramps' (*TN* xviii). If anything, the stylised moving/unmoving, a moving into stasis and silence, epitomised by the play's *Wartestellen* – Beckett's theatrical invariables – promised a greater intensity than the earlier French *Godot.* To echo Roger Fry, even in the most emptied-out abstract painting, purely formal relations of certain kinds do arouse peculiarly profound emotions (see Fuller 1998, 199–201, 177–238). While the sheer self-reflexivity of Beckett's moving-unmoving may suggest that the underlying emotion has been evacuated, it might equally suggest that the emotion has been transformed into something more refined that defies expression and representation. As we shall see, *Warten auf Godot* did not fail to stir aesthetic emotion, in particular feelings conveyed by empty space so aptly represented by the huge Schiller stage, a stage that seemed to engulf and bewilder Estragon and Vladimir. It is perhaps the stage's vacuity that served to heighten and intensify the Vladimir–Estragon bond, their perpetual inseparability.

Seeing the unseen

Beckett's production notebooks are picture books in a way, a blueprint for a theatrical imagination imagining itself, thinking itself, visualising a play that Beckett considered unvisualised. The notebooks also literally illustrate Freud's notion of dream-work and the regressive transformation of thoughts, ideas and words into pictures. 'A dream is a picture-puzzle', Freud wrote in *The Interpretation of Dreams* (Freud 1976, 382). In Bion's terms, Beckett's diagrams are the spatial or even geometrical realisation of 'thoughts'. For example, while we don't know what 'exactly' Beckett may have 'dreamt' or 'thought' in staging his play, we do know that some of Beckett's theatrical 'picture-puzzle' proved to be practically 'untransformable' on stage such as the 'unrealizable trio of Estragon and Vladimir supporting a staggering Pozzo' – in B-4 – who questions them to find out 'what happened exactly' (*TN* 414; and *Schiller nb.*, 46). The diagrams are not, then, the experience of the thing-in-itself, but rather a transformation of an unknowable experience both in conscious and unconscious forms. In other words, the Godot stage can be 'felt' by the uncertainty and doubts it generates and 'known' only by the forms the waiting necessitates. In that sense, the diagrams and sketches, structural devices and divisions, for instance, may be said to constitute a paradoxical positivity for viewing 'the unidentifiable place', a phrase used by Beckett to designate the stage (*Schiller nb.*, 7; *TN* 91, 400).

However, it would be misleading and superficial to empirically reduce the play's qualities of 'uncertainty and irresolution' (*TN* xx) to the 'Doubts, confusions' section of the theatrical notebook (ibid. 79–80, 419). This is a section dealing with verbal motifs as it brings together various entries where 'place, time, the identity of all the characters and the tree, stone and boots are all systematically questioned or denied' (101). For example, under the heading '*Was sagt Ich noch*' – 'what was I saying?', Beckett catalogues points of mental confusion, particularly at places 'where memory fails', as when Estragon, in A-2, casts doubt on their appointment (McMillan 125). But according to Knowlson, such confusion as in lines like 'where was I' (*TN* 97), is more a 'confusion about the fundamental nature of their situation and their radical forgetfulness' (ibid.), and not a mere verbal motif. However, in my view, McMillan, for one, makes a false distinction between the visual motifs – 'the specific associations of the geometric configuration and gestures' and the verbal motifs of uncertainty and 'mental confusion' 'which help to "avoid definition"' (McMillan 125). I would argue that such verbal motifs work more as an echoing device and belong to a wider mental universe of uncertainty and the unknown where it is the visual (or is it the invisible?) that dominates. Examples of this is when Estragon asks: 'you're sure it was here?' (*TN* 13) or Vladimir asks, 'you recognise the place'? (14). But more than just 'another major source of uncertainty in the play' (400–1), the unknown and unknowable place is the fundamental mental image that necessitates thinking and necessitates being thought. This we can see in Vladimir's four inspections ('Inspection place') and the repetitive patterning of movements into semi-circles with their 'incompletion and separateness' (xxii).

But above all Beckett's visual dreaming or scenic thinking draws our attention to the 'radical uncertainty that characterizes the entire play' (xix) – the theatrical condition *sine qua non* of the play. As a ghostly complement or companion to inhabit the 'unidentifiable place', Beckett significantly mentions the existence of an 'unidentifiable being' in relation to Estragon's mysterious persecutors. For the exchange in A-1: 'Certainly they did beat me/The same lot as usual/The same, I don't know' (9), Beckett writes that this is the 'first hint at unidentifiable being' (*Schiller nb.*, 3). This brings me to the mysterious symbol 'O' used by Beckett to refer to the diagram he drew for the departure of the boy at the end of Act 2 (*Schiller nb.*, 51), for it also indicates a point near to the centre of the stage. It is precisely after 'O' that the boy disappears into the darkness which 'momentarily directs attention to that darkness and allows contemplation of what it might contain' (*TN* 143). Might there be an affinity between Beckett's theatrical O and Bion's O, one configuring a zone of absence, the other, a paradigm of absolute reality that remains unknowable but thinkable? But before going any further into the realm of the unknown and the immaterial, we should perhaps have a closer look at the material stage Beckett revised and reconfigured.

The two stage coordinates are of course Estragon's stone and Vladimir's tree, these serving as points in scenic space or pointers of space. Dynamically they provide two differing and irreducible points of view or vertices, of Beckettian emptiness: sky and earth, vertical and horizontal, mind and body, the spiritual and the mineral. Vladimir and Estragon's two views are different vertices of emptiness in the sense of two different fields or orderings of the physical and psychic world (Meltzer 1978, 80–1).[6] It is as if Godot has left these two points in Estragon and Vladimir's physical mental void and disappeared somewhere between them, between the near-stasis, timeless stone – Estragon's mineral abode – and Vladimir's ghastly pale tree. (We could also add that the tree has also disappeared from Estragon's inner world, in that he hardly recognises it at all.) However, Estragon's stone is more than a convenient prop; it is part of the play's wider imagery of a timeless mineral or inorganic universe (already explored to some extent in *Molloy* and *Malone Dies*) counterpointed by Lucky's 'earth abode of stones'. (More about this later.) Finally Beckett 'transformed' one aspect of the Vladimir–Estragon relationship using the Hat–Boot analogy (*TN* 95), the boots (regularised to 'Dreckschuhe' ['mud shoes'] in Schiller) establishing Estragon as more earthbound while the hat establishes Vladimir as more cerebral.

Mental engulfment

Beckett counterpoints the physical uncanniness of his stage by doubling it as mental space or, to be more precise, having it serve the function of a constrictive mental container. Here I am referring to the image of imprisonment (*TN* xxii) that haunts Beckett's notebook, or what he calls the 'caged dynamics' (98) of the Estragon /Vladimir relationship. In fact, Beckett crossed out the suggestion that he might use 'faint shadows of bars on stage floor' (98), finally 'deciding against this degree of "explication"' (xxii). As Knowlson remarks, the theme of imprisonment is one that pervades all of Beckett's theatre, an example being that when the main couple go offstage during Lucky's 'think', 'they merely beat their wings like birds trapped in the strands of the net, bouncing back into the stage space to which they are inextricably tied' (xxii). While Knowlson reads such imagery as 'incarceration in self', pointing to Beckett's remark about May in *Footfalls* as someone 'totally encapsulated within herself' (ibid.), for me such spatial dynamics rather confirms the hypothesis, explored in the previous chapter, of the characters being under the mental control of the Other, or of the unknowable Godot.

Beckett's stage directions go even further in this direction where the stage space may be seen to function very much like a constrictive container. For instance, in advising Alan Schneider for the American première, Beckett made it clear that *Godot* needed 'as closed a box as possible' (98) from which there is no escape for the tramps. It is significant that the boundaries of the action in Beckett's production 'were established by the dark shadows of the lighting' (ibid.) which reinforces not only the doubling of mental space as scenic space, but the sense of a tentative border between the known and the unknown, light and darkness, the conscious and the unconscious, thought and the unthought.

If the stage is rethought by Beckett as being paradoxically the uncontained and uncontainable void and the constrictive container of the Other, such container-contained interplay is reduplicated and mirrored on stage by the revised characterisation. What the Berlin performance underlines is the dynamic interdependence of the container and the contained. Where we had insisted, in our previous reading, on the structuring function of 'Godot' as the mental membrane that differentiates the couples, with Vladimir's thinking serving, for example, to contain Estragon, Beckett's revisions made all four characters interdependent to some extent and mutually conditioned by the *Wartestellen.* The interdependence of the four characters is nowhere better seen as when, in the second act, when lying on the ground, they form two crosses, 'each with an empty centre' (McMillan 107). Equally, as regards the relationship between the couples, the potential for cross-identification between Estragon and Lucky as marginal excluded beings is enhanced through the bone–stone motif.[7]

'It is all about stones, about the world of stones', Beckett said concerning Lucky's famous monologue (*TN* xiv). Beckett gave a clear thematic structure: indifferent heaven, dwindling man, earth abode of stones (*Schiller nb. 57*). Asmus goes on to tell us that one of the actors involved, Herm, checked up the meaning of Apathia, Athambia, Aphasia: 'indifference', 'imperturbability' and 'muteness', to which Beckett concurred (McMillan 138–9) saying that the earth is only good for stones. In section 4 of his monologue in which Lucky discusses 'earth abode of stones', Estragon and Vladimir make coordinated exits and entrances which leave Lucky alone in the landscape and highlight his references to the deeps and stones. Beckett was also able to play on the general mineral association between stone and death as in the play on names in Lucky's speech: Steinweg and Peterman (petra, literally meaning 'rock' and 'petering out' suggesting, among other things, a process of exhaustion). Similarly, Beckett exploits verbal comedy in the German – 'ihn/ihm aufsetzen (I'll put it on his head)' (*TN* 407) – punning on the idea that Lucky might also be putting back on his head and not just his (thinking) hat after his delirious 'think'.

Where we previously stressed the dissociated state of the Pozzo–Lucky couple, the Berlin performance underlines their complementarity. Beckett enhanced the depiction of Pozzo as an intellectual and aesthetic disciple of Lucky's by getting the former to use gestures in his set-piece of the fall of night that are similar to those used by Lucky in his long monologue, emphasising thereby the parallels between the two speeches, one evoking darkness, the other night (121). However Lucky's dependence on Pozzo undergoes a transformation of a sort insofar that Beckett appears to evacuate the physical in favour of a mysterious mental dimension dramatising further what is already in the text, namely that Pozzo is Lucky's mental master. This merits a brief comment.

If Lucky is produced into someone that is mechanically faithful even when not bidden by his master, the suggestion is that he is under the intrapsychic control of his master. Lucky 'is never a moment free of load except 1. To dance 2. To think 3. When fallen' (*Schiller nb.*, 54). At rehearsals in Berlin, Beckett clarified the power–subservience relationship that exists between Lucky and Pozzo by underlining 'Lucky's *unthinking* servility' (*TN* 111, my emphasis) with the added stage direction: *Pozzo goes to Lucky, picks up rope and fixes him with a long hypnotic look* (ibid., 36–7), which Beckett termed 'hypno look' (23). Equally just before the 'think', *Pozzo fixes him* (Lucky) *with a long hypnotic look* (38). Commenting the 'hypno' look, Knowlson writes: 'this look supplants the whip and rope as Pozzo's ultimate form of control over Lucky' (407), which explains the decreased importance of Pozzo's whip, Beckett's listing of the seventeen occasions, when Pozzo might use the whip, being not incorporated either into the text of the performances of Schiller or San Quentin productions (111).

The empty centre

The performance foregrounds empty space as its inner theatrical medium and Beckett's reconstituted need for containment. The Beckettian stage is there to be negotiated, traversed, the characters paradoxically floating in space and yet occupying fixed positions. In constantly ascertaining the boundaries of their world, delineating the bounded spaces in which the play is performed – the circles and semi-circles – Estragon and Vladimir also imply what may lie within or beyond these closed figures with their invisible presences and all too visible absences. The actors invite us as audience to complete the scene – the semi-circles – in our own imagination, the empty circle representing perhaps 'the emptiness from which all existence comes from' (Glover 2004, 12).

In the Eastern mystical tradition, the circle is interpreted as a symbol of the idea of *mushin* roughly meaning 'no-mind' or 'the state of being without mind' (Takahashi 2001, 38) – a mental void. The balletic movements foreground above all the fact that the stage is empty and such an emptiness is foreboding. If there is a theatrical void to be talked of at all, it is then as much a passage as it is a place, an irreducible inter-spacing, between figure and figuration, a precarious discourse that can only be described in terms of its decentering operations and not, by any means, in terms of a graspable entity.[8]

Superficially the decentred effects seem obvious enough; the only character who occupies the centre of the stage for a significant period of time is Lucky; Vladimir and Estragon are for most of the time off-centre. An example of the differential play of Beckettian negativity would be when Vladimir and Estragon unwittingly leave the stage completely empty just before the return of Pozzo–Lucky in B-2: 'off long enough for empty stage to carry', noted Beckett (*Schiller Nb.*, 40). Their exit is provoked by Vladimir's impersonation of the threatening other, that is Lucky's 'think', a moment that mirrors Lucky's 'think' in Act I which almost succeeded in evacuating the stage. Vladimir and Estragon's frenzied trajectories at this point amount to a differential spacing of the play's boundaries and borders between on-stage and off-stage, outer and inner, centre and periphery, near and far. Before exiting simultaneously, the tramps enact a series of large stage movements which form a cruciform pattern, the suggestion being that they are being mentally crucified. For example, the movements back and forth from wings to centre create the two horizontals, the vertical axis being formed when Vladimir pulls Estragon downstage, and they recoil backwards along the horizontal axis to complete the pattern (*TN* 158). The space at the centre of the stage which their brief exits earlier had left vacant 'long enough to carry', remains vacant (McMillan 109). At this particular moment in the play, anxieties and fear oscillate constituting a mini drama of emotional turbulence: engulfment or abandonment, reunion or annihilation, the void within or the void without?

An additional piece of dialogue that restores a passage in the original French – 'Jusqu'au bord de la pente' – is also repeated (qtd in *TN* 103), indicating the whereabouts of the 'absent' Estragon. It underlines the menacing Other world that surrounds the *Godot* stage:

> VLADIMIR: Where were you?
> ESTRAGON: To the foot of the rise.
> VLADIMIR: No doubt we're on a plateau, served on a plateau. (67)

The 'pente' or 'rise' does not only develop the idea that they may be surrounded, but that the stage may lead to the psychic 'pit', 'ringing with [Dantesque] infinite groans' thus explaining why Estragon hurries back (159).

If the active avoidance of the centre reinforces our sense of 'the emptiness of the stage' (Cousineau 1999, 67) and the constant running back to the 'plateau' of the sense of an unspeakable fear of an unknowable Other, the occasional occupation of the centre by Estragon and Vladimir could be seen as an attempt to find inner dimensions for Beckett's gaping stage, a sense of self-location somewhere in the unfathomable expanse of mental space. But, predictably enough, Vladimir's turns culminate in a self-cancellation of their own discernible operation, that is an erasure of place. Such inspecting indicates the possibility of curiosity at the outset, a curiosity about objects (the props on stage), their nature, their possible contents, a curiosity that increasingly declines, the last inspection being considerably abridged, or, in Beckett's words, 'not properly inspection' (*TN* 99). But these inspections hover ambiguously between being both inspections of the space without (geometric space) and the space within, that is inspections of a recessive inner mental space.

A key reference in the second act is Estragon's addressing the audience with: 'es fehlt nicht ja an dem leerem Raum' – there is no lack of void/ ce n'est pas le vide qui manque' (59), the choice of 'Raum' suggesting a more concrete sense of place than the more abstract 'void' or 'vide'. While he says this, Estragon gestures to the auditorium outlining in the air a number of empty boxes, maybe coffins or graves. In doing so, he addresses himself to a missing audience, an intersubjective absence, but certainly an emptiness, an empty theatre as suggested by 'leerer Raum'. The provocative suggestion might be that even if present, the audience is nonetheless devoid of any mental matter, the blank auditorium mirroring the play's own blankness.

Beckett elaborates here what is already implicit in the texts of all his *Godot*s, that is the stage as an image of mental space or an empty mind, and, by extension, thinking as a persecutory act of self-representation, an act of mental terrorism (cf. Ross 1994, 1996).[9] After discovering an outer blankness figured by the auditorium, Estragon is furious to find that in the centre of the stage, there is equally *nothing* to recognise 'there'. The new stage direction, *Looks about in a circle, gesturing with both hands* (149), replaced *Looking wildly about him* (*G* 61), as Estragon dramatically points to the ground with both hands and traces a circle. The direction: *Points to the ground with both hands* was added for 'tell me about the worms' (*TN* 149). 'I tell you we weren't here', he vehemently stresses using his knee (ibid.). But as we have seen in our previous analysis of the text, Estragon refutes the finite and the concrete. Not unlike the scene in *Watt* where Watt notices a curious picture of a circle broken at one point and starts speculating endlessly about the possible relationships between the circle and point and the possible positions of the breach (Takahashi 2001, 38), Estragon too literally hates the possibility of there being a point *present* in his *empty* circle, that is, his empty space being intruded upon by a sense of the determined, a 'here' and 'there'. He prefers that his space be kept wholly other, preferring the space underneath the ground, the horizontal space of the dead to the vertical space of the living: 'Sag mir lieber wie es drunter aussieht' (*TN* 149). (Literally, 'tell me how it looks underneath', the German being more explicit than the cryptic 'Tell me about the worms'). By searching to eliminate literalness and longing for indeterminacy, Estragon harks back to experience prior to either the verbal or the geometric representation of the world as differentiated from the self. For him there is no 'Breisgau' but only the 'Scheisgau' (ibid.), a very angry reference to his undifferentiated body-self from which he fails to escape.

It is in this context of fear and anxiety, that Beckett's particular emphasis on the five sleeping scenes must also be mentioned, that is, sleep as an escape from the void and perhaps a flight into the void. Estragon has three sleeps with dreams and two 'drowses' without dreams. His sleeps produce two negative nightmares, two neutral drowses and one dream of happiness. Sleep while maybe providing narcissistic refuge and solace, can also be seen as being identical with a state of mindlessness – 'buried in who knows what profounds of mind' (*Ohio Impromptu*, in *CSPa*, 288 – and being awake is equally unappealing since this would imply that Estragon is capable of thought. Both states are highly undesirable. Whether sleeping or waking, Estragon struggles not only against the primitive persecutory fears and the associated threat of annihilation of falling, but also against the confrontation with emptiness, which, as André Green shows, 'is probably the most intolerable of states feared by patients and whose scars leave a state of eternal dissatisfaction' (qtd in Fuller 1988, 220).

The unfathomable chasms of silence

> 'We were nearly there'
> (letter to Alan Schneider)

Insofar that Beckett can be said to have had any theatrical aesthetic of absence, it may be said to lie in the *Wartestellen*. They are, after all, the logical development of the 'approach by stages', since they interrupt and arrest the play's moving-unmoving dialect. But the still points are also still moments which in forming a determined sequence of twelve, indicate the temporal spacing of the void – atemporal moments or incommunicable 'visions'. They provide the play's matrix image of absence and emptiness.

Winnicott refers to 'the delicacy of what is preverbal, unverbalized, and unverbalizable expect perhaps in poetry' (Winnicott 1971, 131) and Beckett's theatrical image, in a way, precedes words of any kind, even thoughts, approximating to perhaps what Bion calls in his reference to *Alice in Wonderland*, a 'timeless and spaceless "space"' (Bion 1965, 104), the innermost recesses of mental space. 'The domain of thought may be conceived of as a space occupied by no-things', Bion also reminds us (106) and the *Wartestellen* are precisely ways of seeing and thinking the no-thing. As a figuration of mental space, 'a thing-in-itself' that is unknowable but which can be represented by images, the *Wartestellen* (*W*) project thought as 'stillness', 'blankness', 'silence'. These are Beckett's mode of transforming the unverbalisable into image even if his image has no content and poses as pure blank form. It is as if the void or blankness becomes the ground of the characters' being, their container, but a container that is indistinguishable from its threatening 'content', that is, the engulfing silence – the equivalent of the unknowable but thinkable 'O' – Bionian ultimate reality. The *W* are hints, then, of an ineffable experience, – theatrical 'animism' (Pilling 1997, 153) – that lies beyond the realms of word or thought. This is not unlike what Angela Moorjani poetically expresses albeit in a different context, namely: 'a poetics of resistance and opposition to the known doubled or shadowed by a poetics of un-knowing' (Moorjani 1997, 216). A brief look at the paradoxical and playful functioning of the *W* in relation to the silence, will hopefully illustrate this point.

While they clearly embrace silence, they may also be said to cheat the silence. Becket once remarked that silence 'is pouring into this play like water into a sinking ship' (*TN* xiv). To quote again from Asmus's diary: 'at the beginning when Estragon is asleep sitting on the stone, that is the theme repeated throughout the play. There are fixed moments of stillness, where everything stands completely still and silence threatens to swallow everything up. Then the action starts again' (McMillan 139–40). For Knowlson these moments of stillness allow the characters to 'conjure up other ways of cheating the threatening silence', (Knowlson 1996, 609).

I would be less categorical and insist first on their fundamental formal blankness – Beckett's 'dream screen' of blankness – for it's into this blank space, which is not unlike a potential play-space, that Beckett can 'project' and think the unknowable void in its positive *and* negative features these being inextricably linked. For example, in the same way that Beckett had restructured Lucky's think along the lines of emotional 'shocks, five in all, each marking a structural division and giving rise to a series of reactions from the other characters, the *Wartestellen* equally serve to counterpoint and counteract the text's emotional 'shocks' with silent abstractions or 'thoughts' of these. In other words they may be seen to function ironically as 'silent shocks', emotional shock that finds 'expression' and containment solely in impenetrable silence – the mental space of the thought/unthought. Such shocks defy description since no one knows what is being thought (if anything) at these various points or moments of 'realisation'. Examples might include: Estragon and Vladimir wondering where they are in A-1; Pozzo evoking his loss of memory in B-4 or Vladimir and Estragon 'recognising' Pozzo's 'humanity/otherness' (triggered off by the famous 'Wir sind Menschen' speech also in B-4). Indeed the *W* may be seen to be as much as an intuition of the unknown and the unknowable as a retreat or a defence from the beckoning nothingness with its threats of engulfment and annihilation. While they pose as 'pure' moments of blankness, a potential wiping clean of the slate of consciousness and thinking, they may also double up as moments of *at-one-ment,* succoured quiescence, or 'moments of felicitous enlightenment rather than nihilistic despair' (Takahashi 2001, 37).

The negative sublime

The moon is a more dominant image in this production than in the published text (*TN* 170) Beckett's moon appearing as a transformation of the original moon that inspired him. Here I'm referring to Beckett's reference in his notebook to the symbolic painting *Zwei Männer betrachten den Mond* ('Two Men Contemplating the Moon') by the German Romantic artist Caspar David Friedrich (*Schiller Nb.*, 30), a painting Beckett saw in Dresden in 1937.[10]

The painting is a highly romantic, sombre landscape with two men viewed from the back looking at a full moon framed by the black branches of a large and leafless tree (*TN* 143). Theatrically, in the earlier versions of the play we only have Vladimir who *contemplates the moon* (*G* 52). In this version, at the very end of Act 1 (*TN* 48), Beckett has Vladimir *with back to audience, looking at the moon.* Estragon, on waking, *contemplates Vladimir* – the rhetorical figure of thinking the thinker or the mind of the beholder beholding the mind of the Other. At this point or moment Beckett pencilled in a possible *Wartestellen* before Estragon finally *turns upstage to contemplate the moon* (ibid.). The vivid moonlight may also have cryptic links with Bion's 'negative capability', or, idiosyncratically, the 'beam of darkness', already alluded to in our analysis of the way the characters intuit the unknowable. Beckett's moonlight could be seen, then, as an illumination of the unknown, that is a highlighting of the unknown. Estragon and Vladimir must wait in the dark (literally and metaphorically) and tolerate uncertainty and extreme anxiety without irritably reaching after fact and reason. Their 'negative capability' is put to the test. Estragon contemplates the unknowing Vladimir who contemplates the moonlit unknown, etc. Significantly, the stillness at the tree is never broken and

Beckett felt it necessary to add a *long silence* before *they do not move* at end of Act 1 (*TN* 50) and a *silence* after *they do not move* at the end of Act 2.

For all the play's inevitability as suggested by the synchronic interaction between the boy and the moon, Lucky's automated gestures even when not bidden by Pozzo, Beckett's *Godot* achieves a dreamlike indefinitude with the ghostly interplay between eye and mind, the tree having to be touched to be believed, as Vladimir does in the second act. Beckett gets us to repeatedly hear the silence of Godot, see the vivid darkness. Literally the play emerges from the dark, is played in deepening twilight, finishes in dramatic moonlight and fades back into the dark, a very distant memory perhaps of the three zones of light in *Murphy* (*MU* 65).

In addition to his use of darkness, Beckett's graceful manipulation of blank space or blankness might also be thought as a derivative of the negative sublime. Where the sublime conventionally evokes sentiments of boundlessness, limitlessness and engulfment, inspiring strangeness, Beckett's production, in its explorations of the vacuity of bounded space and the cardinal importance it gives to darkness, silence and stillness, offers us an inversion of the sublime.

I would contend that one way of 'seeing' Beckett's theatrical image of void, would be to see it as a transformation in the painterly idiom of a Natkin or a Rothko rather than some manifestation of a post-romantic sensibility. Here I am referring to the self-annihilating limitlessness of infinite internal space in Natkin's work and his use of a grid that 'binds in his void' (Fuller 210) or Rothko's monochromatic paintings with their deep black spaces of beckoning nothingness and sinister clouds of emptiness (ibid., 222).

Another notion that might be said to traduce our sense of Beckett's negative sublime is what Jean-Luc Nancy terms the unlimited. Nancy likens the important distinction between beauty and the sublime to the irreducible tension between limitation and the unlimited:

> The unlimited as such is that which sets itself off on the border of the limit, that which detaches itself and subtracts itself from limitation (and hence from beauty) by an unlimitation that is coextensive with the external border of limitation. In one sense, *nothing* sets itself off thus. But if it is permissible to speak of the 'unlimited' as of 'something' that sets itself off 'somewhere', it is because, in the judgment or the feeling of the sublime we are offered a seizure, an apprehension of this unlimitation that comes to raise itself up like a figure

> against a ground, although strictly speaking, it is always simply the limit that raises a figure up against a nondelimited ground. In the sublime, it is a question of the figure of the ground, of the figure that the ground cuts, but precisely insofar as the ground cannot constitute a figure and yet remains a 'raising that razes' [*un 'enlèvement'*], an unlimiting outline, along the limited figure. (Nancy 1993, 35, Nancy's emphasis)

Beckett's German *Godot* equally offers us a seizure, a nightly intuition of the unlimited. But to 'see' Beckett's *Godot*, to distinguish the 'figure' from the 'ground' might even require something that would be closer to an act of faith, where seeing is both 'seeing' and 'unseeing'. To quote Rudolf Otto's commentary on the role of void and emptiness in Chinese painting, if 'void is, like darkness and silence, negation', it is 'a negation that does away with every "this" and "here", in order that the "wholly other" may become actual' (Fuller 217).[11]

If psychoanalysis offers us an engagement with the 'terrible beauty' of our absences, to quote yet again Jed Sekoff (1997, 114), it might be equally said that Beckett offers his actors and his spectators an engagement with the sombre beauty of Godot's absence. It is an engagement with an otherly world where the task of waiting for Godot is a resolutely aesthetic one. Estragon and Vladimir have to patiently wait for a pattern to emerge for, as T.S. Eliot wrote in *Four Quartets*, 'only by the form, the pattern/Can words or music reach/The stillness' (qtd in Glover 2004, 18). And as Beckett had also intuited, in his German letter to Axel Kaun, then 'one will already be able to sense a whispering of the end-music or of the silence underlying all' (Beckett's letter to Axel Kaun, 9 July, 1937, *SBL* 519).

Conclusion: By Way of Neither

Steven Connor, in the aftermath of Beckett's death, discusses the question of Beckett's legacy in relation to Joyce's as follows: 'the problem with a legacy is that it is often so bound up with legality and legitimation [...] typically, as we know, the legality of legacy is also a matter of certain kinds of reading, or legibility' (Connor 1992, 105). In addressing the question of legislating Beckett's legacy, Connor reminds us of the danger here of taking upon ourselves too precipitately the task of preserving rather than disposing or distributing that legacy: 'we should not assume or legislate his legacy too narrowly' (107). Ingeniously and provocatively Connor claims that Beckett's legacy can only be conserved by being given away, for only this will maintain that heroic gesture of self-dispossession and self-expenditure which is so thoroughly, and oxymoronically, its own:

> Beckett's legacy to us is that we can now begin to learn how we and others might possibly come to read him. Having so long been read according to the terms and values which it surpasses, Beckett's work may at last begin to be read and understood according *to the forms of thought and imagining which it makes possible*. (Connor 1992, 107 my emphasis)

While this book has not been concerned with the issue of legacies per se, it has nonetheless sought to legitimate the notion of a Beckettian aesthetic predicated on absence and void and its connected issues such as the unknown, un-knowingness or indeterminacy. I have thereby attempted to reveal the relevance of concepts such as thinking, attacks against linking, playing, transitional space, 'according to the forms of thought and imagining' that Beckett's writing makes possible. By looking at Beckett's later directing practice in the 1970s I have been tentatively suggesting that between the novels and the theatre, the page and the stage, Beckett's aesthetic 'object' develops via a series of formal 'thinking' transformations of the unknowable void. But, more than that, I have hinted that the negative *is* the object for much in Beckett. Of course, it is not there in any tangible or empirical sense of the word, but rather more in terms of an 'unlimited' space or spacing that prevents and bars 'presence', yet invites thinking and being thought.

By looking at how Beckett uses thinking and thought, I have tried to give his negative a 'mind' of its own, or to quote Beckett's unpublished German diary, 'an "open-mindedness" that is mindlessness, the sphincter of the mind limply for ever open, the mind past the power of closing itself *to everything but its own content*, or rather its own treatment of a content' (2 February 1937, qtd in Knowlson 1996, 252, Beckett's emphasis). The same concern with open-minded mindlessness reappears in Beckett's later drama:

> What thoughts who knows. Thoughts, no, not thoughts. Profounds of mind. Buried in who knows what profounds of mind. Of mindlessness. Whither no light can reach. (*OH* 288)

Where Leslie Hill (1990) concludes his book by saying that Beckett's negativity does not allow redemption since the force of indifference cannot be incorporated into the writing, I would certainly agree, but would argue that it is the 'unlimited' negative or void that resists and exceeds 'silence', 'understanding', resolution, etc. As we saw in the case of *All That Fall*, the genre of radio drama allowed Beckett to formally explore the relations between darkness and sound or what Kim Connor calls 'the edgeless darkness' or 'edges that can be drawn acoustically and linguistically, without reference to actual vision' (Connor 1997, 307 and 303). The later shorter work allowed him to further problematise the dimensions of all forms of 'presence' in his writing, such as 'character' and its conditions of observability and possibility, bringing to mind what mathematicians call 'quantum intermediacy', that is, something 'unknown in between'.

One thing Beckett and Bion had in common, argues Steven Connor, for example, 'was a highly-developed capacity to confront and contain negativity combined or alternating with a growing impatience with the distorting effects of such saturation' (2008, 32). Like Bion's grid, a heuristic diagram to classify thoughts and emotions according to their genesis (Skelton 2006, 59), Beckett's shorter works seek to fix the forms of encounter between self and other, apprehending their 'transformations and relativities' (Connor 30). The recourse to diagram and scheme in the later plays, with their 'stable structures of repetition and permutation' (32), is not unlike 'the tension between the desire for more and more rigid definition and greater and greater abstraction on the one hand, and greater and greater complexity and reflexivity on the other' (30). But where Bion's later work may be said to put tolerant knowledge 'in the place of negativity' (31), I would argue that in the later Beckett the negative is his sole form of 'knowledge' as the void is increasingly shaped and reshaped.

Already in a text as 'early' as *How It Is* (*H*), Beckett is concerned with the different ways his characters can be said to form 'relations' of suffering and how these can be subject to 'formal' thought (Ross 1995, 59–63). The indefinacy, the generality of characters and their abstract 'outline', allow them to merge into one another, losing themselves, only to be caught up again later and redefined once more. This is not unlike what mathematics teaches us about numbers, namely that anything can be 'thought': ordinal numbers, imaginary numbers, the square root of minus 2, etc.

In *How It Is* an 'infinite' number of relations can be thought concerning the 'presence' of Pim. The model relation is that of sadomasochism as the voice attempts to construct an infinite system of tormentors who turn out to be the producers of (or are produced by) an infinite series of possible sadomasochistic relationships engendered by Pim or should I say, by a multiplicity of Pims. Here, time has no boundaries nor has space if we are to accept the narrator's calculations:

> imagines millions millions (*H* 123)
> [...] million Pims now motionless agglutinated 2 by 2 in the interests of torment ... thousand nameless solitaries half abandoned half abandoning. (125)

The emotional concern here is not so much with sadomasochism as with those feelings conveyed by time and space. The vast stretches of time give rise to intense feelings; the journey through the mud is also a journey through the separation from what the voice knew, remembered, felt, loved. The concern might be said to be with constructing boundaries, outlines, however, vague, however rigorous as the narrator attempts to reconcile his 'intuitive' formulations with 'precise' geometric formulation. He investigates his observation on the basis of the relationship between the representation of the presence and absence of Pim as if all that happens to Pim is nothing but tentative *intuitions*:

> be with Pim have been with Pim have him behind me hear it said he'll come back another will come better than Pim he's coming right leg right arm push pull ten yards fifteen yards you stay quiet where you are in the dark the mud and on you suddenly a hand like yours on Pim two cries his mute. (25)

The narrator's conclusion is either he is alone or else he is part of an endless series of couples of tormentors tied to their victims. Or perhaps the journey he made in the dark across the mud with the sack tied to his neck was the journey he didn't make and then made it again and again (138). Maybe there was 'never any journey never anything but the dark the mud the sack' (139). 'Experience' gives rise to abstractions just in the same way that the space of abstraction can be filled with experience, however daunting and grim that experience may be. It is the generality of formulations that increases the specificity of the uses to which it can be put to use.

Moving to the shorter texts of the eighties, the notion of 'character' may be said to have completely disappeared from the Beckett mindscape and narrative space. A text like *Worstward Ho* is, among other things, the capacity to imagine or think the 'presence' or 'absence' of an old man and a child in an all-pervasive void, the very 'existence' of which is the subject of the voice's rational speculation. All this calls for a certain performativity:

> All save void. No. Void too. Unworsenable void. Never less. Never more [...] Say child gone. As good as gone. From the void. From the stare. Void then not that much more? Say old man gone. Old woman gone. As good as gone. Void then not that much more again? No. Void most when almost. Worst when almost. Less then? ... Enough. A pox on void. Unmoreable unlessable unworseable evermost almost void. (*WH* 42–3)

In *Company*, the narrative of the speaker's past has more the quality of a dream thought than a memory, a thought concerned more with its logical consistency and coherence than its content:

> You first saw the light in the room you most likely were conceived in. The big bow window looked west to the mountains. Mainly west.

> For being bow it looked also a little south and a little north. Necessarily. A little south to more mountain and a little north to foothill and plain. (15–16)

Dream thoughts grow in complexity, sophistication and abstractness where there is less and less evidence for their 'existence' or any 'original' experience. There is hardly any more evidence for the narrator's statements or the 'presence' of character for one is dealing with a reality so slight as to be virtually imperceptible, unimaginable, but which manages to be 'real':

> So he imagines to himself as voice and hearer pall. But further imagination shows him to have imagined ill. For with what right affirm of a faint sound that it is a less faint made fainter by farness and not a true faint near at hand? Or of a faint fading to fainter that it recedes and not in situ decreases. If with none then no light from the voice on the place where our old hearer lies. In immeasurable dark. Contourless. Leave it at that for the moment. Adding only, What kind of imagination is this so reason-ridden? A kind of its own. (44–5)

The overriding paradox of Beckett's late work, then, is that in order to contain the infinitesimal lessness as regards the literal content of the texts, Beckett has increasing recourse to formal structure and rigid patterning. By giving the void, or the nothing, a paradoxical positivity, he thereby deepens the incommensurable gulf between self and other, between the empirical and the insubstantial.

In the television play *Quad* (1982) Beckett formalises the mathematical permutations that allow the four players to negotiate and deviate E, the centre space of the setting that is supposedly a danger zone, constituting 'dread fascination' (Bryden 1995, 112). In Beckett's own words: 'there was something terrifying about (E) ... it was danger' (111).

The four players – in monk-like cowls, 'as alike in build as possible (*CSPa* 293), enter one after the other, and from differing corners (designated A, B, C, and D) follow different courses (1, 2, 3, and 4) as they go along either the perimeter or make interrupted diagonal moves from corner to corner. The players, though in constant movement, remain always separate and intact. As Mary Bryden suggests, quoting Martha Fehsenfeld, 'The unbearable and unrelieved tension strained almost to the breaking point' in the play, 'derives less from its length than from the intensity of its internal patterning' (110). Yet, for all its exhausting rigidity and repetition, it is a play which inhabits 'a zone of indeterminacy and provisionality' (113), a psychic zone:

> Beckett's careful direction – 'E *supposed* a danger zone. Hence deviation' (*CSP* 293: my italics) – does indeed seem to site the threat of the centre point within the psyche. Whether the central cavity or abyss is invented or not, however, its threat is clearly not dispelled or alleviated either by its frequentation or by the presence of others whose passing may or may not be recorded. (Bryden 112)

I would complement this insight by suggesting that the dramatic indeterminacy of the play lies not so much in the unthought or unthinkable nature of E – a possible paradigm of absolute reality that, like Bion's O, remains unknowable but 'thinkable' – as in the *incidental* nature of Beckett's directing notes. For example, Beckett uses the word 'say' to suggest and not to dictate the differential factors between the players: 'say 1 white, 2 yellow, 3 blue, 4 red (113; and *CSPa* 292). It is as if Beckett is giving one possible 'realisation' of *Quad*, one possible way of 'limiting' the play's 'unlimited' mental matrix. He is 'thinking' the play through the use of such concrete coordinates. Beckett's 'say' preserves the zone of indeterminacy and clearly formalises the 'relationships' between E and the players' as essentially inscrutable, beyond the realm of thought. Yet we, as spectators, are incited to think E. As Bryden goes on to explain, it is precisely the existence of E and its nameless fear 'which recruits *Quad* into the human domain and divorces it from the mechanization of the dodged track' (111).

Indeed there is nothing inhuman, sub-human or 'negative' about *Quad*, or indeed about any of Beckett's later texts.[1] Bryden's statement about *Quad*: 'to dehumanize the play would be to subvert its impact' (111) is indeed, in my view, applicable to all of Beckett. The impact of the play lies for me in its call 'for thought', that is to say, in the way E might be seen as a 'thought matrix' that generates an *unlimited* series of thoughts for the players and us to think whether these be: thoughts of fear, of terror, of self-extinction; thoughts of the unthought, or to quote Bryden once more, thoughts of 'potential infinity' (114).[2]

I would like to conclude this study by returning one last time to Beckett's letter to Duthuit about an art predicated to the nonrelation. What fundamentally interests Beckett 'is the beyond of the outside-inside where he [Bram] makes his effort, not the import of the effort itself'

(Gontarski 2006, 19). However, to his horror, Beckett realises that whatever he says about Bram 'will appear to imprison it again in a relation':

> If I say that he [Bram] paints the impossibility of painting, the deprivation of relation, of object, of subject, I appear to put him in relation with this impossibility, with this deprivation, in front of them. He is inside them [...] he is them, rather, and they are he, in as full a manner as possible. (19–20)

This psychoanalytic study has unavoidably put Beckett's writing 'in relation' not only with the conceptual work of analysts and thinkers like Bion and Winnicott, but, more widely, with 'absence', 'void', 'negativity'. The paradox is unavoidable and must not be resolved. I have been trying to invoke the 'impossible' presence of absence in Beckett's writing and, at the same time, the impossible 'absence' of other, or in Beckett's own words concerning Masson's painting of the void, 'the obliteration of an unbearable presence' (*P* 110). This has been my particular way of 'accepting' Samuel Beckett's unique writing. 'My writing is pre-logical writing', Beckett once explained to Patrick Bowles. 'I don't ask people to understand it logically, only to *accept* it' (qtd in Knowlson 2006, 109, my emphasis). In the same way that Beckett saw the significance of Bram's art of nonrelations lying '*beyond* [...] the outside-inside' (my emphasis), similarly Beckett's art of absence brings us beyond divides such as outside-inside, absence-presence, knowing and not knowing. It simply brings us beyond words and thoughts, beyond 'the lug-worms of understanding', to quote Beckett's unpublished German notebook (19 November 1936, qtd in Knowlson 269).

'And to end up with?' [...] 'a little poetry' (*EG* 49)

I would like to take up what Jean-Michel Rabaté said a number of years ago, when in the wake of a plethora of post-structuralist and deconstructionist studies, it was more than ever necessary to foreground Beckett as a poet (Rabaté 1992, 3). If the later plays and shorter texts can be said to be closer to poetry with their enigmatic figurations of the unfigurable, I would argue that the trilogy and *Godot* also carve out a space for the poetic, where the unsayable and the sayable uncanningly 'meet' at that very moment 'of knowing not knowing', to quote an early poem of Beckett's 'Cascando' (*CA* 30). As we have seen, *Molloy* ends on an aesthetic encounter where Moran finally writes (in) the absence of Molloy; the absent-present Malone 'dies' and 'lives' leaving us with a night vision of water, death and madness; the Unnamable is obliged to re-create himself out of his self-engendered chaos, and Estragon and Vladimir think and dream in the void left by Godot. If it is poetry, it is a poetry 'generated by a restless, formless antagonisms' (Boxall 2003, 50) where negative affirmation 'meets' painful awareness of absence.

Therefore there is nothing negative about Beckett's negative way.[3] His artistic way is *not* the way of the negative, theological or otherwise, but, to quote a short text Beckett wrote in 1976, it is 'By way of neither'.

> To and fro in shadow from inner to outer shadow
> From impenetrable self to impenetrable unself. (Qtd in Knowlson 1996, 632)

With its eternally unsaturated voids and enigmatic absences, Beckett's art remains inscrutable, ineffable. His writing is a writing that does *nothing* but begin, never to 'finish'. It undermines every deterministic 'certainty' with mocking doubts. It resists thinking and being thought, particularly by books like this one, with its story of absence – 'the blessedness of absence' (*BT* 204) – and its imaginings about a void, the 'so-said void, the so-missaid' (*WH* 24).

Notes

Introduction

1. Jung's spell-binding phrase first re-occurs in the addenda to *Watt* albeit in a slightly distorted form: 'never been properly born' (*W* 248). For the Jung lecture motif, see Knowlson 1996, 176, 177, 207–8, 375–6, Melnyk (2005), Thurston (2009). James Knowlson tells us that the woman in a later play of Beckett's, *Footfalls*, was specifically linked by Beckett with the young female patient of Jung's, of whom Beckett had heard him speak in 1935. May in *Footfalls* was 'Beckett's own poignant recreation of the girl who had never really been born, isolated and permanently absent, distant and totally encapsulated within herself' (Knowlson 1996, 616). In an article entitled, 'Outselves: Beckett, Bion and Beyond', Luke Thurston (2009) also explores the role of Jung in the Beckett–Bion relationship albeit from the perspective of Beckett's troubled relations with James Joyce and Lucia Joyce. Thurston's article, by stressing the modernist dimension of Beckett's writing and its creative resistance to historicist interpretation, sets out to provide a critique of the historicist empiricism represented by the work of Matthew Feldman. Finally, for a full-length Jungian study of Beckett, see O'Hara (1997).
2. Also see Marius Buning's English version of Sjef Houppermans' introduction to 'Beckett & la Psychanalyse & Psychoanalysis' (*Samuel Beckett Today/ Aujourd'hui* (ed.) Sjef Houpperman, Amsterdam and Atlanta: Rodopi, 1996, V, 5–7). '"Pitiless lucidity", writes Marius Buning, might be a good term to express a Beckettian element in the modern unconscious, we are always likely to have recourse to his obscure light to help lighten our darkness; perhaps a kind of transference and counter-transference goes on between him and us' (Buning 1996, 5).
3. Among such reductive readings see: André Marissel, 'L'Univers de Samuel Beckett: un noeud de complexes', *Esprit,* XXXI, Sept. 1963, 240–55; Brian Shapiro, 'Toward a Psychoanalytic reading of Beckett's *Molloy*', *Literature and Psychology,* XIX, 1969. no. 2, 71–86, nos. 3–4, 15–30; R. Riva, 'Beckett and Freud', *Criticism,* XII, spring 1970, no. 2, 120; 132; Danièlle Bajomée, 'Lumière, ténèbres et chaos dans *L'innommable*', *Les Lettres Romaines,* XXIII, mai 1969, no. 2, 139–58; Guy Barnard, *Samuel Beckett: A New Approach,* New York: Dodd, 1970.
4. For a less biographically oriented use of the 'Imaginary Twin' theme, see Moorjani (2004a), 177–80 and Oppenheim (2001). In another article, Moorjani compellingly uses Bion's concept to explore the intriguing like-mindedness of Beckett and Bion on the fascinating subject of vision and blindness. See Angela Moorjani (2004b), 'Peau de chagrin: Beckett and Bion on Looking Not to See', *Samuel Beckett Today/Aujourd'hui,* 'After Beckett/ D'après Beckett', edited/édité par Anthony Uhlmann, Sjef Houppermans & Bruno Clément, 25–38.

5. I align with Steven Connor's view that there is a familiar kind of psychoanalytic appropriativeness in Anzieu's judgement, for it suggests that, having broken off analysis, the only route to psychic reparation lies in the reincorporation of its procedures. Just as the refusal of psychoanalysis is always read as a psychoanalytic symptom, so the resolution of psychological problems must always it seems be attributable to psychoanalysis carried on by other means (Connor 2008, 12–13). For a critique of Anzieu's reductionism, see Oppenheim 2001 (768–9).
6. Other Beckett critics have, in turn, been influenced by Anzieu's own concepts, in particular, including Moorjani (2000a, 93–9; 2000b, 63–70); Grossman (1998, 38; 50–2), Connor (2008, 11–13, 29, 30).
7. See *Samuel Beckett Today/Aujourd'hui,* XVI, 'Notes diverse holo': Catalogues of Beckett's reading notes and other manuscript at Trinity College Dublin, with supporting essays, eds Matthijs Engelberts, Everett Frost, with Jane Maxwell, Amsterdam and New York: Rodopi, 2006, 157–66. Moorjani (2004a) also addresses the question of Beckett's vast psychoanalytic culture and, in particular, the influence of Rank (173–5).
8. Rabaté (1984) in his stimulating reading of *Murphy*, notes the influence of the theories of Külpe, Koffka and Köhler (139–42); Knowlson (1996) notes the appearance of allusions to Woodworth's text in *Murphy* (177–8, 737 nn. 44–7).
9. Matthew Feldman (2006) insists on seeing Beckett's reading within 'a larger self-education process' (78), more an encounter with erudition than with the personal unconscious. In this respect, Feldman takes Anzieu's work to task dismissing it as pure speculation. For a psychoanalytic critique of Feldman's historical empiricism, see Thurston (2009), 123–4.
10. The other absent analytic figure in this study is, of course, Lacan. This is not to disregard the well-known affinities between all three analysts in question. Winnicott, for example, acknowledges being influenced by Lacan in viewing the individual's ego development being conditioned by the mother and specifically by the use of her face as mirror (Winnicott 1971, 130–8). However, unlike Lacan whose mirror stage, on the contrary, is a phase critically marked by misrecognition since the child's fascination with its own image presents a fiction of a sort, a fantastic unity – 'the Ideal-I' – (Lacan 1977, 2), Winnicott claims that the mirroring role of the mother is fully constitutive of the child's identity since 'what the baby sees is himself or herself. In other words, the mother is looking at the baby and what she is like is related to what she sees there' (1971, 131; see Ross 1995).

    As regards Lacan and Bion, it is well known that Lacan had always been an admirer of Bion (Rabaté 1996, 26; Rabaté 2001, 14), Bion's discovery in the 1930s of 'the nothing' as a fundamental object of unconscious desire being taken up by Lacan in his seminars of the 1960s. As Rabaté outlines, unlike Bion, 'Lacan did not try to align his concepts with those of Locke, Kant or Hegel, but instead continued to criticize philosophy for an original sin that consisted in placing consciousness as the origin of meaning' (2001, 15). From a Lacanian point of view, the 'original sin' of this study is that, theoretically, I am placing the 'object' as the origin of meaning in Beckett's texts. However, as Lois Oppenheim astutely argues, object-relations models in psychoanalysis 'draw attention to a very different (as experiential or non-representational) order of language. Thus, within the zones of transformation and blankness, where Beckett's artistry, for one, is most poignant, they situate the vitality of the individual's endeavor to come to terms with his or her lot' (2001, 781). For my previous discussion of the wider theoretical common-ground between Lacan, Winnicott, Bion and Anzieu, particularly with regard to notions such as 'breakdown', 'foreclosure' and 'negation' and 'skin-container', see Ross 2004, 59–76. For a full-length Lacanian study of Beckett's prose, see Bernard (1996).

11. A second and very different type of book would have been required to show how the counter-transferential relations between Beckett and Bion continued up to the end of Bion's career, as if Bion let himself be 'written' in advance by Beckett, not unlike the way Lacan was 'written' in advance by Joyce (Rabaté 2001, 183). As mentioned, Didier Anzieu, Jean-Michel Rabaté and Steven Connor have all shown, in different ways, how Bion's later conceptual work shows a contradictory fictional structure not unlike Beckett's.
12. Jean-Michel Rabaté rehearses a very similar debate, this time in relation to Lacan's aversion to any would-be application of psychoanalytic theory to literature:

> Lacan's theses do not just 'exploit' literary examples as so many confirmations of Freudian insights, for instance, they also, since they present themselves as fundamental 'literary', give literature a much more ambiguous role to play in them and for them: literature cannot be just an 'object' caught up, traversed or exhibited by a discourse seeking a simple justification though exemplification, it inhabits the theory from the start, and makes it tremble, hesitate as to its own status, it ruins the mirage of a pure and clean theory neatly opposed to a few well-chosen examples. (Rabaté 2001, 6–7).

13. Lois Oppenheim explores similar issues albeit from a slightly different perspective (Oppenheim 2001). Refuting the notion of a profound reciprocal influence of Beckett and Bion, and using a different interpretive framework, she hypothesises that Beckett's 'visual' writing and concern with evocative memory might be more fruitfully analysed in the light of Bion's concepts of transformation and assaults on verbal thought (a point I shall take up later in this book). She relates Beckett's 'dissociative writing' (776), defined as 'the predominance of ego dissolution and a disengagement from any objectifying notion of world' (ibid.), to André Green's theory of blank psychosis and blank mourning.

1 Setting up Shop in the Void

1. As a criticism, one can point to Sartre's analysis of Paul Valéry's bourgeois origins which was shown not to be the ultimate factor in Valéry's radical status as a writer, since not every petit-bourgeois was a writer like Valéry, though Valéry himself was a petit-bourgeois (Sartre 1968, 53–60).
2. On Beckett's childhood see: Bair 1978, 13–60; Knowlson 1996, 1–29; Cronin 1997, 1–38.

3. On Beckett's analysis, see: Bair 153–68; Anzieu 1986, 21–30; Baker 1997, 6; Moorjani 2004a, 173; Ross 2004, 42–9; Connor 2008. (More references will be made in the following chapter.)
4. See: Gérard Bléandonou, *Wilfred Bion: His Life and Works 1897–1979*, trans. Claire Pajaczkowska (London: Free Association Books, 1994) and the comprehensive coverage of his life, career and theories in *The Edinburgh International Encyclopaedia of Psychoanalysis*, ed. Ross M. Skelton, Edinburgh UP, 2006, 55–60.
5. Two examples may suffice: in a letter written to MacGreevy in January 1935, Beckett mentions getting encouraging news about his Proust article: 'I was highly gratified, especially as it cheered up Mother. I had things out with her, mildly & cautiously, & and now things are much more satisfactory' (*LSB* 240). Later that year, on 8 October, Beckett writes to MacGreevy: 'As to going even to Spain, I fear that is unlikely for some time. Mother will be feeling there is a lot of me due to her, & perhaps after all I may find myself immune to Dublin now, & be able to work there. She writes from Killiney more happily I think than since it happened, & with a new sense of how she must accept what is left behind. She went to see Count of Montecristo film with Frank! Miracle' (*LSB* 283).
6. Previous to this letter MacGreevy had written expressing his concern about-Beckett's black moods and recommended the German theologian Thomas à Kempis's *Imitation of Christ* as an alternative way of life from which Beckett might find comfort (Knowlson 1996, 179. In his reply (previous to the quote presented), Beckett dismissed Kempis as 'an abject self-referring quietism indeed' (*LSB* 257). Notwithstanding, the theme of quietism in Beckett has intrigued many critics. See Ackerly (2000).
7. Beckett's personal contacts with the Unanimists, the Surrealists and the Verticalists amply confirm his juvenile avant-gardist affiliation. He did after all translate Breton, Eluard and Crevel's respective works for the 1936 September issue of *This Quarter*. The influential journal *transition* was to publish much of Beckett's earliest work (essays, poems). It should also be remembered that Beckett wrote his first two major works in Paris: the poem 'Whorescope' (1930) and the unpublished novel *Dream of Fair to Middling Women*, a sort of parody, among other things of *Finnegans Wake*. On Beckett's first Paris stay, see Beckett's three biographers who differ little: Bair 1980, 61–102; Knowlson 1996, 87–119; Cronin 1996, 86–102. On Beckett and the French avant-garde, see: Norma Bouchard (1997).
8. On Beckett's Italian translations, see Visconti (1997).
9. This point is made quite clear by the editors of Beckett's published letters who write: 'the restlessness which Beckett experiences during this period allows him to settle only briefly, and he is almost constantly on the move, between Dublin, London, and Paris, taking in Germany too on several occasions, opting finally for Paris in later 1937, just in time to move again in 1940, although by forces largely beyond his control' (*LSB* lxxix).
10. In a letter written to MacGreevy from Paris in the winter of 1937, Beckett likens escaping from Ireland to 'coming out of gaol in April' (*LSB* 567).
11. Asked if he wanted *Godot* to be premiered in Dublin, on Alan Simpson's suggestion that it would be fitting if the first production in English were to be in Dublin, Beckett replied tartly: 'As to the propriety of first production in

English being in Dublin, I'm afraid I have no feeling about that at all' (Letter to Simpson, 9 April 1954, qtd by Knowlson 1996, 784).

12. 'How lovely it is being here', Beckett wrote in a letter to MacGreevy referring to the wall of his room in the Hôtel Libéria in Paris where he had taken temporary lodging in January 1938: 'even with a hole in the side. A sunlit surface yesterday brighter than the whole of Ireland's summer' (*LSB* 596).
13. 'All homelands are more or less violent hallucinations', writes Steven Connor, 'and it is perhaps in this sense that Becket is the most Irish of writers' (Connor 1992, 104).
14. Samuel Beckett's Letter to Nancy Cunard, 5 July 1956, quoted in Knowlson (1996, 428).
15. On Beckett's time in St Lô, see: Dougald McMillan's introduction in Samuel Beckett, *As the Story Was Told* (*AST*) 13–16; Knowlson 1996, 345–51; Knowlson 2003, 27; Gaffney 1999; Pilling 2007, 191–5. For textual analysis of *The Capital of the Ruins*, see Katz 1998, and Ross 2006.
16. Many critics fasten onto Beckett's script, none more than Lois Gordon who goes furthest when claiming Beckett's awareness of the human capacity to endure misfortune going as far as to talk of Beckett's Irish pride (in Gaffney, 266–7).
17. Beckett's poem, Saint-Lô (1946) functions as a consolatory footnote to *The Capital of the Ruins*:

    Vire will wind in other shadows
    Unborn through the bright ways tremble
    And the old mind
    Ghost-abandoned
    Sink into its havoc
    (Original *Irish Times* version, quoted in
    Pilling 1997, 194).

18. I am using Viola Westbrook's English translation of the German. See her discussion on the particular translation difficulties presented by the German letter (*LSB* xliii–xlvii).
19. Such a view is also all of a piece with Beckett's personal fascination with the philosophy of Arnold Geulincx, 'my literary fantasia', wrote Beckett in a 9 January 1935 (for 1936) letter to George Reavey (*LSB* 295). Explaining to Sighle Kennedy the irrationality and negativity of his first novels, Beckett said that the real point of departure of any investigation into *Murphy* should be the concept of 'nothing', a 'nothing' that appears in Democritus's famous 'Nothing is more than nothing' (and later in *Malone Dies*) and in Geulincx's statement, *Ubi nihil vales, nihil veli* [you will not want anything where you are worth nothing] (*D* 113; Rabaté 1996, 25). We now know that in 1936, in the library of Trinity College, Beckett read and took extensive notes in Latin from the *Ethica* of Geulincx. See *Notes Diverse Holo* (2006), special issue *SBT/A* XVI, 141–55, *LSB*, 297 and McMillan and Fehsenfeld 1988, 53–5. (I shall return to this point in the chapter on *Waiting for Godot*.)
20. However, it would be foolhardy to think that the negative principle was something new chez Beckett of the 1940s. As Pilling rightly points out, 'this principle was never more vigorously and variously exploited than at the very beginning of his writing career, in 1931–1932, in *Dream of Fair to Middling*

Women but also in *Murphy* and *Watt*' (Pilling 2005, 174). On a personal front, Beckett seems to have needed to cling to his 'negative' side. For example, as regards continuing his analysis Beckett realises: 'how lost I would be bereft of my incapacitation' (Letter to MacGreevy, 14 February 1935), *LSB* 250, and derides in another letter, just shortly afterwards, 'the intolerable symptoms of an improvement' (Letter to MacGreevy, 20 February 1935), *LSB* 253.

21. The first page of the French manuscript bears the date '9 Octobre 1948' and the last '29 Janvier 1949' (Bair 1980, 323), the general impression of the manuscript being 'one of almost continuous writing' (Cohn 1973, 141).

2 Beckett's Negative Sublime

1. I shall be partly using Nicole Glover's excellent online study of post-Kleinian psychoanalysis and its relevance for art: see Nicole Glover, Psychoanalytic Aesthetics: The British School (2004). http://www.human-nature.com/free-associations/glover/ (accessed 1 February 2008).
2. On this point, see Murray Schwartz's discussion in *Psychoanalysis and The Question of the Text* (ed.) Geoffrey H. Hartman (Baltimore, London: Johns Hopkins University Press, 1978), 1–18, who contrasts classical psychoanalysis, as represented by Freud, with contemporary psychoanalysis, as represented by Winnicott, in order to distinguish between two potential models of literary criticism.
3. Angela Moorjani contends that the overlap in Bion's early essays with Kleinian theory is another reason for the parallels between the English analyst and his Irish patient. There is little doubt, Moorjani continues, that Beckett was aware of Kleinian thought and play technique as early as *Murphy*, where the first zone of Murphy's mind contains 'the world of the body broken up into the pieces of a toy' (qtd in Moorjani 2004a, 180).
4. Keats wrote that a 'Man of Achievement was capable of being in uncertainties, Mysteries, doubts, without any irritable reaching after fact and reason'. Letter to George and Tom Keats, 2 December 1817, in *The Letters of John Keats: 1814–1821*, ed. H.E. Rollins, Cambridge: Cambridge UP, 1958, 15.
5. Meltzer also suggests a link between Bion's O and Wittgenstein's concept of 'seeing as' (Meltzer 1978, 81).
6. In a fascinating Levinassian analysis of the unconscious links between Keatsian negative capability and the Jungian motif of 'never really been born', Dan Mellamphy writes:

> The unknown and unnamed being whose very unknowability and unnameability – whose ultimate negativity – 'Beckett the writer' had initially tried to conceal, revealed itself to be a negativity (a negative) that in no sense manifested itself as a positive *incapacity*; rather, it became for Beckett a negative *capability*, an intuition where intellection reached an impasse, an actual affect (a feeling ill-at-ease) arising at the point where the concept collapses, a certain uncertain 'something or nothing' ('isolated', as Keats would say, 'from the [very] penetralium of mystery') that Beckett, in a letter to Axel Kaun written two years after Tavistock, described as a 'something or nothing' 'leaking' or 'seeping' into consciousness against the grain of language [...]. (Mellamphy 2006, 495)

7. Indeed, according to Glover, it is the notion of the 'transitional object' and 'transitional' or 'potential' space that distinguishes a 'Kleinian' from a 'Winnicottian' account of aesthetics (12).
8. On this case, see Albert Hutter, 'Poetry in Psychoanalysis: Hopkins, Rossetti, Winnicott', in Rudnytsky (63–86).
9. Winnicott does acknowledge that no one will ever be able to explain the creative impulse, and 'it is unlikely that anyone would ever want to do so', (ibid.).
10. Indeed, in a number of correspondences, Winnicott argues that Bion and he are virtually saying the same thing, with Bion doing so in a more abstract fashion. See his letter to J.O. Wisdom, in Rodman (1987, 159).
11. In his analysis of abstract painting and blankness, Fuller (1988) deploys both Winnicott and Bion's account of space without any reference to the very important differences between these two conceptions (201–8, 211, 225–8).

3 Family Matters

1. On the same issue, Moorjani writes: 'For in *Molloy*, Moran's orderly and Molloy's disorderly texts exist as aspects of the artistic process in the manner of the orderly disorder of chaos' (Moorjani 1991, 55).
2. Baker, op. cit. argues that if Molloy's account of his relationship with his mother is shot through with lacunae and denials, it is because Beckett is playing with the idea of repression (5). More convincingly, Baker goes on to show that Molloy's modes of denial follow closely Freud's figure of *Verneinung* or 'negation' in which the subject raises and disowns the repressed material at the same time. 'The most suggestive part of Freud's comment for reading Molloy must be on grounds picked up from his treatment' (ibid.).
3. On the question of Beckett's manipulation of cliché and dead language, see Christopher Ricks, *Beckett's Dying Words*, 1993, 62–78.
4. For theory I shall follow Glover's presentation of Bion's notion of links and linkage (Glover, op. cit., chapter 4 'The Legacy of Wilfred Bion).
5. Hill explores the son–mother relation using the notion of the uncanny (86–7).
6. I am indebted to all of Baker's chapter: 'The Stamp of the Father in *Molloy*', Baker 1997, 37–47.
7. Lacan explains that the Name-of-the-Father is a metaphor, that is, 'the metaphor that substitutes this Name in the place first symbolized by the operation of the absence of the mother [...] to the appeal of the Name-of-the-Father responds, not the absence of the real father, for this absence is more than compatible with the presence of the signifier, but the inadequacy of the signifier itself' (Lacan 1977, 200).
8. Later in his life, Bion came to believe that the process of thinking was indeed a modification of the oral-alimentary process. Moran is thinking and speaking here using oral-excretory forms, not unlike one of Bion's patients who, for example, remarked that he used his intestine as a brain (Bion 1967, 40), or the patient who felt 'that good interpretations from me were so

consistently and minutely split up by him that they became mental urine which then seeped uncontrollably away' (ibid. 95).

9. Anthony Uhlmann also draws on Beckett's Resistance activities, and using Foucault's key dichotomy between the society of spectacle and the society of surveillance, proposes a fascinating account of the Moran–Molloy relationship in terms of surveillance, order and 'open secrets'. See Anthony Uhlmann, *Beckett and Poststructuralism*, Cambridge UP, 1999, 40–57.
10. Bion compares catastrophic change to Keats' negative capability, a notion already alluded to.
11. Daniel Katz makes a similar point when he writes that Beckett's 'characters don't "produce" thought as much as interpret, translate, and repeat the "thought" to which they are subject' (Katz 1999, 91).
12. This echoes the art criticism Beckett wrote just after *Molloy* where he is concerned with the representational crisis in modern painting. Describing van Velde's art in terms of the interior duplication of an impenetrable space, Beckett writes: 'for what remains of the representable if the essence of the object is to elude representation' (qtd in Moorjani 1982, 44: and see 44–5).

4 Playing, Dying and the Art of Being Absent

1. See the excellent entry on Transitional Objects and Transitional Phenomena in Skelton 2006, 468–9.
2. Winnicott was critical of psychoanalysts who had been busy using play content to look at the playing child and to write about playing as a thing in itself, hence the need on Winnicott's part to make a significant distinction between the meanings of the noun 'play' and the verbal noun 'playing' (Winnicott 1971, 46).
3. The space of the *in-between* can also be conceptualised, in my view, by re-deploying Bion's idea of the caesura. Where Freud discovered the caesura between unconscious and conscious, Bion uses 'caesura' to stress two aspects: separation (barrier, pause, cut, screen) and continuity. More widely, Bion saw emotional development taking place by layers where between each layer there are caesuras, birth being only one of them (Skelton 2006, 72). Using a quotation from Freud he wrote: 'There is much more continuity between intra-uterine life than the impressive caesura of the act of birth would have us believe' (Bion 1987, 234).
4. See Daniel Katz's analysis of the inventory motif (Katz 2006, 13–14).
5. James Knowlson tells us that 'Beckett became very nervous at night and would only go to sleep with a night-light and his favourite teddy bear. "He had a teddy bear called 'Baby Jack' and they had brass bedsteads. And it was always tied to the top of the bed, with almost no stuffing left in it at all", said Sheila Page' (1996, 17).
6. Commenting the same passage in *Malone Dies*, Leslie Hill analyses the fate of objects in terms of mourning. 'Objects are not forgotten, but recur like ghosts. Mourning seems never completed and there appears to be a

fundamental obstacle preventing a resolution of the ambivalence inherent in incorporation' (1990, 70–1).

7. In a similar vein, some of Malone's 'treasures' exist in order not to be defined or determined. For example, Malone is unable to determine the nature of 'a little packet tied up in age-yellowed newspaper' (181). The text stipulates that Malone's hand 'understood softness and lightness', but instead of opening the mysterious packet, Malone decides to keep it as 'my little mystery, all my own' (ibid.). Other unknown objects are to be found 'belonging to a third category' of which Malone knows 'nothing' (229–30). Chris Ackerley suggests that the little packet 'may be a frail, desiccated coagulan of apian exoskeletons, Moran's '"dry light ball"' (Ackerley 2007, 15).
8. The novel's first title 'L'Absent' (Cohn 1973, 92) strongly suggests the abandoned child's game with his image in the mirror and the earlier fictional series of self-reflexive games (Moorjani 1982, 52).
9. On the shifting boundaries between Malone and his characters, see Daniel Katz 2006, 13–14.
10. Freud used the term 'barrier contact' to describe a neurophysiological synapse (Skelton 2006, 94). Bion used the same term to designate a mental structure that has both the functions of contact and of barrier, marking both the points of contact and separation between conscious and unconscious elements (Ibid.).
11. For Moorjani, 'the names of both pencil and pen underline the sexual significance of the objects. On both narrative levels, then, it is clear that writing is derived from an unconscious incest wish which has been sublimated'. Moorjani goes on to argue that Malone's pencil may symbolise a weapon of death, and represent 'the sublimation of aggressive drives' (1982, 125). Daniel Katz intriguingly shows how the Venus pencil has stronger connotations with the umbilical cord and, consequently, the room is seen by Katz as a metaphor of a 'giant abdomen' (2006, 15). Hill proposes a fascinating discussion of the play of names in *Malone Dies*, in particular the links between Lemuel and Samuel (107–12). See also Begam who sees Lemuel's mass homicide as an act of authorial intervention (146). Parkin-Gounelas, however, unconvincingly reads the end of the novel in terms of Kristevan abjection and horror (Parkin-Gounelas 2001, 77–8).
12. Eliade writes: 'Above all, stone is. It always remains itself; and, more important still, it strikes. Before he even takes it up to strike, man finds in it an obstacle – if not to his body, at least to his gaze – and ascertains its hardness, its roughness, its power' (Eliade 1996, 107).
13. For a Swiftian intertext of madness and insanity in *Malone Dies*, see Smith (2002 35–7). Smith also argues for the influence of *Tristram Shandy* on Beckett's Malone (see 61–4).
14. As Foucault tells us in his analysis of the famous Ships of Fools in the Middle-Ages, the practice of conveying the insane in boats from town to town, was a means of getting the insane out of the way, ridding the cities 'of their presence' (Foucault 1967, 10). The madman was made into 'a prisoner of his own departure' (11). Confined on the ship, from which there is no escape, 'the madman is [...] a prisoner in the midst of what is the freest, the openest of routes [...] He is the Passenger par excellence: that is, the prisoner of the passage' (11).

15. 'I like that crouching brooding quality in Keats', Beckett once wrote to MacGreevy, ' – squatting on the moss, crushing a petal, licking his lips & rubbing his hands, "counting the last oozing, hours by hours." I like him best of them all, because he doesn't beat his fists on the table. I like that awful sweetness and thick soft damp green richness. And weariness' (Letter to MacGreevy, Sunday [c.27 April to 11 May 1930], *LSB* 21).
16. On this point, Bair tells us that Beckett insists that he was born on Good Friday, 13, April 1906 although his birth certificate gives the date 13, May 1906 (Bair 212 n. 32). See also Moorjani (1982, 123–4).

5 Incomprehensible Damnation

1. As Stephen Barker remarks, it is thinking the unthought that provides Beckett with a 'conceit and an appendix for [the] nothing' (Barker 1991, 128).
2. David Hesla argues us that the Unnamable goes through 'Something in order to arrive at Nothing ... goes through Something and demolishes it on the way in order to get to Something ... unapproachable by any way other than this version of the *Via Negativa*' (Hesla 1971, 115).
3. Compare the Unnamable's 'our hell will be heaven to them' (*BT* 348) to Milton's description of hell in *Paradise Lost*: 'The mind is its own place, and in itself/Can make a Heaven of Hell, a Hell of Heaven' (Milton 2004, 143).
4. Lacan puts this in more jocular witty terms: 'It is sometimes striking that a dimension that is felt as that of Something-else in so many of the experiences that men undergo, not at all without thinking about them, rather while thinking about them, but without thinking that they are thinking' (Lacan 1977, 192).
5. On the disjunction between thinking and what Lacan calls the 'Elsewhere', the latter writes: 'But this aversion becomes quite clear once the conceptual juncture, which nobody had yet thought of, was made, between this Elsewhere and the place, present for all and closed to each, in which Freud discovered that, without thinking about it, and without being able to think he thinks about it better anyone else therefore, it thinks (*ça pense*). It thinks rather badly, but it does think' (193, translator's emphasis).
6. See also Parkin-Gounelas 2001, 69–70.
7. Steven Connor reminds us that later in his career, Bion came to believe that the process of thinking was indeed a modification of the oral-alimentary process. To illustrate the point, Connor fascinatingly compares a case history presented by Bion ('Notes on the Theory of Schizophrenia', 1953), which focuses on the experience of physical dissolution, to Beckett's Unnamable speaker's description of his 'dissolving, dismembered body' [...] 'as he thinks of his hair, eyes and ears falling away from his body' (Connor 2008, 24–5).
8. It is more a case of 'I am amming' rather than 'I am', argues Katz (1999, 122).
9. Barker draws a parallel between Beckett's 'I' and Lacan's 'I' while quoting Lacan's alteration of the Cartesian *cogito ergo sum*, which Barker translates as: 'I am not there where I am the plaything of my thought; I think about what I am, there where I do not think that I am thinking' (Barker 1991, 142). Alan Sheridan's translation slightly differs from Barker's: 'I am not wherever I am

the plaything of my thought; I think of what I am where I do not think to think' (Lacan 1977, 166).

10. Thinking may appear to take on a more metaphorical dimension in the latter part of the novel, insofar that it is the vocality of the voice 'that comes to constitute that frail supporting membrane within, or upon which the work of splitting, fragmentation and disavowal is permitted to occur', to quote Connor's reference to Anzieu (Connor 2008, 29). However, I am arguing that the voice need not exclude the presence of some hypothetical embryonic consciousness. As we have just seen, the orbit of awareness in *The Unnamable* spirals pitilessly and inexorably inwards or backwards, hence my claim that voice and 'mind' are virtually indistinguishable.
11. Winnicott goes on to explain that it is only when integration gradually becomes a maintained state of the individual, that the word disintegration rather than unintegration 'becomes appropriate for description of the negative of integration' (117). A similar emphasis on the link between disintegration and re-integration in artistic activity can be found in Anton Ehrenzweig's Kleinian study *The Hidden Order of Art* (1967) where the function of artistic work is to shape or harmonise what Angela Moorjani calls 'this ordered disorder of the unconscious into the disordered order of a work of art' (Moorjani 1991, 57).
12. Richard Begam comes to a similar conclusion, albeit from a very different perspective and with a different objective, when he reads the image of the tympanum in terms of an interstitial space or space-in-between that collapses any would-be dualist relations between narrator/narrated or subject/object. It is *both* 'identity and difference' (Begam 1996, 177).

6 The Void on Stage

1. There is no overestimating the influence of Geulincx on Beckett's theatrical 'nothing' (already alluded to in our first chapter in relation to Beckett's salutary vision). McMillan and Fehsenfeld show how the *Ubi nihil vales, ibi nihil veles* quote in *Murphy* might be usefully compared to and contrasted with the situation in *Godot* (1988, 53–8). The decisive passage in Geulincx reads: '*Where you can do nothing, there wish nothing,* or in other words *Nothing is to be done for naught* ... [This is) is the highest principle of ethics' (ibid., 54). Where, for Murphy Geulincx represents 'primarily a rationale for escape into a solipsistic "microcosm" [...] Estragon and Vladimir, in contrast, retain more of a "deplorable susceptibility" to external urges and so are more entangled in the futile struggle Geulincx warns against' (55). The same critics explain that in the first French Edition Vladimir did approach Murphy's vision of nothingness. Early in Act II, Vladimir speaks of being happy when Estragon is absent. Estragon questions, 'Happy?' and Vladimir responds, 'Perhaps it's not quite the right word.' Then follows a passage that was crossed out in Beckett's prompt script for the original 1953 production of *En attendant Godot* and deleted in subsequent editions and translations:

    when I close my eyes (*closes eyes and covers them with his hands for more security*) I feel ... yes ... that the light abandons me. (*He opens his eyes*) Now, there you are (*he closes his eyes and concentrates*). Now I feel myself becoming all black inside. (53, McMillan's translation)

'Even the temporary release to the kind of nothing Murphy experiences', explains McMillan, 'is removed as a possibility in *Godot*' (ibid). Ironically, the 'nothing to be done' which opens the play could be read as a statement on subsequent failure to achieve nothingness: 'the "nothing" that "happens" throughout is the other "Nothing" – the circular activity of corporeal existence which Murphy rejects', state McMillan (ibid.).

2. The Wildian echo here is unmistakable. In *The Importance of Being Earnest*, one reads: 'Well, what shall we do? / Nothing! / It is awfully hard work doing nothing. However, I don't mind hard work where there is no definite object of any kind' (Wilde 1966, 23).
3. In relation to the tree, it is worth noting that for the 1961 Odéon revival of *En attendant Godot*, Giacometti designed a minimalist tree made of plaster and thin wire. Jean Martin, the actor who played Lucky, remembers the mutual fascination the tree held for Beckett and the sculptor becoming 'a special emblem of that production: 'every night Sam and Giacometti came before the beginning of the play. Giacometti would change the position of a twig a little bit and then Sam would come later and he would change it. It was just as if it was the important thing. And in fact it was a very important thing you know' (qtd in McMillan 80). As Matti Megged reminds us, Giacometti's stage has its own life, its own reality. On this stage, a sense of space-atmosphere surrounds the objects (with human and inanimate), penetrates them, becomes independent yet related to the world outside, through the field of vision that is created between the objects and the observer [...]. His figures placed on a confined stage and detached from the objective world are surrounded by *empty space*' (in Megged 1985, 21, my emphasis).
4. Beckett's 'psychology notes' of the 1930s clearly attest to his interest in sleeping and dreams, one source being Jones. See Feldman 2006, 79.
5. For a fuller treatment of the ethical dimension to the self–other and we/they relation in *Godot*, see Ross 2006, 75–90.
6. This section is a development of various passages from *Aux frontières du vide*, (Ross 2004, 169–80).
7. Dougald McMillan tells us that, an abandoned title, *En Attendant*, without *Godot* for the French version clearly shows that Beckett originally wanted to displace the emphasis from Godot to waiting. In his own production of the German *Godot*, his deletion of 'wir' from the original title *Wir Warten auf Godot* (*We Wait for Godot*) also placed the emphasis upon the act of waiting rather upon the characters who wait (McMillan 1988, 59–60).
8. On this point, Elin Diamond, partly using Lacan, argues that the pleasure Vladimir and Estragon get from their 'alternative' activities – their duologues – far from being time-passing heroics of existential clowns, lies in the fact that their pronounced sameness makes room for difference. Even when they play at Pozzo and Lucky in the second act, it is a way of keeping the other in view and available for pleasurable mimesis (Diamond 2001, 385 and 386).
9. In the original production of *En Attendant Godot*, Beckett insisted on Estragon's mental acuity being kept to a minimum. An important instance

of this concerns the objection made to Blin about the pants-dropping scene at the very end of the play. Apparently Estragon had kept them half on. Beckett's reply to Blin is worth quoting:

> 'one thing troubles me, the pants of Estragon. I naturally asked Suzanne if they fell well, and she told me that he keeps them half on. He mustn't. He absolutely mustn't. *He really doesn't have the mind for that, then.* He doesn't even realize that they're fallen'. (Qtd in McMillan 79, my emphasis)

10. As regards Beckett and the question of a mineral imagination, Michael Angelo Rodriguez (2004) tells us that as early as 1937, in a letter to MacGreevy, Beckett praised the painting of Watteau for its depiction of people who are 'mineral'. According to Rodriguez, he may also have been influenced by Gottfried Benn's essay, 'The structure of the Personality', an essay that outlined a geology of the self while taking into account recent advances in neuropsychology. Also mining Beckett's texts for mineral strata, Chris Ackerley tells us that a table of geological periods appears in Beckett's *Whorescope* Notebook and in the early drafts of *Watt*, the stated intent is autospeliology, the desire to plummet 'deep down in those palaeozoic profounds, midst mammoth Old Red Sandstone phalli and Carboniferous pudenda' (Ackerley 2005, 179).
11. On the subject of faith and psychoanalysis, see Eigen (1981). Faith is implicit, Eigen argues, in Winnicott's 'transitional experiencing'. In Bion faith is linked with openness to O or the (unknowable) ultimate reality. A certain faith is also required to tolerate the movement of meaning in Lacan's symbolic order (432).

7 Restyling the Ineffable Void

1. This chapter is a development of previous work. See Ross 2001, 64–73.
2. The performance was filmed without audience and it is on the film version as well as on Beckett's production notebooks that this study is based. The audio-visual cassette was kindly forwarded to me by Walter Asmus to whom I extend my gratitude and thanks. All references will be to the revised edition of *Waiting for Godot* in *The Theatrical Notebooks of Samuel Beckett*, Volume. 1, *Waiting for Godot*, eds James Knowlson, Dougald McMillan, London: Faber/Faber, New York: Grove Press, 1993, abbreviated to *TN*. The Schiller production notebook (abbreviated to *Schiller nb*) is presented in both facsimile and transcription in the second half of *TN*, 175–395. When referring to the manuscript, I shall refer to the actual manuscript number and not to the corresponding page number in *TN*. For accounts of the 1975 Berlin *Godot*, see: Ruby Cohn, 'Beckett's German Godot', *Journal of Beckett Studies*, no. 1 (Winter 1976), 41–9; McMillan and Fehsenfeld (abbreviated to McMillan), 1988, 87–136 including Walter Asmus' rehearsal diary (136–48); Ruby Cohn, *Just Play: Beckett's Theater*, Princeton: Princeton UP, 1980, 3, 19–20, 256–67; Julian Garforth, 'A Trilingual Godot', Samuel Beckett Today/Aujourd'hui, 5, 'Beckett & la psychanalyse & psychoanalysis', Amsterdam & Atlanta: Rodopi, 1996, 155–74.

3. It should also be added that using his own German translation of the play, Beckett completely revised both text and stage directions, and these revisions were then incorporated into an English text for subsequent productions by Walter Asmus closely modelled on Beckett's work in Berlin (Bradby, 106). Walter Asmus went on to direct *Waiting for Godot* with the San Quentin Drama Workshop in 1984 (supervised by Beckett) and with the Gate Theatre (Dublin) at the Barbican, London in 1999.
4. This is not to diminish the importance of verbal motifs in the Berlin *Godot*. As McMillan explains, Beckett also listed key verbal repetitions which reflected the larger themes of the play these serving to counterbalance 'the specific associations of the geometric configuration and gestures' (125). Headings such as 'Doubts, confusion', 'Come let's go', 'Help', 'Sleep', are closely related accounts of the mental confusion that permeates the play' (ibid.), in other words, 'the uncertainties of the play which help to "avoid definition"' (ibid.).
5. Oppenheim, in her discussion of evocative memory disorder in Beckett, argues that 'Bion's notion of transformation and, by extension, the grid, are analogous to Beckett's pre-eminently visual use of the word [...] Beckett's profoundly visual thinking is comparable to that of the painter; in modelling his use of language on seeing [...] he makes a distinctly "painterly" use of the word' (771) [...] 'Beckett's visual thinking, generally illustrates Bion's notion of verbal expression as necessarily transformative of experience' (775).
6. Bion uses the term mathematically since he is interested in adapting a scientific method for describing psychoanalytic observation and in particular the thinking processes of schizophrenics. Simply put, Bion is describing the way patients 'split' their world into multiple worlds – bad/good, persecutory/non-persecutory, each 'world' or position constituting sometimes interchangeable and multiple vertices. The vertex is a type of value system or view-of the world which can be empty of meaning or full of meaning.
7. During rehearsals, Beckett explained that Estragon's 'recognition of his counterpart's situation' could be seen in terms of the 'solidarity' of 'two very poor people' (*TN* 117). Significantly, it is Estragon, in the English text, who proposes 'The Scapegoat's Agony' as the name of Lucky's dance (*G* 129).
8. I am inspired here by Derrida's discussion of the Platonic Khora, meaning place as spatial interval, a place of passage or threshold. Rhetorically the Khora is a figuration of the unfigurable. Derrida, in his article, 'How to Avoid Speaking?' shows us how the Khora refuses the consolidation of negativity into something that can be appropriated; it plays against itself and bears the inscription of that something. Paradoxically, it allows us to speak about negativity as interval and hence as the place of inscriptions, while avoiding the fruitless attempt to speak or to figure negativity itself (in Budick 1996, 3–70). Angela Moorjani, in her fascinating philosophical and psychoanalytic inquiry into the radical otherness of *Textes pour rien*, argues that 'Beckett, like so many other writers and artists, derived his form of secular mysticism, which attempts to say the unsayable space, outside the human, and outside the theological, that is the playground of art' (Moorjani, 1997, 213).
9. Interestingly for the thinking sequence which we analysed in the previous chapter, and for the line 'it's terrible to have thought', the acting script

of Bud Thorpe, who played Vladimir in the 1984 San Quentin Drama Workshop production, contains the annotation 'mental murder' with arrows pointing to 'corpses' and skeletons' below (151). Knowlson links this with to Joe's 'mental thuggee' in *Eh Joe* and Hamlet's 'there is nothing either good or bad but thinking makes it so' (II, ii).

10. James Knowlson, in particular, has developed the rich affinity between the play's pictorial and visual codes and Beckett's life-long interest in painting. In his unpublished German diaries, Notebook 5 dated 14, February 1937, Beckett speaks of a visit to the Alte Akademie in Dresden, where he saw the moon watchers and admitted to a 'pleasant predilection for 2 tiny languid men in his landscapes, as in the little moon landscape, that is the only kind of romantic still tolerable, the bémolisé [in a minor key]' (Knowlson 1996, 254). See also 378–9. See also June Schlueter, 'Beckett and the Moonwatchers', *The Beckett Circle/Le cercle de Beckett: Newsletter of the SB Society*, Spring 2002, vol. 25, no. 1, 16–17. Finally, for a Bionian approach to abstract painting, see Peter Fuller's stimulating chapter, 'Abstraction and the Potential Space' (Fuller, 177–238).
11. In *Three Dialogues*, the discussion about Masson is about a very similar issue, that is, Masson as a painter of the void. To quote Duthuit: 'That is perhaps why he [Masson] speaks so often nowadays of painting the void, "in fear and trembling". His concern was at one time with the creation of a mythology; then with man [....] and now .... "inner emptiness, the prime condition, according to Chinese esthetics, of the act of painting"' (*P* 109).

    For the discussion on the negative sublime in painting and the reference to Jean-Luc Nancy, I am greatly indebted to Hélène Ibata.

Conclusion: By Way of Neither

1. James Knowlson also argues for an emotional dimension in the short texts like *Ill Seen Ill Said* or *Worstward Ho*!:

    > Yet the reality of these emotional traces, as well as the sheer courage of such a bold encounter with language, infinity and the void, prevent the text from being arid and utterly inhuman. The imagination however ruined is still alive. In spite of its almost manic wordplay, the text is far too tortured and tormented to be judged a mere linguistic exercise. And there *is* a human sub-text after all, in spite of the narrator's tactics of reducing, shedding and omitting as he strives to 'worsen'. (Knowlson, 676–7, Knowlson's emphasis)

2. In another article Bryden suggests that the middle of the stage's quadrilateral might represent the most terrifying place to be and likens it to the void: 'the middle is uncomfortable because it represents a point of no return, a point of energy, or of spatial dilemma; it may be the eye of the storm, or more terrifyingly, the void or vortex which arrests or displaces movement' (Bryden 1996, 90).
3. Daniel Katz also argues that 'there is no nothing in Beckett' (Katz 1991, 181), his 'stages are never empty or void' (186). Gontarski, for one, points to the

predominance in later Beckett of 'the afterimage that lingers, as a memory, a haunting, a not-yet-vanquished impression' (Gontarski 2006, 3–4). The afterimage 'occupies a space that is not only between different texts, things, and people, but also within those things, something that is there, but not fully present ... no longer there but all the more there in not quite being absent' (4). This is very similar to Jean-Michel Rabaté much earlier analysis of the nothing in terms of ghostliness and spectrification (Rabaté 1996).

Bibliography

Ackerley, C. (2000) 'Samuel Beckett and Thomas à Kempis: The Roots of Quietism', *Samuel Beckett Today/Aujourd'hui* (Amsterdam and New York: Rodopi), IX (eds Buning et al.) – Beckett and Religion/Beckett/Aesthetics/Politics. Beckett et la religion/Beckett/ L'Esthétique/La politique – 81–92 (abbreviated as *SBT/A*).

——, (2005) *Obscure Locks, Simple Keys: the Annotated Watt* (Tallahassee, FL: Journal of Beckett Studies Books).

——, (2007) 'Demented Particularity, or, the Art of Annotation', *The Beckett Circle/Le Cercle de Beckett, Newsletter of the Samuel Becket Society*, Spring, 2007, XXX, vol. 1, 13–16.

Adams, R.M. (1966) *Nil: Episodes in the Literary Conquest of Void during the Nineteenth Century* (New York: Oxford University Press).

Alvarez, A. (1973) *Beckett* (Glasgow: Collins/Fontana).

Anzieu, D. (1983) 'Un soi disjoint, une voix liante: l'écriture narrative de Samuel Beckett', *Nouvelle Revue de Psychanalyse*, XXVIII, 71–86.

——, (1985) *Le Moi-peau* (Paris: Dunod).

——, (1986) 'Beckett et Bion', *Revue de Psychothérapie Psychanalytique de Groupe* V–VI, 21–30.

——, (1989) 'Beckett and Bion', *International Review of Psycho-Analysis*, XVI, 163–8.

——, (1992) *Beckett et le psychanalyste* (Paris: Menta Archimbauld).

Astro, A. (1990) 'Le Nom de Beckett', *Critique*, LXVI, 519–20 (août–septembre), 737–54.

Bair, D. (1978) *Samuel Beckett* (London: Picador).

Bajomée, D. (1969) 'Lumière, ténèbres et chaos dans *L'Innomable*', *Les Lettres Romaines*, XXIII, 2 (mai) 139–58.

Baker, P. (1997) *Beckett and the Mythology of Psychoanalysis* (London: Macmillan; New York: St. Martin's Press – now Palgrave Macmillan).

Baldwin, H. (1981) *Samuel Beckett's Real Silence* (Pennsylvania State University Press).

Barker, S. (1991) 'Recovering the Néant: Language and the Unconscious' in J. Smith (ed.) *The World of Samuel Beckett* (Baltimore: Johns Hopkins University Press), pp. 125–56.

Barnard, G. (1970) *Samuel Beckett: A New Approach* (New York: Dodd).

Beausang, M. (1982) 'L'exil de Samuel Beckett: La terre et le texte', *Critique*, 420, (mai), 561–71.

Begam, R. (1996) *Samuel Beckett and the End of Modernity* (Stanford: Stanford University Press).

Bernard, M. (1996) *Samuel Beckett et son sujet: une apparition évanouissante* (Paris: l'Harmattan).

Bion, W.R. (1950) 'The Imaginary Twin' in *Second Thoughts* (3–22).

——, (1957) 'Differentiation of the Psychotic from the Non-Psychotic Personalities' in *Second Thoughts* (43–64).

——, (1959) 'Attacks on Linking' in *Second Thoughts* (93–109).

——, (1962) 'A Theory of Thinking', *Second Thoughts* (110–19).

——, (1965) *Transformations* (London: Karnac).
——, (1967) *Second Thoughts* (London: Karnac).
——, (1970) *Attention and Interpretation* (London: Karnac).
——, (1979) *A Memoir of the Future: the Dawn of Oblivion* (London: Heinemann).
——, (1987) *Clinical Seminars and Four Papers* (London: Fleetwood).
Bléandonu, G. (1990) *Wilfred R. Bion: La vie et l'œuvre.* (1897–1979) (Paris: Dunod).
Bouchard, N. (1997) 'Rereading Beckett's *Dream of Fair to Middling Women*' in *Samuel Beckett Today/Aujourd'hui*, VI (eds) M. Buning et al., – Crossroads and Borderlines/ L'œuvre carrefour/l'œuvre limite – (Amsterdam and New York: Rodopi), 137–49 (abbreviated as *SBT/A*).
Boxall, P. (2003) *Samuel Beckett, Waiting for Godot/Endgame: a Reader's Guide to Essential Criticism* (Basingstoke and New York: Palgrave Macmillan).
Bradby, D. (2001) *Beckett: Waiting for Godot* (Cambridge University Press).
Brown, L. (1993) *The New Shorter Oxford English Dictionary* (Oxford: Clarendon Press).
Brown, T. (1981) *Ireland: a Social and Cultural History 1922–1985* (London: Fontana).
Bryden, M. (1995) '*Quad*, Dancing Genders', *Samuel Beckett Today/Samuel Beckett Aujourd'hui*, IV, ed. C. Wulf – The Savage Eye/L'oeil fauve – (Amsterdam and New York: Rodopi), 109–22.
——, (1996) 'The Schizoid Space: Beckett, Deleuze, and *L'Epuisé*', *SBT/A*, V, (ed.) S. Houpperman – Beckett & la Psychanalyse & Psychoanalysis – 85–93.
——, (2004) 'Beckett and Religion', in L. Oppenheim (ed.) *Palgrave Advances in Samuel Beckett Studies* (Basingstoke and New York: Palgrave Macmillan), 154–71.
Budick, S. and Iser, W. (eds) (1996) *Languages of the Unsayable: the Play of Negativity in Literature and Literary Theory* (Stanford University Press).
Buning, M. (1999) 'The Play of Negativity in the Beckettian Text' in B. Stewart (ed.) *Beckett and Beyond* (Gerrards Cross: Colin Smythe), pp. 23–31.
Busi, F. (1980) *The Transformations of Godot* (Kentucky University Press).
Büttner, G. (1984) *Samuel Beckett's Novel Watt* (Philadelphia: University of Pennsylvania).
Casement, P. (1982) 'Samuel Beckett's Relationship to his Mother Tongue', *International Review of Psychoanalysis,* IX, part 1, 35–44.
Chabert, P. et al. (2005) *Hayden* (Paris: Fragments).
Clément, B. (1994) *L'Œuvre sans qualités, Rhétorique de Samuel Beckett* (Paris: Seuil).
Cohn, R. (1973) *Back to Beckett* (Princeton University Press).
——, (1980) *Just Play: Beckett's Theatre* (Princeton University Press).
Connor, K. (1997) 'Beckett and Radio: The Radioactive Voice', *SBT/A*, VI (eds) M. Buning et al. – Crossroads and Borderlines/ L'œuvre carrefour/l'œuvre limite – 303–12.
Connor, Steven (1992) 'Over Samuel Beckett's Dead Body', in S.E. Wilmer (ed.) *Beckett in Dublin* (Dublin: Lilliputt Press), 100–8.
——, (2008) 'Beckett and Bion', *The Journal of Beckett Studies,* 17, September, 9–34.
Cousineau, T. (1996), 'The Lost Father in Beckett's Novels', *SBT/A*, 5 – Beckett & la psychanalyse & psychoanalysis – 73–83.

——, (1999) 'Beneath Representation: on staging Beckett's plays' in B. Stewart (ed.) *Beckett and Beyond* (Gerrards Cross: Colin Smythe), 62–9.

Cronin, A. (1997) *Samuel Beckett: the Last Modernist* (London: Flamingo).

Davies, P. (1994) 'Three novels and four *nouvelles*: giving up the ghost be born at last', in J. Pilling (ed.) *The Cambridge Companion to Beckett* (Cambridge University Press), pp. 43–66.

——, (2001) 'On Beckett's Metaphysics of Non-Location: Vagrancy, Void, and Formless Fire', *SBT/A*, XI, eds A. Moorjani & C. Veit – Samuel Beckett: Endlessness in the Year 2000/Samuel Beckett: Fin sans fin en l'an 2000 – 399–407.

Derrida, J. 'How to Avoid Speaking?', in Budick and Iser, *Languages of the Unsayable*, op. cit., 3–70.

Diamond, Elin (2001) '"The society of my likes": Beckett's Political Imaginary', *SBT/A*, XI, 383–8.

Driver, T. (1961) 'Beckett by the Madeleine', *Columbia University Forum*, 4.3.

Eagleton, T. (1996) *Literary Theory: an Introduction* (London: Blackwell).

Ehrenzweig, A. (1967) *The Hidden Order of Art: a Study in the Psychology of Artistic Imagination* (Berkeley and Los Angeles: University of California Press).

Eigen, M. (1981) 'The Area of Faith in Winnicott, Bion and Lacan', *International Journal of Psychoanalysis*, 62, 413–33.

Elevaara, R. (1976) *The Problem of Identity in Samuel Beckett's Prose* (Helsinki: Soumalainen Tiedeakatemia).

Eliade, M. (1996) *Patterns in Comparative Religion*, trans. Rosemary Sheed (Lincoln and London: University of Nebraska Press).

Ellmann, M. (ed.) (1994) *Psychoanalytic Literary Criticism* (London and New York: Longman).

Esslin, M. (1964) *The Theatre of the Absurd* (London: Eyre Spottiswoode).

Feldman, M. (2006) *Beckett's Books: a Cultural History of Samuel Beckett's 'interwar notes'* (Continuum International Publishing Group).

Foucault, M. (1967) *Madness and Civilization: a History of Insanity in the Age of Reason* (trans.) R. Howard (London: Random House).

Friedman, M. (1970) *Samuel Beckett Now* (Chicago and London: University of Chicago).

Freud, S. (1961) *Beyond the Pleasure Principle* (trans. J. Strachey) (London: Hogarth).

——, (1976) *The Interpretation of Dreams* (trans. J. Strachey) *The Pelican Freud Library*, IV (London: Penguin).

——, (1985) 'Creative Writers and Day-Dreaming' in *The Pelican Freud Library*, XIV, Art and Literature (trans. J. Strachey) (London: Penguin), 129–41.

——, *The Standard Edition of the Complete Psychological Works of Sigmund Freud* (trans.) J. Strachey et al. vols 1–23 (London: Hogarth Press, 1953–74 [Abbreviated as SE]).

Frost, E. (1994) '"A Fresh Go" for the Skull: Directing *All that Fall*, Samuel Beckett's Play for Radio', in *Directing Beckett*, ed. Lois Oppenheim (Ann Arbor: University of Michigan Press), 186–219.

Fuller, P. (1988) *Art and Psychoanalysis* (London: Hogarth Press).

Gaffney, P. (1999) 'Dante, Manzoni, De Valera, Beckett ... ? Circumlocutions of A Storekeeper: Beckett and Saint-Lô', *Irish University Review* (ed.) A. Roche, XXIX, 2, (Autumn/Winter), 256–80.

Garforth, J. (1996) 'A Trilingual Godot', *SBT/A*, 5, 155–74.

Glover, N. (2004) *Psychoanalytic Aesthetics: the British School* (http://www.human-nature.com/free-associations/glover/)

Gontarski, S. (1997) 'Staging himself, or Beckett's late style in the theatre', *SBT/A*, VI, 87–97.

Gontarski, S. and Uhlmann, A. (eds) (2006) *Beckett after Beckett* (University Press of Florida).

Gordon, L. (1996) *The World of Samel Beckett.* 1906–1946 (New Haven and London: Yale University Press).

——, (2002) *Reading Godot* (New Haven and London: Yale University Press).

Green, A. (1986) *On Private Madness* (London: Hogarth Press).

——, (1999) 'The Intuition of the negative in *Playing and Reality*' in *The Dead Mother: The Work of André Green,* G. Kohon (ed.) (London and New York: Routledge), 205–21.

Grolnick, S. (ed.) (1978) *Between Reality and Fantasy: Transitional Objects and Phenomena* (London and New York: Jason Aronson).

Grossman, E. (1998) *L'Esthétique de Beckett* (Paris: Sedes).

Gunn, D. (1988) *Psychoanalysis and Fiction: an Exploration of Literary and Psychoanalytic Borders* (Cambridge University Press).

Harmon, M. (ed.) (1998) *No Author Better Served: the Correspondence of Samuel Beckett and Alan Schneider* (Cambridge and London: Harvard University Press).

Harrington, J. (1991) *The Irish Beckett* (New York: Syracuse University Press).

Hesla, D. (1971) *The Shape of Chaos* (Minneapolis: Minnesota University Press).

Hill, L. (1990) *Beckett's Fiction in Different Words* (Cambridge University Press).

Hoffman. F. (1962) *The Language of Self* (Carbondale: Southern Illinois University Press).

Homan, S. (1984) *Beckett's Theatres* (Lewisburg: Bucknell University Press).

Hunkeler, T. (1997) *Echos de l'Ego dans l'oeuvre de Samuel Beckett* (Paris: Harmattan).

Irigaray, L. (2006) 'The Path toward the Other', in Gontarski et al. (eds) *Beckett after Beckett* (op. cit.), 39–51.

Janvier, L. (1986) 'Roman et théâtre', *Revue d'esthétique*, 'Beckett par Beckett' (ed.) P. Chabert (Toulouse: Privat), 45–56.

Jung, C. (1968) *Analytical Psychology: its Theory and Practice (The Tavistock Lectures)* (London: Routledge Kegan Paul).

Junker, M. (1995) *Beckett: the Irish Dimension* (Dublin: Wolfhound).

Katz, D. (1998) '"Les façons d'être nous": sujet et culture dans *Watt*' in E. Grossman and R. Salado (eds) *Samuel Beckett: L'écriture et la scène* (Paris: Sedes), 127–37.

——, (1999) *Saying I No More: Subjectivity and Consciousness in the Prose of Samuel Beckett* (Illinois: Northwestern University Press).

——, (2006) 'Beckett's Absent Paris: *Malone Dies*, Céline, and the Modernist City', *Etudes Anglaises,* 1, eds C. Ross and C. Bonafous-Murat (janvier–mars), 7–17.

Kearney, R. (1984) *Myth and Motherland* (Derry: Field Day Theatre Company).

——, (ed.) (1985) *The Irish Mind: Exploring Intellectual Traditions* (Dublin: Wolfhound).

——, (1988) *Transitions: Narratives in Modern Irish Culture* (Dublin: Wolfhound).
Keats, J. (1958) *The Letters of John Keats: 1814–1821* (ed.) H.E. Rollins (Cambridge University Press).
Kennedy, S. (2004) '"The artist who stakes his being is from nowhere": Beckett and Thomas MacGreevy on the art of Jack B. Yeats', *SBA/T,* XIV (eds A. Uhlmann et al.) – After Beckett / D'après Beckett – 61–74.
Kern, E. (1959) 'Moran-Molloy: the Hero as Author', *Perspective* 11, 183–93.
——, (1970) *Existential Thought and Fictional Technique: Kierkegaard, Sartre, Beckett* (New Haven, Yale University Press).
Kiberd, D. (1996) *Inventing Ireland* (London: Vintage).
Klein, M. (1975) *Love, Guilt and Reparation and Other Works*, 1921–45 (London: Hogarth Press).
——, (1975) *Envy and Gratitude and Other Works*, 1946–1963 (New York: Delacorte Press).
Knowlson, J. (1996) *Damned to Fame* (London: Bloomsbury).
——, (2003) *Images of Beckett* (Cambridge University Press).
Knowlson, J. and Knowlson, E. (2006) *Beckett Remembering Remembering Beckett* (London: Bloomsbury).
Knowlson, J. and McMillan, D. (1993) (eds) *The Theatrical Notebooks of Samuel Beckett*, vol. I, *Waiting for Godot* (London: Faber and Faber; New York: Grove Press).
Kohon, G. (ed.) (1986) *The British School of Psychoanalysis: the Independent Tradition* (London: Free Association Books).
——, (1999) *The Dead Mother: the Work of André Green* (London and New York: Routledge).
Lacan, J. (1977) *Ecrits: a Selection* (trans.) A. Sheridan (London: Tavistock).
Lloyd, David (1993) *Anomalous States: Irish Writing and the Post-colonial Moment* (Dublin: Lilliput Press).
Marissel, A. 'L'Univers de Samuel Beckett: un nœud de complexes', *Esprit,* XXXI, Sept. 1963, 240–55.
McMillan, D. and Fehsenfeld, M. (1988) *Beckett in the Theatre* (London: John Calder; New York: Riverrun).
McMullan, A. (2004) 'Irish/Postcolonial Beckett', in L. Oppenheim (ed.) *Palgrave Advances in Samuel Beckett Studies* (Basingstoke: Palgrave Macmillan), 89–109.
Megged, M. (1985) *Dialogue in the Void: Beckett and Giacometti* (New York: Lumen).
Mellamphy, D. (2006) 'A Look Anew at Beckett's Other Peg', *Modern Drama,* 49:4 (Winter), 491–500.
Melnyk, D. (2005) 'Never Been Properly Jung', *SBT/A* XV (eds M. Buning et al.) – Historicising Beckett/Issues of Performance. Beckett dans l'histoire/En jouant Beckett – 355–62.
Meltzer, D. (1978) *The Kleinian Development* (London: Clunie).
Mercier, V. (1977) *Beckett/Beckett* (New York: Oxford University Press).
Milne, D. (2000) 'Attacking the World's Portadownians: Beckett's Early Politics', *SBT/A,* IX (eds Buning et al.) – Beckett and Religion/Beckett/ Aesthetics/Politics. Beckett et la religion/Beckett/ L'Esthétique/La politique – 279–93.
Milton, J. (2004) *John Milton: the English Poems* (Ware: Wordsworth Editions).

Mooney, S. (2000) '"Integrity in a Surplice": Samuel Beckett's (Post)Protestant Poetics', *SBT/A*, IX, 223–37.
——, (2007) '"Others' Words": Traces of Translation in the Trilogy', *The Beckett Circle / Le Cercle de Beckett, Newsletter of the Samuel Becket Society*, Spring, 2007, XXX, vol. 1, 16–18.
Moorjani, A. (1982) *Abysmal Games in the Novels of Samuel Beckett* (Chapel Hill: University of North Carolina Press).
——, (1991) 'A Cryptanalysis of Beckett's *Molloy*', in Smith (ed.) *The World of Samuel Beckett* (op. cit.), 53–72.
——, (1997) 'Beyond Paradox and Perplexities in *Textes pour rien*: A Psychopragmatic Approach', *SBA/T*, VI (op. cit.), 211–2.
——, (2000a) *Beyond Fetishism and Other Excursions in Psychopragmatics* (London/ New York: Macmillan/St. Martin's Press).
——, (2000b) 'Beckett et le Moi-peau: au-delà du fétichisme matriciel', *L'affect dans L'œuvre de Samuel Beckett*, ed. M. Engelberts et al., X, *SBT/A*, Amsterdam: Rodopi, 63–70.
——, (2004a) 'Beckett and Psychoanalysis' in *Palgrave Advances in Samuel Beckett Studies* (ed.) L. Oppenheim (op. cit.) 172–93.
——, (2004b) 'Peau de chagrin: Beckett and Bion on Looking Not to See', *SBT/A*, XIV (op. cit.), 25–38.
Morin, E. (2006) '" Gathering Thinglessness": Beckett's Drama, Scarcity, and the Irish Literary Revival', *The Beckett Journal of Studies*, XVI, 1–2, 137–49.
Nancy, J.L. (1993), 'The Sublime Offering', in *Of the Sublime: Presence in Question* (trans.) J. Librett (Albany: State University of New York Press).
O'Brien, E. (1986) *The Beckett Country* (Dublin: Black Cat Press).
O'Hara, J. (1997) *Samuel Beckett's Hidden Drives: Structural Uses of Depth Psychology* (Gainesville: University Press of Florida).
Oppenheim, L. (2001) 'A Preoccupation with Object-representation: the Beckett-Bion Case Revisited', *The International Journal of Psychoanalysis*, 82: 767–84.
——, (2003) 'Disturbing the feasible: Object Representation in *Three Dialogues with Georges Duthuit*', *SBT/A*, 13 – Three Dialogues Revisited. Les Trois dialogues revisités – eds M. Buning et al., 75–88.
——, (2004) (ed.) *Palgrave Advances in Samuel Beckett Studies* (Basingstoke and New York: Palgrave Macmillan).
Parkin-Gounelas, R. (2001) *Literature and Psychoanalysis: Intertextual Readings* (Basingstoke and New York: Palgrave – now Palgrave Macmillan).
Parsons, M. (1999) 'Psychic reality, negation, analytic setting' in Kohon, *The Dead Mother* (op. cit.), 59–75.
Phillips, A. (1988) *Winnicott* (London: Penguin).
Pilling, J. (1994) (ed.) *The Cambridge Companion to Beckett* (Cambridge University Press).
——, (1997) *Beckett before Godot* (Cambridge University Press).
——, (2005) 'Something for Nothing: Beckett's *Dream of Fair to Middling Women*' in 'Beckett, Joyce and the Art of the Negative', *European Joyce Studies* XVI, (ed.) C. Jaurretche (Rodopi: Amsterdam and New York), 171–9.
Pountney, R. (1988) *Theatre of Shadows: Samuel Beckett's Drama 1956–1976* (Gerrards Cross: Colin Smythe).
Rabaté, J-M. (1984) (ed.) *Beckett avant Beckett: Essais sur les premières œuvres* (Paris: Accents).

——, (1992) 'Comment lire, comment dire Beckett', *Interfaces*, 'Samuel Beckett: Intertextualités et psychanalyse', Université de Bourgogne, 3–13.

——, (1996) 'Beckett's Ghosts and Fluxions', *SBT/A*, V (op. cit.), 23–41.

——, (2001) *Jacques Lacan* (Basingstoke and New York: Palgrave – now Palgrave Macmillan).

Ricks, C. (1993) *Beckett's Dying Words* (Oxford University Press).

Riva, R. (1970) 'Beckett and Freud', *Criticism*, XII, 2 (spring), 120–32.

Rodman, F. (1987) (ed.) *The Spontaneous Gesture: Selected Letters of D.W. Winnicott* (Harvard University Press).

Rodriguez, M. '"Everywhere stone is gaining": The struggle for the Sacred in Samuel Beckett's *Ill Seen Ill Said*', *SBA/T*, XIV, After Beckett/D'après Beckett, eds. A. Uhlmann et al., 105–16.

Ross, C. (1995) '"Where there were gleams": Between Fantasy, Thought and Logic': (A General Reconsideration of Beckettian Character), *Ranam*, XXV, 1995, 51–64.

——, (1996) 'The Face in the Mirror', *SBA/A*, IV (op. cit.) 123–37.

——, (1997) 'Toute blanche dans la blancheur': La prédominance de la métaphore blanche dans l'écriture beckettienne', *SBA/A*, VI (op. cit.), 267–77.

——, (1998) 'Jeux d'absence ou vers une lecture de l'autre: la place d'*En attendant Godot* dans la trilogie beckettienne', *Samuel Beckett: L'écriture et la scène*, eds E. Grossman, and R. Salado (Paris: Sedes), 13–28.

——, (2001) 'Beckett's Godot in Berlin: New Coordinates of the Void', *SBT/A*, XI, eds A. Moorjani, and C. Veit – Samuel Beckett: Endlessness in the Year 2000. Samuel Beckett: Fin sans Fin – 64–73.

——, (2004) *Aux frontières du vide: Beckett, une écriture sans mémoire ni désir* (Amsterdam and New York: Rodopi).

——, (2006) '"Where do we come in"? Responding to Otherness in *Waiting for Godot*', *Etudes Anglaises*, 1, eds C. Ross and C. Bonafous-Murat (janvier–mars),'Samuel Beckett', 75–90.

——, (2010) (ed.) '"On the black road home": Re-radicalizing Beckett's Irish Protestant Legacy' (A Re-reading of *All That Fall*) in C. Ross (ed.) *Sub-Versions: Trans-National Readings of Modern Irish Literature* (Amsterdam and New York: Rodopi), 199–217.

Rudnytsky, P. (1993) (ed.) *Transitional Objects and Potential Spaces: Literary Uses of D.W. Winnicott* (New York: Columbia University Press).

Sartre, J-P. (1968) *Search for a Method* (New York: Vintage Books).

Scott, N. (1969) *Craters of the Spirit* (London: Sheed and Ward).

Schwartz, M. (1978) 'Critic, Define thyself' in *Psychoanalysis and the Question of the Text* (ed.) Geoffrey Hartman (Baltimore and London: Johns Hopkins University Press), 1–17.

Sekoff, J. (1999) 'Necromancy and the inner world', in Kohon, *The Dead Mother* (op. cit.), 109–27.

Shapiro, B. (1969) 'Toward a Psychoanalytic Reading of Beckett's *Molloy*', *Literature and Psychology*, XIX [first part in] number 2 (71–86) [second part in] numbers 3–4 (15–30).

Simon, B. (1988) 'The Imaginary Twins: the Case of Beckett and Bion', *International Review of Psychoanalysis*, XV, 331–52.

Skelton, R. (2006) (ed.) *The Edinburgh International Encyclopaedia of Psychoanalysis* (Edinburgh University Press).

Smith, F. (2002) *Beckett's Eighteenth Century* (Basingstoke and New York: Palgrave – now Palgrave Macmillan).
Smith, J. (1991) (ed.) *The World of Samuel Beckett* (Baltimore: Johns Hopkins University Press).
Stewart, B. (ed.) (1999) *Beckett and Beyond* (Gerrards Cross: Colin Smythe).
Stewart, P. (2006) *Zone of Evaporation: Samuel Beckett's Disjunctions* (Amsterdam and New York: Rodopi).
Takahashi, Y. (2001)'"On mindlessness": Beckett, Japan, and the Twentieth Century', *SBT/A,* XI (op. cit.) 38–41.
Thurston, L. (2009) 'Outselves: Beckett, Bion and Beyond', *Journal of Modern Literature,* XXXII, 3 (Spring), 121–43.
Trezise, T. (1990) *Into the Breach: Samuel Beckett and The Ends of Literature* (Princeton University Press).
Uhlmann, A. (1999) *Beckett and Poststructuralism* (Cambridge University Press).
——, (2006) (eds S. Gontarski and A. Uhlmann) *Beckett after Beckett* (op. cit.).
Visconti, L. (1997) 'The Artist and the Artisan: Beckett as a Translator of Italian Poetry', *SBA/T VI* (op. cit), 387–98.
Weller, S. (2005) *A Taste for the Negative: Beckett and Nihilism* (Oxford: Legenda).
Wilde, Oscar (1966) *The Importance of Being Earnest* (London: Methuen).
Wilmer, S.E. (1992) *Beckett in Dublin* (Dublin: Lilliput Press).
Winnicott, D. (1953) 'Transitional Objects and Transitional Phenomena' in *Playing and Reality* (1–30).
——, (1963) 'Communicating and non-communicating leading to the study of certain opposites' in Winnicott (1965) *The Maturational Processes and the Facilitating Environment* (London: Hogarth), 179–92.
——, (1971) *Playing and Reality* (London: Penguin).
——, (1974) 'Fear of Breakdown', *International Review of Psychoanalysis,* 1:103–7.
——, (1988) *Human Nature* (London: Free Association Books).
Wolosky, S. (1996), 'Samuel Beckett's Figural Evasions' in Budick & Iser, *Languages of the Unsayable* (op. cit.), 165–86.

Index

GPSR Compliance
The European Union's (EU) General Product Safety Regulation (GPSR) is a set of rules that requires consumer products to be safe and our obligations to ensure this.

If you have any concerns about our products, you can contact us on

ProductSafety@springernature.com

In case Publisher is established outside the EU, the EU authorized representative is:

Springer Nature Customer Service Center GmbH
Europaplatz 3
69115 Heidelberg, Germany

www.ingramcontent.com/pod-product-compliance
Ingram Content Group UK Ltd.
Pitfield, Milton Keynes, MK11 3LW, UK
UKHW020225160926
475607UK00004B/99
9780230575189